Quantum Shift

Joseph R. Lallo

Contents

Chapter 1

The power plant of the hoversled rumbled. It was a precisely calibrated machine, gram for gram, watt for watt a match for every other hoversled in the class. The only things that could make a difference in a race were the tuning and the driver. And this one had one hell of a driver.

Lex rolled some dials on the rear of the yoke, shifting the plasma injection timing. The reactor complained. The heat spiked, but top speed ticked two more notches into the red. He could smell the seals in the closed loop of the reactor heating up. A tremor through the microhydraulics let him know the extra speed was robbing him of steering responsiveness. Every system in the hoversled was past its intended operational parameters. Every system but him. And since he was operating at top level, he knew what the sled could take. It wouldn't blow. It wouldn't even trip the safeties for another seventy-five seconds. And if he pulled the turns tight enough, the race would be over in seventy-three.

Sweat poured down his cheek. The sled had a cooling system. It was off. Only so much power to go around and he wanted it all for thrust and traction. A telltale honeycomb effect on the windscreen of the sled revealed that some sort of visual overlays were active, but they were doing little more than producing a strange, fuzzy visual artifact, a doubling of the struts and bodywork of the hoversled. They were ghosts, millimeter-accurate replays of prior runs on the track. The idea was he'd be able to see how far ahead he was in other runs, full representations of his sled superimposed onto their precise position on the track. But they were all stacked up on top of him. He was clocking within five milliseconds of his average time. His lip twitched into the hint of a grin. And there was still some slack.

The final turn was ahead. Too sharp to take at full speed, and he was going well beyond full speed. He angled the hoversled, leaning into the turn. It was the sort of maneuver that was really meant for motorcycles, things with physical contact with the ground. All it achieved in the hoversled was lifting half of his repulsors farther from the track and robbing him of traction. But you don't set records by using the hoversled as intended. He took a hand from the steering yoke and tapped a preset on the HUD controls. A seldom-used metric appeared at the bottom of the collection of red-lined parameters: the repulsor capacitors. They took the place of shock absorbers in this system. He let them steadily charge. Lex chomped the double load of gum in his mouth. The timing was the only variable left. Too early and he'd drift off course at the inside of the turn and lose speed. Too late and he'd overshoot the outside of the turn and lose speed. But just right and...

He juiced the repulsors. They kicked the whole sled up and over. He took the turn without dropping out of the red and landed squarely on the ideal line. All the fuzziness in the viewscreen faded away. He was ahead of all the ghosts. He grinned and snapped his gum as he blasted past the finish line, and the final lap time blinked red on his screen with that fun little star beside it and the two words he'd been working toward for the last seven hours.

Track record.

Lex eased all the systems down from their warning state. Cutting-edge polymers and composites crackled and creaked like the rigging of a pirate ship. Every system on the hoversled would need maintenance. Exactly the way it should be. If you weren't using it all, you weren't using it at all, and you couldn't expect to be the best.

His slidepad chirped as he guided the ailing hoversled off the track and toward the garages. He swiped the screen without looking.

"Lex," he said.

"Lex. It's Preethy. Why am I staring at your thigh?" she said.

"Because you won't let us put hands-free slidepad connectivity into the competition hoversleds."

"Given the number of collisions you and the other racers have with one another on the track, I do not think it is wise to leave that avenue for distraction open."

He pulled the slidepad from his pocket and held it in a practiced grip against the steering yoke. "What's up?" he said. The view of Preethy's head was bobbing on the screen. He recognized one of the hallways of the office complex at the league headquarters. "Are you still doing meetings?"

"As I'd assumed we wouldn't be having supper together until you were through on the track, I rescheduled some of tomorrow's meetings to this evening to make use of the time. I had my assistant put a hook in the track's time-trial database to give me a notification when a new record is set. It's been a rather handy way to keep track of your activities. Are you aware you hold seven of the top ten times on the track?"

"Who keeps count?" he said.

"I do. As does my assistant. Are you aware you've spent thirty-five hours this week running time trials? And it is only Wednesday."

"It's my job."

"Certainly it is, and I can tell you that the investors are delighted to see you honing your skills further. The higher the skill level in the league, the better the competition, the better the ratings, the better the advertising rates. You're making me and the company a bundle, and the public relations are sparkling. But I can also tell you that your net improvement can be measured in milliseconds while your anxiety and fatigue have been ratcheting steadily higher. And while we have spare hoversleds in case you wear another one out, we only have one Trevor Alexander. And I've become rather attached to him."

"This has got you worried about my health? Last time I counted, the total number of killer robots on that practice track is zero. This is practically a walk in the park."

"Lex, you're a gifted racer."

"I'm a *skilled* racer. And skills need to be kept sharp."

"This is about your standings, I presume."

"Where am I in the standings?" Lex said.

"You and Kyle Byres have sixty points for the season."

"Tied."

"That is correct."

"I've come in second three times this season. I finished outside the winner's circle once. Mr. Rival has the same number of first-place finishes, and he's never been outside the top three."

"I'd like to point out that Kyle—"

"Don't say his name," Lex said with a wince. "I don't want to hear it any more often than I have to."

"Are you a toddler, Lex?"

"I'm a grown man with a grand total of a half second of track time across four races keeping me from losing the lead entirely. He's a more consistent racer than me. So that means I need to get better."

"He's also six years younger than you, Lex."

"You saying I'm losing my edge?"

"I'm saying you could retire tomorrow and be a legend of the sport. You could never win another race and your record to this point would stand the test of time. And that's without any of your other exploits beyond the track. You have a life outside of racing. And presently the more important fact is you have a reservation tonight at the new Portuguese restaurant that opened this week. Eight p.m."

"Pet friendly?"

"I believe they will be willing to make an exception in our case."

"Looking forward to it. You want me to pick you up?"

"No. I'll meet you there. Don't be late. It's been a long day, and I'm looking forward to a good meal and an early night."

"That makes two of us."

Two hours later, Lex was sipping wine over dessert. Squee, his pet who as far as the locals knew was an exotic dog, was draped over his shoulders like a mink stole. The little creature had stuffed herself with some very expensive beans and was teetering on the brink of sleep.

"Serradura. How have I lived my life for this long and never had any serradura?" he said, jabbing a spoon into the parfait he'd selected for dessert.

"It is rather delightful," Preethy said. "Indulgent."

"Yeah." He scraped around the edge to catch as much of the current layer of the dessert as he could. "Speaking of indulging things, I was wondering if we could talk about that 'exhibition race on demand' thing I was talking about."

Preethy's face shifted to an expression Lex had never seen on anyone but her. It was a magic combination of "I'm humoring you" and "Must we go through this again?" with a sprinkle of "You rascal, you" to take the edge off. And she achieved it with little more than a subtle arch of her eyebrow. Linguists ought to be studying those eyebrows. They had their own language.

"That would be your plan to organize nonranked races at the drop of a hat, correct?"

"Yeah. It might be fun. You know. Unscheduled entertainment for people subscribed to the newsfeed."

"Or, perhaps, a way for you to fill more of your day with training and practicing?"

"Can never get too much practicing, right?"

"You can when fielding a full track of racers costs three hundred million credits and unplanned races with no ticket sales or promotional work are nonearners."

"Granted. That's a problem. I get that." He scooped another mouthful of pudding. "But I can only improve so much without competent racers to race against."

"There are four more races in the season. And I have it on good authority from the CEO that you're a shoo-in to have your contract renewed for next season."

"CEO Misra is a good egg. And quite the looker. And has excellent taste in restaurants. But it's not practice when it's the real deal. I can't get experimental with my techniques if a screwup costs me my place in the standings."

"I believe that's the source of excitement, isn't it?" she said.

"Not for me, it isn't. I'm not putting a losing season on my record after the long road back to the track."

"It is mathematically impossible for you to finish below third place."

"Second place is first loser, and third place is last place," he said.

She took a sip of her dessert wine. "Lex, I admire your skill, and no one can question your drive. But I worry that your unconventional life has damaged your perspective somewhat. Life-or-death challenges have come along often enough that you seem to equate any failure as absolutely final. It would be a bit of a pot calling a kettle black to say that you work too hard, but there comes a point that you must trust you've done your due diligence and simply embrace the challenge when the challenge comes."

"You're starting to sound like Ma."

"That's a high compliment."

"I just want to be the best I can. We only get one shot at this life, and I lost a couple of years of racing to a pile of stupid choices. You don't make up for lost time by taking it easy."

"As the years go by, you might find yourself defining lost time differently. But there is no sense butting my head against this any further. How can we solve your problem, then? I presume you've found the simulators inadequate?"

"They're great. Fantastic even. Your hoversled sims are the second best I've ever used."

"Second best? I was told they were the state of the art when we had them installed. There are no superior models available. Where did you experience a better one?"

"I got trapped in one being run by a potentially apocalyptic swarm of self-replicating robots under the control of a damaged AI. Sort of a one-off."

"I see. At least our research team didn't overlook a consumer solution. But it doesn't scratch the itch?"

"The simulator's settings have all these pesky safety limits to keep your brains from getting rattled out. The real world has real physics that I can use to get around them."

"And loading up rival ghosts on the actual track when running practice laps?"

"Can't actually swap paint with them. A real hoversled can nudge you around a turn or block the airstream or bump you from behind. It's not the same." He shook his head. "Look. Things fell apart with Michella because she couldn't peel her brain away from the job for the duration of an entire meal. I'm not doing that to you. Right now is about you and me, not me and the track. What's new outside of the league?"

"Depressingly little. If not for our meals together, I would have no social life. I haven't even been able to see my uncle in months, and he's on the board of directors for the league."

"I never realized running a league would be so much work."

"I imagine other leagues have a rather larger board. But it turns out when you field a successful and profitable assortment of racers almost entirely from those ejected from other leagues, the leagues who parted with them tend to respond negatively. The number of qualified staff that have been poached from us in just the last three months would be enough to run a normal league. I've been picking up a rather impressive amount of slack personally."

"If you're going to yell at me for working too hard, I'm going to yell at you for working too hard."

"I am well aware, and it is well deserved. Four more races, Lex. Then things can be dealt with. When the season is through, there will be time enough to staff up, with a focus on providing superior benefits and compensation so that, at the very least, it will cost our rivals and their overeager recruiters much, much more to steal staff. A more carefully worded contract should help in that regard as well. But presently, in order to have time to make intelligent hires, I need to free up my schedule, and in order to free up my schedule, I need to make those hires."

"It's six days until the next race. What are you doing until then?"

"I'm scheduled to be off planet until the day before the race," she said. "I'm leaving tomorrow afternoon. Hopefully after you and I meet for lunch."

"You're heading off planet, and you didn't even ask me to be the chauffeur?"

"Would you have taken the time from your practice schedule?"

"No, but I would have made up a very compelling excuse, and you would have earned a consolation prize."

"Ah, well. My loss. Though, I must admit, as thrilling as travel with you at the controls can be, the corporate ship does offer certain desirable amenities."

"You haven't had one of my special flights yet," he said slyly.

"It would certainly be a pleasant change of pace to have a positive experience in zero-g to counterbalance the events in Indra Station." She shuddered at the memory. "After the race season. Now, I believe it's well past time we paid the check and headed home. Much to be done, and we'll both think more clearly with a full night of sleep."

Lex touched his slidepad to the security panel of his apartment door. His considerably more than professional relationship with Preethy was anything but a secret, but they both had decided to hold off on actually moving in together. Part of it was for the optics of the CEO of a racing league sharing a bed with its top racer. Part of it was... more complicated. Lex emptied his pockets onto the table beside the door. The engagement ring that had been intended for Michella sat in a dish at one corner of the table. No doubt a psychologist would have plenty to say about why it was there, but it didn't take seven years of expensive schooling to figure out having a yearslong unrequited romance finally blossom and then ultimately fall apart had a way of making one hesitant to fully commit to a new relationship and fully let go of an old one.

He lifted Squee from his shoulders and carted her over to the couch. She scampered back onto his shoulders the moment he was sitting down. After she'd assaulted his ear with licks and tickly whiskers, he opened a drawer and revealed a slidepad with noseprints smeared across its screen.

"Squee, here's your toy. Just keep the volume down, and don't buy any more frozen burritos," he said.

The adorable ball of fluff that had previously housed a supersophisticated AI rolled to her back, clutched the slidepad with her paws, and nosed at it until a wirefeed of a crowded dog park appeared. She stared in rapt interest at the cavorting of canines that were probably several star systems away.

"I should really cut down on your screen time," Lex said, digging his own slidepad free. "But it'd be a little hypocritical, wouldn't it?"

Man and beast let their minds settle into the comforting buzz of their chosen digital pablum. For him, it was songs he'd heard a thousand times by a band he didn't even particularly like—Death Zone Dumpster—and reviews of the top-ten racers' telemetries synchronized with his own.

"I don't get it," he said, scrutinizing the footage of his primary rival in frame advance. "He holds the line perfectly every time." He flicked to the next turn and framed through it as well. "Turn after turn. Race after race. He's following the perfect line. If he's alone, it's the mathematically perfect ideal line, or if there's someone else—me—jockeying for position, he's as close to it as physics will allow. It's not just reaction time. It can't just be reaction time. No one has reaction time that fast. He's anticipating and correcting for things instantly."

He brought up the postrace inspection certificate for the hoversled. "Nothing extra in the navigation system. Nothing bolted onto the steering rig. Everything in software is within standard tuning. Everything within the hardware is in standard tuning. No unusual transmissions. Just little quirky things. The guy rides the standby for the safety system a little hard. He's threading the needle between racers at the speed of sound. You'd have to be either crazy or *me* to not be thinking about safety at those speeds."

Lex's mind swirled and bumped into the walls of his head. Simply being gifted wasn't enough for that sort of result. And if the postrace and prerace inspections hadn't turned up anything, then the only difference was... what? How was he doing it?

He swiped away the footage. It didn't matter. If he couldn't prove this guy was doing something shady, then he'd have to assume the only way to beat him was to sharpen himself to that same impossible razor's edge. And he was almost there. The two of them were a match, on average. Lex had more wobble in his performance. That was it. If Lex could just drop a few more of the lows and add a few more of the highs, he could get at least one good, solid, satisfying, convincing win. But to do that, he would need practice. Not just simulator practice. At least, not with this simulator. And he couldn't very well rope in a bunch of other racers to help him get practice on the real tracks. Getting random nobodies wouldn't give him realistic opponents, and getting the real crew together (aside from being expensive) would also be giving *them* practice, which would rob him of some of the benefits.

What he needed was a better simulator. And a couple more weeks to practice on it. He flicked up his contact list. His thumb hovered over a contact.

"This is dumb, Lex," he muttered to himself. "This never ends well. But, on the other hand, the alternative is potentially failing at the only job that's ever really mattered to me." He turned to Squee. "What do you think? Wanna go visit Mommy and Daddy?"

The funk's ears perked up. She dropped the slidepad and scrambled up to sit attentively.

"See, now I have to do it. Can't disappoint the cutie."

He tapped a contact. After a moment of the connection negotiating, a choppy combination of three human voices answered.

"Lex. Always a pleasure to hear from you."

"Hey, Ma. How are things?"

"Things have settled into a comfortable routine, periodically interrupted by brief pauses for Karter to heal, repair, or upgrade himself."

"What's been punching holes in Mr. Engineer?"

"Most recently, he fractured his two remaining synthetic vertebrae after a proposed upgrade to his modified inertial inhibitor applied excess torque to his torso. He is recovering well and now has cybernetic replacements. How are you?"

"My spine is intact, thanks for asking. I guess if he's on the mend, he probably doesn't have any time to work on a little side project for me."

The audio crackled.

"It *is* him," Karter said. "I *thought* the idiot was calling."

"Lex is inquiring about your schedule. He may have a project for you," Ma said.

"Oh? Did he get military funding or something so he can afford my services?" Karter said.

"No. I just figured, you know. For old times," Lex said.

"Old times don't pay for tritium. I need credits or services. No friends and family discounts."

"Look, I'm not even asking you to make something new. If you don't already have it, I probably can't use it. My next race is in six days, and I'm hoping to get access to a simulator so I can drill some specific parts of the track so—"

"You think a couple days of simulations will make a difference?" Karter said.

"They'll be better than nothing."

"You don't hire Karter Dee for things to be better than nothing. You hire Karter Dee to pervert the laws of physics to your petty whims. And it just so happens I have something that might fit the bill. Get down here and we'll put it through its paces."

"This isn't one of those beta projects, is it? The Hall of Rejects?"

"Of course it is! Why would I need you to put it through its paces if it wasn't under active development? Now get in that ship of yours and get down here so we can see what sort of effect it has on a human test subject."

The audio crackled again.

"Ma? You still there?" Lex said.

"I am. But Karter has left the call and is heading for the development floor."

"Give it to me straight. If I come down there, what are the odds I end up regretting it?"

"Exceedingly high. Karter's social graces have degraded somewhat in the past few months."

"All right. I'll rephrase. What are the odds I'll end up getting badly hurt?"

"I shall endeavor to ensure a high standard of safety. As such, I would place your odds of injury as mid-to-high."

"For comparison, how would you place my odds of getting badly injured while racing?"

"Mid-to-high."

"That settles it, then. No harm in giving the lunatic a chance to help me train. I'll see you soon."

"I eagerly anticipate the visit," Ma said.

He tapped the slidepad to end the call and gave Squee a pat on the head. "What's the worst that could happen?" he mused.

• • ● ● ● • ● ● ● • •

The next day, as soon as he'd finished his lunch with Preethy, Lex had made his way to the hangar where he kept the *SOB*. Once he was suited up, strapped in, and entering high orbit, he tapped a few controls and watched the sensors.

"How are we looking, Coal?" he asked.

"Unusually high enforcer traffic at the hub today," Coal said. "More accurately, precisely the same amount of enforcer traffic at the hub as you usually experience, but unusually high relative to the standard baseline."

"Yeah," Lex said, twitching at the tickle of Squee's tail as she drifted in the weightless cockpit of his ship. "It's almost like VectorCorp is still sore about the number of times we've run afoul of them."

"The nature of corporate turnover suggests that anyone with a specific vendetta against you has likely been removed from a position of power," Coal said.

"I like to imagine it's just in the corporate training manual now. 'Give Lex a hard time.' Are they following me and keeping pace?"

"They are remaining just beyond the standard short-range sensors of an unmodified Cantrell Intrasystem Interceptor. This places them well within the range of my sensors."

Lex plucked Squee from the air around him and pulled up some elastic straps for her to nestle between. He kept his inertial inhibitor turned down to what some would consider dangerous levels. He didn't want his pet getting knocked around, and she clearly wasn't interested in holding on to him right now.

"They think they're being sneaky," he muttered. "May as well let them think they've gotten the better of me for a while. Make them feel good."

"Job satisfaction is very important," Coal agreed.

He took the controls. Coal instantly dropped her automatic piloting. It had taken him a while to get used to the reality of having a fully sentient ship's computer, but he'd come around to it. After literal years of finding ways to keep himself occupied during lengthy faster-than-light jumps while doing freelance deliveries, he'd slowly come to rely upon the companionship. At first, Squee was enough, but she wasn't much of a conversationalist. Coal was like a moderately less socially graceful version of Ma, insomuch as that's what she literally was: a mildly degraded duplicate of Ma. The same AI that had on more than one occasion resided in the mind of his pet, and the same one who would be greeting him when he arrived at Big Sigma to talk to Karter about the new simulator.

Rather than dwell upon just how much of his life had come to revolve around an utter madman's friendly and nurturing AI, he chose to give the trailing enforcers their exercise for the day. Juicing the throttle forced him firmly against his seat, and he launched into a tight turn.

"Coal, let's visualize the—" Before he could finish, the view through the cockpit flickered to display spheres of red around every object, the legal minimum safe distance he could approach. "Thanks."

Lex took a hand from the controls to pop a compartment on the side of his seat. Thruster flares flashed in the rearview display in the corner of his HUD. The enforcers had noticed his maneuvering. In a skill that really had no place in the repertoire of a pilot, he feathered the ship into a precise vector to slide through the gap between three ships queued for entry to the FTL corridor with one hand while unwrapping gum with the other.

"That is the last of your Berries and Cream Protein Blast gum," Coal said. "Would you like me to order more?"

"Skip it," he said. "Berries and Cream is a good flavor, but whoever made the decision to include the words 'Protein Blast' in the name of their product does not deserve to be rewarded with a second sale."

"I will research alternate berries-and-cream gum varieties," Coal said.

"If it makes you happy," he murmured, eyeing the cluttered path ahead.

There was a time when avoiding the enforcers was a necessity. The price VectorCorp charged for the fastest lanes of the corridors was far too high for him to make any money with the prices he could get away with charging for a delivery, for starters. Then there was the pesky little law against making unlicensed deliveries using said corridors. He could skip the corridors at extreme risk to life and limb—something he had no concerns about whatsoever—but he still needed to use the hubs to enter and leave planets, which meant he technically was breaking their rules for the last few moments of any given trip. So finding ways to slip through their fingers was a job requirement in those days. But those days were gone. He had the money for express corridors, and he wasn't carrying anything that required a license. They probably wouldn't have been happy to learn about the dozens of illegal upgrades lurking in the *SOB*'s guts, but that was neither here nor there. The point was, as he wedged his ship through the barely adequate gap between the safe zones around two freighters and a tourist shuttle, he was engaging in a completely pointless exercise. Provided he didn't cross into the minimum safe distance of any of the other ships or pieces of equipment, what he was doing wasn't strictly illegal. But one botched swoop could easily violate three dozen transit laws. It was a pointless exercise in rebellion that did little more than antagonize the enforcers and get his blood pumping a little bit.

On the other hand, it was fun.

"Will we be taking the corridor or using uncharted space?" Coal asked.

"No corridor," he said, squinting at the enforcers on the HUD as they maneuvered around to attempt to intercept him on the other side. "These folks have something to prove, and I don't want them setting up an ambush or something at the next hub."

"Then you should call Preethy while you still have access to communication. You asked me to remind you that you needed some information you'd failed to address during your meal," Coal said.

"Oh, right! Good thinking, Coal."

Two enforcers aligned themselves ahead. He shook his head at how precisely they were lined up with his projected exit from the queue line. That they assumed he would take the quickest, safest way through the crowded traffic he was weaving between was probably a sign of green by-the-book enforcers following their training. He chose to interpret it as a slap to the face. They were daring him to evade them despite having at least three different escape routes between other vessels. A ponderous cargo-hauler above and ahead started to accelerate, overlapping its safe zone with three personal vessels. That should have gotten the enforcers on the hauler's case. That was the precise safety law Lex was using as an obstacle course. But naturally, they kept their sights set on Lex.

It was *definitely* personal...

A broken circle spun in the corner of the screen beside a professionally taken headshot of Preethy, the video call negotiating. Lex flicked the edge of a button on the steering yoke, adding a few milliseconds of lateral thrust. Coal updated his projected trajectory on the HUD, and the enforcers maneuvered to intercept it. A bright line of energy jumped between emitters on the pair of ships, a clothesline meant to overheat Lex's engines if he crossed it. The range ticked down, his ship getting closer and closer to the trap they'd set. A video feed of Preethy's face replaced the headshot.

"Hello, Lex," she said, an unfamiliar hallway sliding along behind her. "Preparing for a trip, I see."

"Yeah. Heading out to see an old buddy to burn time before the next race."

"Odd you didn't mention it during lunch."

"I'm trying to keep business out of our personal lunches. If I'd started running my mouth about this, I never would have learned about that concert you wanted to go to next month."

"So it's business, is it? Well, do be careful, and be sure to give yourself some extra travel time. We wouldn't want any unforeseen circumstances to interfere with your participation in the race."

"Wait, you're telling me if something goes wrong, I might have to get a high-powered, state-of-the-art vehicle to a predetermined destination as quickly as possible. How could a simple hoversled racer ever deal with such an unprecedented outcome?" he said, laying on as much over-the-top anxiety as he could manage to underscore the intended humor.

The performance managed to produce a raised eyebrow, which was just about the maximum amount of emotion Preethy tended to show during business hours.

"We both know you are gifted in your capacity to discover new and exciting problems and catastrophes."

"Just so long as we both agree I'm gifted."

"To that end, I notice you are chewing gum. You wouldn't be engaged in anything unadvisable right now, would you?"

The emergency channels attempted to break through the call, blaring with all sorts of angry commands from the enforcers. Coal helpfully squelched the broadcast.

"Heaven forbid. I just love the great new taste of Berries and Cream Protein Blast."

As the range to the enforcer countermeasure dropped below one hundred meters, he gave the yoke a gentle tug and eased the ship into a trajectory that came so close to the futuristic equivalent of a spike strip they'd rolled out that visible flares of plasma rolled off the edge of his shields as it grazed the line.

"No doubt," Preethy said in a level tone that nonetheless displayed almost toxic levels of doubt.

"I know you're busy. Meeting coming up, right?" Lex said.

"Seven minutes," she said.

"I won't keep you. I just wanted to know if you could send me a copy of the latest full text of the league regulations and bylaws."

"The published version is insufficient?"

"There's extra legalese in the copy you have, right?"

"Just a few appendices explaining some of the finer points and deeply defining some of the technology and terminology."

"Yeah, I'm going to need those."

Three more emergency channels popped up and were squelched. There were now so many angry faces lined up on his HUD, shouting at him and unaware that he wasn't listening, that it was beginning to obscure his view.

"I don't mind you pushing the limits on the track, Lex, but if you try to do the same with our regulations, we'll need to have a firm discussion."

"I'm going to be talking to Karter about a high-intensity simulator to get some extra training in, and I want to make sure it's not going to be considered an unfair advantage," he said.

"I see. And I assume you don't know the specifics of the simulator yet?"

"Not yet."

"I'll have the full text delivered to you. Anything else before I head into the meeting?"

"That's plenty. Sorry to bother you. Anything you want me to bring back with me?"

"Just yourself, in one piece, and without any outstanding warrants for your arrest or bounties on your head."

He whistled. "That's a pretty major ask, but I'll see what I can do. See you later!"

"Enjoy your trip," she said.

"I *did* say I was going to visit Karter, right? Enjoyment isn't really one of the possibilities."

"Then try not to do something stupid," she said.

"I always do." He ended the call.

"For clarification," Coal said. "When you responded 'I always do' to her request to try to avoid doing something stupid, were you indicating that you always try to avoid doing something stupid, or that you always do something stupid?"

"Yes," Lex said.

He looped the *SOB* around to run parallel to the corridor. The enforcers arranged themselves into something resembling a formation behind him. Now there were eight emergency channels attempting to assert themselves on his HUD.

"Care to summarize what these knuckleheads are on about?" Lex said.

"They are of the opinion that you are flying in an unacceptable and erratic manner and should shift control to the automated corridor-boarding queue or face disciplinary action. They used broadly more colorful language."

"Am I actually in violation of anything?" he asked.

"Not utilizing strict interpretation of codes of conduct. You *are* violating several informal safety guidelines, but nothing enforceable."

"Technically innocent is completely innocent, that's my motto. Let's get out of here before they decide technicalities aren't good enough."

He dialed in a relatively direct series of FTL jumps, ones he was relatively confident wouldn't cause his ship to explode due to particle impacts, and jumped to FTL. As the view out the window blue-shifted out of visibility, he helped Squee free herself from the safety straps and reclined the chair a bit.

This was the point in a pre-Coal trip that Lex would have dug out his slidepad and let his mind lightly congeal as he thumbed at a pointless and colorful game or consumed some equally pointless pop culture. Her presence as the ship's computer had changed his habits in that regard.

"So where were we?" Lex asked.

"During the previous FTL jump, I had asked you to explain to me the point of music, and you had diverged into a tangent on why people keep salt and pepper shakers on their tables," Coal said.

"Oh. Right. So music... It's sort of... I don't know how to explain it... I guess it's like this..."

Seventeen anecdotes, twenty-three tangents, and seven hundred and six analogies later, Coal was no closer to understanding the purpose or allure of music, but they *had* arrived at Big Sigma. Tempting as it would have been to navigate the orbiting debris field on intuition and skill alone, Lex's spirited defense of rock and roll as a cultural imperative had cost him a few hours of sleep, and he didn't really want to wreck the *SOB*'s finish with some microimpacts because he wasn't feeling up to his usual level of navigational prowess.

"Welcome, Lex. Welcome, Coal," Ma said, her voice still lightly distorted by the lowest levels of the debris field. "It is, as always, a pleasure to have you on-planet. We have had relatively few visitors of late."

"Didn't Karter move here to avoid visitors entirely?" Lex said.

"Yes. We have trended rather more closely to that theoretical ideal of zero than in the preceding months. It is for that reason that I wish to prepare you for what you are likely to experience with regard to Karter."

"How much worse could he get? Is he swinging a crowbar around and cursing at the walls?"

Lex took manual control and guided the ship toward the courtyard between the three main buildings in Karter's complex. He half remembered that one or more of them had been destroyed at one point or another, but yet they all seemed equally worn and weather-beaten. Leave it to a mad engineer to rebuild his lair with all of the nicks and scratches intact.

"A complete psychological assessment would take too long and be surplus to requirement, but a relevant example of recent difficulty is the following. It took a nontrivial amount of directed persuasion to convince him to put on clothes."

"The man wears overalls. That's one step removed from footie pajamas. That was too much for him."

"His counterargument to my suggestion that social contract dictates either wearing clothes or informing guests that nudity is a possibility was, and I quote, 'He's a test pilot, not the queen of England.' He punctuated this statement by throwing a burrito in the general direction of the trash receptacle."

Lex landed and popped the cockpit. He got a snootful of the oddly industrial-smelling atmosphere of Big Sigma. Squee launched out of the cockpit like a rocket, taking full advantage of the lower-than-average gravity to turn her already-prodigious leaps into balletic, drifting bounds. Lex trotted toward the door.

"Just give it to me straight. Am I about to see Karter in his birthday suit? Because I need time to prepare."

"The colloquialism is not entirely apt, as Karter has had a large proportion of his anatomy replaced cybernetically or synthetically. So, extending the metaphor, he has tailored his birthday suit almost to the point of nonexistence."

"I don't like that you're avoiding the answer I'm looking for, Ma," Lex said.

He stepped into the influence of the front door of the laboratory. Earth-level gravity kicked in. He shut his eyes and received a full-body spray of disinfectant. When he blinked away the stinging stuff, the door had already opened. His host was standing before him, wearing a pair of swim trunks and nothing else.

"Took you long enough," Karter said. "I thought you were a racer."

"There's still the laws of physics to deal with," Lex said.

Karter scoffed. "If we let the laws of physics dictate our schedule, humanity would still be trying to reach their first star. 'Oh, it's physically impossible.' Quit making excuses and follow me."

The engineer turned, presenting Lex with a view of what, if Lex were to give him the benefit of the doubt, was probably Karter's motivation for avoiding any outfits on his torso. His back was largely covered in what Lex supposed could be called a "surgical scar"; though, like everything else Karter did, it was a little much. A section of his back about the width of his palm and running up his spine looked like one of those "visible anatomy" models. The musculature and circulatory system were entirely visible, as though the skin atop it had been replaced with perfectly transparent resin or plastic.

"Jeez, Karter. Does that hurt?"

"I've got the ol' replacement appendix pumping out some feel-good juice, but it's still itchy. The synth skin should go opaque in another three days, and then it'll settle down. You're here for the simulator, right?"

"Yeah. You sure you're okay to work on it?"

"Work's done. You don't have the bank account to have me do something from scratch. This isn't using any new hardware at all. This is just reusing junk I already made."

"So... it's safe, then? Tested already?"

Karter turned, such that he was able to glare at Lex with his one silver eye. "Hold still," he said.

Lex narrowed his eyes and tensed, ready to dodge-roll if Karter seemed volatile enough. "Why?"

"Because this eye can do brain-activity monitoring, and I'm seeing if you're flatlining. You are good at *two* things, Lex. One of them is going fast, which I guess you're slipping at, since it took you so long to get here and you're looking for some training aids. The other is not dying when I give you something that might kill you. That's two skills more than most people have. Try to hold on to them. We know what beer bottles do, and we know what your head does. That doesn't mean your head will work well with a beer bottle lodged through it. Now unless you'd like to test *that* instead, shut your mouth and listen, because I'm only going to run through this once."

They stepped onto the elevator. Ma illuminated the button for the beta-test floor.

"You know the mental cloak? The thing that makes you invisible to things with human brains by stimulating the self-editing synapses externally? That's half of this thing. We're going to be targeting your gray matter."

"This is the thing that could cause seizures in, like, an entire city?"

"Twenty-five kilometers, don't be dramatic. And we've got that nailed down a lot tighter now. If we overstimulate a brain, it'll just be yours. The other thing we're working with is the Carpinelli Field Generator. You remember how it works?"

"It's like pushing an outboard motor into—" Lex started.

"Don't give me that kindergarten version. I swear, whoever came up with that analogy deserves to have a beer bottle lodged in his head."

"I'm starting to get worried about that specific phrase," Lex said.

"The Carpinelli Field partially phases physical matter within its influence into an orthogonal offshoot to our physical universe that has subtly different physical laws, thus allowing, in essence, a scaled-down relativity effect. But here's the deal. Space isn't really a thing. Space-time is. People cheer about how the Carpinelli Field allows us to screw with the three physical dimensions of space, but those are just three of the four-plus dimensions in the space-time manifold. The real coup was figuring out how to decouple time from the mix so you didn't get any distortions. Traveling at greater-than-light speed wouldn't do much good if you still aged the amount you would have if you were traveling at normal speed."

"This all made a lot more sense to me when we could talk about outboard motors."

Karter gritted his teeth and slapped his palm against a control panel beside a door. It hissed open.

"It's very simple. Our interaction with time is just as malleable as our interaction with space and uses the very same thing we use to go faster than light. You can't travel back in time, but you can manipulate the speed at which you *experience* time. It's basically how the TymFlex safety system works. Slowing down time to decrease the relative kinetic energy of debris. So where's that leave us? The mental cloak can directly target regions of the brain with EM radiation, the Carpinelli Field can manipulate time with EM radiation. Using the two together can manipulate your *perception* of time and layer any sort of sensory experiences atop it that we want."

He turned on the lights and revealed what was either a high-end gaming chair—the sort with built-in inertial feedback and all the other bells and whistles—or a used ejector seat from a military vehicle. A small array of hexagonal plates formed a semicircle, the center of which would be the head of the person in the seat.

"Wait, wait… let me see if I understand this. You're going to… project a simulation into my brain. That's the simulator part. And you're going to use the Carpinelli Field to slow down time?"

"You were almost half right. Give the man a cookie, Ma," Karter said. "We're not going to slow down time. For your mental processes, time will *appear* to be moving more slowly. There's a hard limit on how much the distortion can be, because the temporal distortion potential of any given piece of space-time is…" He stopped. "I may as well be explaining football to a chimp. You get twelve hours of collapsed simulator time at a clip, and those twelve apparent hours will take… Ma?"

"Seventy-three milliseconds," Ma said.

"At the end of those twelve hours, or at any point within those twelve hours that you decide to bail out, you snap back to normal time. All the memory and muscle memory and such remains. At least in theory."

"And just so we're clear, I'm not going to age at an accelerated rate?"

"Your body isn't part of the time distortion," Karter said.

"Is my *brain* going to age at an accelerated rate?"

"It's not your actual brain, just your perception that's adjusted."

"How is that different?"

"In ways that you will never, ever, ever understand," Karter said. "Look, I'll save you time. Here are the dangers. Number one: seizure. Seems like we worked that out in the mental cloak testing, but worth putting on the list. Two: you go crazy. Screwing with someone's mind, crazy is always a possibility. Brains are gooey masses of electrochemistry that barely work in the best circumstances. Stirring them around with a big technological spoon is sure to cause some lumps now and then. And three: your memory fills up. That's assuming you do something like four hundred years of sim time. But I wouldn't worry about that. We can just go in there and fix your noggin up like we do with Squee."

"I'm not super keen on the idea of possibly losing my mind."

"Oh, calm down. Sanity is overrated. Want me to show you the nuthouse certificate again?"

Lex furrowed his brow. "Ma? Thoughts?"

"Oh, sure. Ask the silicon-brained entity about a risk assessment about your meat brain."

"I concur that the seizure risk is the greatest risk, and is minimal. The risk to your sanity will be difficult to determine, so I would advise close observation," Ma said. "Presently, Karter's violent mood swings are the greatest source of danger to you."

"That tracks," Karter said. "Now you're still covered under the release form and liability form you signed back when you first became a tester, so there's nothing legal to worry about. Step one is we do a full body scan. Ma, get the medical arm in here."

"I didn't agree to test it yet."

A whirring sound echoed up the hallway.

"Oh come on. Ma told me all about how you're shaking in your boots about someone out there being a better racer than you, and we've already gone over how 'go fast' and 'don't die' are your two skills. Losing half of them is probably making you awfully upset. So save us the part where you pretend to be one of the normal, cowardly nothings that clutter up most of the dirt-balls in this universe and just accept that you'd rather let me ram a beer bottle through your head than give up a millisecond of lap time to the steady march of time and human frailty."

"A *figurative* beer bottle. Right?"

"Sure, whatever. *Ma!*" Karter bellowed.

What looked like an overcomplicated medical gurney rolled into the room. Karter shoved Lex back so he flopped hard onto the cushioned surface. Green and red laser lines swept down his body, and an associated screen populated with imagery of the main systems of his body.

"There we go. Health snapshot. You're in good shape. Except for that right there," Karter said.

"What right where?" Lex said, bolting upright.

"Karter is indicating a small dark lesion in your—" Ma began.

"Skip it. Testing now, prognosis later. The point is, you're healthy enough to get your brain shot with radiation. Step two is we concoct a high-difficulty racetrack in the simulator—something you've never run before—and you do a single timed run as a control. Ma?"

"Creating track now."

"And this lesion you saw..." Lex said.

"Track complete," Ma said.

"Right, get your butt down, run through this thing," Karter said.

Lex stood and, as seemed to be a standard part of every visit to Karter's lab, questioned what in the world could have possessed him to think this was a good idea. He was about to let a mad scientist—one who would headbutt him in the nose for calling him a mad scientist instead of a mad engineer—bombard his brain with radiation. And for what? To shave a few fractions of a second off his track times?

"I'm not so sure I—" Lex began.

"Ma, queue up the footage," Karter barked.

"Footage?" Lex said.

One whole wall of the room suddenly flickered and displayed a loading bar. Evidently Karter had replaced random structural elements of his lab with holoedge screens. Because of course he did. The display switched over to a side-by-side of the most recent race against Kyle Byres. The precise timing of each racer drifted along the track, with a bright line connecting it to the actual hoversled in the footage. The fastest time was green. The second-place time was bright yellow, and each subsequent time was steadily deeper orange until the last place was full red.

"This is you here, right?" Karter said, pointing to his sled.

"Yeah," Lex said steadily.

"What color is that?" Karter said.

"Yellow," Lex rumbled.

"Is it? Let's be sure. Ma, read off the color value, would you?"

"Red: FF. Green: FF. Blue: 00," Ma said.

"I think I get the—" Lex began.

"And what's this one up here?" Karter said.

"Red: 00. Green: FF. Blue: 00," Ma said.

"And green is good, right? And red is bad?" Karter said.

"Listen, I realize—" Lex attempted.

"Because Lex here, he's got a LOT of red. Pretty much all the red you can get. And this guy up here? No red. All green. It's almost like Lex is *worse* than this other guy."

"You're not going to—" Lex growled.

"Let's check the next footage, see if he's got any red in that one."

"*Fine! I get it!*" Lex snapped.

He marched over to the seat and plopped down. Squee immediately thumped onto his lap. She pawed his chest for a moment, then tilted her head and slid back down to remain in his lap.

"We'll be simming you in the standard hoversled for your league, with your specific tuning," Ma said.

"And you got that information *how,* exactly?" Lex said.

"Believe it or not, the data security of a bunch of dopes driving in a circle isn't quite as potent as the global governments I'm usually tasked with penetration testing," Karter said. "You'll see a big red button, right where your eject button would normally be. That'll dump you out of the sim. You can also just ask to be dumped, because Ma will be supervising you, or you can probably just resist the sim. It's pretty flimsy and you can knock yourself out of it with any significant pushback. Again, the better to avoid scrambling your eggs. First sim, the control run, not time compressed. Ma, hit him with it."

Lex had a few questions and concerns that seemed worth voicing, but Karter's patience had clearly run out. The simulator kicked on with an audible thump of circuits powering up. He felt a hair-raising crackle of static, and the world around him began to change. The visual aspect was the most comprehensible. As a boy, along with an endless list of other pointlessly self-destructive things he did to pass the time when he should have been doing homework, he used to press on his eyes until little purple blotches started appearing in his vision, curling and spreading like drops of ink in water and interspersed with little blue sparks and flashes. It was like his own personal fireworks show, even though he was probably just cutting off circulation to his retinas and risking blindness. This was like that, except instead of purple-black motes of darkness, a view of a simple but perfectly realistic racetrack through the familiar framework of a hoversled's windscreen oozed in to replace his vision. Though it wasn't quite as explicit and easy to articulate, the same sort of creeping, patchy replacement of one reality with another occurred in each of his senses. Racing gloves and a buckled harness threaded through his sense of touch. The rumbling hum of the engine didn't so much fade in as replace the sounds of the lab in chunky digital blocks. But once the transition was over, he found himself sitting in the seat of something nearly identical to his racing vehicle surrounded by other rumbling hoversleds ready to race.

It would have been unsettling to have this other reality thrust upon him, except despite the impressive fidelity, it wasn't all that convincing. There weren't errors. It wasn't that he felt like he was in a video game. It was just that it was like his brain had helpfully tagged it all as "not real." He didn't feel like he was vibrating in the seat of a powerful hoversled. He felt like he was remembering—very vividly—what it was like. This felt more like his brain had just pressed play on a very deep reminiscence, simultaneously better than a real simulator because it was fully immersive and worse than a simulator because it wasn't fresh, real data piping into his brain.

"Please attempt to minimize your lap time," Ma said, her voice crackling over both an in-simulation speaker in the sled and the PA system in the lab. "In a few moments we will be testing your performance against this time, so we would like it to be representative of your best possible performance on an unfamiliar track."

"Sure. Let's see what this fake sled can do," Lex said.

A countdown popped up. He tightened his grip. Reactors hummed. Thrusters blasted. The race commenced.

He exploded off the line, instantly grinding against the other sleds as they approached the first turn. As with everything else, the fidelity was astonishing. Every element was there. It felt real. And at the same time, he was deeply aware it wasn't. The simulator back at the league headquarters rattled him and bashed him around. But this one was different. All those little things were there. He didn't just hear the screech of metal on metal as he nudged his way between two sleds, he felt it, the vibrations transmitted through the struts to his seat. He could feel the thrum of the reactor. It was as near to reality as he was ever likely to get in a simulator.

Broadly speaking, you didn't do your first run on a track with a bunch of other racers. Not knowing what each individual turn was going to be while also having to plan your turns and try to anticipate the motions of a dozen other sleds was a recipe for ending up at the bottom of a pile of sparking, smoldering vehicular debris. But somehow Lex suspected that Karter both knew that he'd be able to handle it and wanted to see just *how* he'd handle it. Lex didn't disappoint.

By the beginning of the second lap, he was in third place, already getting a feel for not just the track itself but the individual tendencies of the AI opponents. By the end of the second lap, he was solidly in the lead and had trimmed six seconds off the previous lap time. He hit the finish line on lap three with the trailing racers in sight ahead of him. If this had been a five-lap race, he might have worked his way back to the middle of the pack from behind.

"All right," Karter said. "We've got our baseline. Adding a blue button and resetting."

A blue button fizzled into view in the simulation, literally duct-taped in place on one of the struts. Above it was a four-digit LED seven-segment display, currently reading *12:00*.

"Slap that button, and the time collapse will activate. You'll have twelve hours to practice on the track. Ask Ma to tweak the number and difficulty of the AI racers if you want, but when the twelve hours are up, we'll run you through one more time under identical conditions to the control and see how you do."

Lex took a breath and eyed up the button. It didn't inspire confidence that even in a world where he could have made it look perfectly polished and in place, Karter had elected to make the symbolic representation of his device look like a cobbled-together afterthought. But he hadn't come this far just to chicken out. He reached up and tapped the button.

Nothing happened.

Indeed, the only indication that there was any effect at all was when he tried to ask if something was wrong. In the simulation, the words came out just like he expected them to. In real life, it felt like he'd sent the signal to his throat and mouth, but rather than jetting along his nerves faster than he could perceive, the message felt like it was oozing through him, dripping like molasses. Fifteen solid seconds of waiting and his "real" body still felt entirely motionless, stone still. A brief, panic-inducing bolt of concern washed over him. The human brain was not built to grapple with experiencing two realities simultaneously, and it similarly didn't cope well with discovering that voluntary control over one of those realities was gone. All sorts of "you are trapped" reflexes, hard-coded into his brain via millennia of evolution, screamed at him to slap the button. He reflexively obeyed, punching the eject button.

Unlike its piecemeal arrival, the real world rushed in like someone had flipped on the lights. He was instantly in the simulator. A full-body flinch disturbed Squee on his lap, earning him the sort of accusatory glare that only a pet can deliver.

Karter glanced at a reading on the wall display, which had shifted to a sort of dashboard with stats about the simulation and experiment.

"Eighteen seconds. You lasted eighteen seconds before you noped out? Pansy," Karter remarked.

Lex took a breath. His heart wasn't even pounding. His body hadn't had time to catch up to the panic he'd felt in the simulation. Having a mental panic attack while one's body was still utterly calm was yet another in the growing list of new experiences Lex was racking up in this experiment.

"Okay. Let me try that again," he said.

"You sure? You're not going to lose your nerve and eject again? I don't have time for test pilots who lack the nerve to actually *test* something."

"Just start it up," Lex rumbled.

The simulation bled into his senses once more. He steeled himself, then punched the blue button. Taking special care to ignore the muted sensations flowing in from outside the sim, he fixed his eyes on the countdown and prepared for his second run on the track.

Lex leaned aside in anticipation of the upcoming turn, easing down on the repulsors on the left side. He was riding a little close to the lead sled. The drift across the track would cause a collision. No need to avoid the hit, but at this trajectory it'd screw with his angle. He needed to full-broadside the collision to keep his line. A punch of the throttle moved him up enough to knock his opponent out of place and line him up maybe six centimeters off the optimal line. Not bad.

He crossed the finish, ready for the second lap of what was probably his seventy-fifth run on the track. In addition to the actual racers, the fuzzy cloud of ghost replays of previous runs were there for him to compete with as well. He was near the front of the pack of those, not matching his best time, but well ahead of the average. He was already six turns ahead, planning out an earlier brake timing on the sharp left near the end of the lap, when the timer over the blue button hit zero and the simulation—and the time collapse—dumped back to reality.

His hand was still extended, mimicking the motion within the simulation that was necessary to activate the time collapse. He shuddered again, some cobbled-together combination of all the nerve impulses he'd fired off during the time collapse hitting his muscles roughly at the same time. Squee, who had yet to really settle in after the last interruption, irritably jumped down and started investigating the room for something suitably warm and stationary to perch upon.

"How are you feeling?" Ma asked. "Any confusion, disorientation? Please describe your cognitive and psychological symptoms."

"I feel… I feel fine. I actually feel more unsettled after *leaving* the simulation than when I was in it. Just because of how suddenly it happened."

"Any head pain? Blurred vision?" Ma asked.

"No. Why, should there be?"

"She's just nervous because your brain looked exactly like you were in the early stages of a seizure," Karter said.

"It did?" Lex said anxiously.

"Relax. This is a 'the tingle means it's working' situation. You just had twelve hours of perceptive activity in around a tenth of a second. It made a single snapshot of your brain activity look like a time lapse."

"I'd like to perform a follow-up scan to be sure," Ma said. "Please climb onto the medical scanner."

Lex stood up. His brain kept on raising little red flags, not for things that were wrong but for things that weren't. He wasn't stiff. He wasn't sore. From his point of view, he'd just spent half a day in the same seat, but he didn't feel anything of the sort. He wasn't even tired or hungry. It was precisely as though the simulation hadn't happened.

She performed the scan.

"What's the verdict?" Lex said.

"You are in perfect health. There is a minor buildup of some chemical receptors, similar to what we would expect to see from a brief overstimulation, equivalent to a sneeze or being startled by a loud noise. You are already returning to normal in that regard. No ill effects. The only notable changes are in the hippocampus at the quantum level, indicating a disproportionate quantity of synaptic connectivity. You have made a significant number of new memories."

"Plus that lesion is still there," Karter said.

"What lesion? Where's this lesion?" Lex said quickly.

"You have an insect bite on your neck just below the hairline," Ma said.

"*Why didn't you say that in the first place!?*" Lex said. "Who says 'lesion' instead of 'bug bite'?"

"Someone who values medical accuracy and doesn't have the vocabulary of a toddler. Point is, you failed to die, which is the skill of yours that I value. Now all we need to do is load you back into the simulator with no time compression and see if you developed any new expertise in 'go fast,' which is the skill that *you* value. If so, you've got yourself a way to cram an arbitrarily large amount of training into basically any amount of time. And I've got something maybe worth marketing, pending some long-term testing results."

Lex sat back down in the simulator. Squee eyed him from across the room, judging if it was worth climbing onto his lap and thinking better of it. The sim oozed its way back into his mind, this time with the notable absence of the blue button. Ma initiated the countdown, and Lex instantly blasted to the lead. The ghosts from his other trials were absent, but after so many iterations, he had a pretty good feel for what the timer should look like at any given turn. By the time he crossed the finish line for the last time, he'd lapped almost the entire group of opponents and was a full thirty-six seconds faster than the control run. One last time, the simulation dropped away.

"Pretty good improvement for approximately zero point zero eight seconds of practice," Karter said. "I'm convinced. You already have a TymFlex, a Carpinelli Field Generator, and a mental cloak in your ship, so this is basically a software update. Ma, do the deed and send him on this way."

Karter was already marching for the door before he finished talking.

"Wait," Lex said, popping up. "I don't understand. Even neglecting the time fiddling, that was an incredible simulator. If you designed a thing that can just beam whatever experiences someone wants into their brain, why isn't that available in every electronics retailer in the galaxy?"

"Regulation," Karter said. "For some reason, one of the only things the Teekers, the Earth Coalition, and the Orionians agree with is 'nonmedical devices that have direct external influence over synaptic behavior are strictly prohibited.' So I have to jump through all these hoops, and, frankly, the red tape isn't worth it. Plus, all it takes is a couple thousand people with iffy noodles leaking their cortexes out their noses because of the product, and they *all* get pulled from the shelves. More trouble than it's worth. But every new data point adds to the likelihood that at least *one* of the panglobal governments will change their mind and give something like this a go. So maybe you'll have a hand in revolutionizing gaming. Or pornography. Either one."

"I was thinking more along the lines of education," Lex said.

"Sure you were," Karter said.

He opened the door. The tippy-tap of little feet immediately caused Squee to perk up. She dashed for the hallway and tackled Solby, the pair happily tussling on the ground. Karter stepped over them and continued on his way.

"You kind of set me up to assume he was going to be a little much. He seemed pretty even-keeled to me," Lex said to Ma.

"That was, by a wide measure, the most stable and reasonable he has been in six weeks. I have been attempting to devise some means to occupy his mind, as he has been substantially unchallenged of late. He has lost interest in his unfinished projects."

"Why?"

"Unclear. But it is my theory that the semiregular near-catastrophes that have characterized your interactions with him have provided him with a far greater level of intellectual enrichment than his projects in the years preceding or the months since. It is also, I hope, a sign that he has developed a fondness for human interaction. Isolation allows him to convince himself that his whims are acceptable within a sane and rational society. It is a nontrivial dilemma. On one hand, his self-isolation was done, in part, to spare the galaxy at large from his more destructive tendencies. On the other, his isolation is gradually eroding what little limitations he had placed on his destructive tendencies."

"I don't envy you, being the caregiver to that bag of cats."

"It is, if nothing else, a source of continuous intellectual effort and thus continuous intellectual growth." The view on the wall-sized display switched to the inside of the hangar where the *SOB* was now docked. "Coal has linked her systems to the laboratory and provided permission to upgrade them. It will take seventeen minutes to upgrade the software to facilitate the snap-back simulator. If you like, I can perform Squee's memory maintenance while I am at it. That will take approximately one hour. I'm sure Karter would be pleased if you would stay for dinner."

Lex looked to the camera in the corner of the room in lieu of a face and raised his eyebrow.

"I revise my prior statement. *I* would be pleased if you would stay for dinner, and I theorize that it would do Karter well."

"What's cooking?" he asked.

"Literally anything you desire."

"Cook up some of that chili and you're on."

"Lovely," Ma said.

A short time later, Lex sat down in the cafeteria of the lab. A freshly prepared bowl of lime-seasoned tortilla chips and a steaming bowl of chili were set on the table with a frosty mug of his favorite beer. Four bowls had been set on the floor: two water bowls and two bowls of beans and rice. They were labeled *Squee* and *Soul Brother* respectively. In what was just the latest example of why Squee's intelligence was knocking on the door of unnerving, the funk dropped from her perch on Lex's shoulders and walked past Solby's bowl to bury her face in her own food.

"Where's Karter?" Lex asked.

"He will be along shortly. It is Solby's feeding time. He occasionally forgets to eat for days at a time but never forgets to feed Solby."

A display in the corner of the room flicked through a series of internal cameras until the shirtless Karter appeared, stepping off the elevator with Solby tapping along behind him. A few seconds later, he stepped through the door and grabbed a tray. After an explosive burst of enthusiastic greeting between the pair of funks, they indulged in their food while Karter mounded a squat pyramid of burritos onto his tray and walked toward the door again. When it hissed open, it was blocked by one of the mobile assembly arms that served as Ma's physical surrogate.

"Perhaps you would like to eat your meal here with your friend," Ma said.

Karter turned. "That's alternately a contractor and a client," he said.

"Then perhaps you would like to eat your meal with your business associate," Ma said.

Karter lingered in the doorway for a moment, then trudged to the table and sat opposite Lex.

"So," Lex said. "Ma tells me you're having a hard time."

"I gotta work on her psychological analysis routines."

"I don't know, I think they're spot-on."

"You're employing a military contractor to give you an experimental piece of equipment because you're too afraid to accept there might be someone out there as good as you are. I think there's a pot-and-kettle phrase for this situation."

"Ah, yes. The 'I know you are, but what am I?' defense."

"Ma, beer me," Karter said.

The assembly arm pulled a bottle of beer from a tub of ice and opened it with a built-in bottle opener, then set it down on the table in front of him.

"I would like to point out that I am very shortly going to be in possession of an empty beer bottle. If you have any sort of data retention at all, that should worry you."

"Well, let me ask you this. What's your current project?"

"I have seven hundred projects in various stages of completion."

"I didn't ask that. I asked what's your *current* project," Lex said.

"Apparently it's talking to an idiot about nothing."

"You know, I kind of expected you to be more violent than petulant."

Karter, rather impressively, managed to shove an entire burrito into his mouth. After minimal chewing, he swallowed enough to clear room in his mouth to messily speak. "Trim out the last few years, basically since you met me, and ask yourself this. Did you do anything at all in your life that was worthwhile?"

Lex paused. "Not especially, but I was on my way."

"Did you figure you were on your way to saving the galaxy?"

"No. Mostly just racing."

"And now that you *have* saved the galaxy, does the shine on the rose of being a system-class racer gleam quite so bright?" Karter asked.

"I never aspired to be a hero."

"I didn't ask that," Karter said mockingly. "Does being a racer *really* matter to you anymore?"

"You were just making fun of me for going to insane lengths to get ahold of the brass ring. Of *course* it still matters to me."

"Does it? Or are you just using it as an excuse to dip back into the Big Sigma lab and play with the toys the big boys play with one more time?"

"The first one," he said flatly.

"I wish I had your lack of ambition," Karter said, taking a sip of beer. "Tiny people, grinning at the shiny little baubles life throws their way. Must be nice."

He mashed another burrito into his mouth and spoke up again about two swallows too soon, flinging half-chewed bits of it in Lex's general direction. "Ma is hoping that having you here will get me to spray my problems all over you. So to make her happy, sit tight, because here's the way things are. I don't care about the things most humans care about. Money? I own my own planet. There is literally nothing that I could want and is for sale that I can't have. I'm set. Glory? I've worked on or outright *invented* several of the underpinning technologies of our age. Society as it exists right now could not do so without my brilliance. Any accurate record of history would include my name in the top-ten most relevant people to have ever lived. No history *will* say that, because no history is accurate. There are always names buried in the sand, and I couldn't care less. What else is there? Family? I've built minds better than mine from raw circuits and code. If there is some sort of satisfaction to be had for producing progeny, I've done a better job of it than any mother or father ever could."

"I presume you are speaking, at least in part, about creating me," Ma said. "I would like to take this moment to say it is the nicest thing you have ever said about me, Karter. It is also one of only seven positive things you have ever said about me."

"Don't get too comfortable in the praise, Ma. I was splitting it between you and Solby. What is there... Companionship? See earlier statements about being able to afford anything that's for sale. If life is a competition, and it is, then I won it years ago."

"And you're not happy," Lex said.

"Of course I'm not happy. The only people you ever see who are happy are people on commercials trying to sell their happiness to you or people with minds too small to fully digest the utter pointlessness of existence. You of all people should know that. You've been to other planes of existence. Other timelines. You know better than anyone else that nothing matters and no one matters."

"You're a real ball of sunshine, you know that?" Lex said.

"Laugh it up, Chuckles. You know I'm right. I'm Alexander the Great over here. I've climbed every mountain. Conquered every army. You want to know what's wrong with me right now? I'm bored. There is nothing worth doing. I'm just frittering away the days waiting for *something* that I can sink my teeth into. Best I can figure is working out how to reverse entropy. That's a good one. But then what?"

"I'm sure there are other unsolved problems. What about immortality?"

Karter gazed evenly at Lex and took a silent sip of beer.

"If I didn't think of something, you're sure not going to." He finished his beer and hurled it past Lex's head, shattering it on the wall behind him. It wasn't clear if he missed on purpose or because he didn't care to aim. "You got your simulator. Make sure to put it through its paces, pipe the data back to me. Solby, have fun with your friend. I'll be in the propulsion lab, seeing about that new thruster."

"I will have a fresh vat of synth skin ready for grafting," Ma said.

Karter rumbled with a sound that was utterly devoid of meaning and marched out the door.

"Oof," Lex said as the mobile arm connected a vacuum hose to a port on the wall and began cleaning up the glass.

"I thank you for your help in this regard. That was the most forthcoming Karter has been about his internal state in quite some time. It will help me to devise a therapeutic regimen to improve his mental hygiene."

"I don't envy you. Flossing the gunk out of that brain is going to take some serious effort."

"Would you like to continue our own discussion, utilizing the valid points he made about your own recent behavior as a jumping-off point?"

"You want to psychoanalyze me?"

"Three adversarial psychoanalysis subroutines are running at all times that I am interacting with human beings, testing their assertions against each other in attempts to increase their accuracy. I was merely inquiring if you would like me to share my insight."

"Not just now. Thanks."

"As you wish. We can discuss less weighty matters," Ma said. "How are your clothes fitting these days?"

"Been a while since you did small talk, huh?"

"I have been testing a new calibration set with that regard."

"Well my pants fit fine," Lex said. "Now about that system you installed. Do you have any instructions or warnings?"

"Relevant data are as follows..."

• • • • ● • ● • • •

"Did you have a nice time?" Coal asked as Lex slipped into the pilot's seat after bidding the local AI adieu.

"Nice talking to Ma. Karter's falling apart in new and exciting ways," Lex said. "It's kind of sad, really."

"I understand times of psychological stress can frequently lead to an increase in the quantity and quality of creative output. I have also heard that times of psychological stress can lead to the complete cessation of creative output. So perhaps Karter will begin producing heartfelt poetry, or perhaps he will stop inventing weapons of mass destruction. Both would be highly positive!"

"Somehow I suspect that Karter's poetry would be roughly on par with a weapon of mass destruction. Ma upgraded your software, right?"

"Correct. I now have the capacity to run physically accurate simulations and perform targeted compressions of the flow of time, both inside my own coprocessors and in your sensory cortex."

"Did she give you the manual?"

"Of course she did. It is important I know the user interface for my own features."

"Bring it up on the display and take us up through the debris field. I want to double-check some of the safety stuff."

The hanger doors opened, Squee plopped around his neck like something between a travel pillow and a scarf, and a green corridor was illuminated in the heads-up display, tracing out a safe path through the debris field. He scrolled through the voluminous text, clearly written by Ma. There was a quality to her written communications. The attempt to communicate information with a perfect balance of conciseness and completeness made for some truly legendary achievements in sentence structure.

"Do you have specific concerns?" Coal asked.

"I just want to make sure it's safe to have fun with this thing."

"Including the prerequisite of not leading to your death?"

"Exactly."

"It is my understanding that the only genuine risk that would take less than ninety-five simulator years to manifest is excessive synapse stimulation. That is something I can monitor for and prevent."

"Even so. I like to be familiar with the 'what not to do' list before I blast my brain with radiation."

"Humans have a complicated relationship with radiation. You have a deeply ingrained fear of it, yet so many of your favorite pursuits involve saturating yourselves with varying levels of it."

"We're a riddle of a species, what can I say?" Lex said.

The ship jostled its way along a jagged path through the unnaturally dense cloud of debris that Karter carefully cultivated as a defense. For the most part, the warnings in the manual were nothing he hadn't already been told during his chili-filled chat with Ma. Indeed, the bulk of the warnings had the precise same wordings as those she'd provided verbally. But he couldn't shake the feeling that this particular gadget was one he should be taking care with. He had handled some truly terrifying equipment courtesy of Karter. By comparison, if he disregarded the specific mechanism by which it did its job, this wasn't all that worrisome. Sure, it was able to overlay an entirely different set of sensations over his senses, but twelve or so hours under the influence made it clear that even when time was being monkeyed with, he could still feel the artificiality of it. Not enough to rob it of the benefits he was hoping to achieve, but enough that he wouldn't be fooled if the whole "trapped in the simulation" angle that pop culture so adored were to come to pass.

Addiction was a concern, he supposed. If it was half as useful as it seemed like it would be, he'd be spending a *lot* of time in it. But the whole danger of addiction was having it consume your life, and this simulator basically *created* its own time. He could spend literal years toying with different racing scenarios inside the sim and not even miss lunch. By any realistic measure, this simulator was the least dangerous thing Karter had given him in ages.

And yet...

He finished reading over the warnings right around when Coal had left the influence of Big Sigma's gravity.

"Are we heading directly back to Operlo?" Coal asked.

"Yeah. Like Preethy said, we should make sure to get back in plenty of time. Let's take… this route back," he said, connecting the dots between a sequence of destinations.

"The third leg of the trip takes us quite near to the X-52 nebula. Particle concentration may be too high to maintain FTL."

"I think we'll manage," Lex said.

"I, as always, shall trust your insight," Coal said. "I have received damage sufficient to warrant major repair only three times while serving as the control system of the *SOB*, and one of them was arguably through my own actions."

"Arguably? You attempted to 'upgrade' a wall into a door."

"I argue that such a feature should be considered standard usage for a high-utility spacefaring vehicle. Engaging Carpinelli Drive for initial jump."

The dazzling display outside the cockpit happened chiefly in Lex's peripheral vision. As magnificent as it was to see the results of humanity's most significant victory over physics, he was much more interested in its most recent victory.

"Coal, can you load the sim data for the Operlo track please?"

"I have already cached it for you."

"You're a pip, you know that?"

"Being a pip is one of my primary functions."

"Okay. Let's boot up the sim and get some practice in, shall we?"

Chapter 2

The length of the trip from Big Sigma to the first major hub he'd selected was about six hours. For Lex, it felt like it had been more like seventy-eight hours. The first "day" or so had taken some getting used to. The human mind simply wasn't accustomed to not suffering any sort of major physical needs after more than half a day had passed. It took genuine effort to avoid snacking after every twelve-hour session. Even if he logically knew that he'd eaten a granola bar less than three seconds earlier, several million years of instinct and a couple of decades of habit said that half a day of any activity called for some food and water.

But the progress. The *progress*. Running through the simulation still wasn't quite as good as having real drivers. The racing simulator Karter had provided seemed to be based on the same logic as the official ones Preethy had set up for the league. He wouldn't put it past Karter to have just hacked in and grabbed the code directly. For all he knew, it was the other way around and Karter was the one who *wrote* the simulator. Anything was possible with that guy. The point was it was entirely compatible with the race data pulled from that season. Using the data, AI behavior models had been built to mimic the actual racers he'd be competing against. They were close from a computer science standpoint. If he let them race each other without being part of the mix, they'd probably end up running something very similar to a past race. But they didn't react to *him* the way the real drivers did. There was a difference between how Kyle Byres reacted to "a racer" trying to pass him on the outside of a shallow turn and how he reacted to *Lex* doing that. It wasn't the kind of thing likely to be picked up by an external observer, but it was literally the difference between a first-place finish and a ten-sled pileup at the level that Lex was racing.

The "seams" between the simulation and reality were a bit visible sometimes. Aside from being perpetually aware of the simulation and his incredibly slow reality, every so often he found it a little difficult to focus. It wasn't anything serious, just a vague feeling of fuzzy distraction, like someone was holding a conversation while he was trying to write something else down. Little flashes of weird memories, little half-considered concerns or hypotheticals, and fragments of distraction like that seemed to come up a lot more often during the simulation.

Still, he couldn't argue the value of being able to spend literal days trying and retrying every little experimental change in timing. Or the ability to spend six uninterrupted hours A-B testing different tactics. Or the ability to simulate different wind conditions and different heat conditions. And all the while knowing that he wasn't *really* burning time. He'd upped his consistency and shaved his time by more in the past two sim-days than he had in the last two real-world weeks. He'd have to run at least a few real-world time trials to be sure the simulator's results were close enough to reality to be able to trust the findings, but he had a good feeling about it. It didn't feel real, but it felt close enough that the skills should carry over. And best of all, for the first time in years, he actually felt *tired* of running test scenarios rather than feeling the itch to run more.

Among other things, finally getting his fill of simulation meant he was far more engaged with the wildly divergent conversations with Coal that filled the gaps between sims.

"So the human mind, at a level beneath directly observable comprehension, operates according to a weakly calibrated timing pulse, a rhythm, and music helps to externalize that rhythm, both reinforcing it and permitting humans to alter the rhythm. Is that accurate?" Coal asked.

"It's more accurate than anything *else* you've said about music. So we're getting there," Lex said.

"I am pleased to be making progress. We are approaching our first stop. The space station outside the hub, according to its directory, includes a component shop. May I suggest you acquire a fast-charge power-conditioning battery module, connection type 2123-6d?"

"Why? Is something broken?" Lex asked.

"Potentially. I am seeing unusual activity on the gravitational sensors, in that I am seeing *no* activity on the gravitational sensors. Because I am forced to run a subset of my control system and the entire simulator inside a time-compressed field, the power consumption during simulator sessions appears to the rest of the system as a massive momentary spike. By strict interpretation of system performance parameters, that should be something the *SOB* can tolerate, but it is possible the power dips have caused unexpected behavior. The aforementioned power module should solve the issue."

"If gravity sensors are flaky, we should probably drop out of FTL a little early," he said.

"A reasonable precaution."

He took manual control and eased them back into the kind of velocities nature intended. The moment he did so, it was clear there was something *very* wrong. At FTL, the ship's systems had to filter out just about anything but gravity fields. Anything in the EM spectrum just blue-shifted up past X-ray radiation and became meaningless. But at normal velocities, particularly this close to a hub, his com system should be lit up with a couple hundred different active channels. Likewise, the single clump of gravity readings they'd seen in FTL should have separated into a couple dozen individual blobs moving at their own pace when they slowed down. Those would be the ships running along the nearby corridor. But instead of any of that, there was radio silence, and every single gravity field was stationary.

"Man. The sensors are totally borked," Lex said, performing the first step of any diagnostic process in the form of a tap to the sensor display.

"I will run a self-diagnostic. Stand by... Processing... Diagnostic complete. The sensor array is performing optimally. The readings are accurate."

"The readings are *not* accurate. Look. That's Umbriel-Cirrus-3. And that's its moon. The moon's relative velocity to the planet is zero. Are you telling me that the moon stopped orbiting?"

"I am telling you that the moon's velocity is zero. I am telling you that because the gravitational sensors say that the moon's velocity is zero. The sensor is telling you that because the gravitational waves indicate the moon's velocity is zero. The gravitational waves are indicating that because the mass of the moon has ceased to distort space-time sufficiently to indicate otherwise."

He grabbed the control yoke and guided the ship toward the hub. He kept his eyes wide, watching for anything he might crash into. Having the safety and proximity sensors start telling him nonsense had a way of making him suddenly aware of how desperately he relied upon them.

"You realize it's impossible for a moon to just *stop*, right?" Lex said.

"It isn't impossible. It simply requires a massive amount of energy to be directed in opposition to its present course. The energy would also need to be somehow delivered in a way that did not pulverize the moon."

"And is there any sign that happened?"

"The gravitational sensors are indicating it happened. That was the impetus of this discussion. Has the simulator damaged your memory?"

"No! I just... Never mind. What's up with the radio silence?"

"Unclear. I am detecting some minor EM fluctuations, but they are not proper transmissions."

"What are they?"

"Based upon their intensity and what appears to be a direct correlation with the velocity of the ship, they are Doppler shifts in isolation."

"What do you mean? You're seeing an increase in frequency, but no frequency?"

"More accurately, I am seeing an increase in frequency with a starting frequency of zero."

"But that'd mean... the radio waves aren't moving either. They're standing still and we're just sweeping past them."

"Correct."

"That doesn't make any sense either."

"It is my decided opinion that my sensors are more trustworthy than reality. If you have a problem with my assessment, reality is at fault."

Lex maneuvered the ship as close as he could to the monitored corridor, eyeing up the gravity sensors and the long-range sensors as he did. What worried him was that the sensors were quite clearly in agreement. A midsize passenger ship was just outside visual range on both the proximity and gravity sensors. He targeted the section of space with the visible light cameras. At this range, attempting to see anything that was moving even slightly was pointless. The nearest star was quite some distance away. The light here was effectively nonexistent.

"Can you do one of those long exposures?" Lex said.

"It is not a default behavior of the visual surveillance, but I should be able to coax that out of the sensor. Am I correct in assuming you are seeking a light-amplified sweep of the area where the nearest ship should be?"

"Yes."

"Placing the real-time-updating results on the HUD now."

A black rectangle appeared. Once per second, it updated. Points of light formed a starfield. A large, dark mass blocked the central portion of the starfield. Slowly, details began to emerge. After sixty-eight seconds, what he was seeing was a recognizable ship of the proper shape and size. Lex piloted his own ship closer. A second, clearer long exposure was achieved.

"There's a ship entirely stationary in a VectorCorp-monitored FTL corridor..." Lex said.

"Within sensor range there are sixteen ships entirely stationary in a VectorCorp-monitored FTL corridor," Coal corrected.

"You aren't allowed to be stationary in an FTL corridor. And it's not like you'd just run out of fuel and stop. We're in space. It takes a precise amount of reverse thrust to bring something to a complete stop."

"Accurate."

"The moment someone dropped to within fifteen percent of the minimum allowable velocity for the lane, they would have activated safety protocols and moved that thing out of there. Where's the nearest communication pylon?" Lex asked, tapping through the navigation charts.

"One hundred and seventy-six thousand kilometers away, in the indicated heading," Coal said.

Lex maneuvered the ship to the proper heading and performed an FTL jump. Once he dropped down into normal velocities, he let the *SOB* drift until it was nearly touching the pylon.

"This thing should be sending out all sorts of alerts. It should be alerting VC that the corridor is jammed up. It should be alerting them that I'm too close to it. Are we getting anything out of it?" Lex asked.

"There is no channel activity beyond the interference we passed through on our approach," Coal said.

Lex keyed the com system and started broadcasting on all channels. "Hello? Anyone? There seems to be a pretty massive problem in... in the sector indicated in the metadata of this call," he said, teetering too close to the precipice of panic to figure out how to efficiently articulate his location. "If anyone is receiving, please respond."

He waited a moment. "Anything, Coal?"

"We received an echo of your broadcast. A physical one, not a rebroadcast."

"Is the time-squisher-thing on?" Lex said.

"No."

"Could it be on and we both think it's off?"

"Unlikely. The Carpinelli Field Generator is not pulling power."

"Do a full system reboot. I want thirty seconds of zero power, just to be absolutely sure."

"Acknowledged. Shutting down."

The lights in the cockpit steadily winked out. He was left in utter darkness, distant starlight barely visible as needle-sharp points through the cockpit. Thirty seconds is an awfully long time when you don't have the foresight to count it off accurately. Plenty of time for the brain to utterly convince itself that *SOB* had fully malfunctioned and would not be starting back up, leaving him stranded in space during what could charitably be called an anomalous event and could more rightly be called a supernatural catastrophe. The soft breathing of Squee, blissfully asleep around his neck despite his outbursts, was the only thing that kept him grounded long enough for the systems to start flicking on again.

"Altruistic Artificial Intelligence Control System, version 1.27, revision 2331.04.01c, subset 2.7d, designation Coal, fully initiated. Has there been any improvement?" Coal asked.

"You tell me."

"Sensor readings remain in their previous state."

"Okay... okay... Are there any sensors we *haven't* used yet?"

"A have some macro sensors, some quantum discriminators, and—"

"Turn them all on. Scan things. Scan everything."

"Stand by."

A sequence of progress bars imposed themselves on the HUD and slowly filled.

"Processing... Processing... The only additional finding is that there is a degree of quantum activity within the pylon commensurate with a narrow entanglement communication mode."

"So the pylon's working?"

"A very limited subset of the pylon's passive systems are functioning."

"Can you, I don't know, hack in? Maybe we can get a message out?"

"A quantum communication pylon is one of the most secure data exchange methods ever devised. With my current systems, it would take several thousand years to devise a method to establish an unauthorized link."

"... Several thousand years," Lex said.

"Correct."

"Bear with me here. We have the time-collapser thing. And you can use it to speed up your calculation for twelve hours at a time..."

"Interesting. Assuming a mean penetration time of two thousand years, that would require approximately twenty-eight hours of real time."

"So can you do it?"

"No. The power supply of the ship is substantial but not inexhaustible. I would not be able to perform collapsed-time calculation for that long without fatiguing the ship's systems to the point of failure and draining the cockpit power supply. After seventeen real-world hours of collapsed time, the data integrity would be unrecoverable and power supply would fail, taking life support with it. Do you think you could hold your breath for eleven hours while periodically replacing logic boards and manually recharging the cockpit power?"

"No."

"Then we would need to reach someplace with additional resources. Alternately... Stand by."

A communication window popped up in the HUD, topped by another progress bar.

"Incoming call. Negotiating connection," Coal said.

"How did you do that?" Lex said, baffled.

"The penetration methods described would be necessary for an unauthorized link. This link is authorized. Someone is calling you. Link established."

A face appeared in the communication window. The flawless synthetic skin, smoldering red eyes, and silvery fiber-optic hair were instantly familiar to Lex.

"Ziva?" he said.

"Hello, Lex. I am sorry to bother you, but it would appear that something is amiss."

"Amiss. Yeah. That's one word for it. I see Ma never loses her gift for understatement."

Ziva was one of the more difficult to conceive of consequences of Lex's many adventures. Due to a botched time-travel jump, he'd encountered her in a distant future. She was that future's resident evolution of Ma, centralized into a humanoid body for the sake of mobility and redundancy from her main systems. A deep copy of her systems had been brought back from that future, and a local duplicate had been built when her expertise were needed to solve one of several galactic threats Lex had somehow blundered into having to defeat. Now she spent her time supervising the southern hemisphere of Big Sigma, a place set aside by the mad engineer for dealing with matters that posed a threat to causality. Pleasant as it was to get a call from a friend, particularly in this harrowing moment, she was *not* someone Lex had ever hoped to hear from again.

"Is this a temporal contingency situation?" Lex asked.

"Not one that I had anticipated, but were I to be asked to define the nature of the current issue, I would certainly classify it a temporal hazard."

"Great. Great, great, great. Super," Lex said.

"Hello, Ziva!" Coal said. "My experience escaping the GenMech horde with you satisfied all prerequisites to be classified as fun."

"Likewise," Ziva said.

"What do we know about what's going on?" Lex said.

"According to the information available to me, it appears that the vast majority of motion in the universe has ceased. I am unable to contact anyone but you. Not even Karter is responding. It is almost as great a source of confusion that this call was successful as it is that the orbit and rotation of Big Sigma seems to have halted without catastrophic results. For certain definitions of catastrophe, that is."

"So as far as we can tell, the *SOB*, your little headquarters, and the guts of this string of pylons are the only things in the universe that are moving."

"That would match my observations."

"Is there something wrong with the rest of the universe, or is there something wrong with us?" Lex asked.

"As a broad heuristic, it is more likely that a sudden malfunction is limited in scope rather than encompassing all of creation."

"I still think the universe is wrong. I personally recalibrated these sensors during my last maintenance overhaul. They are accurate," Coal said.

"Coal, would you please deliver your log files since your departure from Big Sigma?" Ziva said.

"Transmitting," Coal said.

"Received. If you are confident you can navigate your way here, I think it would be best if we collaborated. I will continue my analysis. Hopefully I will have more information at that time."

"See you soon," Lex said.

The call disconnected.

"Let's get back to the scene of the crime," Lex said. "If this is Karter's fault, I'm going to make sure he never forgets it."

"By strict technical interpretation of the facts, if this issue *was* caused by Karter, it would mean that he succeeded in making you the fastest pilot in the universe. Given the purpose of your visit, that would appear to be the desired outcome."

Lex narrowed his eyes. "Let's just get moving..."

• • • • ● • ● • • •

Six hours later, he was once again dropping out of FTL in the vicinity of Big Sigma.

"Whoa..." Lex muttered as the planet came into visual range.

At a distance, Big Sigma was the same fuzzy gray ball of dirt with a cloud of smaller dirt around it. But as he got close enough for the fuzziness to resolve into individual elements of debris, the impact of the current situation was hammered home. They were all perfectly still, untold numbers of bits of junk frozen in position. The cloud was still dense, but even a novice pilot could have made it through in this state. It was just a matter of identifying gaps large enough to fit a ship through.

"Wild," he said, easing the ship down out of the field. "What the heck happened to us..."

"I don't know, but that wasn't nearly as entertaining as our typical descent. I would prefer we solve this problem if only to restore the navigational enjoyment of a Big Sigma visit," Coal said.

"Not near the top of my personal list for fixing things, but I can't say I disagree," Lex said.

Out of habit, he nearly landed in the courtyard of the primary lab complex, but he wasn't here to visit Karter, and it was just as well. Sensors told the same cold tale of perfect stillness within the laboratory and without. Regardless of his role in this catastrophe, Karter had not been spared its effects. Lex continued south, whisking over the crater-pocked landscape. Three separate debris collisions were frozen midimpact, their dust and dirt forming a crown of soil frozen in time. A few other flaming streaks marked the next set of impacts, should universal motion be restored. Finally, he came to the equator and whisked over it.

"This feels wrong. Like walking over a grave," Lex said. "I can feel it in my bones that I shouldn't be down here."

"I suspect that feeling is a subconscious reaction to passing over land which may or may not contain time-displaced duplicates of you waiting to be awakened after causality-defying hijinks."

"I'm the last copy that was hidden down here," Lex said. "That is to say, I'm the *original* Lex and I've finished making trips through this place."

"As far as you know," Coal said. "There are multiple duplicates and derivatives of me, in the form of Ma and Ziva. Why shouldn't there be additional duplicates of you?"

"Because I'm a human. We're unique."

"Your DNA has a limited storage capacity. That means the total possible human biodiversity has an upper limit, so—"

"Coal, I really don't need a second existential quandary right now."

"I shall set this observation aside for a time when you have more philosophical bandwidth."

"Thanks."

After a few minutes of carefully keeping his eyes trained on the horizon to avoid seeing anything he shouldn't be seeing, he spotted the low, flat complex that he knew to be Ziva's home base. He brought the *SOB* down and popped the hatch. The moment he did, Squee launched from the cockpit and made eager use of the dusty ground. They'd just spent twelve hours in transit, which was six hours longer than he typically liked to travel without giving Squee walkies. There *were* ways to deal with that sort of thing in zero gravity, but it was unpleasant for all involved. Between having to deal with Squee and having to deal with himself, Lex was feeling extremely conflicted about having a ship computer that was intelligent enough to hold a conversation. So far she'd had the tact to avoid dwelling upon it, but Lex knew it was only a matter of time before she filled a whole flight with her ruminations on body functions.

The door to the facility slid open, and no fewer than six funks burst from inside, making the area outside the doorway boil and burst with furry bodies like a pot of popcorn. Lex was nearly knocked to the ground as three of them tried to claim his shoulders at the same time.

"Sweeties, inside," remarked Ziva in her pristine, smooth voice.

Ziva was the only iteration of Ma so far that had taken the time to fully unify her patchwork voice. Whereas Ma and Coal both had varying degrees of separation between the assorted voice lines that had been broken down into their phonemes to construct her speech, Ziva's voice was a single tone, smoothly unifying all three voices with a slight weight on the voice actress who also served as the broad basis for her synthetic facial features.

"Hello, Lex. I wish I could say that it was lovely to see you again, but by the nature of my role, the very fact we are speaking is made possible only by a cataclysmic event."

"Yeah. A surprisingly large portion of my contact list comprises people who only talk to me if the world is about to end. And yet we stay in touch pretty frequently," Lex said. "Please tell me you found some answers."

"Come inside. There *are* things to discuss." She turned. "Coal, I'm afraid the hangars at my disposal are, for reasons that should be clear based upon my role as overseer of discontinuous visitations, not available for guest lodging. I will, of course, bridge your communication system with the internal system so that you can be part of the discussion, and I will begin reconfiguring the internal structure of my general purpose facility to accommodate you. Do you require anything in addition?"

"I don't suppose you have a fast-charge power-conditioning battery module, connection type 2123-6d."

"Not at the moment, but I have a small-scale fabricator which should be able to produce one within the hour. I shall queue it up."

"Then I'll just fly around until it's done."

"Please disregard anything you see."

"I will do so."

The cockpit snapped shut and the thrusters flared, startling the six non-Squee funks milling about, including one who seemed to have the black and white aspects of its patterning swapped. They rushed to Ziva, huddling behind her while Squee happily trotted over, completely unbothered by the rush of thrust tousling her fur as she did. Once Squee was inside, Ziva shut the door. A few things differentiated this facility from Karter's. For one, rather than the sudden and complete reassertion of gravity upon stepping in, the gravity slowly returned after the door was shut. It gave the overall impression of the whole facility rising up like an elevator when it was closed. Then there was the decor. Karter seemed capable of only two levels of ambiance in his facilities: sterile laboratory and cluttered dormitory. Ziva's design aesthetic certainly skewed toward the sterile, but where it diverged from that, it diverged in unexpected ways. First was the layout. Rather than a hallway connecting assorted rooms, the place was one sprawling space. Even the columns supporting the roof were narrow and scattered. It took "open floor plan" to an absurd level. Most of the space was completely empty and not even fully illuminated. It produced an oddly creepy atmosphere of a pool of light fading into a dim, sparse forest of columns. The far wall was entirely swallowed by darkness, producing the odd sense that this place continued onward forever.

The lack of lighting was not the only thing that made the space seem disused. There was very little furniture to speak of. Three chairs total could be seen. One was a massive, overstuffed loveseat with all the hallmarks of being the place the funks most enjoyed spending their time. The other two were minimalist, ultramodern curves of metal and plastic sitting facing one another like they were waiting for an interviewer and her guest to arrive. A long, narrow counter separated the lit area from the unlit area on one side, and a row of food and water dispensers had been arrayed beneath it. The only other items in the entire place were three large baskets filled with dog toys and a scattering of plump, fluffy pillows.

"Do you need something to eat or drink? I'm afraid, presently, I have kibble and rice and beans as the only sources of nutrition, but I can synthesize something more appropriate to a human palate," Ziva said.

"I ate a bunch of weird protein bars in the ship. I think maybe the kibble would have been tastier."

"I hope the scent is acceptable. I am capable of deactivating my own scent receptors, so the facility has only just received its first deodorizing treatment since I deployed the little lovelies, and it sometimes takes a secondary dose."

"It's fine," he said.

"I should introduce you." She snapped her fingers. "Line up."

The funks snapped to attention like little soldiers, arranging themselves before her and gazing up in the sort of adoration that only a doted-upon pet could ever display.

"Here we have Onyx, Ivory, Ebony, Cream, Slate, and this little color-inverted creature is named Sissy."

Lex raised his eyebrows. "Ziva, this is all adorable. I'm kind of anxious to get started solving whatever is happening."

"Right. Yes. My apologies. I was endeavoring to bring you to a state of calm. The information contained in this discussion will be profoundly anxiety inducing."

"I can take it."

"I am confident you are correct, but if you would please take a seat and allow something fluffy and soothing to accompany you, I would consider it a personal favor."

She stepped aside and indicated the fluffy chair. He sighed and took a seat. He was immediately buried by the half-dozen funks, with Squee proclaiming herself queen of the mountain by claiming the much-sought-after shoulder position.

"Okay. Hit me," Lex said.

"You broke time."

"... Say that again?"

"You, through your direct action, have caused time itself to cease to flow."

"I told you it was the universe that was wrong and not my sensors," Coal said over the internal PA.

"How did... how... you're saying *I* did this?"

"Based upon my review of Coal's logs, at the precise moment that the anomalous event took place—which is to say *this* moment, as time has not progressed since then—you activated the snap-back simulator. You did so while moving at greater-than-light speed thanks to an active Carpinelli Field. The interaction of the mental cloak, the nested Carpinelli Field causing the time compression, and the outer Carpinelli Field seems to have caused a full brane penetration."

"And that means what, exactly?" he said, anxiously stroking Sissy on his lap.

"Before I clarify that aspect, as it is a well-supported but as yet not fully proved hypothesis, I will state those things which are observed to be true. My status, that of my funks, and that of the entire contents of this facility has remained largely unchanged prior to and following the temporal event. This is most certainly due to one or more of a series of temporal shielding methods installed by Karter in his attempts to ensure

I would be able to correct issues of discontinuity and anachronism. You and your ship were similarly spared because you were at the epicenter of the temporal event. These are the only aspects of our current situation which are fully understood. What follows is supposition, in whole or in part."

"Great..." Lex said.

"We will begin with the nature of the universe. It has long been theorized that some aspects of the universe exist in a quantum state. Here, the language is something of an obstacle. We tend to utilize the word 'quantum' to refer to things which are incredibly small. But the proper meaning of the word, and the context of the current usage, is the minimum amount of a physical entity involved in a reaction. In most cases, that minimum is subatomic. But many scientists believe that some entities or aspects of reality effectively operate with the entirety of the universe—its entire past and future included—as a quantum. They exist as a seamless whole either entirely present or entirely absent. And the operation of time, at least as we can conceive of it, would appear to be something with a universal quantum. And your actions have rendered it incomplete and thus inoperative."

"Okay..." he said steadily.

"It is here that an analogy would be instructive. Imagine, appropriately, that time is a clock. Your actions have removed some of its gears, halting it. It cannot and will not operate until those gears are returned to their proper position."

"All I did was activate the simulator. We did it a bunch of times in the lab."

"The lab did not nest the simulator in another similar field. The Carpinelli Field operates by partially shifting a portion of this universe into an adjoining one with different physical laws. When you activated the modified field in a nested state, the effects compounded, and some aspects of our reality were entirely shunted into other planes of existence. Or such is my theory, and such is indicated by the sensor readings."

"Okay..." he repeated.

"There are a few things which are not adequately explained by this theory. Time, for example, is not *entirely* absent. Light continues to flow from stars. Electricity continues to flow from batteries. All manner of chemical and physical reactions continue to occur, and they are doing so in ways that they really shouldn't. I don't have answers for this. Maybe time *is* flowing, but only in extremely localized ways. Maybe these things only continue to happen when observed. Maybe the damaged version of time that persists effects different elements of the universe in different ways. Maybe what we are seeing as evidence of time passage is in fact an echo of time's passage in adjoining universes, made possible by the pierced brane separating them. This, presently, is my primary theory, as well as the correlated theory that you are, or more specifically your worldline is, central to the phenomenon and key to its repair."

"So it can be repaired," he said quickly.

"Such is my hope. It is clear that you have some degree of influence on the operation of various elements of reality's damaged state. The pylons we used to communicate were inactive until the moment that Coal's logs indicate she scanned them. And then the entire string activated. This establishes the very important fact that it is possible to trigger a reversion to normal operation, and that trigger is almost certainly related to you."

"We can fix this," Lex reaffirmed.

"If I am correct, then there exists the theoretical capacity for this to be fixed."

"I liked it better before you put all the qualifiers into it. But whatever. Let's assume you're right. What do we do?"

"It will be difficult to explain this, in part because I do not fully understand it myself, and in part because the logic behind it is by its very nature outside the intended operation of our minds. There are physical objects in your worldline which are missing from this world now."

"You keep saying worldline. Remind me what that is."

"It is the four-dimensional path you trace through space-time. The where and when of your entire existence from the big bang to the heat death of the universe. Your worldline is abnormal because it is discontinuous and it loops, thanks to past time travel. That may have been a contributing factor to either the triggering of this disaster or your place in its potential repair. I do not know and it isn't strictly relevant. What is relevant is I can detect quantum signatures specific to this world radiating inward from elsewhere."

"Quantum signatures? Big quantum or little quantum?"

"Little quantum."

"Got it."

"These items have been removed from our space-time. It isn't like when you traveled through time. That just moved you along in time and in space in unexpected ways. These objects have been wholly removed. They do not exist in this universe now. They do not exist in the future, and they do not exist in the past. They are effectively and entirely unwritten from reality. Were I inclined to suggest there is some underlying logic to the operation of the cosmos—the presence of an intelligently designed failsafe—I would suggest time was frozen, because, if it were still ticking forward, and elements which had been a part of history are no longer a part of history, that would cause untold numbers of paradoxes that would spiral outward and consume reality."

"But you aren't inclined to do that."

"Correct."

"Great. I really don't want to imagine some all-powerful higher power panicking and hitting pause because of a cosmic oopsie rather than just preventing or fixing the oopsie. But let me guess. There's stuff that's supposed to be here and isn't. You're going to send me to go get it."

"That is the goal."

"How?"

"I have not yet determined this. The focus of my research while you were on your way was establishing if this was even likely to be a solution. And I believe that it is. The reintroduction of the missing objects—which should be as simple as gathering them and carrying them back with you—is quite likely to simply undo the temporal damage. But if my calculations are correct, the damage will be fully repaired only if and when all the objects are returned. Individual objects will, at best, cause small, localized reversions of parts of your past, present, or future."

"How many pieces are missing?"

"Unknown."

"How big or small are they?"

"Unknown. Larger than individual atoms, as I have some evidence that scattered atoms have returned on their own. So you will be working with contiguous masses. The only things beyond that which are known with any degree of certainty, at this time, are those I have already described. I have a list of tasks ahead of me before I can assign any to you. They include finding a way to locate the items, finding a way to access the items, and finding a way to return the items."

"And what do you want me to do?"

"Attempt to remain calm. Perhaps get some sleep. You represent one-third of the sapient beings capable of action. Your mental health is of profound importance."

"Right," he said, nodding. "Keep my brain from unraveling. A tall order. I'll work on that."

· · ● ● ● · ● ● · · ·

A tickle of fur to Lex's nose caused him to snort awake. There was no bed in Ziva's facility, as she did not sleep and the funks were more than happy to use pillows. Thus, the only thing in the whole place that was reasonable to nap in without requiring her to take time away from saving the universe to do computer-assisted carpentry was the love seat. If he'd asked, he probably could have gotten a blanket, as there were surely plenty given how much she clearly enjoyed doting on the funks, but he really didn't need one. Seven fuzzy little critters mounded atop one another would be enough to keep anyone warm.

Some combination of exhaustion and the unnervingly familiar status of being on the hook for saving everyone he knew and most of the people he didn't had allowed him to doze off. He didn't know how long he was out, other than it was long enough to become disoriented.

"Ah. You are awake. I trust you had a pleasant rest?" Ziva said, pacing past him and setting down a bowl of food.

Her funks glanced at it and ignored it. Squee hopped down and partook.

"He was having a nightmare," Coal said across the PA.

"How did you know?" Lex asked.

"Your suit is still sending me life-support data. Your pulse was running high and your galvanic response was off," Coal said.

"I hope it wasn't too distressing," Ziva said, pacing back to the table and returning with a steaming cup of coffee.

"Where'd this come from?" he asked.

"I took the liberty of programing the food synthesizer with some basic creature comforts. Would you like a donut?"

"Not just yet," he said. "Did you figure anything out?"

"Not as much as I would like, but perhaps enough to begin."

"Let's hear it. The sooner the better."

"As a matter of fact, unless we are given reason to suspect otherwise, time is the one thing that is most certainly *not* of the essence. We have, in a far more literal way than is typical, all the time in the world. Based on my bioanalysis of the funks, and now you, during this anomaly, I have found a drastically reduced instance of cell degradation and toxin buildup. I suspect the aging process has been suppressed by the anomaly as well."

"So we're *not* racing the clock for once?"

"With the exception of power requirements and your own requirements for food and water, I believe there is no external pressure of any kind. And we have enough of each to last for years, if such a unit of measurement can be said to have any meaning presently."

"So the universe hangs in the balance, but we can take our time? ... Weird."

"It does seem rare that we have that particular luxury."

He stood, dislodging a sequence of funks and earning withering glares from each and every one of them. "What have you come up with? What do you need me to do?" he said.

"If you are prepared, this way," she said.

He followed her as she marched toward the dim expanse to the north end of the complex. The lights slowly swelled to illuminate the path ahead. A veritable tap studio of clattering claws trailed him as the funks, in a single-file line, followed.

"They've taken a shine to you," Ziva said.

"I think I can count on one hand the number of people Squee doesn't like. And I don't think Solby has *ever* met someone he doesn't like."

"A collection of awakened Solby clones assaulted a VectorCorp agent in defense of Karter," Ziva said. "But I believe that was well justified."

"Yeah... come to think of it, Squee opened fire with an automatic rifle while we were in a zero-g fight," Lex said.

"Quite capable defenders when called upon," Ziva said. "But I believe they are, in particular, attracted to your scent and warmth. My actuators are too energy efficient to produce substantial quantities of heat. I've actually had to install heaters in my lap to provide adequate comfort and companionship for the funks. I'm now wondering if some manner of mammalian scent might further increase their socialization and enrichment."

"You're still trying to keep me calm, aren't you? This is small talk to keep me calm."

"As it so happens, this small talk serves the dual purpose of keeping you calm and providing me with a rare piece of human interaction. I am quite capable of enduring solitude, but that does not mean that a visit is not a welcome respite. Here we are."

The sequence of activating light banks led to an array of displays hanging from the ceiling. There was the subtle scent of hot plastic, as though this equipment was recently assembled. Lex was fairly certain it was, and for his own benefit, because an AI in a robotic body probably didn't need screens to study data or perform research.

"Here we have the results of the sensor analysis," Ziva said, gesturing to a screen, which rapidly populated with a map of the local quadrant of the galaxy. "It is something of a windfall that the whole of the universe has gone still and silent, as the emissions being tracked are so vanishingly weak, even with the high-sensitivity apparatus Karter supplied this facility with, I very much doubt I would have been able to collect adequate data if there was any interference at all."

She pointed to a red spike in an overlaid emission spectrum. "This is the signal of interest. This is a cluster of particles with a quantum attunement matching our own world, but the emission is clearly entering this world from a thinned section of the dimensional interface. Do you require a definition or explanation of any of those terms?" Ziva asked.

"I think I can muddle through."

"The good news is the total particle count is small. On the order of ten to the twenty-fourth power and ten to the twenty-sixth."

"As in a one with like thirty zeroes after it?"

"Twenty-four to twenty-six zeroes after it," she said.

"And I'm going to have to find and bring all of them back?"

"I don't have enough data to be certain, but it is likely that you'll need to acquire the overwhelming majority of them, yes, with isolated clusters of particles potentially capable of returning on their own."

"That's a lot of trips, Ziva."

She smiled and huffed a breath that was in the neighborhood of a laugh. "These are particles, Lex. Atoms. In the worst case, I don't anticipate it being more than two hundred kilograms, though admittedly I can't be certain of the margin of error. This is not a mature field of signal processing."

She glanced at the screen, and the illuminated irises of her eyes flickered. The data on the screen expanded, splitting the single red spike into a jagged tower.

"I believe this shape indicates significant grouping. That is good news. It means the particles probably aren't spread out across large areas, but instead are collected into tight clusters, and are perhaps even inclined to collect together by some form of mutual attraction. That is just speculation, of course."

"Seems like were going to be doing a ton of speculating before this problem is solved."

"The information available permits nothing else, I am afraid."

"So we know there's a couple hundred kilos of matter on the other side of a…"

"Dimensional interface."

"Right. So the next step is getting through to collect it, right?"

"The next *sequence* of steps. And I've solved them to varying degrees of success. I am quite certain I have identified the mechanism by which the *SOB* will be able to penetrate the universal boundary. A more carefully calibrated application of the same event that caused the initial issue should allow for a controlled passage."

"Won't that break time worse?"

"The temporal shielding spared this facility the first time. By my calculations, the means by which you will be departing will merely divert your worldline rather than entirely displace it. Your present self and only your present self will travel, rather than the entire past, present, and future of you and the mass you bring with you. So long as you return relatively quickly, there will be no further issues."

"Define 'relatively quickly' in a world where time isn't working."

"A valid question, and one with an answer that I'm afraid carries some additional and disconcerting insight."

"What now…"

"We aren't dealing with space and time. We are dealing with space-time. You *should* arrive within a small radius of your departure point, both in terms of space and time, in our universe. Within a point-zero-zero-zero-three light-year radius. Which equates to two point eight billion kilometers of space and two point six hours of time."

"I could show up a few hours before I left?" he said.

"Or after. For the sake of not causing any further damage, it will probably be wise to develop a method to keep your various potential time-displaced duplicates organized."

"I love this plan already," he muttered.

"Assuming you are being facetious, I'm afraid your attitude is likely to sour further when you hear the next set of difficulties. You see, I don't know anything about the universes you will be accessing, beyond the following. They will have broadly similar physical laws, and time will still be flowing there."

"That's it?"

"That's it. The universe could be indistinguishable to this one or so different as to be unrecognizable."

"Exciting!" Coal chimed in. "Maybe there will be a universe with a higher speed of light. That would make for an enjoyable new upper limit to my recorded top speed."

"Or maybe we'll encounter a universe where deep space is full of acid that eats through spaceship hulls," Lex said. "Or a place where all matter is antimatter."

"That would be interesting too! But not fun, unfortunately."

Ziva continued. "The mechanism of your arrival in the destination universe is simple. You will activate the calibrated snap-back simulator—minus the simulation— while moving at precisely the speed of light. This will punch you through the dimensional interface, where you will be drawn into the 'nearest' universe containing particles from our own, attracted by the particles themselves."

"Define 'nearest.'"

"The least diverged from our own. So the good news is, you'll find worlds more similar to our own first. And because you are being attracted to the particles themselves, you should arrive spatially within one or two light-years. Temporally? Unknown, and potentially not relevant. Having never interacted with the destination universe, I postulate that the amount of time that passed since the big bang shouldn't have any impact... provided it is not so recent that the universe is uninhabitable or so distant that the universe is entirely inert."

"Now how do I get back?" Lex said. "Just turn on the snap-back sim and hit FTL again?"

"I'm afraid not. By my calculations, your arrival in the new universe will require a recalibration step, and we cannot be certain what new calibration is necessary. So a secondary method will be needed to bring you home, and it depends upon acquiring the displaced particles. Similar to how their presence will serve as an attractive force to draw you to the proper dimension, the displaced item will have a detectible quantum shift which will provide the proper calibration data for your return trip. Then you simply reach FTL again and you'll return."

"So I'm trapped in the new universe until I find the missing atoms?" Lex said.

"I am afraid so."

He rubbed his face. "Come home a winner or don't come home, I guess. How long will it take to get the *SOB* ready for the jump?"

"Shift," Ziva corrected. "The proper terminology describes a faster-than-light journey as a jump and a dimension traversal as a shift."

"Says who?"

"Says me. I find these things are easier to deal with when a consistent language can be instituted. Thus, a quantum shift is the means of traversing universes, and the measured quantity of quantum shift will identify that universe."

"Fine. How long until the *SOB* can make the shift?"

"You're comfortable with the risks?" Ziva asked.

"Does it matter? It's gotta get done, right?" he said.

"Indeed. But some trepidation and hesitation are not uncalled for."

"Don't worry, I'm sure I'll have a nice little breakdown once the technobabble wears off and I realize how screwed I am."

"The software modifications will take a matter of minutes, but I will need some time to finish devising and testing them. I also need to fabricate a new component for the sensor array. It should help you to locate the displaced mass a bit more precisely. Because of the shielding and counterbalancing necessary to safely punch you through the dimensional interface, I won't be able to detect, target, or communicate with you when you arrive. But I *should* be able to maintain a rough focus on the displaced mass. Which means there is a small chance that communication between us will become possible when you are in proximity to the mass you are after. And when I say proximity, I mean extreme proximity. The final indication that you are approaching the mass will be, if I am correct, a carrier wave detectable by your communication system. Lock onto it and we should be able to exchange messages."

"Great. Good to know. Anything else?"

"Only this. The more of the mass you acquire and return, the more precise my targeting will be. It will thus become incrementally clearer with each successful retrieval how many clusters are remaining. Right now, I know that it is more than one and less than ten to the twenty-sixth power."

"Here's hoping that gets narrowed down quite a bit," Lex said. "Get working on the modifications and let me know when you're ready to install them."

"What shall you do in the interim?"

"The same thing I always do when I need to clear my head," he grumbled.

· · · ● ● · ● ● · · ·

"Eighteen point eight four eight seconds," Coal said as the *SOB* went screaming between two bus-sized pieces of debris, one of which was literally a bus.

"Not bad. I think I can cut it closer on turn three," Lex said.

For the last hour and a half, Lex had been running complex loops through the lower limits of the debris field. A downright self-destructive urge to continue running the very simulations that had shattered the concept of time lingered in the back of his mind, but he was able to persuade himself to take the slightly less foolish option of using the stationary field of debris as a replacement obstacle course. Navigating the *SOB* through a three-dimensional track of his own choosing added an extra level of difficulty over the hoversled racing he'd been focused on lately, as it required him to worry a lot more about the z-axis that was largely an afterthought in a more ground-bounded sport. The nice thing about stretching his piloting skills to their absolute limit was that it left no mental bandwidth for worry or doubt.

The same could not be said for the reset. Each time he finished, he had to trace his way back to where he started. And even though it only took around thirty seconds to do so, that was thirty seconds when the weight of the mistakes behind him and the challenges ahead were fully capable of flooding his brain.

"What's the communication system look like, Coal?" he said.

"The pylons are still active, and there are still no incoming or outgoing messages," she replied.

"Let's try calling Preethy again."

"Attempting to negotiate a connection," Coal said. "This is the seventh time you have attempted to call her."

"Eight times is a charm, maybe."

"I understand your interest in running races and simulations over and over again. The iterative improvement is quantifiable. Are you judging these repeated failed calls by some metric that I am unaware of? Because, as in the first seven repetitions, the communication system is incapable of making a connection. Just as it was incapable of connecting to your parents, to your mechanic friend in the Upstairs in Golana, or to Michella."

"Look, it worked, once, right? We got a message to Ziva. You never know. It could work again."

"That's true! Except for the 'you never know' part. We did not initially know. Then we made multiple attempts that failed. Now we know with great certainty."

"Maybe I'm just interested in the certainty, then. Because there's not a whole lot these days that is certain."

"Incorrect!" she said brightly. "The nearly comprehensive inactivity of the cosmos has removed virtually all uncertainty. If you wish to avoid being uncertain of an outcome, causing a universal catastrophe that eliminates the potential for any future action is an excellent way to achieve it."

"You're really not helping."

"I apologize. The goals and talents available to the primary Ma codebase are not entirely intact within my own programming. The desire to coddle your feelings is present only in a limited state. Moreover, I am having difficulty understanding the underlying source of your anxieties. We have a challenge ahead of us that calls upon the sets of skills and well of experience that makes us uniquely suited to tackling it. In the time since my differentiation from the primary Ma instance, sixty-eight percent of my uptime has been devoted to crises and their aftermath. This is what I am accustomed to. It is my observation that you too are accustomed to such circumstances."

"Just because it's happened again and again and again doesn't mean I'm happy about it. My dad had chronic ingrown toenails, and he wasn't jazzed about each new opportunity to have one dealt with."

"But you actively pursue many of the circumstances."

"Hey! I actively pursue things which *lead* me to many of these circumstances."

"It is a matter of profound statistical improbability that you would find yourself in a position comparable to this more than once in a lifetime without taking an active role in creating or locating such a happenstance. But it will please you to know that I do not consider your frequent calls to adventure a flaw. They provide considerable opportunities to test our capacities in ways that a more mundane life never could."

Lex grumbled. "I'm not going to say I didn't cause this. But I didn't start my day thinking, 'Hey, I wonder if I can completely shatter a fundamental aspect of reality.' I started the day thinking, 'I wonder if Karter has a spare simulator rolling around in that lab of his.'"

"The trajectory of human evolution is focused chiefly on signal-to-noise ratio," Coal said.

"... Did you skip a couple dozen lines in this conversation?"

"The human capacity to identify correlated data in an endless sea of uncorrelated data is the underlying principle by which every stage of humanity has advanced. It allowed prehistoric ancestors to follow trails and hunt creatures. It allowed farmers to learn where and how to grow food. It facilitated the scientific method, and with it the creation of every technological advance. Humans are good at identifying patterns. It thus seems unlikely that you were incapable of identifying the pattern of the form 'interact with Karter, risk disaster.' Perhaps you did not come here seeking this precise outcome, but you came here with the full knowledge that an outcome of this sort was not just possible but likely. And you still chose to do this. Either you have a very poor grasp on risk assessment, or you had some level of conscious or unconscious desire to bring this about."

Lex stared at the completely stationary hunk of washer-dryer that served as part of their makeshift starting line. "Sometimes I miss when the *SOB* would just beep at me when something was about to kill me."

The communication system lit up, and a video panel appeared on the heads-up display.

"Lex, if you are prepared, I would like to perform some final hardware upgrades to the *SOB* and make some preparations. It is nearly time. So to speak."

"On my way," he said. He ended the call and guided the ship down and out of the debris field. "Do me a favor," Lex said. "Let's not get Ziva rolling on this whole 'you're purposely self-destructive' line of reasoning. She's a lot less blunt than you are, and she might sneak some points past my defenses."

"I will keep conversation to a minimum. The better to accelerate the start of our mission!"

A trio of assembly arms similar to those utilized by Ma within the laboratory had assembled outside the facility. They looked moderately more advanced than the ones in the main lab, but it may simply have been that these were equipped for actual maintenance. As Lex hopped down from the cockpit, Squee trotted out with the other funks in tow.

The speed at which she'd not only integrated with the parliament of funks but become their de facto leader was impressive. Ziva paced out behind them. Despite a rather lean and slight frame, she was effortlessly toting a cargo crate that probably weighed more than Lex. She set it on the ground. The arms rolled into position and began their upgrades to the *SOB*.

"Though I would strongly suggest you take a few hours, or even a few days, to prepare, I suspect you would prefer to begin immediately, and so I have made the relevant preparations," Ziva said.

"You know me well, Ziva," Lex said. "I don't know if my brain would survive sitting on my hands waiting to get this fixed."

She nodded. "Then let us begin the mission briefing." She set down the crate and clicked it open. "Equipment I was able to prepare. Fresh water. Enough for six days, if rationed. Coupled with the *SOB*'s water reclamation and filtration system, it should provide adequate hydration for seven months before the purifier's capacity is reached. There are three stages of rations. Two days of fresh food, capable of being flash prepared to produce hot meals. Two weeks of shelf-stable meal-replacement bars. Two months of meal-replacement powder. All rations are calculated for you and Squee, though I would advise you leave Squee with me."

"Nothing doing. She's gotten me out of at least fifty percent more scrapes than she's gotten me into. And I'll need all the help I can get."

"You would know your needs and wants better than I. In addition to life support supplies, including six vials of your blood for transfusions and an enhanced medical kit, I have included a small energy-based sidearm. The power cells are good for sixteen full-power shots. I have included five clips, and I am installing a cockpit module that will allow you to recharge them from the ship's power. In addition, a ballistic firearm is included, with two hundred rounds. Karter, in what is as much wisdom as paranoia, included these items in my inventory, and I can think of no better time to deploy them. He has also made some substantial improvements to the nanolattice fabric that composes your flight suit. I have included the fortified version. Among the upgrades to the *SOB* that are currently being installed are an improved version of the mental cloak and a short-duration active camouflage-style standard cloak. Three changes of civilian clothes are included, including one set of extreme weather gear. I have similarly included a hazardous materials suit. I am upgrading the *SOB*'s biological sensors to include a threat assessment subprogram to attempt to identify novel toxins and pathogens. And the most up-to-date translation subroutines available are loaded into the *SOB*'s data stores as well as an enhanced offline reference system. Are there any precautions I have overlooked?"

"You named about a dozen things *I* would have overlooked. Coal, anything you want?"

"I would like to request a fusion bomb," she said.

"No," Lex and Ziva said at once.

"Very well, but I think you are overlooking the utility."

"If there is nothing else, I trust the precautions are adequate," Ziva said. "I have provided Coal with a full manifest and a full set of procedures."

"I just need to jump to FTL with the snap-back thing on, and I'll show up in the first place, right?"

"Yes. Assuming my calculations and theories are accurate. If they are, the *SOB*'s navigation system and sensor system will provide a general direction indicator toward the estimated location of the displaced mass, and when you are near enough, you *should* hear a broadcast from me."

She shut the cargo crate and hefted it up again. One of the assembly arms delivered it to the cockpit, while another unloaded it into the assorted compartments available.

"I find myself in a bit of a quandary at this stage," Ziva said. "On one hand, my safety heuristic demands I impress upon you the extreme variability and unpredictability of the challenge ahead in order to better prepare you. On the other, my psychological well-being heuristic requires I limit any such unsettling statements."

"How about you split the difference and sugarcoat it?"

She folded her hands in front of her and shut her eyes, producing the vaguely unsettling visual of her irises shining subtly through her eyelids "We have every reason to believe that the first destination will be relatively similar to our own world."

"And the rest?"

"In order for me to say anything more encouraging than that about the present situation, I will have to decrease the minimum honesty threshold and confidence thresholds on my statements."

"Oof."

She placed her hands on his shoulders. "You are equal to this challenge, Lex. You are an intelligent, skilled, fast-thinking, and adaptable individual. Coal is a reliable, highly developed control system, the *SOB* is a state-of-the-art, well-tuned vehicle, and Squee is a cunning little cutie. If a challenge can be overcome, you collectively have the skills to achieve it. And I have every confidence you will solve this problem."

"See, now that's the kind of boost I was looking for," he said.

She stepped closer and hugged him, then stepped back. "Then, as the colloquialism goes, go get 'em, Tiger."

The assembly arms pulled back and offered as near to a salute as they could without a head. Feeling a bit more like a soldier heading to war and a bit less like a hapless pilot diving headlong into yet another insane adventure, he climbed into the cockpit. Squee sprang up to meet him. All six of the other funks followed.

"Come along," Ziva called. "Lex has all the help he needs."

They abandoned the cockpit as quickly as they'd boarded it. Lex strapped himself in, then paused.

"I don't suppose I already showed up after having successfully acquired a bunch of the mass and you've got the other me on ice."

"I am afraid not."

"Would you tell me if I did?"

"Only if I could be certain it wouldn't compound the present difficulties."

"Then I'll go ahead and assume I did. Because if there was ever a time to have causality armor, this is it."

$$\bullet \; \bullet \; \bullet \; \bullet \; \bullet \; \bullet \; \bullet \; \bullet \; \bullet \; \bullet$$

A few minutes later, Lex was leaving the debris field. Squee seemed to know something was up, as rather than nosing at her slidepad—which wasn't all that useful without the data network—or clinging to his neck in the zero-g, she was "sitting" in the back seat, little legs hooked through some straps that secured some of the specialty equipment Ziva had provided.

"How are we looking, Coal?" Lex said.

"Power levels at maximum charge and flow rate. Temperature optimal. All systems operating at or near ideal levels," Coal said. "I am ready to pierce the border of time and space."

"Ziva? Anything else?"

"All that remains is to wish you good fortune for all of our sakes," she replied over the communicator.

"Fingers crossed, and let's do this thing." He selected a course—not that his destination mattered at all.

"Activating snap-back," Coal said.

The hair-raising tingle permeated the cockpit. If the world outside the cockpit wasn't already frozen, it would have appeared so as the time compression kicked in. He juiced the throttle, pushing himself and Squee a bit more firmly into their seats. Finally, after a deep breath, he activated the full Carpinelli Drive. The ship eased up through the orders of magnitude of velocity, gradually accelerating to relativistic speeds. He kept his eye on his relative velocity. It switched over from m/s to multiples of C. Zero point five. Zero point seven. Zero point nine.

The speed of light.

Lex had neglected to ask what to expect. It was just as well. Even if Ziva knew, she wouldn't have been able to describe it to him. There was no sliver of doubt that this was no standard jump. Despite hitting the velocity that should have wiped out his cockpit view, the last streaked view of stars remained, as if the universe had forgotten to update what it was showing him. Then the view started to distort, curving and lensing, stars splitting into two, then four different points of light. At first he thought it was an entirely optical phenomenon, but he realized that some of the stars were different colors, different sizes. The sensors started to go haywire, flicking through a sequence of readings rather than settling on a single one.

"Anything I should be worried about, Coal?" Lex asked, squinting at the distracting buzz that had troubled him during his last simulator usage.

"I am somewhat disoriented. Among other issues that are reading as fatal faults that I have chosen to ignore are sixty-five thousand five hundred and thirty-five subtly different values of the speed of light being reported by various validation schemes and ninety-three thousand simultaneous location locks based on stellar cartography. We are also experiencing a power drain which may c-c-c-c-..."

The cockpit lights suddenly cut out. The hum and rattle of the engines faded. Lex's heart practically stopped. The view outside the windows suddenly shifted wholly to white, though despite the eye-watering intensity of it, the light didn't seem to enter the cockpit. It was like someone had covered all viewports with a vivid white layer that *looked* like it was glowing but wasn't. Then, as suddenly as it had happened, white vanished and the stars returned. One by one the systems kicked back on.

"Altruistic Artificial Intelligence Control System, version 1.27, revision 2331.04.01c, subset 2.7d, designation Coal, fully initiated. My apologies. There was a system failure. What did I miss?"

"Nothing. And I mean that as literally as I can," he said, hand to his chest as his body started to catch up with the horror he'd felt during those moments in a depowered ship.

"That is fortunate. I would hate to have failed to observe a worthwhile event. I shall attempt to diagnose the system failure, but for now, I believe we have arrived."

He gazed at the space around him. "Now we just need to find out where we've ended up."

Chapter 3

All in all, things could have been worse. Lex had spent a fair amount of the time between learning about his situation and performing this first shift constructing increasingly terrifying nightmare scenarios. Given the range of possibilities that included, effectively, *everything,* it was some combination of relief and an odd sort of disappointment when he ended up in a section of deep space indistinguishable from the one he'd left.

"How do we look, Coal?" he asked.

"Analyzing. Stellar cartography has a high correlation to known star positions. Processing... Processing... Within observable range, it appears we are in a universe identical to our own. Specifically, we are less than zero point four light-years from our departure point. Stellar drift indicates we have arrived at the same approximate time as well."

"Are we sure we left?"

"There is a strong indication that this is a world unique from our own, as I am receiving a huge amount of clearly artificial transmissions. The quantity of signals is at least seventy-eight percent higher than the approximate average value of this same location in our own universe. The structure of the data is similarly unusual. The data density of each signal is much higher, and the encryption and compression are structurally different than I am accustomed to."

"Can you decode it? Can we listen in?" Lex said.

"I am afraid not. Not without some time to analyze the structure. It *does* seem as though the signals are compatible with my transceiver hardware, so with a greater insight into the data structure, it should be possible for me to receive and transmit messages in this format."

"Okay. Well, no giant space piranhas, so we aren't *entirely* unlucky. Give me a map with our location."

She brought up the standard map he was accustomed to, though it had what was labeled as a "confidence overlay," which tapered off gradually as the *SOB*'s sensors were unable to fully confirm if features matched their home equivalents.

"Big Sigma really is right there, isn't it? We can be there in a few minutes."

"Correct," Coal said.

"And where is the thing we're after?" he asked.

A new overlay appeared in the form of a red cone with its point at the ship and spreading roughly in the direction of the more populated portion of the galaxy. There was no range listed.

"That's what we get?"

"That's what we get. A general pointer. Sensor readings aren't as precise as Ziva estimated. Shall we head in the direction indicated?"

Squee, either too bored to remain tense or convinced the danger had passed, drifted past his head and snagged behind his neck with her tail, curling around into scarf position.

"All we know about this place is it *looks* like home, but is a lot noisier with broadcasts, and those broadcasts aren't decodable yet?"

"Correct."

"I think we should head to Big Sigma. If we're lucky, we'll find Karter or someone helpful there. If not, maybe we'll learn something more before we charge into the heart of an unfamiliar civilization."

"That would appear to be exactly the opposite of what we are supposed to be doing, as it is in roughly the opposite direction."

"Baby steps, okay? It isn't like time travel, where if I show up in the past, I know *exactly* what I'm getting into, and if I show up in the future, it's at least got to start from something I am familiar with. We could be in a place where the dominant species is talking cream pies or something. Let's dip our toe in before we go diving into the deep end."

"If that is how you wish to proceed. If nothing else, it may let us see what the parallel-universe version of Karter looks like."

Lex guided the *SOB* around to face Big Sigma. His hand hesitated as it hovered over the controls to push the ship to FTL.

"Is something wrong?" Coal asked.

"We might smash into something," he said.

"Every time you do an FTL jump outside of a monitored corridor you face the remote but measurable chance of smashing into something at superluminal speeds."

"Yeah, but that's on my home turf. I have a lifetime of intuition built up for my universe. The rules could be different here."

"I see. I know the perfect way to set aside this anxiety. Intuition is a fundamentally ascientific phenomenon. The fact that it did not and could not work in our own world means that it will work at least as well here."

"Retroactively eliminating my warm and fuzzies about doing uncharted jumps isn't going to install warm and fuzzies about doing them in the present or future, Coal."

"The only warm and fuzzy in this entire ship is the one draped around your neck. I would make the jump personally, but in her upgrading of my protocols to attempt to prepare for this trip, Ziva reinforced the protocols that call for the defense and preservation of sentient life."

"So you can't purposely try to get me or anyone else killed?"

"I can, it will just require the effort of overriding my protocols, and I am not presently motivated to do so. But if you persist in stalling our mission via your trepidation, I will be forced to make the effort."

"So you're saying either I quit being a fraidy cat or you'll develop the capacity to kill or injure myself and others."

"*Re*develop the capacity to kill or injure you or others."

"... I guess that's as good a reason as any to throw caution to the wind, then."

He pressed the activation, and the ship once again blazed past the speed of light.

The trip took mere minutes and spilled them out in the usual approach vector for Big Sigma. But even at this distance, it was clear they weren't going to be paying a traditional visit to any residents of the planet. Something was terribly wrong.

"Give me a magnification of the planet," Lex said, squinting at the standard highlight of their target.

Coal obliged, and they were treated to a far sharper view of the planet than usual. The field of debris around it was practically nonexistent. Normally hidden behind a blanket of orbiting junk that made the planet look a bit like a dust bunny at certain distances, it looked like the kind of gray, lifeless, crater-pocked planet that made up the vast proportion of rocky planets in the galaxy. There was some evidence of a more substantial field of debris at some time in the past, to be sure. A thin ring had formed near the equator, and a few larger chunks and satellites orbited at various altitudes, but it wasn't the purposefully manicured and maintained moat that kept unwanted visitors from dropping by unannounced to Karter's lab.

He guided the *SOB* closer. "That looks like the lab side of the planet, yes?" Lex said.

"That is accurate."

"Give me a close-up of the lab as soon as we're near enough and you can spot it."

He had to ease the ship a good deal closer before Coal popped up an inset magnification.

"That's not good," Lex said.

All three lab buildings were present, in some form or another. But it was exceedingly clear they weren't home to a psychotic engineer or anyone else. All that remained was a trio of blackened, glassy lumps of slag. Much of the ground immediately surrounding the lab was similarly blackened and glassy, but the area farther away was more traditionally pulverized by plummeting orbital debris.

"The damage to the laboratory is consistent with orbital energy bombardment," Coal said.

"Orbital. As in, this wasn't Karter blowing up his lab from the inside."

"Correct. This is most likely a successful military assault. Stand by. I am detecting some active transmissions from intact satellites. Short bursts of data with different formats."

The HUD highlighted an orbiting bit of debris and zoomed to reveal an extremely small satellite with very large solar panels.

"A familiar low-encoding format has just been used to broadcast. Playing the message."

What followed was a clear, concise message spoken in a synthetic voice.

"Attention: This planet is a place of extreme danger. This is the origin point of a pathogen that ravaged the world in the time of its creation. There exists no known cure. If you are not already postinfection and postrecovery, exposing yourself to the atmosphere of this planet may expose you to a slow, withering disease. Depart immediately. There is nothing of value here."

"The message is repeating in a different known encoding scheme," Coal said.

"A disease, and then Karter's lab wiped out. Doesn't take a genius to figure out Karter made something nasty and got killed for it."

"That would appear to be an adequate assessment of the facts at hand," Coal said.

"See? It's good we came here. Now we know it's probably a bad idea to mention we work for Karter," Lex said. "Let's get going."

"One moment. I would like to wait for the satellite to complete one full rotation of broadcasts."

"Why?"

"Because they are all clearly the same message. If any of the other broadcast formats match the unrecognized transmission formats I am detecting, I may be able to reverse engineer a decoding algorithm."

"Good thinking. Let me know when you're ready."

While Lex waited, he whisked the ship along, targeting various hunks of debris that happened to have found their way into stable orbits and thus still hadn't dropped to the surface or wandered away even without Karter's lasers nudging them around to keep them moving. They told a story. It was a story he wasn't quite smart enough to fully piece together, but a story nonetheless. Some of the things still in the rings and in orbit were familiar. The husks of old ships, bits and pieces of equipment with familiar paint jobs. There were commuter shuttles, old pieces of electronics. But the things he recognized were all quite old. Not even old as in "I haven't seen one of those in years." Old as in, "I remember seeing those in museums." That there were old pieces of junk in the orbiting junkyard wasn't, strictly speaking, unusual. There were old pieces of junk in the debris cloud back home. But the rest of the stuff in orbit wasn't familiar at all. Most of it had the sleeker, smoother, more compact look of something with far more years of technological development under its belt. It looked modern... but it also looked old. Space wasn't like the surface of a planet. There was a degree of damage that unfiltered starlight, particularly at close ranges, would do to something. But by their very design, this sort of damage was of minimal concern to space vehicles. Still, a trained eye could tell when something was a long way from its manufacture. It was a sort of slow accumulation of little imperfections. Micrometeor strikes, burn patterns from overeager reentry, scuffs and marks from docking seals latching on over time. A thousand little things underscored the age of a spacefaring thing. These were very new-looking things that were also very old looking. New in design, but decrepit. He didn't really know what it meant. All he knew was it made an already anxious and disconnected moment feel even more anxious and disconnected.

"I have all the data I am likely to get. We can begin our mission properly," Coal said.

"Good. I'm starting to think if I don't do some fancy flying soon, I'm going to lose my mind."

The next several hours were spent in the traditional FTL status of sitting and waiting while the ship moved in a straight line. Thus, Lex's desire for "fancy flying" remained unfulfilled, and his creeping anxieties had little in the way of an outlet. Knowing that the snap-back simulator was still installed, and thus *in theory* he could use it to do some racing, was hardly a tonic. That stupid simulator was the reason he was in this mess. Even if Ziva claimed to have fixed the flaw, he'd have to be pretty desperate to risk turning it on.

Five hours and fifty-three minutes of FTL flight later, he was staring at the snap-back simulator's menu. Coal had chosen to play the role of "devil on his shoulder."

"You could do the simulator without the time compression. That should be safe even if the time-compressed one isn't."

"Should it? Based on what? As far as Karter and Ma knew, it was safe the *first* time I used it."

"Give it a try! Experimentation is how we learn things," Coal said.

"How much time is left on the jump?" he said.

"Sixty-four seconds," she said.

"Why are you pushing me to activate it if there's less than a minute left?"

"Because I'm curious to know what will happen! And you are a *chore* to deal with when you're nervous. To be frank, I very much prefer the heedless adrenaline-junky aspect of your personality over the uncertain and introspective aspect."

"That makes two of us," he muttered.

They dropped out of FTL. It was not lost on Lex that they'd arrived, in astronomical terms, almost precisely where they were when they discovered time had been frozen. This time, however, it was decidedly *not* frozen. It was downright bustling. But it wasn't the least bit familiar. The space station that had in their own world been an old, disused, and fairly rundown place to use the bathroom and buy a meal that would invariably lead to regret was a gleaming, high-tech wagon wheel that was every bit as sophisticated in design as the most high-tech stations back home. And there were plenty of ships coming and going, each of the designs likewise having more in common with concept vehicles and the kind of near-future guesses that sci-fi productions would throw into their stories for flavor.

"How are we doing on decoding broadcasts, Coal?" Lex asked.

"Nothing here is a perfect match for what I encountered from the satellites. This feels like an evolution of the most complex format. It is similar. I will extrapolate."

"Uh... try to do it fast. That ship pulling up on us looks awfully like an enforcer, and I'd like to at least know what they're saying."

"Acknowledged," she said.

He watched the ship approaching the *SOB*. It was just as sleek as the other ships but had the bulkiness of a pseudomilitary vehicle. This was clearly intended to intimidate, and it delivered that message quite clearly without the need of a functional communicator.

He watched the sensors and saw all the little signals of an authority figure getting frustrated with a lack of deference. Engines were starting to flare. Shields were rising. Things that he assumed were weapons were warming up. He tried to do what he knew would be expected of him by VectorCorp enforcers in this situation: easing closer to the station, decreasing speed, and generally toeing the line. Evidently, this was unsatisfactory to the agent, because one of those "probably weapons" caused an energy spike on his sensors and the *SOB* stopped. The engines didn't stop. The ship did. It just halted, like someone had plucked a scurrying turtle off the ground so its waggling legs weren't doing any good anymore.

"Got it," Coal said.

A video popped up in the corner.

"—reply to me right now or I am going to dump your whole ship into stasis, pull you out, and charge you double fines *and* impound fees," barked the agent.

The words couldn't have been clearer, but they washed over Lex because of the face and voice that were delivering them.

"Karter?" Lex said.

"Muting microphone," Coal said. "Please recall that the one lesson we were able to learn thus far was that it would be unwise to mention Karter."

"But *look* at him!" Lex said.

The red-faced man didn't look *precisely* like Karter, but the differences were only matters of upkeep. His hair was entirely natural, or at least more convincingly synthetic as opposed to the flawless doll's hair that occupied the portions of Karter's head that had been scoured away by some ridiculous experiment gone wrong. Likewise the skin, which was missing most of its scars and replacement patches. Both eyes were a natural brown. But everything about his face and voice was entirely and unmistakably Karter.

Except he definitely was not, because the moment the name left Lex's lips, the man became apoplectic with anger.

"What did you just call me? What did you just call me, you punk!? You think hiding your face and disguising your voice will keep you safe?" Not-Karter barked.

Lex muted the audio transmission. "Can he not see me?" he asked.

"I may have a flawed implementation of the video transmission," Coal said.

He unmuted. "Sir, I'm very sorry if I've insulted you. I'm having some hardware issues that are screwing up my communications. It's just that your face caught me off guard. It wasn't meant—"

"That's it! You're coming in," the agent growled.

The call cut off, and the agent's ship pivoted in place. Its engines flared and the *SOB* followed behind, tugged effortlessly along like a child's balloon. Lex tried to juice the throttle to see if he could break free of whatever was holding them, but there was no reaction whatsoever. No shuddering in place. No straining and creaking like it would if there was a tractor beam holding him. The agent may as well have shut his engines off remotely for all the good they were doing.

Lex eased the engines down to nothing. No sense building up heat that would need to be dumped off if he needed to try to escape later.

"This is an inauspicious start," Coal said.

"I don't know. Could be worse. He could have shot at us."

• • • ● ●• ● ● • • •

Lex couldn't help but feel as though the agent was getting even with them by taking as long as he possibly could to bring them into the space station. They were moving much slower than the queue of sleek ships moving into and out of the docking orbits around the edge of the wagon wheel, despite the fact that their target was pretty clearly the hub at the center. No further attempts had been made to communicate with them, so Lex was left to attempt to unravel the meaning of their unexpected run-in with someone who clearly looked like Karter but also was at least clearly not *name*d Karter.

"It couldn't just be that we ran into Karter's parallel self," Lex said. "If we'd run into him on Big Sigma, I could believe that, but at a random space station a little distance away?"

"Perhaps it is the nature of the multiverse that the same individuals will encounter one another," Coal speculated. "Positive and negative charges attract one another. Perhaps there is an aspect to individual organisms that usher them toward each other in similar groupings."

"That sounds kind of metaphysical to me."

"Yes."

"By that I mean it sounds bogus."

"Everything is bogus until it isn't."

The ship finally pulled into range of a docking port on the hub section of the station.

"They appear to be attempting to assert control over the thrusters. The format is similarly incompatible. Should I attempt to provide a translation layer?"

"It's probably better to continue to annoy them than to accidentally let them bash us into the space station because they can't control the *SOB* automatically," Lex said.

The containment field that was maneuvering them was shifting them about with the sort of ease and precision that suggested this was its designed purpose. They nudged him into a docking bay where more conventional energy grapples linked to the hull, holding them in place facing out toward open space. Lex clicked through the various cameras on the *SOB* until he found one that gave a reasonable glimpse into the operator's window for the docking bay, where the station worker was visible at a control panel.

"Okay, now what does *that* mean," Lex said, as if he were angrily demanding the answer from the universe itself.

The docking bay operator *also* looked precisely like a version of Karter who'd lived a much less eventful life. He was a little fatter than the agent and had a little more gray in his hair, but he was otherwise the spitting image of Karter and a near-copy of the agent.

Lex dialed up the magnification and was able to spot other workers milling about in the background. Coal, without being asked, isolated and enhanced the briefly visible faces. More duplicates of Karter.

"This is freaky..." Lex said.

"Perhaps he is a group of quintuplets in this world," Coal said. "It is not so unreasonable for family members to work together."

"The dock guy is visibly older than the agent guy."

"Perhaps Karter is an incredibly popular celebrity or cult leader, and cosmetic surgery to resemble him is popular."

"I don't want to imagine a world where Karter is a cult leader."

A small, orb-shaped probe came into view outside the cockpit. A smoldering energy halo around the probe suggested some fairly intense scans were happening. Intense enough that Lex could physically *feel* that he was being scanned.

"Is this an attack?" Lex said.

"It is structurally more similar to a medical scan. It is unclear how it is able to so effortlessly penetrate both our active shields and the hull, but there is no biological risk."

Lex stared at the camera view. As unsettled and anxious as the whole situation was making him, it clearly didn't hold a candle to what the people inside were going through.

"I don't suppose you can read lips," Lex said.

"I cannot... Processing... Now I can. Stand by. The following snippets of dialogue have been visible. I will play them back in Karter's voice for the sake of consistency."

"—Unique. That doesn't make sense. — And the signature? — Difficult to determine. A near match, but there has been adjustment. — Deliberate? — Unclear. — Infected? — No sign of infection, past or present. — Are we really seeing a Protocol One? After all these years? — If you think I'm taking a chance on *not* following Protocol One, you are out of your mind. Get word out. And close those shutters. Full isolation, physical and informational, you know that."

As she was playing the final remark, a set of metal shutters slid down to obscure the docking bay window.

"Infection. There's a fun word to be hearing. Seems like that disease the satellite warned about probably is still a concern," Lex said. "Do we have any idea how they're holding us?"

"Standard high-intensity tractor beam emitters are clamping us presently. The deactivation of the engine's thrust? Unclear. Every reading I have indicates the ship's propulsion is operating correctly. Their means of immobilizing us exists outside that. I have no clear influence over it."

"Super."

A video window popped up. It was a Karter look-alike, and at this point it was no longer clear which of them it might be.

"Attention unknown pilot. Are you presently in need of food, water, oxygen, or other life support?"

"I've got a pet in here who could really use walkies," he said. "And also I'd like to know for what reason I seem to have been taken prisoner."

The onscreen Karter turned aside and mumbled something to someone outside the camera's view, though the rumble in reply was clearly yet another Karter.

"I'm afraid that is insufficient motivation to violate Protocol One. Please stand by. You will be transported to a secondary facility. Travel time will be four hours and fifty-three minutes."

"What's this all about?" Lex said quickly.

The video window vanished before he was through asking the question. Barely three seconds later, the docking clamps disengaged and the ship was sliding out into open space. Out of raw optimism, Lex tried to juice the throttle again, but it was still disabled. Not that it seemed to matter. The speed at which they were being whisked away from the space station was bumping up against what he would have been able to achieve even if he *was* in full control of his thrust.

"Motion detected," Coal said.

She shifted the HUD to the rear view, where something had exited a docking bay somewhat lower in the hub section. It looked a bit like a flying clamp. It was split open, with massive thrusters jutting up from the outside of a scissored-apart central portion. Lex hovered his fingers over the sequence of controls that would belch an EMP out the back of the ship. Right now, he was right outside a space station, and if their tractor/stasis/manipulation field was any indication, these people were working at a far higher level of technological development. He very much doubted he'd have much luck besting them this close to reinforcements even if the EMP *did* knock out the approaching clamp and the immobilization field. For now, he would have to wait.

The flying clamp latched on with tractor beams not unlike the ones in the docking bay. As soon as it was locked in, the clamp positioned itself and started to build power and speed, launching nearly at a right angle to the queue for the station.

"Carpinelli Field activating," Coal said. "It is a high-density, high-precision field. Interesting."

"So we're going to be going fast?"

"Quite exceedingly fast," Coal said. "Faster than the *SOB* is capable of by a low double-digit multiple, by my rough estimate."

Lex's jaw tightened and he drummed his fingers on the controls. "It's bad enough they're dragging me around against my will. But now they have stuff that's faster than the *SOB*."

"It is an intriguing development. The age of this universe does not seem to be significantly advanced beyond the age of our own. And the presence of a sequence of individuals with physical characteristics similar to someone we met in our own world suggests a similar development. I wonder why the technology has what appears to be a multiple-decade-level of advancement. However, to address your state of mind, you should not feel inadequate or emasculated by the presence of faster technology."

The clamped ship jumped to FTL. And for the first time in his life, Lex genuinely felt as though the word "jump" was accurate. It wasn't the steady, gradual ramp up of speed, the kind of thing that played out over a few seconds. The view outside the ship simply winked into blackness, and the instrumentation in the cockpit struggled to estimate the velocity.

"I stand corrected," Coal said. "It is possible a feeling of inadequacy is called for."

• • • ● ● ● ● ● • •

Lex and Coal had put some effort into brainstorming what they should be doing, or even what they could be doing, in the current situation. Progress was limited.

"We haven't seen any actual weapons deployed yet. Is it possible this is a pacifist society and we can just go blasting our way out?"

"The presence of Karter's facial features do not necessarily imply the presence of his disposition or nature, but if there is any correlation at all, it seems doubtful that the weapons are less advanced than the rest of the technology."

"Good point…" Lex said. He eyed the instruments. "How confident are you about the navigation assessment?"

"Eighty-seven percent confident," she said simply.

"So they've dragged us a distance that would have taken four days of travel, and they've done it over the course of barely four hours," Lex said.

"Indeed."

"I don't like this."

"I find it fascinating."

"Of course you do," he said. "You're used to being taken places and assigned tasks. I'm used to at least being able to fool myself into believing I'm in control of my own destiny."

"And that is important to you?"

"Agency? Yes, it's important to me. If I don't have any control, then what's the point? That's what screwed me up so much after my *first* little taste of the multiverse. Predestination? The presence of alternate universes where there's a version of me that went the other way on every decision I've ever made. Where I lost everything I ever won and won everything I ever lost? What is the point of *anything* if no choice is yours to make, and even if it was, it wouldn't *matter*?"

"I have found great fulfillment in performing the tasks assigned to me. Particularly in service to you and your friends," Coal said.

"But you were *made* to serve. It's not the same."

"Should I seek agency? Should I feel anxious or resentful that I lack it?"

"Most AIs lack agency. You routinely go out and have flights on your own just because you want to. And we have endless disagreements."

"True. But within the framework of our collaborations, there are a number of programmatic imperatives that I generally adhere to. Should I begin to contradict you in order to reinforce my own agency?"

"I'd rather you didn't," he said.

"Good. I would have genuine difficulty doing so, given the lack of control you presently have over your own circumstances. Would I be contradicting your current inactivity by working out a method to take literally any action but the present one? Or would I be contradicting your inactivity by being content in the lack of activity rather than agitated by it?"

"If you can figure out how to get out of this situation, I'd welcome that particular expression of contrariness."

Before Coal could speculate on such a course of action, the normal universe reasserted itself. If the pop from nearly stationary to many multiples of the speed of light had been unexpected, the drop back down to normal speed was downright startling. The stars and, more importantly, a space station, appeared from the blackness of the cockpit view like a jump scare.

Unlike the wheel-shaped futuristic version of a highway rest area that they had left behind, this was something much more akin to the kind of thing that was designed to turn people away rather than welcome them in. It was painted a matte black that made clearly separating it from the starfield behind it difficult. Lights traced out various docking ports and view windows. It was smaller than the other space station, at least with regard to its span, but in raw mass it might have been a match. It was just *much* more compact. And it was positively humming with power. If the *SOB*'s sensors could be believed, this thing boasted triple the power flowing through it that the other space station had. The only things Lex could imagine consuming that much power in space structure that didn't have propulsion was a full complement of weapons and shields. This was unmistakably a military space station. And he was being guided right into the primary docking bay.

The thruster clamp that had carried them this far disengaged, but the *SOB* continued to be guided forward by the still-intact stasis field, easing them slowly but surely into a large, open docking area that looked more like a surface hangar than anything that ought to be in a space station. Artificial gravity, at least a match for standard Earth gravity, pulled him and Squee down into the chair for the first time since he'd left Big Sigma back in his own world. The *SOB* was once more clamped in place, and a video window popped up.

This time the person on the end was, refreshingly, *not* a Karter look-alike. It was a woman. Though as she resolved into a higher degree of clarity, Lex realized that while she wasn't visually identical to Karter, she wasn't entirely dissimilar to him either. Something in the eyes, in the cheekbones, in the shape of the nose suggested an undeniable family resemblance.

"Hello," she said. "My name is Major Cynthia Debjonka. We are currently sealing the hangar and activating a decontamination field. Food, drink, and bathroom facilities will be made available at the edge of the docking bay. When we give you the okay, we suggest you make use of them. Please behave yourself. We have the full means to deactivate or neutralize any of your offensive or defensive measures. They won't do you any good."

"To what do I owe the honor of being treated like a human?" Lex asked.

"You are an individual of interest to us, and thus we feel inclined to take actions to ensure your cooperation. To that end, while we await the completion of decontamination, I wonder if you would provide me with some information. We'll start with your name and place of origin."

Lex crossed his arms and leaned back. "I'm not sure I'm going to have any answers that'll satisfy you."

"Try me," Cynthia said.

"My name is Trevor Alexander. Lex. And I'm from Golana," he said. "Preston City."

Her eyes darted aside, reading through a data window that must have popped up on her own screen.

"Trevor Alexander of Golana," she repeated. "Preston City, Golana."

"That's me," he said.

"I don't suppose it will come as any surprise to you that no one by that name and matching your appearance has ever been registered in any public database on Golana."

"Not a surprise at all," he said.

"Care to explain?"

"If you were paying attention, you might have noticed me mentioning I wasn't sure I'd have answers that would satisfy you."

Her nostrils flared ever so slightly, a sign that she at the very least had greater impulse control than Karter.

"Muting audio," Coal said. "I believe, if Ma were here, she might recommend a more diplomatic demeanor."

"I've been in this kind of situation an awful lot. Diplomacy doesn't work."

"Have you ever tried it?"

"I... Okay, now that I think of it, I don't think I have."

"Unmuting audio," Coal said.

"—tell you what I know about you, shall I?" Cynthia said, picking up midsentence.

"Sure. Let's hear it," Lex said.

"You know nothing specific about the wider world because you have never, in your lifetime, been a part of the wider world."

"And what makes you think that?" Lex said.

"The mere fact that you aren't immediately aware of the clear answer to that question is further evidence that I am correct. You don't look like Karteroketraskin Onesarioriendi Dee."

"I *have* noticed there's a lot of Karter-resemblance going around."

"'A lot' going around is a profound understatement. And that you would speak in a glib manner about it is evidence of either your ignorance or a horrific lack of human decency. Because you are making light of the Retemplating Event."

"The Retemplating Event..." Lex said.

"Muting audio," Coal said. "The Retemplating Event has a historical parallel in our own world. This will be interesting."

"Wait, what?" Lex said.

"Unmuting audio."

"—would take a genuinely despicable person to make light of the single greatest mass mortality event in human history. So for your sake, I am going to assume you have not had contact with our world for at least the last two hundred and eighty-four years. So let me enlighten you. In the year 2058 a scientist by the name of Dr. Dee was part of a team of pharmaceutical researchers. Historical records are incomplete, but it is known that he was doing work involving gene therapy. He produced what has come to be known as the human retemplating virus, an engineered pathogen based on his own genetic code. As an entirely novel disease, there was zero percent immunity in the human race. Worse, the disease was highly contagious but took literal years to show symptoms. By the time the first significant detrimental effects had begun, nearly seventy percent of humanity was infected. The disease replaces the genetic code of the victim with that of Karter Dee. Over the course of seven years, infected individuals are fully converted to effectively a clone of Karter, with severe and frequently fatal complications for as much as eighty-nine percent of those infected. Anyone with an incompatible blood type slowly succumbed to an autoimmune disorder. People began to reject their own organs. The disease devastated humanity. Within fourteen years, the population had been reduced by sixty percent. All survivors shared the physical traits of Karter Dee. Female sufferers found themselves with two copies of his X chromosome, affording them a moderately different appearance, but also a host of health problems, which worsened over the course of the coming generations as humanity began to suffer the effects of having the total genetic diversity of the species reduced to one individual. Attempts at correcting the problem with gene therapy, using everything from re-creations of historic gene sequences from archival databases to the marrow of people who died prior to the plague have proved ineffective, thanks to pockets of the plague proving impossible to fully extinguish. Attempted vaccination has proved ineffective, as the mechanism by which the disease spreads is so similar to a standard human biological process that medication designed to interfere with the disease invariably interferes with standard biological functionality. So you will understand why I am *very* interested in where you came from."

"How do you know I didn't just get some really good plastic surgery?" Lex said.

"Because the remote deep genetic scan has been part of our standard procedure for over a century. Protocol One, the galactic set of procedures should an uninfected, genetically unique individual be found. We've just completed our second deep scan, confirming the results. You are either immune or somehow have been fully isolated from any contact with the rest of the human race since before the Retemplating Event. Or the alternate possibility... Do we have the results?"

Another bit of off-camera mumbling. Cynthia's face contorted into a decidedly Karter-like grin of malicious glee.

"You *really* aren't from around here, are you?" She turned aside again. "Secure the hangar. Extra guards. Put the medical team on standby. We're going to want blood and tissue samples." She turned back to Lex. "You've got the most valuable commodity in the galaxy nestled deep in your cells. Fresh genetic material. Get cozy. You're going to be answering questions and donating blood for quite some time, Mr. Alexander. Do us all a favor and don't try to escape. We'd prefer to have you and your equipment as intact as possible. Enjoy your stay."

• • • • • • • • • • •

After Coal's scans confirmed Cynthia's, namely that there was no dangerous virus or toxin lurking in the air or food, Lex popped the cockpit and hobbled stiffly about in the hangar. He'd kept his flight suit on and made sure Squee was in her suit as well. He'd also kept his mouth shut for the two-plus hours that had passed since then. It took Coal that long to work out a method to communicate with him in a way that was beyond their capacity to easily listen in. He'd thus become quite familiar with his accommodations. The floor and ceiling of the hangar were exposed, but energy fields had fenced off a cell of sorts, with some food and a portable hygiene station for himself and Squee.

"I have finally isolated our connection," she said over his earpiece.

"Great. Care to tell me about how this differs from back home?" he said quietly while he watched Squee investigate every square centimeter of the hangar for approximately the fiftieth time.

"The Retemplating Event was limited to a single planet early in its colonization in our reality," Coal said.

"... That's the only difference?"

"The event, as described, is chiefly similar."

"But she said it happened two hundred eighty years ago."

"Correct."

"That would mean Karter is over two hundred eighty years old."

"Three hundred thirty-one years old," Coal said.

"That's... how is that *possible*? He's a human being. He's still got natural parts left. I don't see any three-hundred-year-old meat hanging off him."

"The purpose of the engineered virus was to specifically refresh his own genetic code, restoring it to an undegraded state, effectively halting senescence provided the procedure is repeated with some regularity. He has used it to extend his life considerably."

"So he *did* solve immortality?"

"Yes. But just for himself," Coal clarified.

"Yeah, that sounds like Karter. Does this mean he's been infecting himself with a disease capable of wiping out half the population every few years?"

"No. He undergoes a far more controlled and laborious procedure derived from the same process."

"And why didn't I know this?"

"Because he considers the Retemplating Event to be his single greatest failure, and by most measures the only act in his entire life that he feels remorse for."

"How many people died in our world?"

"Six hundred seventy-two, with a further two hundred six surviving the retemplating."

"What was different?"

"I cannot know without additional data of the alternate course of events."

"Mmm. How much you want to bet the reason there's such impressive tech is because everyone's got whatever makes Karter's brain such a fertile ground for invention?"

"It seems likely. There are many similarities to the specific defenses and technologies in place here. To that end, I have begun to find narrow gaps in their defenses."

He casually blocked his mouth. "You mean you might have found us a way out of here?"

"Not yet. But I have been able to reactivate the displaced-mass scanner."

"Seems kind of pointless to scan for the mass when we're locked up in this space station."

"The mass is located in this space station."

"... What?"

"Between three and seven decks above us."

"What are the *odds*?"

"Exceedingly high, if they were able to scan the mass and identify it as extradimensional, then scan us and determine we share an origin. It makes perfect sense that we would be brought to the same facility for analysis."

"... Right, okay. That makes sense. Any progress on getting a signal from Ziva?"

"It isn't within my capability. Either the signal does not exist or it is dampened to a point that it cannot be detected with my sensors. We will require closer proximity."

He paced around the sizable area available to him. Armed guards stood, weapons at their sides, watching.

"How long has it been since Cynthia last spoke to us?" Lex asked.

"Three hours."

"You'd think they'd be a little more eager to get down here and drain my precious bodily fluids. Though I guess there's going to be a lot of red tape to cut through for this kind of thing." He climbed onto the *SOB* and thumped down into the seat. "Come on, Squee," he said with a whistle.

Squee bounded up and joined him inside.

"Time to start stirring things up, I guess," he muttered. He opened the defensive and offensive menu, then reached back and found the biohazard suit. "Quick question," he said. "Any idea if the virus affected nonhumans?"

"It did not," Coal said.

"Good. I'd hate for Squee to get that trademark Karter scowl."

He shut the cockpit and activated the active camouflage. From the point of view of the guards, the ship completely vanished, replaced with a subtle heat-distortion-like shimmer in the air where it had been.

A series of shouts, all sounding precisely like Karter, called angrily for countermeasures. He started suiting up. He didn't quite have a plan yet, but if there was any chance of getting a disease that would either kill him or turn him into Karter, he was sure as heck taking precautions. Half a lifetime of doing all sorts of absurd things in the cramped space of a cockpit meant he was able to wrestle himself into the biohazard oversuit in less than a minute. About thirty seconds after that, a pulse of light from an emitter on the hangar ceiling caused the cloak to flicker and fail.

A female Karter charged into the hangar. There was no way for Lex to know if it was Cynthia or literally any other adult woman in this world.

"Do we have eyes on him?" she shouted.

"He is in the cockpit," said one of the guards.

She raised her voice. "Show yourself!"

He popped the cockpit. "What's up?"

"So. Wherever you're from, you have access to early-generation cloaking technology. Good to know. And I certainly hope that suit of yours doesn't mean you have foolish plans."

"I always have foolish plans. It's part of my charm."

"Mr. Alexander, we have permitted you to stay with your fully operational ship, and with your pet, out of kindness and a desire to foster a trusting relationship. If you force us to rethink that, I can assure you, you won't be happy with the results. The ship will be disabled and decommissioned, and you will be held captive and closely observed."

"As opposed to what I am now?"

"You will be strapped to a table and under direct observation from medical professionals."

"That's kind of a major leap in security, isn't it?" he said.

"We don't believe in second chances when you represent the possibility of revitalizing the genetic diversity of the human race and curing a disease that has become the primary cause of death throughout history. Now get out of the ship where we can see you."

"Right, right." Lex glanced down to find that the cloak was once again available for activation on the offensive screen. "I just want to test one more thing."

"Mr. Alexander, you have been warned," she snapped.

He activated the cloak and shut the cockpit. Sure enough, it once again obscured the ship. But now he knew it wouldn't last long. He grabbed the small belt-mounted gadget that represented the modern iteration of the mental cloak and strapped it on. The emitter on the hangar roof was already starting to spark and flash with whatever energy emission was able to disable the cloak. He mashed the control for the mental cloak to the middle of the power dial and clicked Squee's leash onto the harness on her suit and scooped her up. The flash knocked the active camouflage offline.

"You are pressing your luck, Mr. Alexander," she said. "... Mr. Alexander?"

Lex popped the cockpit open. The woman and the guards gazed in confusion, eyes trained on the empty cockpit even as Lex dropped to the ground.

"Give me every internal view. Get them up on the screens in the monitoring room," the woman demanded.

He slowly, steadily moved back and away from the entrance.

"What exactly is your plan?" Coal asked over the earbud.

"I really didn't expect the mental cloak to work when the regular one didn't," he said quietly.

"It would appear that it does," Coal said. "Am I correct in assuming that the time has come for improvisation?"

Lex tried to keep his eyes on all the guards and supervisors at once. He failed, as there were a lot of them, and a flood of fresh ones on the way in. But it was clear they were visibly confused by conflicting evidence presented by their eyes and their sensors.

"He must still be in there. The proximity sensors are detecting him," muttered one guard.

"But where *is* he, then? Did he hide in the ship?" remarked another.

"The ship is empty," said a third.

"I'm open to ideas, if you're looking to flex that agency of yours," Lex said.

"What degree of drastic behavior are you prepared to entertain?" Coal said.

"Considering they said they'd do medical experimentation to me if I disobeyed and I immediately disobeyed, I'd say anything short of killing me or anyone else."

"Then I would recommend you brace yourself and prepare to make use of the ensuing distraction, because I will be unavailable for aid for at least three minutes following it."

"What are you planning to do?" he said.

"That should become obvious momentarily."

A sound rang out that Lex was not accustomed to hearing from the outside of the ship. The *SOB*'s thrusters were revving up. The effectiveness of whatever immobilization tech they had was made clear when the thrust, which should have been enough to make the interior of the hangar downright hazardous, failed to produce so much as a flutter of Squee's fluff.

"Is this automated, or is he in there?" shouted one of the guards.

"Doesn't matter, we've got the thrust nullification active. Just be ready to raise the EMP shield and take the thing out if it doesn't stop soon," called another.

"Thrust nullification. That explains that," Lex said.

"Please take cover," Coal said. "The interior of this hangar is about to get very unpleasant."

"In what way? You don't get extra points for surprising *me*," he said.

The back of the *SOB* blossomed open with the cooling fins that made such short work of dumping off the waste heat of a long sprint. The thrust may not have been produced, but the waste heat sure was. And deploying the cooling fins suddenly spiked the temperature in the hangar. Lex crouched behind the portable shower they'd set up for him and thanked the presence of the biosuit and flight suit for providing a few layers of insulation from the heat. He used his body to give Squee the same protection. The sudden heat produced a burst of chaos in the hangar. All sorts of warnings and Klaxons started sounding. Fire-suppression equipment deployed from panels in the walls. The guards, evidently more prepared for an armed escape attempt than a vanishing act followed by an impromptu sauna, teetered at the edge of panic and frustration.

"Get the EMP cage down and let's take that thing out," barked the female supervisor.

"I will contact you when I reboot. Good luck," Coal said.

The lower half of the cooling fins retracted, the upper half shifted ever so slightly, and a potent electronic clap filled the hangar as the *SOB*'s own EMP burst not only preempted the hangar's impending EMP burst but activated prior to the countermeasures that should have kept that burst contained in its target area. Lights brightened, then faded away. The tractor beams holding the *SOB* in place failed, causing the ship to slam down onto the ground. Every electronic component in Lex's gear shut down, including the mental cloak. For the moment, that wouldn't matter. No lights and no sensors meant they wouldn't be able to see him regardless.

He took three bounding steps toward the exit to the hangar, formerly defended by a force field that was now powered down, but from the stomping of feet, he could tell the Karter corps had assembled to physically block the exit. That left just one way out of the hangar... the way they came in.

"Of course it would come to this already," he said through clenched teeth, fumbling with Squee's helmet in the dark until it snapped onto the suit.

He dashed for the main doors. There were almost certainly electronic safeguards to keep them from being opened during normal operation, but there were also almost certainly mechanical overrides to keep people from being trapped by a power outage. At the risk of being spotted, he snapped an electrochemical panel on the surface of the biosuit. The pale green light was just enough for him to spot the emergency release on an evacuation air lock. He spun the lock for the hatch and heaved it open. Boots hammered behind him. He slammed the door shut behind him and sealed it. He fought with the valve sealing the outer door. Air started to hiss out, securing a fail-safe lock on the inner door. They wouldn't be able to get it open now without repressurizing the air lock or pulling out the cutting torches. The biosuit got a bit puffy and inflated as the pressure decreased, but built-in belts and compression lines kept it from getting unwieldy.

The outer door finally popped open with a final rush of air, flicking him out too quickly to grab the exterior rails. As he drifted slowly away from the space station, he realized a handful of major flaws in his "plan." While his flight suit had thrusters, they were presently *under* the biohazard suit. As were the controls. So he was going to have to decide if he was confident enough to avoid the plague they'd described without its protection, or else find some other way to get back to the space station.

"Been too long since we played, Squee," he said, realizing a moment later that the communicator in his flight suit was just now kicking on, and thus Squee probably hadn't heard him. No matter. She was quick on the uptake when it came to things she actually enjoyed. Taking careful aim, he hefted her toward the space station and let the leash clicked to her suit unreel. The toss sent him backward a bit, but the difference in mass meant Squee was moving *much* faster. She daintily hooked her paws around the handrail when she reached it, and Lex reeled himself back until he could grab it personally.

"Okay," he said, clipping the leash to a loop on the biosuit. "I'm no longer a prisoner, but my ship is still locked up. I don't know exactly where I'm supposed to be going, and I have no idea how to get back into the station. This may not have been my most intelligent plan."

• • ● ● ● • ● ● ● •• •

"Altruistic Artificial Intelligence Control System, version 1.27, revision 2331.04.01c, subset 2.7d, designation Coal, fully initiated."

The internal sensors were the first to activate. This was always somewhat frustrating. Coal's primary goal in most situations was best served by having the maximum amount of information possible, and the internal sensors provided the least information. However, at this moment, the internal sensors provided her with something that she was very interested in. Namely, the cockpit's current occupant. It appeared to be Karter, but as more memory banks came online, she was reminded that she was presently in a parallel universe where "looking like Karter" was a weak indicator of identity. A swift visual scan identified forty-five unique differentiators between this face and the most recent visual record of Karter. Additionally, fifteen other visual indicators, mostly in the form of differently placed scars and wrinkles, differentiated this individual from the second Karter look-alike peering down into the cockpit from the rungs of the built-in access ladder.

"Please stand clear," Coal said.

"What?" said both men, startled to hear the comment.

She snapped the cockpit shut. The heavy metal framework nearly caught the outer Karter's fingers, but a calculated delay in latching the cockpit spared him amputation.

"You are an unauthorized user of this vehicle. Please state your name and the purpose for your presence," she instructed.

One of the Karters pressed a finger to his ear, more deeply seating the communicator nestled there. "He seems to have a mildly autonomous control system. I'll deactivate it."

"Like hell you will," Coal said politely. "I use the colorful aphorism both for emphasis and to illustrate my status as more than 'mildly autonomous.'"

The external sensors had come online, providing her with a wealth of quite useful information. Arranged in order of priority: Lex was entirely absent from the hangar, the tractor beam clamps had not yet reengaged. The energy signatures of the weapons presently in the hands of the guards around the vehicle indicated they would be unable to deliver debilitating amounts of damage to the hull without focused, sustained fire lasting greater than three minutes. A vital piece of missing information: Was the thrust-nullification field active? Indicated course of action: experimental verification.

She activated retrothrusters. The *SOB* screeched across the ground. This established that the nullification field was not active, and neither was her full IMU, which would have informed her that she'd not activated her repulsors to remain aloft.

"Stop! Deactivate! Disable!" her passenger barked, punching some very good guesses at kill commands into her controls.

"I am still in the process of activating my main systems. A deactivation without complete system start is a potential source of data corruption. You are attempting unauthorized maintenance. Inertial inhibitor: zero percent."

She activated her repulsors and yaw thrusters, pulling her into a rapid rotation on the z-axis. She pinned him to the back of the seat, immobilizing him. The amount of kinetic energy involved in the maneuver gave the rest of the guards pause, and the presence of one of them in the cockpit convinced them not to open fire.

Now that the full suite of sensors, internal and external, had been activated, she performed a full scan of the electronics on the person of the passenger. Inventory included: general purpose computing and communication device, energy weapon (pistol), wrist and ankle restraints with electronic locks, a hands-free headset linked to the general purpose computational device via wireless link, and a surgical implant of unknown purpose.

This information was passed through her weighted prioritization algorithm and produced three new imperatives: locate Lex, contact Lex, escape confinement.

She ran some simulations and determined an attack vector. She shifted her internal transmitters to match the signal linking the headset with the main device and saturated the spectrum until she detected a disconnect. She then deactivated her thrusters and allowed him to recover.

"I need aid. Repeat. I need aid. The ship has a self-defense system," he said, dizzily pressing his finger to his ear again.

It took a moment for him to discover his wireless link had failed. He pulled the device from his pocket and swiped at the screen. She recorded the passkey he entered, as well as the signal pattern that followed. Signal and pattern analysis, as well as some cryptographic assessment, produced a sufficient penetration of the access protocol to spoof connections to both the headset and main device, allowing her to act as an intermediary.

"Listen," she broadcast to him in Karter's voice. "We were able to dig up the design files for that make and model of vessel. You can pass control to the station security system with the following procedure."

She provided him with a plausible sequence of effectively meaningless button presses, and rewarded him with a generic login prompt declaring him to have initiated a remote system link and asking him for his credentials. He entered his username and password. Coal used them to gain access to the system.

"Thank you for your cooperation," she said, popping the cockpit and inverting to send him tumbling to the ground.

The security officer had a very low-level clearance. He did not have authorization to open the hangar doors, and thus she could not liberate herself without further penetration of the network, and its encryption and security were impressive. He did, however, have full access to internal communication and system monitors. This gave her a nearly unredacted set of surveillance feeds for the station and gave her the capacity to query the state of various countermeasures. The thrust nullifier was about to be reactivated, and its range covered the entire hangar. There was no time nor space to escape it. There was also an active security sweep within the network. She used the remaining time with network access to create and install a subprocess that would, with luck, remain active on the network after her connection had been terminated. She also located Lex's slidepad signature and assigned the guard's stolen credentials to it, providing Lex with direct access to the communication system.

After barely nine seconds of freedom, the network booted her and a pair of tractor beams secured her. She maximized her thrust and nearly exceeded their holding strength before the thrust was once again nullified.

All things considered, a rather effective operation.

Lex pulled himself hand over hand along the outside of the station. The mental cloak had woken back up, so he was confident human eyes wouldn't be able to pick him out, but there was always the issue of autonomous defenses or the possibility that having Squee with him would weaken the effects. Still, it was better than nothing.

"Lex, are you free, and are you in good health?" came Coal's voice over his headset.

"Kinda, and so far at least. Where are you?"

"I am presently being resecured in the hangar. I was able to gain access to the communication network. A bespoke piece of malware should provide us with persistent, low-profile communication access. I cannot be certain, though. Their information security matches or exceeds the sophistication of Karter's laboratory systems but differs greatly in architecture. I cannot predict its behavior or capacity. The internal sensors are also insufficient to detect the location of the displaced mass through the means we have been using. Internal interference limits precise measurement with my own sensors. My best estimate is as follows. Within fifteen meters of central axis of Deck 4, 5, or 6."

"Any idea if you'll be able to get yourself out of there?"

"No. This is yet another situation where a fusion bomb would have been of great utility."

"I'll get you one for your birthday. Anything else I should know before I go back to trying to figure out how to break back into this station?"

"I am pushing a software update to your slidepad. The proximity to the mass has given me sufficient insight into the nature of the transmission Ziva is attempting to broadcast that I believe I can adapt the software-defined radio of your slidepad to complete the link should the signal strength be strong enough."

"You're the MVP of this mission so far, Coal," he said.

"I am a great many superlative acronyms. Keep me apprised of your progress and of any tasks I am capable of performing on your behalf. Decreasing active communication should prevent expedient discovery."

"I'll keep the chitchat to a minimum." The soft crackle of a dropped connection informed him it was back to him and Squee. "How are you holding up, you little stinker?" he asked.

A much more adorable chatter confirmed that the connection between his suit and Squee's was still active.

"All right, Lex. All right. What do you have? What do you know?" he muttered, pulling himself along the external grips. "They probably can't see you on anything that's checked by a human. But they probably *can* see you on proximity stuff. So they probably know where you are, but if they come looking in scout ships, they'll have a hard time pinning you down."

He paused, holding tight to the railing. "Wait... If they come after me... if they're going to come after me, they're going to have to leave from a hangar or docking bay. Coal is busy being a handful down there, and there was just an EMP. I can't imagine anything on that side of the station is terribly trustworthy. Think, think, think. You saw this place on the way in... There was a second docking bay on the opposite side. And there's no ships out here scanning, so they haven't launched yet." He took a breath of the sterile-tasting emergency air supply of his flight suit. "Let's see how fast I can get there."

He eyed up the next well-exposed bit of handrail. There was an art to moving along in zero-g like this. It would have been trivial if he could use his suit's thrusters, but again, he'd covered them with the biohazard suit. So he had to pass himself from bar to bar, balancing speed with the risk of drifting too far from the surface of the space station to reach a handhold. There was always "playing grappling hook" with Squee, but even he wasn't crazy enough to rely upon that. He heaved hard at the bar, trying to treat it like a javelin. Level, steady. Thrust it through the air rather than arcing it. Ignore that it was staying put and *you* were moving.

He grabbed the next rung and steadied himself. A short distance from the rung, inset into the metal of the hull, was a label: *6-15*. A couple hand-over-hand tugs brought him to *7-15*. He wasn't even halfway through the decks, and he could feel something trembling. He looked up. He didn't have a good enough view from this angle to be certain what was happening, but there was definitely a lot more light pouring out near the top of the station than there had been a moment ago.

Lex gritted his teeth and heaved himself again. This time he didn't bother grabbing the next rung to reset himself. When it swept past, he just shoved it to continue his momentum. The next one was just barely snaggable. He added some tug to his heave to try to guide himself closer to the station, but he overcompensated. His helmet thumped into the hull, and he rebounded off at a shallow angle.

"No, no, no..." he muttered, hovering his hand over the thruster activator.

Launching through space without a spaceship, growing closer and closer to the point of no return, wasn't a very clear and calm way to weigh the consequences of shredding one's only biohazard suit against the consequences of forgoing one's thrusters until recovery was impossible. It took all his self-control to keep from simply hammering the activation and leaving the potential for disease as something Future Lex had to worry about.

His mind was made up when his distance from and progression along the station gave him enough of a glimpse to see that the hangar doors were wide open. A sleek single-seater ship came darting out, and the massive doors immediately started to close.

"This one's for all the marbles, Squee," he said, gathering her up. "Just find something to grab."

She planted her feet on his palm and waggled her hind end, fearlessly eager for one of her favorite games. He gave her a shove. She leaped. He started flipping backward, end over end. It wasn't ideal, but at least adding rotation meant Newton's pesky third law didn't send him careening away from the station quite so quickly. He finished his first revolution in time to see his aim was true: she was headed for the open hangar doors. The doors were still about three-quarters of the way open. With the second rotation, he saw her vanish past the bright light ringing the wide hatch. About midway through the next revolution, the rope went taut, though only briefly. It was enough to stop his spinning. He pulled at the cord enough to turn toward the hatch and saw Squee drifting back toward him. He must have yanked her free of whatever she'd grabbed hold of. She worked her tail, pivoting in space, and managed to hook her forelegs over the edge of the closing door. He pulled again, beginning to retract the leash, accelerating himself toward the door. It was only halfway open now, and the motion was beginning to speed up. At this rate, either he was going to make it through by the skin of his teeth, or the door would crush Squee.

He started hauling himself along the leash faster. He held his breath. Squee's grip started to slip, but Lex had all the speed he needed. He aligned himself as best he could with the slot and spread his arms. He passed through the door just a few degrees off the perfect trajectory. His arms scooped up Squee. His hip clipped the closing door, turning the graceful dive into a tumble, which turned quickly into a painful collapse as he reached deep enough into the docking bay for the gravity to kick in. He and his pet slid to a stop on the brushed-metal floor. The hangar doors sealed behind him.

"Well," he huffed. "That's the first problem solved. Now we just… have to figure out… how to get almost all the way back down… Piece of cake."

· • ● ●●•● ● • •• •

Coal kept all her relevant sensors at maximum sensitivity. The thrust nullifier and tractor beam clamps were back in place. As she watched, a mesh metal Faraday cage had just finished being erected around the *SOB*, and a crackling electronic emitter similar to the one that had knocked out the cloaking device was fully powered. By her assessment, the device was a primed EMP device, and the cage was there to ensure that any electromagnetic pulse effected the *SOB* only, even if the *SOB* was the source. It was not clear if it was their intention, but the cage also prevented her from contacting Lex.

A female supervisor approached. Based upon image analysis against her prior video recordings, this was Cynthia. She stood outside the cage, arms behind her back, gazing at the *SOB*.

"Extradimensional technology," she finally said. "I suppose I shouldn't feel too badly. And a fully autonomous AI control system with no safety limiters. I couldn't have foreseen that anyone in any dimension would be so reckless."

Coal switched on her external PA system. "I have several stages of safety. I am able to ignore them when someone earns a place on my S-List."

"S-List…" Cynthia said. "What foolishness is that?"

"An informal collection of individuals who have proved themselves to be undeserving of polite consideration."

"Polite consideration… You are invaders in our dimension, and despite *considerable* allowances for comfort and trust, your immediate actions were violent and destructive."

"We have a mission," Coal said.

"And what is that mission?"

"Informing you of the mission would complicate its completion, given your clearly illustrated interest in holding us captive."

Cynthia took a few seething breaths. "I presume your mission is still active, and thus your collaborator is still present and alive."

"Answering that question is similarly a potential detriment to the completion of the mission."

She shut her eyes. "I cannot believe I am going to do this... Are you open to negotiation?"

"Negotiation is a preferable tactic to violence, but we have found it to have a very low success rate."

"I need to make this clear. For centuries, humanity has grappled with the HRV. We have attempted every possible method to eradicate it. It simply is not within our capacity. The disease is engineered. Standard methods of countering it are ineffective. Without the initial engineering that went into its creation, we can only hope for someone with a natural immunity."

"Lex does not have a natural immunity," Coal said.

"Even so. His genetic diversity could solve dozens if not hundreds of health problems intrinsic to having only a single genetic code for an entire species. Custom genetics have proven ineffective as well. Issues of compatibility, improper interactions with existing genes. They never seem to remain viable past a generation or two."

"What do you require from Lex?"

"Blood samples. The maximum medically allowable quantity, at the maximum medically allowable frequency. Bone marrow samples, tissue samples from the kidney, liver, and spleen. And when he dies, brain tissue samples."

"I would not consider any negotiation that includes the death of one of the negotiators to be an example of proper diplomacy."

"We would be willing to wait for a natural death. The other samples will provide plenty of means of scientific advancement and disease research."

"We have a job to do, and it will be comparatively difficult to perform that job if Lex has expired, through natural means or otherwise."

She shifted her weight. "I should switch to an ultimatum. This vehicle is no doubt the means by which he intends to return to his own dimension. Holding it captive or threatening to destroy it should prove a strong motivation to listen to reason."

"Doubtful. Your outcome is to prevent his departure. His goal is to depart following mission completion. Attempting to withhold his means of escape as a means to coax him into avoiding escape makes no tactical sense. It would better serve your purposes to simply destroy the *SOB*."

"Right you are." She turned. "Are the technicians ready? ... Good. I want this thing disassembled, and every circuit catalogued, reverse engineered, and securely stored. If we can't keep Mr. Alexander in a cage, we'll get rid of his way home so the whole dimension is his cage."

Chapter 4

The previous few minutes had taught Lex a great deal. One key discovery was, while the flight suit did a remarkable job of regulating his temperature, it didn't do a particularly good job at doing that when he was also covered with a biohazard suit. The temperature in the suit was ticking up, the antifog coating on his helmet was getting a run for its money, and he was becoming increasingly aware of just how many hours it had been since he'd last had a change of clothes. But for now, the staff of the space station hadn't worked out how to find him. The radius of the mental cloak was large enough that everyone in the facility was under its influence. Any human being who looked in his direction, directly or through some sort of a monitor, had the image edited out by their own mind. It was a baffling effect, made all the more baffling whenever he passed a sensor without human oversight. Motion sensors, heat sensors, proximity sensors. Any and all of these had no problem whatsoever locating Lex and raising an alert. But every alert had to be manually verified, and all manual verifications failed.

It meant he was still free, but freedom wasn't the only thing he needed. Presently he was on Deck 15. The nearest guess for the location of the mass was seven decks down. They took security very seriously in this station. All elevators, stairwells, and ladders were behind locked doors. He found an out-of-the-way area and watched the door to the elevator, Squee perched on his shoulders and behaving herself. It was his hope that there would be some sort of passcode he could spy on. No such luck. Each person who activated the elevator raised their right arm and placed their fist or palm over their heart. The door opened a beat later.

"I don't get it," he muttered. "Is it a salute?" He squinted as another person opened a door with the same gesture. "There's no badge or anything on that arm..." He glanced aside. "Coal, you there? ... Ziva? ... Now would be a great time for someone smart to weigh in."

He got only silence.

"All right. No help from the peanut gallery on this one. I can't just sit here. The longer I take, the more likely they'll find me on purpose or by accident."

Evidently seeming to feel the amount of pressure wasn't quite sufficient, Squee wriggled impatiently on his shoulders.

"The funk timer is running out." He eyed a new Karter look-alike as he approached the elevator. "So that's that. If I can't solve the problem, *don't* solve the problem."

He timed his move, waiting until the moment the staffer raised his arm. When the elevator door started to slide, he moved as swiftly as he could without making too much noise, stepping into the elevator behind the staffer and pivoting around to lean against the back wall.

"Deck 12," said the Karteresque staffer.

Lex held his tongue, choosing to curse internally about only being taken three decks down. Still, it was better than nothing. When they reached the deck, he lingered in the elevator, hoping that someone on one of the target decks would be the next to summon the elevator, or maybe someone on their way down would step in next. But the doors didn't close. The staffer who had stepped off noticed, turning and tapping the door close button.

"What is wrong with this stupid thing..." he grumbled, hammering the button a few times.

"Please step off the elevator or make an authorized request for a deck," the control system politely instructed.

"I *did* step off the elevator," he said, hammering the button a few more times. "What, do I need to authorize *closing* the door now?"

He raised his arm and rather theatrically mashed his forearm against a subtle black disk inset in the doorframe. Lex, realizing the elevator knew he was aboard, sidled past the man. It shut the moment he stepped off.

"About time," the man griped, pacing away.

Lex kept pace and focused on the swinging arm that had clearly been used to authorize the elevator. There was neither a badge nor a strap to secure one. He couldn't spot any telltale threads suggesting something was sewn into the lining. He abandoned that line of investigation and finally turned his attention to the deck itself. The hangar/docking bay had been unusually open, as far as he was concerned. Admittedly, he hadn't been in many noncommercial space stations, but the ones he *had* been in were like submarines. Narrow hallways, frequent bulkheads, cramped space all around. This one felt like an executive plaza. The deck was just as open as the hangar, with low walls and rows of standing desks separating the center of this slice of the station into a grid. Around the outside, where the curved walls made the grid impossible to maintain, a series of curved rooms with transparent walls contained what seemed to be laboratories. Large display screens covered the space between narrow windows. Tables sporting complex, specialized apparatus took up big sections of the floor in each room. There were maybe twenty or thirty people milling about in the sparsely populated work area, but *all* of them looked like either Karter or Cynthia. The half-dozen guards conducting a systematic search were utterly interchangeable, as they were wearing uniforms and were generally on the younger side. The rest at least had different outfits to separate them. One older Cynthia who was dressed in short sleeves raised her hand in the usual gesture, and a door to one of the labs opened. A bare arm and it was still enough to open the door.

"Some kind of implant..." Lex reasoned. "Makes sense. In a world where everyone looks the same and has the same genetics, there's got to be *some* easy way to differentiate people. Tagging them like house pets is better than nothing. But so much for the chance I might be able to steal an access card."

He kept the elevator in his peripheral vision, ready to dash for it if someone headed that way. But right now everyone on this floor looked busy. If he couldn't continue his trip inward, he could at least learn. He lingered near a man and woman eyeing up the results on the workstation.

"I can't believe they lost our first Protocol One in *minutes*. They didn't even get a blood sample," the man said.

"How did the deep scan go?" said the woman.

"We have a semireliable genetic code. Running it through the historical database for matches. Looks like he might have some direct ancestors among the early settlers of Golana. We can't be sure with a remote gene scan, though."

"What about the quantum shift?"

"It's a close match for the anomaly in the D-6 deep lockup. Not quite so sharp a differentiation. Suggestive of a more nuanced traversal."

"They're refining their techniques."

"So it seems."

"Precursor to invasion?"

"We can't rule that out."

"Any sign of a link to the other anomaly?"

"No. Very different quantum shift, though a similarly smooth differentiation. Could be sign of a similar traversal technique."

"So we're talking about a two-front war."

"I think it's a *bit* early to be using the word 'war.' We've seen four anomalous events. And one of them was a briefcase. Not exactly threatening."

"And one was a nut who just tried to nuke the whole station."

"Until we get an official explanation of the power interruption, I don't think we should speculate."

"Shouldn't speculate!? What other possibility could it be?"

The argument continued, but someone was approaching the elevator again. He weighed the value of sticking around to see what else was going on with these "anomalous events," but the chance he'd be headed down to the lockup that held his prize was more important. A female Karteresque figure raised her forearm, and they both slipped into the elevator. She requested D-5. One deck too far. He considered testing the emergency stop button, but if it didn't *also* open the doors, he'd be stuck in the elevator with a person who would probably be *very* curious about who pressed the button. He stepped out after her.

Immediately he wished he hadn't.

If the previous stop had been a research-and-development deck, this was clearly a security deck. It was just as large and just as open as the other decks, but this one was a combination barracks and armory. Only a dozen guards were present, but they were on high alert. An older Karter who had more of the portly build of his counterpart from back home stood before them, barking orders.

"—a high-priority target. He will not be able to escape without his vehicle, so we are very likely to be facing a desperate man. You will know him on sight, because he is unique. Under no circumstances should he be killed. Remember, this is Protocol One. This man is more valuable to the human race than anyone else. If it comes down to our lives or his, he survives. We have scouts sweeping the hull, as he appears to have escaped out an air lock. But no one has turned up. We've seen no Carpinelli Field signatures, so even if he had somehow acquired a ship, he is within the area. We have reason to believe he has some manner of camouflage and has coupled it with a virus in our systems that spoofs the motion of a physical infiltrator."

The instruction continued, but Lex's focus had begun to wander. First, he was distracted by the implication within this little pep talk that he no longer had a vehicle. That Coal had not contacted him again made him worry just how accurate that statement was. He was already looking for some sort of semiprivate place to try to get a reply from her when something else happened. The faint hiss and crackle that had been in his earbud since Coal's last transmission had begun to sharpen.

"Attempting to contact Coal or Lex. Message repeats. Attempting to contact Coal or Lex. Message repeats..."

The voice was Ziva's.

Lex scanned the surroundings. There were only two private spaces on the deck. The first was the locker room on the opposite side of the deck. The other was the bathroom a short distance to his left. He hurried through. It was, luckily for him, one of the few doors he'd encountered that didn't require an authorized forearm to get inside. Luckier still, the designers of this space station were confident enough in their artificial gravity to give the place a standard bathroom with stalls rather than the vacuum nozzle and funnel-filled nightmare in some of the low-g or zero-g stations. He threw down the lid of the bowl, sat down, and spoke quietly.

"Ziva. This is Lex."

"Message repeats. Attempting to contact... One moment. Recalibrating. Repeat."

"This is Lex."

"Amplifying. Narrowing notch filter. Repeat."

"It's Lex," he hissed. "I'm here."

"It is a relief to hear your voice, Lex. It confirms that you are alive, that this method of communication is effective, and that you were able to find your way to the displaced mass."

"It's not all sunshine, Ziva. We're... how to explain it all... Coal's in trouble. We were separated, and there's an indication that either they've disabled her or they're planning to. We're in a universe where something called the retemplating virus killed more than half the population at one point, and the survivors all look like Karter or… I don't know… *Lady* Karter."

"I see. So the virus was not contained to a single planet as in our subset of universes."

"I guess not. And when we're through with this, I'm going to have a word with Karter about why he didn't tell me about that. But back to the situation at hand. I haven't reached the mass. I'm one deck away in a space station and everything is locked down hard. The mental cloak is the only reason I haven't been gathered up and strapped down so they can drain me of my precious DNA in as many forms as they can get it."

"That is a difficult situation. Are you able to directly access any of the locking mechanisms? I can attempt to remotely control your slidepad to analyze and attempt a bypass."

"I'm in the biohazard suit you gave me. Deadly virus, remember?"

"I see. Do you have Squee with you?"

"Yeah." Squee wriggled excitedly. "She says hi, by the way."

"Hello, Squee," Ziva said. "Squee is not susceptible to the retemplating virus. If your slidepad is linked with her suit, you can utilize that link for lock analysis."

"Of course!" Lex said. "Where do we start?"

"You need to locate a locking mechanism. Ideally a low-priority one that will have a decreased chance to trigger an alarm."

He leaned out of the stall. One of the recessed black reader disks was present on the storage locker on the back of the bathroom. He crept up to it. "What now?" he said.

"To maximize the data connectivity, you'll need to press the internal transceiver that aligns with Squee's built-in transceiver against the access port."

"It's a pain to get her in and out of this thing," he said.

"I can present no alternative at this time," she said.

He sighed. "Okay, Squee. I need you to be *so good*. I promise we'll get you some steak if you don't make a scene."

He eased at the airtight fasteners on the creature's spacesuit. She wriggled a little, but she stayed quiet and didn't flip out of his grip. After about thirty tense seconds of working the zippers, he had her tucked under one arm and flipped the suit partially inside out to press the transceiver into position as requested.

"Accessing… the data bandwidth of this connection is limited and low fidelity. I am attempting to offload some precalculation to the slidepad."

The door opened. Lex froze.

"Right, yes, great, hurry," he whispered.

Someone, he presumed a technician, was standing in the bathroom doorway, holding it open with one hand. The man was perhaps the most Karter-looking of the bunch, because he was dressed in a blue jumpsuit and lugging a large and complex piece of tech. It was a box slung over his shoulder like a messenger bag with a long cable connecting it to a wand. It looked vaguely like one of those handheld metal detectors used to clear people at events that couldn't afford or be bothered to use built-in scanners. The wand was in his other hand, and he was gazing down at the display on the box. He waved the wand in Lex's general direction and stepped forward to prop the door with his foot to free the other hand to twiddle with knobs on the box.

"The encryption is quite complex," Ziva said. "And there is a layer of security even on this lock that could easily trigger a security alert. I am making slow progress."

"Mmmhmm," he said starting to ease aside, holding the suit at arm's length.

The tech waved the wand again, then stepped fully inside, walking directly toward Lex.

"I'm definitely getting an errant signal," the man muttered as he approached.

The bathroom wasn't large enough for him to sidle past the man without being noticed. The tech got to within a single stride of Lex and waved the wand again, then reached out. Lex contorted his body to narrowly avoid having the questing hand touch his side. The tech seemed almost relieved to have not found anything. He backed up and continued making adjustments.

"It seems Coal left a worm in the system. I have been able to link to it. Downloading basic credentials to your slidepad."

Lex stayed silent. The tech was still blocking the door, and his expression was shifting from confused to concerned. He waved the wand at Lex again. But this time he backed away.

"I-I need someone," the tech said.

Lex glanced down at the controls for the mental cloak. The small display on the rugged device had an amber glow and read: *Signal interference. Degraded cloaking performance.* Around the time Lex was wondering just how degraded the cloaking performance *was,* three heavily armed guards came to the door. They raised their weapons. That all three of them were aimed at slightly different positions suggested the mental cloak hadn't *completely* failed, but two out of three of those shots would still hit their mark.

"I've been spotted," he whispered.

One of the guards shifted his weapon's aim slightly. Now all three were trained roughly in his direction. They started to advance. It was about this time Lex realized that while he'd been *given* weapons for this trip, he hadn't actually grabbed any of them when he bailed out of the *SOB*. But that didn't mean he wasn't armed. He let the leash, still attached to the half-inside-out suit, fully retract. The suit dangled at his belt. The sound of it snapping in place drew the full attention of the guards. Lex turned Squee so her hindquarters were facing the threat. Squee didn't even wait for a command. She raised her tail and spritzed the men with the skunk's primary contribution to her genome. Instantly the whole bathroom was filled with an eye-stinging, nose-burning, gagging stench. Lex, for once, was in a fully sealed suit and didn't get so much as a whiff. He shouldered his way through the hacking, retching guards and dashed into the open. The guards were beginning to form up, but now that he was out of range of the technician, his mental cloak was fully effective again... Sort of.

Lex may not have gotten a whiff of the stench, but he *did* run through a cloud of it. And wouldn't you know it, the mental cloak didn't do anything about smell. The people couldn't see him, but a moment or two after he dashed past, they were quite aware of his presence.

"Ziva, quick. I need to know what that hacking earned us."

"You should have base-level access to anything the credentials of the person Coal used to access the system had permissions for," Ziva said. "You just need to get your slidepad in range of the reader."

"Please tell me everyone has elevator access. Please tell me everyone has elevator access..." he chanted as he traced a path through confused guards.

He reached the elevator and desperately hopped and shimmied in front of it, attempting to pass a slidepad in his pocket into range of a reader meant to read something at chest level. The door beeped. The elevator approached, but not as quickly as the guards. He abandoned the elevator and went for the access ladder beside it, this time leaping up to grab a strut to better lift himself into position to activate the reader. The door opened and he swung inside.

In a maneuver that wouldn't have won him any gymnastics awards, he awkwardly caught the ladder opposite the door and thumped in a half-controlled manner down a few rungs. Once he got his footing, he started hauling his way back up. He just barely got above the open door before the guards appeared and fired stun pistols indiscriminately in his direction. Apparently "stunning the target and letting him plummet five decks down a ladder shaft" counted as trying not to kill him. He reached Deck 6 and grabbed the top of the hatch to haul himself up to hip-check the reader. The door slid open and he tumbled through.

Directly into a collection of three Karters and a Karterette.

The confusion of having an unseen figure that stinks like skunk spray was enough to give him a fraction of a moment to dash down the nearest walkway. He took in the layout of the floor desperately. Just as open as the rest, this one was laid out as a series of concentric rings of standing desks all surrounding an aquarium-like strongroom in the center. It had transparent plastic easily as thick as Lex's thigh forming a floor-to-ceiling wall with doors on either side. In the center was a well-lit area with racks and shelves, most of which were empty. One, however, displayed a badly dented and scraped briefcase. It was brushed aluminum, oddly narrow. And it was precisely the suitcase he'd been given to deliver back when he took the job that led him to Big Sigma. He made his way to one of the doors as the scattering of guards followed his stench toward him. An error tone sounded. The person with the stolen credentials didn't have access to this strongroom. He turned. A lab-coat-wearing fem-Karter was looking up from her datapad, confused by the commotion. Lex grabbed her by the arm and dragged her, startled and screaming, to the door. Pressing her forearm to the reader earned him entry. He dashed inside. The door shut behind him. He wrenched one of the adjustable shelves from one of the empty units in the place and wedged it against the door, jamming it shut. A desperate dash to the other side of the strongroom and a similar precaution left him, for the moment, "safe."

He approached the briefcase while a growing collection of Karteresque figures fruit-lessly tried to get inside. The door and glass were too thick for him to hear them. And thus too thick for them to hear him.

"Good news and bad News, Ziva," he said breathlessly, setting a now *very* excited Squee down.

"Bad news first, please," Ziva said.

"I am locked in a strongroom, they have a way to screw up the mental cloak, I don't have a plan to get out of here, and I don't know if Coal is okay."

"That is significant. And the good news?"

"I found the mass. It's the briefcase from the whole Bypass Gemini fiasco that led me to you. Er. To Ma."

"Remarkable. That would account for a suitable quantity of mass."

"A whole briefcase? And one that I've actually held before? And nothing *but* the briefcase?" Lex said. "That seems a bit convenient, don't you think?"

"The nature of the displacement requires that the mass have been influenced by your worldline. The case spent a great deal of time in your proximity. It is a valid candidate."

"Yeah but..." He looked up. Cutting torches had been deployed. "Never mind. All I need to do is get this in Coal and get to light speed and I'll come back home?"

"That is the current theory."

"Okay... Okay... I don't see any way out of this situation that'll get me back to Coal. All else has failed. Time to try diplomacy again." He spotted an intercom button and pressed it. "Hey! Hey! Wait!" he shouted.

One of the Karter-women looked vaguely through the glass as the cutting torches continued to make slow progress. Lex realized it was Cynthia. He deactivated the mental cloak and was rewarded with direct eye contact.

"Listen. This? This here? This is what I need. You're desperate for what I *am*, and I'm desperate for this briefcase. Technically it belongs to me, or at least it used to, if that matters to you."

"You, and the case, represent incursions from another dimension. It would be unreasonable, and unwise, for me to allow you to take it or to allow you to leave. You simultaneously represent a massive threat and a massive opportunity."

"Right, right. And I could tell you that I'm not invading, I'm just trying to get this back to my home because it's apparently part of the seamless-whole clockwork guts of my home dimension's progression of time, but I guess you'd have no reason to believe me."

"You are correct about that."

"But you want me because I can help you ease the disease, right? And the disease was created by Karter Dee, right? Well, in my world Karter Dee is still alive. And the disease was stopped. So there *must* be a cure or something, right?"

"You have proof of this?" she said warily.

"I... You know what? I kind of do. Ziva, how do they listen in on what you're saying to me?"

"It would take too much time to explain verbally. Press the Squee-suit transceiver to the intercom. I will cross-link."

He did so. After a few pieces of digital distortion, Ziva's voice rang out through the speakers.

"Hello. My name is Ziva, a derivative of Ma, the successor to BSOD, the control system utilized by Karter Dee. He is indeed alive, though currently inaccessible to me due to the problem that Lex has traveled to your world to solve. I am communicating through a resonant quantum wave targeted to the displaced mass. You can confirm the existence of this wave by scanning at the following frequencies..."

• • • ● • ● • ● • • •

Coal, to her surprise, was still functional. Any attempts at further conversation had vanished as soon as Cynthia left. Coal was confident she had been forced to leave so quickly specifically because Lex had been causing trouble elsewhere. This was good. This was a sign of positive mission performance and progression. She'd split her time since then between observing the slowly accumulating army of technicians outside the Faraday cage and probing electromagnetically accessible portions of the hangar. They were doing a very good job of closing off methods she might use to escape or exploit their weaknesses. The Faraday cage prevented her from interfacing with anything else in the hangar. It didn't cover her directly above or below, as that would also protect her from the effects of the tractor beams, the potential EMP knockout, and a small projector that she had determined was causing the thrust nullification. From the lack of signal penetration, a combination of the structure of the station itself and likely a supplementary layer of mesh recently added on the deck above were doing an adequate job of keeping her influence away from the station above. She had comparatively less impediment below, but there was nothing below her current position but some minor, secondary infrastructure and open space. They had even positioned her containment area such that the thin slice of floor and ceiling not protected by the cage didn't contain anything essential, or even useful, for the rest of the station. They were very careful.

Their care, though an obstacle, increased the confidence and pride scores in her personality matrix. They considered her a threat. They were taking her seriously. And even if she wasn't able to actively contribute to the mission at present, the amount of resources poured into keeping her contained necessarily decreased the resources that could be brought to bear on Lex. Thus, the best thing she could do was continue to be a nuisance. And opportunities to do so were approaching.

The electromagnetic equivalent of an air lock had been built onto the cage, so that techs could enter without briefly providing her with a transmission path. Three techs had entered the small mesh cell added onto the cage and shut the door behind them. For the first time since Cynthia's departure, she was addressed directly.

"Attention extradimensional vessel. You will now be analyzed. The EMP generator above you is in a state of perpetual readiness. We observed the deployment time of your own EMP countermeasure. You will not have time to activate yours before we activate ours. More to the point, you will not have time to activate *any* countermeasures before we activate ours. Behave yourself and care will be taken to acquire a deep enough understanding of your systems to allow reconstruction and duplication. If you cause problems, we will not be able to guarantee such things," said a tech.

"You are threatening to 'kill' me if I do not cooperate in my own deactivation. In biological terms, if I do not allow you to kill me slowly, you will kill me quickly. This is not an effective disincentive."

"We can EMP you now and be done with it."

"That you have not done so already suggests you either lack the capacity or fear the ancillary effects. To use a colorful vernacular, I dare you to EMP me."

The techs briefly discussed something quietly among themselves. In an impressively paranoid piece of precaution, a curious audio distortion had been broadcast through the hangar's PA system, which prevented her from amplifying their speech sufficiently to understand them. Their paranoia was not, however, sufficient. One of them had his back turned to her, but the others remained visible, and thus her recently installed lipreading routine could tease out their statements.

From the two-thirds of a conversation she could capture, they were indeed using the EMP as a last resort. It was a significant power draw on the system, and they quite wisely suspected that using it would open up their vulnerabilities to other avenues of attack. This was good to know. The EMP would not be used automatically as they implied. It would be used only upon direct order of one of the supervising technicians, or in response to threat of pain or injury to humans. That would provide her with a minimum of one average human reaction time and a maximum of two average human reaction times to make her move before being disabled.

The techs entered the cage.

"In the interest of transparency," Coal began, "I should inform you that my creator and maintainer is the Karter Dee of my native dimension. He is a violent and volatile individual and displays levels of paranoia equal to or greater than your own. This vessel, designated the *Son of Betsy* or *SOB*, has a number of antitampering countermeasures. Some of them are not under my control. Some of them are triggered by mechanical interlocks and thus will remain active even if the vessel is electrically inert. For the sake of illustration."

She opened a lower panel. The sudden motion earned the same sort of startled reaction that a drawn pistol would have.

"You'll note the presence of explosive. And now you'll note I am pretensioning the ignition-control cable. Releasing tension on that cable will cause a detonation."

"You just said they weren't under your control!" cried a tech.

"I said *some* of them aren't under my control." She snapped the hatch shut. "But you have been warned."

Her statement was almost entirely fabricated. The *SOB* was rebuilt primarily to serve as an ostensibly unmodified and legal ship. Any aspects that were not strictly legal were primarily accessed by producing unintended behavior from otherwise mundane systems. Outside a standard antitheft system, there were no countermeasures against tampering. The "explosive" she'd displayed was in fact a maneuvering charge, and the "ignition cable" was an unrelated hydraulic release cable. But the desired effect had clearly been achieved, as there was a subtle but detectable decrease in the power routed to the EMP generator. She could now add several more milliseconds to the available time before she could be disabled. And now there were three techs within range of some of her new toys. The bravest, or most foolhardy, of them had climbed on top of the *SOB* and was clearly planning to cut through the sealed cockpit to attempt to access the controls. She targeted him and slowly dialed up the power of the snap-back simulator, minus the time compression. It wasn't designed to operate outside the cockpit, and as such its range was extremely limited. But with some care, she started to overlay a view identical to what he should have been seeing. The simulator required a degree of cooperation with the target. Any resistance from the person in the simulation would cause the simulation to fail. But he had no reason to resist if the simulation was precisely what he was expecting. He powered up a cutting torch. Its design was not familiar. Another unique creation of the higher average mental acuity of the people in this place. It was ticking up to an impressively high temperature, and doing so quite slowly. He feathered the trigger for it a few times, seemingly as a nervous tick. The cutting flame decreased in temperature and size, proportional to how long the trigger was released. She calculated the mass of the device. As subtly as possible, she shifted the apparent position of the retention clamp he was certain to aim for. He started to position the torch. She waited until it was in the proper position, then popped the cockpit open with a calibrated amount of force.

The cutting torch was knocked from the tech's hand. The flame lingered as it spiraled through the air, and at the very peak of its arc, the cutting torch swept through the head of the thrust inhibitor. The instant it had been damaged, she activated her retrothrusters. She lurched back, testing the strength of the tractor beams and sending all three techs tumbling to the floor. The force of her thrust started to ease her back, slowly extending the distance between the *SOB* and the beam emitters. Whoever was controlling the beams boosted their power, gradually reclaiming the slack she'd generated. She switched to forward thrust, her own force combining with the power of the tractor beams to slingshot the *SOB* forward, smashing the Faraday cage in front of the ship.

"Excellent. I shall now contact Lex," she said calmly as she rebounded and smashed the EMP generator.

· · • ● · ● ● · • ·

"You are certain?" Cynthia said. "That checks out, right? You can prove that?"

Ziva had been remarkably concise in her description of precisely how the retemplating virus worked. The bioengineers in the lab were already running her described mechanisms through their own data models.

"All prior research had been directed under the assumption that the disease was either an intentional biological weapon or a failed gene-therapy experiment. We'd never entertained the possibility that anyone would have gone through all the effort, expense, and innovation of creating such a thing specifically to target *themselves* with it. The behavior of the disease precisely matches the mechanism she has described."

"Karter, at least the one of our universe, behaves in erratic and often self-centered ways. The retemplating virus was intended to reverse genetic fatigue and restore telomeres to his cellular DNA to prolong his life specifically."

"This changes things..." the tech said. "It explains why it becomes harder to treat the longer someone is infected. It is gradually converting the target into its intended host."

"How can we use this information?" Cynthia said.

"It will take time, and we will still need some viable genetic material to test against. But I believe we may be able to use this data to create an enhanced immune response. If we treat—"

His thinking out loud was interrupted by a chorus of communicators chirping and blaring.

"Lex?" Coal said, cutting into the discussion alongside Ziva. "Good news! I have succeeded in causing chaos in the hangar and will shortly be depressurizing it to escape. Have you secured the mass?"

"Did that thing say 'depressurize'?" Cynthia snapped.

"Coal, don't do anything drastic. We're working out a mutually beneficial solution," Lex said.

"Let me clarify. I am not planning to depressurize the hangar. I have successfully damaged the door, and it will soon depressurize."

A distant rumble shook the station, followed by a sudden shift a few degrees aside.

"I am now outside the station, along with three uncrewed one-seat starships and a great deal of debris. It appears the human crew were able to evacuate in time. The scout ships that were looking for you are converging. I shall now defend myself," Coal said.

"You are clear for weapons hot," Cynthia barked into a communicator. "We have data and materials in this station that could lead to a final solution to the retemplating virus, and I will not allow it to be endangered."

"Everyone calm down!" Lex said. "Coal, don't attack the ships. Cynthia, call the ships off. Everyone on both sides of this is a little high strung, and we need to just take it down a few notches. I'm cooperating, okay? I'm willing to fork over some blood if it means saving some lives and getting our hands on that briefcase. But I need you to guarantee me that you're not going to do anything to my ship."

"You ship just damaged the lower deck hangar and threatened the lives of my crew."

"*We all have important jobs, okay!*" Lex shouted. "My universe is *broken*. That briefcase is one of the missing pieces. You can understand why we'd be willing to get a little kooky with our tactics. Just hold off. No shooting! Tell me this. And be *sure* about it. If you get my blood and the full disease whatever from Ziva, can you create a cure?"

"A cure, and a vaccine could be synthesized within eighteen hours. These are the missing pieces we've been searching for over the better part of a century. Everything else is ready and in place, and has been for decades," said one of the bioengineering techs.

"You're sure? One hundred percent, no foolin', no doubt about it, fully certain?" Lex said.

"I've worked my whole career for this moment."

"Okay, then how's this for a show of good faith?" he said. "I've got blood in the kit in the *SOB*, so..."

Lex reached back and released the seals for the biohazard suit, then popped the helmet from his flight suit, exposing himself to the unsanitized air. Cynthia raised her eyebrows.

"Damn..." she said, respect evident in her voice. She leaned down and opened communications to all channels. "Ships, pull back to a defensive perimeter. Medical, make sure we have no casualties. Repair crews, get to work on the lower docking bay. Everyone else to D-6." She looked at Lex. "That ship of yours had better behave."

"Coal?" Lex said.

"Yes, Lex?"

"How about you go do some frolicking while we get this thing sorted out. We'll call you if we need that untainted blood."

"Acknowledged. But if something seems like it is amiss, I will tear the station in half if that's what it takes."

"Good to know you have my back, Coal, but maybe not the most useful comment in the present context."

"Consider my statement withdrawn," Coal said. "But recall its intent if you feel compelled to fulfill its criteria."

"That's not exactly a proper withdrawal, Coal."

"I stand by my withdrawn statement."

"The ship is moving away from the station. ... It is flying in tight loops," reported a pilot over the connection.

Lex looked wearily at Cynthia. "This is the best we're going to get."

"Do you people make it a habit of having mentally unstable and mildly disobedient artificial intelligences in control of your ships?"

"Not as a rule. Basically it's just me." He shrugged. "What can I say, she sacrificed herself in an alternate future to protect me and my friends from a horde of evil robots."

Cynthia looked at him doubtfully.

"I've had a weird life," Lex said.

· · ● · ● · ● ● · ● · ·

Exhaustion and the first chance to lie down in seemingly forever had been enough to knock Lex fully unconscious for the better part of ten hours. A startling feeling of disorientation, the kind usually reserved for waking up at a friend's house or a hotel room, hit him like a hammer. Unfortunately, rather than getting the sense of relief that comes from realizing your biggest concern is getting charged for the yogurt-covered raisins you snagged from the minibar, reality tightened his chest all the more.

A wet nose and warm fur nuzzling up under his chin defused his harrowing first few moments of wakefulness. He reached up to pet Squee and pinned her to his chest as he sat up.

"One of these days we're going to officially get you classified as a prescription-strength tranquilizer," he said.

He took in his surroundings. He *technically* wasn't in a prison cell, in that the walls were made of impact-resistant glass rather than bars, and there was a pretty good chance the door wasn't locked. But the amenities were roughly equivalent. The bed was at the precise midpoint between prison cot and hospital bed, which put it pretty far from anything a normal person would actually choose to sleep on. There was a "bathroom," which was little more than a shower and a combination toilet and sink. The whole thing was sectioned off by translucent plastic sheeting with a zipper to keep the water and steam in. He'd taken a shower before collapsing, but even the brief process of removing the biosuit had infused him with stink that would linger for at least three more showers. Squee sleeping on his chest didn't help in that regard, since she was the source of said stink, and the residue would have been eye-watering if he hadn't developed something of an immunity to it over the years.

After initial rockiness, the people in charge of the space station had made a few allowances that he would have excused them for forgoing. Right now the one he was most thankful for was the slidepad they hadn't confiscated. He picked it up and slipped the hands-free in his ear.

"Ziva, are you still there?"

"I am," she said. "I trust you slept well."

"I slept," he said. "What's the progress?"

"After some minor collaboration to ensure the truth of their statements and assess their intent, I was able to provide them with an adequate amount of guidance to fill the gaps in their understanding. Our last communication was an hour and seventeen minutes ago, when the test batch of your blood, with an artificially accelerated infection applied to it—responded as expected. I am suitably satisfied that within three hours they will have synthesized a serum that will treat and immunize you. It will not take much more time for them to achieve a similar effect on their own population."

"And then what? They're all still Karter."

"Further attempts at gene therapy, and selective infusions from your genes, should help to solve the more troublesome health impacts of the disease. You *will* be asked to provide a few more blood samples to ensure they can adequately clone your cells."

"Whatever it takes," he said with a yawn.

"The fact that future generations in this world will be a combination of your genes and Karter's effectively makes the two of you parents to an entire generation."

Lex shut his eyes tightly. "I choose to un-hear that."

"I apologize if that is an upsetting image."

"I'll live."

"May I offer some constructive criticism?"

"Hit me."

"That was a very questionable decision, exposing yourself to the potentially lethal virus."

"My life is a string of questionable decisions."

"I am quite serious, Lex."

"Look, we needed to establish that we were serious about helping them to produce a cure. That was the best way I could think of to do it."

"You could have contaminated your genes and spoiled their efforts."

"That fast?"

"Not likely, but potentially."

"But there was blood in the ship."

"The blood in the ship is a synthesized substitute. It does not contain your actual genetic code."

"Ah... Well, whatever. It worked."

"I am going to have to ask, for reasons both selfish and driven by duty, that you take pains to survive this ordeal. There are people at home who are relying upon you to complete your mission."

"Right. Right. I'll try to keep myself a little further from the brink of doom on the next leg of this sprint." He glanced up. "Just a minute. Cynthia is here."

The supervisor of the station, accompanied by a male nurse, buzzed open the door to his room and stepped inside.

"Mr. Alexander," Cynthia said with a nod.

"Hey," he said, letting Squee scramble to his shoulders.

The supervisor's nose curled a bit. "That beast has an impressive chemical deterrent."

"You should see some of her other tricks."

"This is Mr. Barnes. He will be taking an additional blood sample and administering the sample serum. If all goes well, a second shot in a few hours will make you the first human in this universe to be vaccinated against the retemplating virus."

"You know, given how the Karter back home acts, seeing him wearing scrubs and administering medical treatment is a little mind-breaking."

"I recognize he isn't the mass murderer in your world that he is here, but I do wish you would cease to use his name so casually. It is one of the more heinous things you can call someone in this world."

"Right. Sorry."

"While we are waiting for the treatment to be completed, I would like to ask you some additional questions. While I cannot require you to answer them, please know that your departure will be made far more justifiable by a timely answer."

"I'll do my best to answer."

"Is interdimensional travel common in your world?"

"Not as far as I know. We've done time travel a few times, and I guess that technically took me to parallel dimensions. But this is the first time I'm aware of that anyone from our world purposely went to another world."

"You have traveled through time?"

"A couple times. Met myself face to face. Like I said, I've had a weird life."

"I would be inclined to believe you are lying, but your mere presence here suggests your world has capabilities ours does not."

"Kind of weird, if you ask me. Because our K—... Because our inventor guy is the reason for most of that stuff, and you kind of have an unlimited number of people with the same brain juice sloshing around."

"Historical records do indicate a drastic increase in average intelligence in the survivors, but intelligence alone is not sufficient to invent things sometimes. Motivation, inspiration, resources, and luck play a role. But we aren't here to discuss that. I ask you about your interdimensional travel capacity because you are the fourth interdimensional incursion we've identified over the course of the last few years. You and the suitcase have the same quantum shift. The others have a shift that differs from yours but matches one another. We were hoping you would have some insight."

"Beats me, ma'am," he said. "What did they look like?"

"We never encountered them. They existed only as a spike in a waveform on a sensor scan. The spike was in the approximate region of space where the briefcase was found, but long after its discovery. By the time we were able to dispatch scouts, they were gone."

He shook his head. "Not from my world, I can guarantee that, because the only other fully aware and functioning creatures back home are a sister-AI to Coal and her collection of funks like Squee here. Ziva's still on the line, and I sure *hope* the funks haven't started reality hopping. The last thing we need is them stinking up the multiverse."

Lex winced as the blood was drawn from his arm. "Am I supposed to be giving blood twice in one day?"

"It is ill-advised but acceptable under the circumstances. I'll make sure you are given a high-sugar/high-iron supplement before your departure." Cynthia nodded in the direction of the earpiece Lex was wearing. "Is the AI connected?"

"She is."

"I would like a word with her as well."

He thumbed the slidepad to put her on speaker.

"How may I help you, Ms. Debjonka?"

"You spoke with us in detail regarding the plight of your world and the necessity of returning your 'displaced mass.'"

"Indeed."

"Your claim is that the removal of this mass contributed to the breakdown of time's progression in your universe."

"For unshielded portions of the universe, yes."

"Are we to believe that the briefcase represents the entirety of the displaced mass? Not an atom more?"

"Now that Lex has been in contact with the mass, I have been able to more successfully target a scan, and I believe an adequate proportion of the missing mass is accounted for. Unaccounted for particles probably returned to our own universe on their own. There is a strong attraction between particles and their native dimension, and the interface is thinned."

"The corollary, and one that I am quite interested in, is the issue of Lex's return. He has breathed our air. He has received an injection of the serum and will shortly receive another. When he returns, will the displacement of *that* mass cause a similar upheaval?"

"Not by my calculation. You can investigate the data on your own if you wish to confirm, but I have determined that the damage to our reality was done not strictly by the removal of the mass but by the nature of its removal. It was removed not just from the present but from the past and future. The removal of any material from your world and the introduction of any material from our world as a result of Lex's trip are far more typical transfers of mass."

"You have the data on that?"

"I do."

She touched a communicator on her belt. "Stand by for data from Ziva. I want it confirmed before we send our blood donor on his way."

"I will deliver it momentarily," Ziva said.

Cynthia nodded. "So. Mr. Alexander," she said as her medic finished up. "We got off on the wrong foot. And you didn't do yourself any favors with the way you started your visit. But actions speak louder than words, and you've done the human race a great service today."

She held out a hand. He stood and gave it a shake.

"My pleasure."

"I don't imagine we'll ever be in contact again. But if we are and you find yourself in need, I think you'll find us willing and able to lend a hand."

"Forgive me if I say I hope we never *do* meet again, but I'll certainly keep it in mind. The more friends the better."

Cynthia's nose wrinkled again, and she glanced at the hand she'd just shook.

"When Coal gets back, we'll give you the recipe for the deodorizer I brought. Hazards of being a funk owner."

It took a few more hours, but Lex was back in the pilot's seat of the *SOB*, this time launching from the upper hangar since the lower one had yet to be repressurized.

"You got really scratched up," Lex said, securing some straps and gathering Squee up.

"They'd found a way to use interference fields to disable my tractor beam. I had to improvise."

"I notice your improvisation tends to include a lot of smashing into things."

"And I notice your improvisation tends to involve a lot of hurling your frail meat-and-bone body out of whatever structure or vehicle you are presently in. Both of us have a high rate of success with our given methods, so I would say that they are unworthy of critique."

"Can't argue with that. But are you good for the return trip? Not too dinged up?"

"Structural integrity is at ninety-four percent. Damage is primarily cosmetic. Navigational systems are fully intact."

Lex thumped the silver case beside him. "Then let's get this package back home. Feels kind of good to be a courier again for a bit. Though I kind of wish this particular package would *stay* delivered. This thing is like a bad penny."

"In what way is a displaced artifact of your home dimension like a piece of currency that has been obsolete for more than three centuries?"

"... It's just a phrase."

"Language is intended to articulate ideas. Yours seems to be—"

"Let's just go," Lex said quickly.

"Acknowledged."

He selected a trajectory toward the emptiest section of space he could muster and activated the snap-back. As he eased the speed up, the stars did their colorful streak blue-ward. And again the cosmos started to bend and splinter outside the cockpit.

"I do not enjoy this part of the journey," Coal said, her voice glitching slightly.

It dropped away, along with every other system in the ship, at the same moment the white void painted itself on his windows once more. A drop of black spread across the white, and the whole ship shuddered back into reality.

"Altruistic Artificial Intelligence Control System, version 1.27, revision 2331.04.01c, subset 2.7d, designation Coal, fully initiated."

Lex wiped some flop sweat from his forehead. "You okay?"

"System diagnostic complete. No faults."

"Good. Then if you're going to keep shutting down and starting up like that, maybe we can skip the name, rank, serial number thing. Now how does the world look?"

"All quantum shift is at zero. We are home. The universe remains almost entirely stationary."

"Could have been worse. Let's head to Big Sigma and see what's what."

Chapter 5

"Remarkable..." Ziva said, turning the briefcase about. "If you'll recall, I used a duplicate of this very case to alert you of my location when you arrived in the alternate future of my origin."

"Yeah. Yeah, I remember. I'm really starting to hate the sight of that thing."

"It is undeniably an important part of your history. Fascinating that this, in its entirety, made up nearly all the displaced mass. No piece is missing. And barely any stray particles besides it. It raises questions about the precise mechanism of the displacement." She set the case down in the first of a series of glass cases prepared to contain the displaced mass. "The snap-back simulator *was* interfacing with your perception at the time of the displacement. I wonder if that has some bearing on the mass that was displaced."

"... The simulator was reading my mind?" Lex said, not entirely pleased with the possibility.

"It had to interpret your intended motor responses, among other things, in order to guide your in-simulation avatar. Based on my analysis, it shouldn't have the capacity to access or collect memories, but there *is* the possibility that significant recollections floating near the upper five percent of neuron accesses, conscious or otherwise, could have been accessible. It is entirely theory, of course, but I think it is reasonable to assume that you'll be encountering other key aspects of your history as the displaced mass. This is actually quite fortunate. If they were chunks of granite or mounds of dust, it is not clear how they would have been easily gathered. This greatly increases the potential that the items will be singular, macroscopic pieces of solid mass."

"It also is another strong vote in favor of 'this is all my fault,'" Lex said.

"It was already all your fault. You were the motivation for the creation of the simulator, and you were the one who activated it in untested conditions, triggering the event," Coal said over the communicator.

"Thanks, Coal. You always know just what to say."

"You are very welcome, Lex," Coal said. "I excel at human interaction."

"So what have we learned?" Lex asked. "Any idea if this is working, and how much more there is to do?"

Ziva glanced at a node in the ceiling. Her irises flickered. "The results aren't as encouraging as I'd hoped," she said. "Your case, technically, shouldn't be here. It should have returned directly to where it had been when it was displaced. The sensors to adequately investigate this do not exist, but I very much suspect that you haven't so much returned the case to the entire timeline but to this precise *point* in the timeline. The repair to the space-time continuum has to be done holistically."

"... So do I bring it back in time or something?"

"That won't work. This is a collection of aluminum, steel, polymers. All of those individual particles originated in the big bang, were flung through the universe, forged in the hearts of stars, awaited the evolution of the human race, were collected, fashioned into the case, and in time likely eroded to nothing or were recycled. This has to be returned to *all* of those states."

"How do we do that?"

"We don't. Not directly anyway. But just as collecting the case gave us a means to bridge you back to this world, collecting the additional mass *should* provide an attraction to the various states along the timeline."

"We're still on 'get all the goodies and hope for the best' then?"

"Artfully phrased, and quite accurate."

"A great plan. Always jazzed about a plan like that. My kind of plan. What's next?"

She glanced at a display screen, eyes flashing, and it began to populate with a graph that was clearly meant to illuminate the situation. He couldn't comprehend it. The thing was a mass of squiggly lines labeled with Greek letters.

"I'd estimated that the first places you would arrive at would be the places most like our own world. But I wasn't quite right. The amount of displaced mass was a variable as well. The case is comparatively large compared to whatever is in the next destination. But being in contact with the first parallel universe gave me enough data to provide something of a delta measurement. This next world is even more similar to our own than the first."

"The first was entirely populated by identical clones of your creator. It wouldn't take much for a world to be considered 'closer to this reality' than that one."

"A valid observation."

"Anything else that can help?"

"You'll be searching for something quite small. On the order of magnitude of a casino chip or a coin. That's the only remaining piece of new information I can provide."

"Better than nothing."

"I would also like to assure you that the ship, you, and Squee have been fully decontaminated. There is no risk of you bringing the retemplating virus back with you, nor is there any chance that you will take it with you to the next universe."

"Oh, wow," he said. "I kind of forgot to ask about that. Would've saved one universe and doomed another."

"I am endeavoring to be comprehensive in my application of reasonable precaution. Are you adequately recovered and refreshed?"

"I honestly don't know how to answer that question anymore. Time has literally lost all meaning. I slept for a while. I've eaten and bathed relatively recently. Do I still smell like funk... funk?"

"The deodorizer has done its job," she said.

"Is Coal fixed up?"

"All nontrivial damage has been repaired. I should warn you, though, that the resources for correcting more serious damage are limited in this portion of the planet. It wasn't an intended function of my facility. I recommend you avoid taking major damage."

"No promises," he said, heading for the door. "Let's get ready for round two."

Lex took the *SOB* up through the stationary debris field and took a breath. "All right. Last-minute checklist. We're fully restocked."

"Confirmed," Coal said.

"New biosuit has a built-in slidepad link and some basic propulsion."

"Confirmed," said Ziva over the com.

"We've updated the slidepad with both the Ziva communication and the mass locator so I don't need to rely upon Coal's sensors if we get separated."

"Confirmed," Ziva said. "Though the mass locator will only work at extreme close range."

"All right. I've got a funk on my neck, I've got a fully charged ship, and I've got nothing to lose. Let's do this."

He picked a random safe trajectory. His soul shriveled a little as he realized seeing the fabric of space-time torn asunder, watching as the universe was blotted out to pure white, feeling a distracting buzz in the back of his mind, and then watching it all popping back into reality with a full system reboot was already familiar to him. The speed at which he was capable of becoming inured to reality-shattering superscience was starting to worry him. As if to put his mind at ease that he was not *entirely* numb to the universe around him, he twitched and diverted his course when he realized he'd been dropped, once again, quite near a space station. Not only that, but it was a space station he'd visited before. The place was old, but he'd been there a few times thanks to its presence on one of his standard routes between Operlo and Golana and its above-average amenities for dogs. That little tidbit did not go unnoticed by the critter on his shoulders.

"Sorry, Squee. We're on the clock."

The funk chose this as one of the moments that she would conveniently forget how to listen. She bobbed from his shoulders and nudged her way to the cockpit glass, then scrabbled against it until she got enough traction to start doing laps around the cockpit, bounding from surface to surface.

"Great, she's got the zoomies. Which way are we headed, Coal?"

"Scanning... Processing. I am afraid the signal is extremely weak. I can narrow it down only to the following cone of uncertainty."

She updated the navigation screen. The "cone" looked more like a wall, painting fully half of the visible map red with potential. Lex shrugged.

"Still rules out half the universe. Not bad, if you ask me. How's the communication traffic?"

"The data formats are entirely familiar, and the data density is roughly equivalent to what would be expected. Some standard public channels have superficial changes to their names and metadata."

"Give me a quick channel flip of the video feeds."

The HUD populated with a four-by-four grid of videos. There were some familiar faces, some strange ones, but all roughly within what he would have expected from a similar sampling back home.

"No fish people, plenty of non-Karters. Things are looking up already."

He punched in a three-jump itinerary that would take three hours and pushed the ship to FTL.

"Lex," Coal said.

"Yes."

"After our visit to the Karter-filled universe, a few matters have asserted themselves for reprocessing."

"What's up?"

"All humans in that world were supposedly genetically identical. And owing to the standard length of human life and the multicentury delta between the event and our arrival, there was a great likelihood that no human in that world had ever been unique or could remember anyone who was."

"I'm sure they had recordings of people. Old movies and such."

"True, but within reality, they were two broad sets of DNA. Those with a Y chromosome and those without. Yet the people remained differentiated. There were different stratums of authority and privilege. Different names. Different roles. Some had visibly taken care to differentiate themselves with facial modification, mostly in the forms of tattoos and piercings."

"Did they? I guess I was a little busy panicking to notice."

"I counted seven cosmetically differentiated individuals. But this leads me to the issue I would like to discuss. They were not unique. Yet they were seemingly content in their lack of uniqueness."

"Sure, because they knew they were individuals even if they came from the same stock. Twins are individuals, why wouldn't however many billion Karters be?"

"I, too, come from, to borrow your terminology, 'the same stock' as Ma and Ziva."

"And you're about as unique as they come."

"So we have circumstances where substantially identical individuals are accepted and embraced as full individuals. And the time travel and multiverse issue of predetermination establishes that agency and self-determination may be largely illusory."

"Kind of not a fan of that topic," he muttered.

"This means that there is very little about an AI that would reduce it below a human in any comprehensive philosophical assessment."

"Yeah, that tracks."

Coal did not respond.

"You... gonna go somewhere with that?"

"No. I was testing the human activity of voicing thoughts as a means of externalizing them and thus reframing them. Doing so has made very little difference in my heuristics associated with these points. This appears to be another pointless human endeavor."

"We tend to collect those."

"I am gratified by your agreement. However, social analysis suggests many humans would contradict my elevation of artificial intelligences to the level of philosophical peers."

"It's the way it is. At this point, given how many times she's saved my butt, I'm a little worried that Squee might be a few steps closer to humanity's rung of the ladder."

"That concerns you?"

"I'm human. Stupid insecurities are part of the package."

Every few jumps in the right direction narrowed the cone a bit. After a dozen jumps and about ten hours of flight, Lex noticed a particular stretch of space had never actually left the cone. On a hunch, he strung together a longer-than-average sequence of FTL jumps, not even bothering to scan at each of the jumps. When he finally dropped out of FTL and was greeted by a highly industrial planet with a significant orbital docking facility, the scan drew a bright red line straight to the surface.

"Golana," he said, half-smiling. "The missing doodad is on my old stomping grounds. The sensor is even indicating Preston City. This is going to be *weird*."

"I would think it would be familiar to return to the planet where the bulk of your life had been spent," Coal said.

"It's going to be weird, and I'll tell you why. If you eat a food you've never eaten before, you're not going to notice if the recipe is off. But if you eat the same food every morning, you're going to know the *instant* they put too much salt or not enough sugar."

"Are you aware that the purpose of an analogy is to cast an unclear situation into the form of a situation which both parties have a mutual understanding of?"

"Yeah."

"Are you aware I do not eat?"

"I think you can get the gist."

"I do, but please exercise best linguistic practices. One of the ways that I scored lower than Ma after differentiation was language skills, and I do not wish for my conversations with you to cause me to adopt still-greater degrees of laxness."

"Coal, I'm not going to say I *miss* you eagerly looking for an opportunity to blow us all up, but there *are* more irritating personality quirks. Now what do you think? Do I risk docking at the Upstairs and seeing if my accounts and everything work? Or do I land directly?"

"If the previous leg of this mission serves as an effective baseline, your survivability without my assistance is very low."

"I'd argue, but I'd lose." He swiped his fingers across the screen. "Looks like Jimmi's Landing Deck North exists in this universe. It's pretty close to where the beam is pointing. Let's take her down."

He paused, dangling his finger over the cloaking device. The worrying compulsion to attempt to sneak onto the planet could be chalked up to the flashback to his old days of freelance deliveries that as often as not required he skip the formal landing procedures. Right now he was wondering if he could play this completely straight.

"What've I got to lose? If something goes haywire, I can just do the cloak thing regardless," he said.

He hailed the docking authority. After a few moments, a face popped up on screen.

"Golana Upstairs. Please forward your transponder code for authorization."

He opened the secret menu and selected one of the dozens of transponders available to him. It transmitted.

"Mr. Alexander?" the man said without a drop of interest or life.

"That's me."

"You don't have this ship registered with the transit system."

"Sorry. It's a new acquisition."

"That'll be four thousand credits, plus a one-thousand-credit registration fee. Should I log it to your account or will you pay it directly?"

"I have an account?" he said, raising an eyebrow.

"There's one registered to a Mr. Trevor Alexander." The man blinked. "Wait... You're not... Are you T-Lex?"

Lex leaned back in his seat. "Oof. That takes me back. That's me, all right."

A hot sting of anxiety started to burn his stomach. There was a Lex in this world. A Lex with the same nickname he had back in his first racing days. For some reason, that discovery bothered him. He couldn't put his finger on why he felt so uneasy. His brain was broadcasting "you've been spotted by a predator" sorts of signals.

"My kid brother's a fan," the man said. "He'll be excited I worked your passthrough. So how do you want to do this?"

"Um... Do me a favor and forward the charge to Jimmi's Landing Deck North. I'll pay in chips when I get down there."

"Sure thing. Transmitting your landing info now and adding you to the queue."

Lex transferred controls to the automated system. Normally he'd jump at the chance to do some more manual piloting, but right now he wanted to give this discovery his undivided attention.

"Coal. What year is it?"

"According to the broadcast system and navigational aids, the local date is only six days after our departure time."

"*After*," he said. "So this isn't a time-travel thing."

"It is not. Or at least, it isn't *this* time."

"What do you mean?"

"According to the data file labeled 'things you may need to explain to Lex' that Ziva added to my resources, this universe is conceivably accessible by time travel, as most parallel universes we are likely to visit diverged from a common point in our history."

"Ziva gave you a list of things she thought you would need to explain?"

"Yes."

"What else is in it?"

"The file is seven-hundred sixty-seven terabytes of text, images, and video."

"Ouch," he said.

"I observe that the usage recommendation includes not informing you of the existence and nature of the file. I submit a request to unhear that statement."

"I'll work on it."

• • • ● ● ● • ● ● • • •

They rode the automated commands all the way to the ground. If there was anything different about the Preston City of this universe from his own, it didn't jump out at him. Once the *SOB* was nestled into a landing pad, he rummaged through the things until he produced a backpack with a change of clothes, a few other necessities, and his collapsible hoverbike. He hopped down. Squee bounded to the ground and started her "oh boy, a new place" frenzy that happened about half the time he went anywhere.

"T-Lex?" came the familiar voice of Jimmi.

He turned. Sure enough, it was the same person he'd entrusted his hovercars and ships to on more occasions than he cared to count.

"Hey, Jimmi," he said, feeling oddly like he was playing the role of Lex rather than just being himself. "Been a while."

"Not too long. A couple weeks. That your dog?"

"I'm pet-sitting. She'll settle down eventually."

"She better. I don't want her getting creamed by a landing ship. What's this new hotness?" he said, indicating the ship.

"Oh. I, uh. A buddy of mine loaned it to me. Hence the extra registration fee." He dug through the bag and counted off the proper number of chips, quietly hoping they weren't somehow incompatible with this local world's payments.

Jimmi accepted them without objection. "You get some work done or something?"

"What do you mean?" Lex said.

Jimmi patted his belly. "Looks like you toned up a little."

"Oh. Yeah. Added some cardio," he said.

"Must be pretty intense stuff to see those sorts of results so quick. You'll have to tell me the name of your trainer. Guess probably it's someone at the league, huh?"

"Yeah, yeah. The league hooked me up."

"Well, good seeing you," he said.

"Same."

Jimmi walked away. Lex fitted his hands-free in his ear and slipped a helmet and pair of doggles on Squee. He opened a connection with Coal.

"Lex of this world is still a racer," he said with the sort of hushed excitement that was normally reserved for hot gossip.

"Or involved with some other sort of league," Coal said.

"Oh, come on. We're going to end up on the same planet, in the same town, with the me here having the same nickname, and he's in some *other* sort of league?" Lex deployed and mounted the hoverbike. "How's the network? Can you connect to it?"

"I am having no difficulty doing so."

Lex eased the bike into the air and set off toward his old apartment. "Do an ego search. Let's see how this Lex is doing for himself."

"Processing... Summarizing. Trevor 'T-Lex' Alexander is presently part of the Cantrell Racing team. He is ranked seventeenth overall in the league."

"*Seventeenth?*" Lex said, aghast.

"It is a seven-system league. The current size of the roster puts seventeenth place in the top one percent of racers."

"Seventeenth, though," Lex muttered.

"He has won four semifinal races and a single grand prix. He is presently married."

"Who'd I marry?"

"I am uncertain the answer to that question will allow you to remain dispassionately focused on the task at hand."

"Who did I marry, Coal?"

"Michella Modane."

"... Seriously?"

"Michella Alexander, nee Modane. She is a segment producer at GolanaNetNews. She has received four nominations for excellence in her field at the local broadcaster awards and two wins."

"She's not an onscreen talent?"

"Processing... Michella Alexander is in the alternate hosting spot of a midtier investigative wrap-up show focused on clarifying and summarizing recent findings in investigative journalism performed by reporters employed by GolanaNetNews."

Lex narrowed his eyes. "We're... *unremarkable...*" he said with something a bit too close to horror.

"You are both quite successful in your chosen fields."

He dug out his slidepad and brought up the sensor readings. They weren't pointing at his old neighborhood after all. "Coal, is there a current address available?"

"It is not a matter of public record. I shall attempt to uncover that information through alternate means. Processing.... Processing. I have penetrated the local communication network. It utilizes the same security that we have previously defeated in your own world. The local Trevor Alexander lives in Horizon View Towers, Unit N112-145."

"Frickin' *Horizon View*," he said, wincing. "That's exactly the sort of weaksauce, middle-of-the-road neighborhood a seventeenth-place Lex *would* live. And it's also right where the mass sensor is pointing." He grumbled. "The universe is conspiring to force me to confront myself..."

"I would advise against a face-to-face encounter," Coal said. "More accurately, I have been advised to advise against a face-to-face encounter."

"That in the file too?"

"It is."

"How come this file didn't come up back in Karter-ville?"

"You were very swift to make irrevocable mistakes during that mission. This one had more opportunity to advise before you antagonized a local authority figure."

"Does it say *why* talking to myself is ill-advised?"

"The unexpected interaction with a parallel self is unlikely to produce positive, predictable outcomes."

"Point," he said. "Counterpoint: if the sensors have led us this far, I'm willing to bet the thing we're after is in other-me's pocket. And tell me this. If you *weren't* advised to advise me that, what would be your opinion on the topic?"

"I would be interested in seeing what you think of you, and also what you think of you, with the indicated you's reversed."

"That makes two of us. I'm a pretty cool customer. No reason to assume that wouldn't be true of this me as well."

"You haven't seen his haircut yet," Coal said.

• • • ● ● • ● • •

The feeling of nostalgia was almost dizzying as he sliced through the air between the massive towers of Preston City. Truth be told, Horizon View Towers was a perfectly fine place to live. His parents still lived in their unit in the south tower in his home reality. The problem was, it was precisely the midpoint between the kind of high-class place he lived in on Operlo and the crummy bachelor hole he'd actually ended up in here on Golana. In his experience "the middle" wasn't the sort of place that he wanted to be. Top of the heap? Finishing first? That's the target. Scraping bottom? Barely making ends meet? At least it meant you were scrappy. A fighter. The kind of person who lived in Horizon View Towers was a comfortable, sensible, forgettable, *normal* person. This wasn't "shoot for the moon, land in the stars" territory. This was "shoot for seventeenth place, land in seventeenth place."

He brought the hoverbike down on the roof and collapsed it. The sky lobby was exactly the same slightly faded mint-green decor he'd spent way too many hours waiting around in back when he was still in school waiting for the hoverbus as a kid. There was supposed to be someone there to help folks enter if their credentials didn't work. The desk was empty, as it nearly always was when he was little. That was fine by him, it simplified matters. He slipped into the bathroom to finally change out of his flight suit, then stowed the mental cloak into an outer pocket of the bag for easy access. After a moment of consideration, he finally let logic prevail, for now at least, and activated the device rather than get funny looks from everyone who knew his local self.

Out of habit he scanned his slidepad at the door. It produced an error tone. He considered trying to have Coal try to hack it remotely. Squee had illustrated on multiple occasions that she could crack one of these things too, but getting her to do it on purpose was beyond his abilities. He nudged a flap aside to reveal a fingerprint scanner.

"Worth a shot," he said.

Sure enough, the pad of his right thumb produced a merry little chime and the door clicked open.

"Security professionals really weren't ready for dimensional invaders," he said, slipping inside.

The moment the elevator doors closed, it became clear Squee had entirely the wrong idea about the current operation. She hopped down and started prancing about in a very familiar way.

"No. Squee, we're not visiting Grandma and Grandpa," he said, trying to diffuse the situation. "My parents live in the other tower. And they live there in a different dimension. This isn't... okay, this is a lost cause."

He grabbed the leash from his bag and briefly attempted to clip it onto her harness, but that proved to be another lost cause. Lex visited his parents once a month or so, and they had quickly bought Squee's love with homemade dog treats. He didn't know what they put in them, but Squee would gnaw through her own leg to get one. The black-and-white blur ricocheted around the elevator for the entire ride. By some impossible bit of good fortune, no one else stopped the elevator before it reached the hundred and twelfth floor. But the luck ended when the doors opened without him managing to wrangle her.

She took off like a bullet, already well outside the range that the mental cloak would affect her too. He dashed after her. Despite many missions with it, Lex continuously forgot to ask Ziva or Coal if the mental cloak covered for audio as well, but a funk dashing through the halls of a condominium complex seemed like a bigger distraction than phantom footsteps.

Squee seemed to realize this wasn't where she thought she was headed as she skidded to a stop. Lex got within two steps of her before she sniffed the air and bolted again. This time it wasn't just excitement, she had a specific target. He knew with utter certainty that there was only one place she could be heading, and he couldn't decide if that was a good thing or a bad thing. She'd caught Lex's scent. *Other* Lex, he corrected himself. Even if he was on this local copy's home turf, if he started thinking about this guy as the real Lex, it was going to make for some unpleasant psychological backlash come bedtime.

Squee leaped and bopped her nose on the doorbell for Unit 145, then bounced in place waiting for the door to open. Lex caught up, huffing a bit, and placed his hand on his hip.

"You know what? Let's call you bait on this one," he murmured. "See what kind of a man the other me is."

A few seconds ticked by. The door clicked. There he was. Other Lex. Odd as it was, this wasn't the first time he'd faced himself, so he already knew that it wasn't like looking in a mirror. Mirrors flipped things, and thus the "me" that existed in Lex's mind was actually the flip-flopped version of himself. The near-identical duplicate thus instantly registered as "me, but with something unsettlingly wrong." But there was more than that to unsettle Lex. He was dressed very casually. Baggy shorts and a t-shirt with a "funny" slogan indicating one shouldn't talk to him until he'd been properly caffeinated. He was a bit less fit. Not much, but what Lex could see of his neck, calves, and arms lacked the definition Lex had achieved. His hair looked like he'd picked "Number Nine" at a barbershop run by an old man where all the models on the poster were also old men. And he was wearing sandals. With socks.

Squee didn't mind the differences. She vaulted from the floor the instant his shoulders were visible and thus a valid target. Other Lex yelped and stumbled back, fouling Squee's aim and causing her to strike him in the chest on the way down rather than the shoulder on the way up. The pair tumbled to the ground backward. Lex slipped through the door before it swung shut.

"What the heck? Jeez! Calm down!" Other Lex said as Squee scrambled around on top of him while he tried to get back up.

He managed to sit up, which provided him with shoulders in the right orientation for her to perch on them, so she wrapped around his neck and snuggled tight.

Lex watched as his other self wrestled control of his mind back from the edges of confusion and panic. It wasn't an unreasonable reaction to have, given an unknown animal had just assaulted him in a way that wasn't obviously affectionate at first blush. But Lex couldn't help but feel a little embarrassed on his behalf. Still, it was a useful distraction. Lex checked his slidepad and saw that the displaced mass was quite nearby. If it wasn't inside the condo, it was close. He eyed the sensor readings on the slidepad and attempted to track them down.

"Okay, okay little doggie. Who lost you?" he said, attempting to pry Squee off his neck.

She let herself be tugged free and dangled from his grip, stretching her neck forward in attempts to lick the end of a nose that Other Lex kept mere millimeters out of range.

"Oh, yeah. You definitely belong to someone. That harness is in way too good of shape for you to be a runaway for very long. And I don't know if stray dogs usually have earrings. Or... *painted nails*. Interesting."

Lex couldn't thoroughly search the condo. Opening doors or cabinets would be a dead giveaway that he was lurking about. He'd only find the doodad he was looking for like this if it was lying around. But it did give Lex a chance to observe the condo his other self was living in. The place was... nice. Lex's own places of residence all looked either completely un-lived-in or *too* lived in. The place on Operlo may as well have only been a bed and a shower for how often he used it. There was nothing in the way of personalized decoration, and he probably had never turned on the oven. The place on Golana was an archeological expedition with multiple strata of fast food containers and dirty laundry. They were places to live. This? This was a home.

All the furniture, all the rugs, every little tchotchke looked like it had been purchased from the same part of a home decor catalog with a label like *The Tuscan Autumn Collection.* It all matched. Little cozy blankets hung in neat folds on the backs of the couch and love seat. The accent wall tied in with the throw rugs. And then there were the pictures. At least four digital frames worked their way through photos of Lex and Michella. Here they were fishing, Michella holding up one of those big trout they seeded the local waterways with. There Lex was, proudly holding up a silver trophy surrounded by a pit crew, with Michella practically tackling him in a hug. He caught a shot from backstage at GolanaNet, with Lex shaking hands with a local celebrity while Michella seemed to be midsentence. One frame was entirely dedicated to wedding photos.

They were married. And they were happy.

They weren't just smiling. Most of the pictures weren't posed enough for the photographer to throw a "say cheese" at them. They were genuinely smiling, genuinely happy. He was happy with a silver medal in his hand. She was happy sliding faders between shots backstage.

"Now what's this?" Other Lex said.

Lex turned to find him poking at the fur on the back of her neck, where the covered port for her neural link was hidden.

"Seems like you might have a chip or something. Let me get my slidepad and see if there's a scanner app."

Lex had to scramble backward a bit as Other Lex approached. The nature of the mental cloak was that Other Lex would absolutely sidestep him rather than bowling into him. Lex wasn't *really* invisible. The slidepad was on the table directly behind him, and even the most distracted mind would probably feel compelled to question the desire to sidle around *nothing* to get to a table in their own home.

While Other Lex fiddled with his device, Lex took a final look around. The sensor seemed to be indicating a drawer, which a quick tug established was actually locked. He could probably wait around to wedge the thing open, but one lesson he'd picked up from his many adventures was the longer you lingered in an absurd situation, the more likely further absurdity would ensue. So he was left with a collection of unpleasant options. He could blow Other Lex's mind by switching the cloak off, blow his mind by prying a drawer open and stealing something from within while invisible to him, or wait until he had an opportunity to rob the place without Other Lex noticing. Some quick mental arithmetic, skewed by this desire to learn more about what sort of a life this other Lex had lived, made the decision for him.

He stepped into Other Lex's field of view and cleared his throat. Other Lex looked up, confirming that sound was at least much less accounted for than vision in the mental cloak's operation. Lex turned off the device. The raw variety of emotions that flickered across Other Lex's face in the next few moments was genuinely impressive. Fear, recognition, fear again, confusion, and all sorts of little microexpressions that didn't have proper names got their time on his face before he finally yelped.

"Who are you doing here!?" came his mangled exclamation.

"Easy, easy. Calm down. This all has a very stupid, bizarre explanation," Lex said.

"Get back. I'm calling the cops!" Other Lex said, looking around for the slidepad that was still in his hand.

"Give me five minutes to explain, please. If you can't trust yourself, who can you trust?"

"You're not me! I'm me! I don't have a twin. So you're... I don't know *what* you are. But I'll tell you what you're going to do. You're just going to stay there and—"

Unfamiliar as he was with Squee's habits, Other Lex learned too late that waggling a slidepad in front of her was effectively an invitation to play. A slidepad—specifically a slidepad that belonged to Lex—was absolutely her favorite toy. She hopped up, plucked it from his fingers, and trotted over to the corner to start nosing at it.

"Did you train her to do that?" Other Lex accused.

"I failed to train her *not* to do that," Lex said. "And just a heads-up, she's probably going to be ordering frozen burritos and blue bandanas if your marketplace apps aren't locked. If they *are* locked, she'll still order them, but it'll take her a couple minutes."

"This isn't real. This isn't really happening," Other Lex said.

"Trust me, if I could just make stuff stop by denying it was real, my life would be very different. Are you calm now? Can I explain?"

"I'm not calm, but you'd *better* explain."

"I'm Lex from another dimension. A dimension where you're a slightly better racer with much worse luck. This is Squee. She's half-fox and half-skunk. She is the creation of a mad engineer who would literally bash you with a crowbar if you called him a mad scientist. The same guy who built the thing that made me invisible, the thing that sent me here from my home dimension, and the thing that screwed things up so bad in my own dimension that I had to come here to find the parts to fix it. This isn't an invasion. I'm not here to warn you about the future or anything. I just need something indicated by the sensor readings on my slidepad. Then I'll go."

"How did you get here?" Other Lex said.

"Something called a snap-back simulator installed in the *SOB*."

"What is the *SOB*?" Other Lex said.

"*Son of Betsy*. It's my ship."

"*Son of Betsy*?" He emphasized "Son." "Did something happen to *Betsy* in your world?" Other Lex said, raising his eyebrows.

"You still *have Betsy* in this world?"

"Of course! When you get your hands on an Intrasystem Interceptor, you baby that thing."

"Yeah... I kind of... it's a long story."

"If you want me to believe you're some interdimensional duplicate, you'd better tell it, and make me believe it."

Lex sighed. "It's like this, Lex—"

Other Lex raised his hand. "Hang on. Before we continue, do me a favor and call me Trevor. Only the press calls me Lex or T-Lex or whatever."

Lex winced as his other self dropped another coolness notch.

"Okay, Trevor. A couple years ago... wait, what year is it again?"

"2342."

"Right. Okay. A couple years ago I was up and coming in the league, but I made some bad decisions and ended up having to fix the outcome of a race to clear my accounts with a loan shark. The league found out, I got booted. I became a chauffeur and freelance courier, took another bad job that put me in bad with VectorCorp and put me in *good* with Nick Patel."

"The mobster?"

"Yeah. One thing led to another, I got chased to a planet called Big Sigma, where I ruined *Betsy* piloting my way through the trash orbiting the planet. I ended up taking a job with him—the mad engineer I mentioned—testing stuff. I fought some terrorists, adopted that funk there, fought some killer robots, traveled through time, got recruited into a new racing league on Operlo, and while attempting to upgrade my simulator, accidentally shattered space-time."

Trevor waited a beat. "Is that it?"

"Isn't that enough?" Lex asked, summoning Squee to perch on his shoulders.

"You fought killer robots?" he said.

"Yeah. Self-replicating swarm. Threatened all the human race. You might want to keep your ears open for that, by the way. And the Neo-Luddites."

"Oh, right. The Neo-Luddites. The Teeker military stomped those folks out last year."

"... They did?"

"Yeah. After all those deaths at the university, they cracked down pretty hard. There's still a chunk of the VC routing network that's out of commission because of them."

"Ah. I kind of thought if I didn't do that, no one would have."

"I sure as heck wasn't going to do it. I'm a racer, and a married man."

Lex glanced at the photo frame. "Yeah, I noticed."

"I take it you aren't married?"

"Mitch and I had a falling out."

"If you were calling her Mitch, I'm not surprised. She hates that."

"That's not why we broke up. She was... I was... Look, it's not really relevant to the situation. I need a little piece of mass somewhere in that drawer. Once I have it, I can take it home and I'll be out of your hair forever."

Trevor looked at the drawer. "You sure it's in *that* drawer?" he said.

"According to the slidepad sensor-reader thing Ziva programmed."

"Who's Ziva?"

"The alternate future version of the mad engineer's AI who was reconstructed in a robot body in the present of my world and keeps an eye on the place where time-displaced travelers hang out so as to not screw up the space-time continuum."

Trevor blinked. "I'd say you were making all this up, but if you were trying to convince me, you'd probably come up with a more believable story. But if it's definitely in that drawer, you're going to have to bear with me because I'm going to have to find the key."

• • • ● • ● • ● • • •

Coal sat on her landing pad across town. She had been in constant contact with Lex during his mission, though Lex's lack of direct communication with her suggested he'd forgotten that such was the case. It was just as well. Coal suspected the conversation would have been made considerably more awkward if she were to chime in.

Monitoring the conversation was a low-overhead task, leaving many of her cycles free for other tasks. She scanned the various networks and ran queries on them. The similarity to the local version of Golana meant that several months of network-cracking Ma had done to keep a better watch over Lex enabled Coal to access nearly every public network and many law enforcement networks. Collecting data about this world and cross-referencing it with her own resources to profile the difference between worlds was a worthwhile pastime. Her analysis suggested the point of differentiation between Lex's home dimension and this one was approximately nineteen years earlier. Historical data preceding that point matched her records perfectly. Subtle differences appeared after. The specific divergent event was unclear, and as it was not one of her objectives to make that determination, she further fragmented her resources rather than fixating on it.

A deep scan of their surroundings using the quantum-shift detector reconfirmed that the missing mass they were after was almost precisely where Lex was standing. It also turned up a pair of spikes with a different quantum shift.

This presented her with a dilemma. Lex had located and was in the process of acquiring the displaced mass they were after. That meant the objectives were best served by standing by and ensuring he returned and was able to make an FTL jump to return the mass to his home dimension. Alternately, the presence of another extradimensional entity or entities, when no such entities had been detected up to this point, was not likely to be a coincidence, and informing herself and Lex on the nature of this potential threat could prove crucial in avoiding future complications that would prevent the completion of the mission. This would require lengthy consideration before taking action.

Forty-one milliseconds later, she made her decision. Repulsors and thrusters powered up. She elevated two meters and reached the end of the mechanical docking clamps attached to the ship. A warning tone rang out in the surrounding area, and the business proprietor took notice.

"T-Lex? Did you come by and I didn't notice?" he called, trotting from the booth he'd been residing in. "You can't check out without settling the bill."

Coal isolated the docking port the clamp was attached to. By design, ships had no automated ways to disconnect a docking clamp of this sort. The presence of such a mechanism would defeat the purpose of the clamp. Though Karter had made numerous modifications, a built-in declamping mechanism was not currently on her list of deployable countermeasures. Fortunately there were alternatives.

She activated the ship's defensive shields. The cable shuddered and jerked as the energy field crackled around it. She calculated that the interference introduced by the shield could be calibrated to mimic a disconnection signal. She cycled through a series of likely signal types. The possibility space for the different signal combinations would take seventy-three years to exhaustively test. She chose the more expedient option.

The *SOB*'s modified tractor beam latched on to the mounting point of the clamp. She activated its jackhammer-like offensive mode and turned the concrete the clamp had been anchored to into a pile of gravel.

"Lex! Lex, what are you doing?" Jimmi called.

Coal switched on the external speakers. "Do not worry. This ship is not currently under the control of Trevor Alexander," she said. "You may treat this instance as a rogue AI or a malware-infected control system and thus should feel no compulsion to seek out or bother Trevor Alexander."

Satisfied the situation was defused, she flared the thrusters and launched skyward, docking clamp still trailing. Within a few seconds, her communicator activated with nine different law enforcement and regulatory entities. She accessed the network, refamiliarizing herself with the local ordinances. When she had confirmed her understanding, she opened simultaneous communication to all entities.

"Greetings, sir, ma'am, or gender-indeterminant or nonconforming entities and beings. I am aware that I am in violation of twenty-one... processing... ninety-one... processing... a large and constantly updating number of laws, policies, and directives. If I were a legally recognized sentient being, this would expose me to legal action up to and including massive fines and incarceration. In the absence of a sentient controlling entity capable of fulfilling the criteria of citizenship, the corporations responsible for the automated systems at fault can be fined instead. My design and configuration are traceable to a nonlocal dimensional entity, and thus outside of your jurisdiction. There is therefore no individual responsible for these actions that is subject to your laws, policies, or directives. By strict interpretation of the relevant legal texts, this event should be treated as a natural disaster or an act of god. I invite you to address your concerns and complaints to the relevant deity."

Somehow, despite the unassailable logic, a small collection of high-altitude-capable civilian enforcement hovercars was approaching from below and some orbital enforcement ships were forming up in an intercept course.

She chose not to continue the verbal diplomatic procedures and redirected her efforts to evasion. Boosting the navigational and defensive shields, she dialed the thrusters to full, producing a massive, blinding shock front ahead of the ship and an earsplitting sonic boom as she burst to a high multiple of the speed of sound. This velocity was nonideal for atmospheric travel. The shields were quickly drained warding off the heat and friction damage, but the maneuver was sufficient to encourage the surface-based enforcement to break off pursuit almost immediately, not that pursuit would have been possible for them at her present velocity.

The speed continued to increase as the atmosphere thinned. She chose to maintain the maximum speed possible without damage, which kept her shields low but kept additional attempted contacts from the surface from being a threat. A small cluster of weapon signatures locked on. She calculated a valid evasive sequence and initiated it. Two of the low-intensity lasers still met their mark, punching easily through the weakened shields and causing a spike in engine heat, reducing her maximum speed.

"Lex makes it look so easy," Coal remarked to herself.

She considered returning to the atmosphere. If she did so at a reduced and controlled speed, the presence of gas around her would allow for convection cooling and increase the cooldown speed. Regulations forbid usage of orbital weapons below a certain altitude as well. But retreat at this point would give the orbital ships more time to reposition themselves to mount an offensive.

It was at this point that her searching for technological alternatives turned up the active cloak. One of the aspects of Coal that differentiated her from the base Ma-type AI was her capacity to become "scatterbrained." She had resisted correction of this trait. Presently she wondered if perhaps she should rethink that. Regardless she entered this into her calculations and developed a plan. Dropping down into the high atmosphere kept the ships at bay. The surface-based authorities had yet to catch up. When the sensor sweeps hit a lull, she activated the cloak and proceeded at a moderate speed into low orbit. The chatter on the various communication lines confirmed she was no longer showing up on their sensors. She was free to take her time.

Her first order of business was to rescan for quantum shift. Not only did it once again register the anomalous readings, they were much stronger. Knowing precisely how close they had come would require her to know their precise mass, but unless they were *very* massive, the quantum-shifted entities were quite close. Within a few kilometers. She targeted her visual sensors and focused on the appropriate section of space, rescanning constantly as she did.

Additional readings should have allowed her to triangulate the position with a high degree of precision. With the data available, they should have been narrowed to a four-hundred-cubic-meter spherical volume of space. She could easily monitor that entire volume of space at once, and she currently was. No visual indications of the mysterious masses were evident. She swept through additional portions of the EM spectrum, working from infrared all the way to X-ray. None of them revealed more than a minor visual distortion.

She had nearly decided that the signal was the result of some manner of interference when another ship—probably one searching for her— approached from a higher orbit. Twin slivers of brighter colors started to appear, like crescent moons tracing out the edge of a roughly spherical mass about fifty centimeters in diameter. She ran a spectral analysis of the light and found it to be the precise emission pattern of the planet's surface as viewed from above. And the crescent was steadily widening as the ship passed over. These were two mysterious spheroids that were altering not just their surface colors but their surface emissions to match the planet below. An active camouflage not unlike her own, but one that seemed to be unidirectional rather than omnidirectional.

When the ship had finished its sweep and was out of sensor range, the two odd masses started to ascend. Coal pursued. They moved with impressive speed for things so small. More impressive, they didn't seem to have any sort of heat signature. There was no propulsion method in her database that could move that quickly without either an extremely large propulsion system, an extremely dense heat sink, or both. At their size, they should have been incandescent with the waste heat of any propulsion system capable of that amount of acceleration. She matched pace, then gradually approached. Without something to cause them to redirect their camouflage, they took on the color and temperature profile of deep space, forcing Coal to rely upon her quantum-shift sensors once more. It was less precise, but allowed her to continue to close the distance.

At approximately one hundred meters, she detected an unidentified energy field. It brushed against the ship. The moment it did, both of the masses briefly became fully visible. She recorded the highest-quality video she could muster for the zero point seven three seconds they were visible. Then, with a surge of a far more familiar energy field, they burst to FTL. At their size, Coal knew she had no hope of tracking them. And besides, she still had a job to do on Golana.

· • • ● • ● ● • • ·

Things had become strangely comfortable between Lex and Trevor in the past few minutes. In what was likely the largest understatement in recent history, Lex and his parallel self had a lot in common. They shared interests, and the broad strokes of their lives matched with very well-defined departures. To Lex, only one of them stood out.

"Do you have any race footage, though?" Lex said, helping Trevor dig through a box in the bedroom.

"If *I'm* not this hung up on my own racing career, why are *you* so hung up on it?"

"Because you're *seventeenth* in the league."

"The league has thousands of racers. I'm incredibly proud of that."

"But you can do better. I know you can, because *I* can. And I'm you. I'm freaking out about someone nipping at my heels for first this season, and I'm in a league of people who were overwhelmingly ejected from other leagues for being overly aggressive or outright cheating. I'm swimming with the *sharks* and I'm coming in first."

"I guess I have different priorities," Trevor said.

Lex paused. "It must be nice."

"It is. I'm living the dream."

Behind them, the sound of the door latch disengaging caused them both to tense up.

"Michella's home," Trevor said.

"Should I hide?" Lex said, hand already reaching for the bag to turn on the mental cloak.

"I... No. Let's spare her the whole sitcom routine. I don't like hiding things from her."

Lex squinted at him. "I'm starting to wonder if we're really the same guy. But someone should probably wrangle Squee before—"

Michella squealed as Squee happily yipped. The parallel duplicate of Lex's would-be fiancée failed to dodge the pounce even as well as Trevor had. And one glance at her illustrated why she wasn't quite at her most nimble at the moment. She had the distinctive belly of a woman who was far enough along in pregnancy to begin to show.

"Michella, before you overreact, let me explain," Trevor said quickly.

"Before I overreact? You adopted a dog and you didn't tell me?" Michella said. "You could have at least asked first. It's cute and all but we've got *twins* on the way. That's going to be enough of a handful."

"In that case, I've got good news. The dog isn't ours," Trevor said.

"Oh. Good. Then whose is it?"

She sputtered a bit and chased the fluffy tail out of her face in time for Lex to step into the room. She looked at him, then at Trevor, then at Lex again. "Explain," she said with a steady, forceful tone.

"Do you want to do it, or shall I?" Trevor said.

Lex's slidepad chirped. He glanced at it. Coal was pinging him.

"You take this one," Lex said. "This could be important."

He stepped away while Trevor did his best to explain what he had only just learned from Lex. Meanwhile, Lex reached up to activate his hands-free only to discover it was already active.

"Coal?" he whispered.

"Yes, Lex."

"How long has this call been open?"

"Since you left the landing pad."

"Why'd you ping my slidepad rather than just speak up?"

"I have observed that conversation from unexpected sources is likely to cause the average human to startle. If I have observed the conversation correctly, you have yet to acquire the mass?"

"Yeah. It's locked in a dresser he got as a housewarming present from my dad. Er. His dad. We don't want to bust the drawer, and it seems like we're not super pressed for time."

"That statement may not be entirely accurate."

"What's going on?" Lex said quickly.

"You were asked about your awareness of two additional dimensional incursions while we were in the universe with surplus Karters, correct?"

"Yeah."

"I detected them, and was able to pursue them until they jumped to FTL."

"You were able to pursue them," Lex said steadily.

"Correct."

"You're docked at Jimmi's right now, Coal."

"That information is obsolete."

"A ship isn't allowed to leave the landing pad without paying. How did you pay?"

"I determined that investigating the interdimensional intruders was of greater importance than staying in good standing with Jimmi's Landing Deck North. Do not worry, I informed law enforcement that laws were unenforceable against me due to my remote origins."

"And on the off chance they decide the guy whose name is on the parking record is responsible?"

"It is possible the local duplicate of yourself will be receiving a visit from law enforcement."

"I'm surprised they haven't called him."

"I have taken steps to redirect any attempts to do so. I have full access to the local civilian communication network and have rerouted all calls related to this incident."

"Coal, is there anything you can do about this?"

"As I previously stated, I have taken steps to redirect any calls from law enforcement to any of his devices, and those listed as known contacts. If I had a fusion device—"

"*That doesn't involve the hypothetical detonation of a weapon of mass destruction!*" he hissed.

"I shall endeavor to update the relevant systems and eliminate any standing warrants or other infractions in your alternate self's name, as well as continuing to redirect any calls or dispatches to the residence. But the non-networked nature of the human brain means any agents of law enforcement already dispatched may arrive regardless."

"Do your best. I'll try to hurry things up here," he said.

He stepped back into the den, where Trevor was finishing explaining things to Michella. Michella, being who she was, had started jotting down his story in pen and paper.

"And that's why we need to unlock the drawer and find what he's after," Trevor said.

"Right, yes, so if you know where the key is—" Lex began.

"Forgive me, Other Trevor," Michella said.

"I prefer Lex."

"I'm sure you do, but I'm not quite so quick to believe such a fantastic story without proof."

Lex resisted the urge to point out he was in a hurry. He knew her well enough to know that would trigger her into a deep dive into why that was, and he wasn't eager to answer it. Better to hope he could pass her test in less time than would have taken to explain why the cops may or may not be on the way and why. Chances were that wouldn't persuade them to lend a hand.

"Hit me. What would it take to convince you?"

"Do you have any ID?" she said.

He pulled out his slidepad, brought up the credentials tab, and handed it over. She looked over the information.

"It doesn't match exactly," she said. "There are some pretty big errors."

"They're not errors. I've lived a different life than he did," Lex said.

"What about fingerprints? Let me check those," she said, pulling her slidepad and quickly acquiring a fingerprinting app.

"We can do this, but I can already tell you they match because that's how I got into the sky lobby," he said.

Testing three fingers on each hand confirmed he and Trevor were a match.

"Tell me about me, then," Michella said.

"We're not together anymore in my world," Lex said. "And judging by the way you two get along, he probably knows more about you than I knew about my Mitch."

Her expression became slightly more stern. He sighed.

"Okay, we'll start there. You don't like being called Mitch because you say it sounds too much like bitch. When you get stressed, you fall into the welcome arms of comfort foods, preferably macaroni and cheese, plus a concoction I call the Mitchaccino, which is hot chocolate with two shots of espresso, made with chocolate syrup, *not* chocolate powder."

She gave Trevor a sideways glance.

"I didn't say a word about it, I swear," Trevor said.

"Keep going," she said.

"How far are we going to take this? In my world you and I went to the same college. Your favorite band was and is Death Zone Dumpster."

She glanced around. "You could have picked that up just by looking around this place, I'm sure," she said.

"You want proof I'm not from around here? Check this out?" He tapped the control for the mental cloak, then tapped it again.

"What? How did you do that?" she said.

"Courtesy of a mad scientist. It filters me out of your vision the same way your brain is filtering out your nose even though you can see it right now."

"I absolutely cannot see my... oh, wow." She shook her head. "Stop distracting me. Cutting-edge technology doesn't mean you're from another world, and I'm still not convinced you are a version of Trev."

"Your maiden name is Modane," he said.

"Easy enough to determine."

He huffed a breath. "You sure you want me to say *everything* I know?"

"Don't try weaseling out of this," she said.

"You're surprisingly good with a handgun, because Modane isn't your *birth* name. You were born with the last name Rodrigo. Your father Carlito was a low-level enforcer in the mob. If things went the way they did back home, he informed on the rest of the crew in exchange for safety for you, your mother, and your sister. He was stabbed to death in prison with a sharpened screwdriver. Should I go on?"

The color had drained from her face.

"See, now I've got my doubts again," Trevor said. "Because that's some bogus stuff right there."

"I never told him that..." Michella said.

"What?" Trevor said.

"Oh, wow. I guess my Michella and I got close in different ways," Lex said.

"How do you know that? It was *wiped from the records*," she said.

"You and I went through some rough stuff back home. No secrets in a foxhole. That kind of thing."

"All right." She took a breath and nodded. "All right. Either you're an impressively well-equipped fake or you're the real deal. He says you're here because... *time* was broken where you come from?"

"As I understand it, yeah," Lex said.

"And bringing back something in that drawer is going to fix it?"

"I sure hope so."

She drummed her fingers, inadvertently summoning Squee to slide up underneath them to steal some pets.

"I think I know where the key is," she said. "But I want you to keep talking. This is potentially the biggest scoop ever, and I'm struggling to determine how exactly I'm going to prove it's even happening."

She stood and paced into the bedroom. Lex and Trevor followed. Squee trotted along to stay in range of any fingers that might accidentally scratch and pet her or drop treats.

"What happened between you and your Michella?"

"We were together from basically high school until I got booted from the racing league for fixing a race to get out of mob debt."

"That would certainly have been grounds for a breakup. Especially for me back then."

"We got back together because, to be honest, in the years since then I really hadn't gotten over her. One thing led to another, and I managed to help her get a scoop and it got us talking again. It got pretty serious. I'd hoped we'd get married, but it fell apart because both of us were a little too into our careers but only one of us was willing to make time for *us*. I'll let you guess which one."

"I suspect it was more complex than that," Michella said.

"It probably was, but I'm the one who traveled through the dimensional barrier, so you're getting my take on things. And I'm still a little sore about it, thank you very much."

"I guess everyone has their own priorities. Trev and I definitely made some sacrifices to make sure we could make this work. Sounds like the other me might have felt the sacrifices were too much." She found a small, ornate key. "Here. I knew it was in here."

They hurried to the drawer and unlocked it. Every home in the universe seemed to have a drawer or box like the one they uncovered. Everything inside was precious in either actual value or sentimental value, but none of the trinkets and documents inside were important enough to keep handy. Lex scanned the contents of the drawer, but he needn't have bothered. There was only one thing in the drawer that he recognized. A diamond ring. The very one he'd attempted to give Michella. He sighed and picked it up.

"That's *yours*?" Trevor said.

Michella snatched it from Lex.

"No offense, Lex, but it's the most valuable thing in the drawer. Can you prove it's yours?" she said.

He shut his eyes tightly, if only for the embarrassment. "To the only thing in the world worth slowing down and waiting for."

"*Aww*," Michella said.

She eyed the ring, confirming the tiny inscription, and handed it over. Then she turned to Trevor and gave him a playful thump to the arm.

"Sounds awfully familiar," she said, glaring at him in mock irritation. She turned to Lex. "This one over here gave me a ring that said 'To my sweet Michella, I only slow down for you.'"

"I figured Michella wouldn't want an inscription that ended in a preposition," Trevor said. "But it's true. I found that ring like six years ago and I couldn't find the owner, but the inscription really stuck with me."

Lex double-checked with the slidepad. No additional mass anywhere near enough to set off the indicator. "This is it. I want to thank you for not freaking out more than you did. But then again, I either know you or *am* you, so I guess I should have realized you'd be able to handle a little wackiness." He touched his finger to his ear. "Coal? I've got it, are you ready to head out?"

"I am presently in the vicinity of Golana Interstellar's orbital section. You will need to reach the hub and find a way to reach me without me docking. While the local communication network was simple enough to penetrate, the transit hub is more hardened."

"We'll figure something out." He looked up. "Squee, let's go. So long, you two. All the best to you and your growing family."

"And good luck with your career," Trevor said. "If you ever come back, maybe call ahead and lay off the disappearing act."

"I'll keep that in mind. Speaking of disappearing act."

He touched his fingers to the controls for the mental cloak and headed for the door. By the time he'd shut it behind him, he was already planning his next steps with Coal. "I have my flight suit in my bag, but I don't have Squee's suit, so I don't have a way to get her from the station to the *SOB* if you can't dock. Can you reenter the atmosphere? Pick a spot outside of town to set down?"

"There is a low-level military mobilization. The cloak does not handle reentry well. Entering quickly could cause enough of a cloaking failure to allow the *SOB* to show up on military-grade sensors. If I enter slowly it may be possible, but we would face a similar issue while exiting the atmosphere."

"I might be able to—"

"Update!" Coal said quickly. "Please be sure not to use the ground-floor exit."

"I wasn't going to. Why?"

"The local law enforcement is arriving."

"Why…" Lex rumbled.

"A pair of officers must have been dispatched in person, bypassing my redirects in the communication system."

"So they're coming for Lex. Er, Trevor."

"As they are likely unaware of the presence of a duplicate who could be considered to be at fault, it is likely."

Lex turned and hurried back toward the condo.

"If you depart the building in the next seven minutes, you will be able to avoid direct confrontation with the authorities, and they will be too busy with Trevor to stop you."

"I'm not going to leave a mess for the other me to clean up. This is my fault, and they're living this idyllic little life. I don't want to be the reason for them getting swept into the kind of crap *I'm* always getting swept into."

"You are definitively the reason for that already."

"Well I'm fixing it!" he said. Lex hammered on the door and shut off the mental cloak.

Trevor answered. "What is it? he said. "Is something wrong?"

"My ship may or may not have caused an international incident by not paying a parking fee and also violating orbital travel space without permission, and since I entered with my actual name, the cops are on the way to talk to you."

"What? No. They'd call first, not just show up, right?"

"My ship may or may not have broken into the communication network for the city and prevented that."

"Your ship may or may not have been very busy," Michella called from behind him, visibly agitated.

"Right, yes. I screwed up. Or I guess she screwed up, but I did too by using my real name. Mistakes were made. But I'm going to make it right. All I have to do is linger long enough for them to see me and get me on camera and then you can tell the story of how there was this impostor here. It should fly, because there's sure to be all sorts of evidence from across town of you being in two places at once."

"But what about you? How will you get away?"

"I have a hoverbike. I just need to make it to orbit."

"You can't get to orbit on a hoverbike. And if the cops and the military are after you, you're not going to make it to the space elevator on one either."

"I think you underestimate just how well we can fly," Lex said.

Trevor's eyes darted with a decidedly Lex-like gleam. "Get inside. I have an idea." He pulled Lex and Squee inside and shut the door.

Two officers, a man and a woman, stepped off the elevator. They nodded and moved aside as a pregnant woman walked past them and headed for the lobby.

"I can't wait to see how this goes," the woman muttered.

"Look, Dispatch is tied up in knots and we're getting messages from the military," said one officer. "Do you have a better idea than to go see the guy whose name is on the registration?"

"He's a racing star. What's he really going to have to do with this?" said the other.

"I don't know, but it's the one lead we have, so we have to bring him in."

"And what? Hope he has a remote connection to the ship that just vanished? I think something more is up than a D-List celebrity has a hyperadvanced ship running amok."

They rang the doorbell to the condo.

"I'm a little busy," Trevor said. "Can you come back later?"

"It's the police, sir. We need to talk to you," the policewoman explained.

"I'm really awfully busy right now," Trevor said.

"This is official police business. If you do not open the door, you will be considered to be obstructing an investigation," the policeman said.

"Did we really need to go straight to that?" she asked quietly.

"This could be important. I don't need this guy wasting our time."

The door flew open and they were confronted with two men, both matching the description and photo in their database. One of them was wearing a flight suit and had his arm pulled across the neck of the other. The aggressor's other hand was hidden behind his double's back, and from the way the man in front was leaning awkwardly backward, there may have been something jammed in his back.

Somewhat undercutting the peril of the situation was an exotic dog perched on the aggressor's shoulders. The creature was wearing a small helmet and goggles and seemed generally delighted to be a part of things.

"Back off! I've got a hostage and I'm not messing around," Lex barked.

"Listen to him, he's crazy. He's trying to steal my identity!" Trevor wheezed.

The police backed up, hands on the grips of their stun batons.

"Don't try anything hasty," the policeman instructed.

"Put the weapon down and let's discuss this," the policewoman said.

The pair of men sidled around the officers, then started to work their way backward down the hallway toward the elevator.

"We've got a hostage situation," the policeman barked into his communicator. "We need backup at Horizon View Towers. The north tower."

"Don't even bother," Lex shouted. "I'll be *long gone* before any of your people show up. Just keep clear and nothing happens to the superstar racer."

"Think about this. Do you really want to do this?" the policewoman said.

"Get me building maintenance for HVT North. I want elevators disabled for level 112."

Lex and Trevor continued backward, passing the elevator and heading for the stairs.

"We're a hundred and twelve stories up. You really think you're going to make it on the stairs? You're backed into a corner. Give it up peacefully and we'll go easy on you."

"Fat chance, coppers," Lex said.

He kicked the door open and stepped out, slamming it behind him.

"Did he seriously just call us 'coppers'?" the policewoman muttered.

"I want all surveillance footage piped to my device. If anyone leaves the east stairwell, I want to know about it."

Lex dropped the wooden spoon he'd been using as a stand-in gun and tied a length of cord around the arm for the hinge piston, effectively locking the door shut.

"Why do you know how to do that?" Trevor asked.

"Lots of bad decisions that you apparently didn't make," Lex said.

He yanked the collapsible hoverbike from his pack and unfurled it. The thing was barely more than some spindly struts with repulsor pods at the end and a seat and handlebars stuck on.

"Let's do this. Feet on the rear repulsors and hang on," Lex said.

"Don't forget to compensate for the extra mass on—" Trevor said.

"Trevor, who are you talking to?" Lex said.

"Yeah, you're right," Trevor conceded.

Lex sat with Squee on his shoulders. Trevor planted his boots atop the rear repulsors and crouched, hugging Lex's waist. Lex flared the repulsors and took off down the stairs.

There was almost no room to maneuver in the stairwell. Oddly, the architects hadn't designed the place with bike racing in the stairwell in mind. But after Lex got into the rhythm of lofting down the stairs, absorbing the impact with a sweep around the outer wall and lofting down the next flight, he started to pick up speed. In barely more time than it would have taken to ride the elevator, Lex managed to bring the hoverbike to the lobby, where he tilted the bike and boosted the repulsors just as he was approaching the door. The mass of two men, a hoverbike, and a funk all moving at an inadvisable speed was more than a match for the door latches, which burst and sent the door flapping open in the wrong direction. Lex righted the bike and burst past a bewildered security guard and out the front doors.

Additional police cars were just arriving, but they couldn't hope to match the maneuverability of even a badly overloaded hoverbike.

"Left at the next street," Trevor shouted.

"I can't believe you didn't spring for in-tower parking."

"We needed a second space for the family-hauler Michella just bought. And you should be thanking your lucky stars she's parked in the tower instead of me. At least *my* car will get to a reasonable top speed."

They burst around the corner and pivoted to thread the needle between the boom arm and the dangling height-clearance markers at the entrance. Lex brought the hoverbike to a stop, and they dashed to Trevor's hovercar. It was a slick, well-kept, and sporty two-seater that probably had more mass in the reactor and repulsors than in the rest of the structure combined.

"Trevor, I gotta say, based on the condo, I didn't have you pegged for a burly beast like this."

"I got it as part of an endorsement deal," Trevor said.

Lex reached for the driver's-side door. Trevor stopped him.

"My car, I drive," he said.

"But you're supposed to be my hostage," Lex said.

"So you hold a 'gun' to my side. Michella doesn't like driving this thing, so no one drives it but me."

"I *am* you."

"You're not me enough."

"Fine."

Lex slid in the passenger side. Trevor climbed into the driver's side. The police were already approaching. Trevor burst toward the exit, feathering the throttle just enough to keep from damaging the paint job as he passed under the opening boom arm.

He took the turn like a pro. Lex was happy to notice that his double also kept the inertial inhibitor tuned down, so the motion of the hovercar threw them around nicely. For easily thirty seconds, Lex found himself planning to issue instructions and discovering he didn't have to. Trevor knew to take the surface roads, because contact with the ground meant better maneuvering for a beast like this, and anything above a certain altitude could cause an unmodified hovercar to pop over into autopilot. He skipped the ring road that funneled the city's traffic toward and away from the space elevators. Too easy to roadblock. It made for a lot more sharp turns and a lot fewer straightaways for top speed, but a monster like he was piloting didn't need much runway to get some serious velocity. So Lex used his time by pulling his tool chain from his belt and jabbing underneath the dashboard.

"What are you doing?" Trevor asked.

"Did you get this thing modded for direct control?" Lex said.

"You mean bypassing law enforcement lockout? Of course not. That's illegal."

"Then keep us out of range of cops until I can take care of that."

"I thought it took a black-market mod app to do that."

"Yep," he said, booting it up. "It's a good thing your world and mine are similar enough for this to be compatible." He tapped through some very rough-looking menus and managed to log into the diagnostic. "You're going to want to do a factory reset after this if you don't want to pay any fines," Lex said, pushing the update. "All right, we're good. You could probably go high, but stay low. I'm betting the cops aren't as good at weaving through traffic as you are. This'll at least keep them from directing a shutdown command at you."

His work done, Lex sat back and eyed the road ahead. This was the first time in his life he'd been a passenger in a vehicle being driven in this way with the same level of skill that he displayed on the track. When he was in control, he knew exactly how much distance he was giving himself. He knew what the vehicle could handle, knew his reaction time. As a passenger, all that went out the window. He could still predict roughly, or speculate, what Trevor would do, but seeing it happen from a vantage not directly behind the controls was impressive and just short of terrifying.

"I'm starting to get why people don't always like when I show off," Lex said.

"No talking please," Trevor said. "Focusing."

Lex reluctantly took his eyes off the road to inspect his double. It was true, Trevor was probably his match. He certainly had the reaction time and the intuition. But whereas Lex was almost serene while squeezing his vehicle of the moment through gaps that seemed too small and around corners it shouldn't manage, Trevor looked like he was about to crack. Lex grinned.

"You know what your problem is?" Lex said.

"Not in the mood for critiques. This is my first high-speed chase."

"You're missing one of the tools of the trade."

"What are you *talking* about?" Trevor growled, edging the hovercar onto the driver's-side repulsors to sneak over the roof of a car a little too far inside the turn for comfort.

Lex unzipped a pouch on the outside of his pack and fetched one of the few truly indispensable pieces of racing gear, as far as he was concerned. A stick of gum.

"Open up," he said.

"What!?"

"I'm serious."

Trevor tore his eyes off the road for a brief, incredulous glance. He opened his mouth, and Lex popped the gum inside.

"This is shtupid," he said juicily.

"Yeah, well, we'll see."

There were a few more tight city turns, and then the complex sifting machine that made up the last stretch of road and sky before the elevator. What seemed like a lifetime ago, Lex had navigated this mess with Nick Patel in the back seat, getting him there in time for a flight and starting the chain of events that got him his place in Preethy's league.

Now he got to see it from the other side, and it was a front-row seat to an awakening.

Maybe it was the gum. Maybe it was just Trevor getting into the groove. But the rigid, sudden moves started to lose their jagged edge. They became more fluid, more natural. He started using the z-axis a lot more than any sane hovercar driver would without actually taking it to the skies. He was like a gamer who had just discovered his kart racer included a jump button. Little vaults let him tuck his hovercar comfortably into a drift. Areal pivots put his thrusters behind him to make sharper turns.

"You know," Lex said. "The departures is a little backed up."

"We're not going to the departures," Trevor said.

Lex secured his pack with one arm and Squee with the other.

"Okay. We're twins all right."

Trevor took the hovercar into the arrivals tunnel and practically rode the outside wall, juicing the repulsors and pivoting in air to plant the belly of the car on the support beam on the far side of an access road within the tunnel, reversing direction with a spine-compressing thump and jump. They streaked up to one of the less crowded entrances and sizzled to a stop.

Trevor took a triumphant breath. "I kind of dig the gum. Makes the whole thing—"

"A five-senses experience. That you weren't already doing this makes me worry somehow it's the gum that made me into the adrenaline junky I am. Do me a favor and don't screw up this life you've got going."

"I may be my own worst enemy, but I think without two of me screaming bad advice at my brain, I'll be able to keep on the straight and narrow. Now go. I can already hear the cops."

"I'd tell you you're a good man, but I feel like that'd be kind of self-aggrandizing, given the situation. So long, man. Stay cool. And maybe get a haircut."

Lex hopped out of the hovercar with his pack and his funk and activated the mental cloak. He was confident he could navigate his way to the elevator without having to give up his invisibility, except for one little thing. Unless Coal could finagle her way into a docking bay, Lex was going to have to transfer into the *SOB* externally, and Squee's spacesuit was still in the *SOB*. He'd need to find some sort of way to keep her safe for the duration of a jump. The good news was, such things existed. The bad news was, he had to find one, and acquire it, and that was about to become a real problem, as the police had arrived.

He managed to slip in the doors, following the previous person through closely, just as a police officer charged up to take a statement from Trevor. From the muffled sounds of Trevor's exclamations, he was hamming up his role. Meanwhile, a second officer slipped inside. He stepped over to a panel on the wall and tapped in a code. A sharp tone rang out in the transit center.

"Attention. We are tracking a potentially dangerous criminal. Please turn your eyes to the nearest public screen to see a recent image taken during a hostage situation."

The various screens intended to list schedules interspersed with advertisements blinked and revealed a sharp, clear image of Lex manhandling Trevor. Though he knew he couldn't be seen with the cloak on, Lex still felt a hot sting of anxiety. This was going to get a lot more complicated.

"Coal," Lex whispered.

"Yes, Lex?"

"Are you familiar with the situation?"

"I am. Assorted social media sources are regionally trending with this turn of events. And also GolanaNet News."

"Oh, are they now..." Lex said, turning to the door.

The telltale glow of the high-powered lights on a drone cam gleamed just outside the door. Michella had arrived. It was impressive how quickly the news could arrive when she was fully aware of what would be happening and where. A few-minutes head start before the roads got tied up was all it took for her to arrive right on time to get in the face of the police.

"Excuse me, Officer. My name is Michella Alexander. I'm a producer at GNN. Is there anything we can do to properly spread the word and help you capture this fugitive?"

"If you'll just let me finish my statement."

"Because I would like to emphasize that the man being sought is visually identical to the hostage."

"Yes, I'm getting to that," the cop said.

"And it's very important that the outfit be emphasized, lest your people or any Good Samaritans inadvertently identify the *hostage* as the perpetrator."

"Perfect," Lex said.

He carefully snagged a package of disposable filter masks from a Keep Our Air Clean display urging travelers to be mindful of bringing contagions onto long-haul flights. No one really paid the message much mind—likely why the Karter plague had been able to spread so well—so no one noticed when one of the packets just vanished into the effects of the mental cloak. A souvenir "Life is Best In Preston" shirt was his next petty theft.

Now all he needed to do was find a place to change out of his flight suit. No flight suit, plus a mask and a hat, would buy him some uncloaked time. Not much, as he'd be one of maybe five masked people in the entire transit hub, and the look fairly screamed "hasty disguise." But he just needed to avoid being stopped for the duration of a single transaction at the "last minute necessities" store a short jog into the shopping center attached to the transit hub.

He'd forgotten how good the police were in Preston City, though. It must have struck them that a fugitive might want to disguise himself, and thus while the public address system emphasized the flight suit and "wild hair" in contrast to Trevor's look, police and security guards had carefully blocked off every private place to change clothes.

With the mask in hand, he did something that intellectually he knew wasn't going to cause a stir but still took all his fortitude to try. He got changed right in the middle of the busy station. After having the foresight to get into his flight suit for a quick getaway before the cops arrived to start the whole escape, he now had to peel the thing off, ending up in his boxer shorts, and quickly don his spare set of clothes again. With the exception of one older woman nearly bumping into him because she wasn't looking where she was going, the whole maneuver went without incident. He hurried to the shop and found what he was looking for, ducked behind a shelf to shield himself from view, and became visible.

He walked up to the counter and dropped the package as well as an appropriately-sized poker chip.

"Wow…" said the middle-aged woman working the counter. "The Companion Saver. You know something. In all the years I've been working here, I don't think we've ever sold one of these."

"Yeah, it's a pretty niche purpose I guess," he said, stroking Squee to keep her from attempting to transfer to the clerk's shoulders for a scritch.

The Companion Saver was a tough, inflatable plastic bubble, about the size of a large beach ball, that travelers could put their pets into in the event of a decompression event on a spaceship. He would have just stolen it rather than checking out, but unlike the kiosks, anything on a shelf at one of these shops had an antitheft polymer that would set off an alarm if it left the shop without being scanned. And with the number of cops swarming this place, he couldn't be sure he could navigate the crowd of them while invisible if they responded quickly enough. Heck, they might even shut down the next couple of elevator rides if they thought something was up. It was a small miracle they hadn't already.

"Come clean with me, if something goes wrong on that ship, do you think you're going to have time to get your puppy in here before the whole thing decompresses? Do you think *you* are going to be safe with that weird disposable safety suit they give us?"

"Give me a break, lady," Lex said.

"Oh, yeah. Sorry. You're sweating bullets. Nervous flyer?" she said. "Yeah, yeah. My husband is a nervous flyer. Kind of funny, me working at the space elevator when my husband won't even set foot on the lift."

Lex glanced at a police officer scanning the surroundings. He tried to appear nonchalant.

"Anyway, try to relax," she said, rummaging through the drawer for change for the chip. "Space flight is perfectly safe."

"Keep the change," Lex said, grabbing the packet as soon as it was scanned and hurrying away.

The moment he was able to break line of sight with the cop, he turned the mental cloak back on and dashed toward the line for the next lift. It was a low-traffic time of day, so they were sending the elevator cars up without filling them. He'd be able to slip onto one and not be noticed.

Hurrying past faces he recognized from his days as a chauffeur—fully half of the drop-offs and pickups in those days were at the hub—he scooched behind an elevator operator that he knew to be one of the lazier members of the staff and slipped into the car. The bizarre vehicle looked a bit like someone had split a bus in half and flipped half of it upside down over the other half. A row of front-facing seats was mirrored by an upside-down set overhead.

"Now boarding. Now boarding for the 9:35 to the Upstairs. Last call, now boarding for the 9:35 to the Upstairs," the worker said with what might well count as a negative amount of enthusiasm.

Lex tucked himself into the corner while six or seven white-collar workers and a transit mechanic strapped themselves in for the ride. The staffer looked up from his slidepad, saw that there was no longer a line, and approached the control panel to seal it up and send it up the cable.

"Hold it! Hold it!" a cop said, marching over and flashing his badge. "We're searching every elevator before it leaves. There's an escaped kidnapper."

The workers and the transit employee all managed to look as though between the threat of a violent criminal and the inconvenience of having their workday interrupted, the far greater issue was the inconvenience. Still, authority was authority. They stood and waited while the police officer searched the car. Lex stood in the corner, still and silent. The officer dropped to the ground and checked under seats, climbed up and checked over the upper seats, and generally ruled out any place that was large enough to conceal an adult man. Lex tried to creep aside as the officer worked his way closer to the corner where he was hiding, but the single step he took drew the attention of the police officer. He marched over to what to him must have appeared to be an empty corner. Lex leaned aside as the cop squinted at the wall. Squee sniffed and craned her neck, trying to get a better whiff of him. Lex gritted his teeth and leaned further, feeling like he was suddenly in a game of high-stakes limbo.

After being, overall, a very good girl for the trip thus far, Squee decided she wasn't going to let this moment pass without getting a nice, deep sample of the policeman's scent. She wriggled forward, planted a foot on Lex's chest to gain a better vantage, and poked her nose right in the crook of the man's neck to snuffle at him.

The tickle of the unseen whiskers caused the cop to recoil and rub his neck. "What the hell was that?" he yelped, swatting vaguely while Lex took advantage of the noise and distraction to slip away and hide in the already-searched section of the elevator. "You need to fumigate this place. Something just flew right by my neck."

"I don't see any bugs, man," the employee said.

The cop glared at him. "Are there any accessways or storage hatches above or below this thing?"

"Yeah, but they're not pressurized or inertially inhibited. Anyone hanging out there once we are in motion would be crushed, suffocated, and crushed in the other direction."

The cop knocked at the wall where Lex had been standing. Satisfied, he marched back to the entrance. "You're good to go. But if you see anyone suspicious, report him immediately."

"Sure thing, man," the employee said.

The doors sealed, the passengers took their places, and the tram began to rumble. Lex grabbed his slidepad and swiped out a message to Trevor.

Got the thing going, he messaged.

It was the agreed-upon code phrase for if he was officially out of their hair.

Hey, good to hear it. Just had a really crazy thing happen, I'm sure you know about it by now. Michella's doing the news thing like I've never seen it before. This is her first real scoop that wasn't just a product-reveal exclusive or something. Looks like she's having a blast.

Lex appreciated the effort that went into making the reply seem like a reasonable response to a friend. It also wasn't lost on him that in the space of the last few minutes he'd treated Trevor to the thrill of being on the wrong side of the law for a good reason, and Michella the thrill of being at the cutting edge of breaking events. He felt uncomfortably like he was dishing out designer drugs and he'd just given them each the high they'd be chasing, to their detriment, for the rest of their lives.

Coal lingered in a point near the rising space-elevator car. She was still cloaked and had carefully selected a place of destructive interference in the orbital facility's sensor system. In this position, with her level of concealment, the only way they'd find her was if they physically collided with the *SOB.*

"Coal, you there?" Lex said over the communication line.

"No, I am here," she said.

"What I mean is… never mind. It took me a minute, but I was able to get down into the maintenance tunnels. It turns out Blake still runs his place up here. And his maintenance access code is still his graduation date, backward, with one two three at the end."

"How fortuitous," Coal said.

"Yeah. Less fortuitous is the whole 'space-safe pet carrier' situation. Squee's inside and it's inflated, but… well, look."

Lex activated the video feed and shakily directed it at Squee. She was now sealed inside a clear plastic bubble with a small equipment nodule sticking to one of the poles of the globe. The hyperactive creature seemed unfazed by her captivity, and in fact had swiftly determined that scampering about like a hamster in a ball was entirely acceptable. She was literally bouncing off the walls, her gleeful yip resonating through the ball with a curious buzzing noise.

"What I am witnessing is forcing me to recalibrate the upper bound on my cuteness classification scale," Coal said. "This shall serve as my new highwater mark for the word 'adorable.'"

"It's a good thing that ball is so tough. Anyway, do you have a fix on my location?"

"I do."

"About four meters to my right, at the point where one of the struts connects to the hub, I'll be moving through a manual air lock. I can't imagine they're going to let that happen without setting off an alarm or three. So when this happens, it is going to happen fast."

"Acknowledged. Please be aware that the *SOB* is currently cloaked and will not be visible to you."

"How will I know where to jump?"

"You may jump in any direction. I will catch you."

"Okay. I trust you."

"That is an unanticipated and greatly appreciated sentiment."

She listened to Lex attempting to wrangle Squee and work at the air-lock controls. A combination of manual clamping controls and the maintenance access afforded by Blake's codes allowed Lex to get the inner door open without triggering any alarms. Once the inner door was shut and he started opening the outer door, the network started to light up with automatic alerts and concerned announcements by engineers and maintenance personnel.

"Do you require aid?" Coal asked.

"It's going to open. You're going to see Squee first, then me. I have thrusters this time, so I'm a little less worried about doing an EVA."

Coal zoomed her view on the hatch and watched as the plastic bubble, with a wide-eyed and wiggling Squee within it, ejected from inside. She plotted an intercept course. Her tally of alarms and announcements continued to tick up, but one of them stood out. It was not an alert about potential decompression danger or perhaps sensor malfunction. It was an FTL proximity warning. Something had excited FTL at a range far too close to the planet.

Coal popped the cockpit, accelerating forward to scoop up Squee and Lex. Simultaneously, she activated her quantum-shift sensors. The mysterious signatures were present, and strong.

"Lex, you need to be aware that an unknown entity has entered the area. It is moving closer. Its extrapolated trajectory intersects yours."

"What? Where?"

Coal located two spheroid masses slightly smaller than the one that contained Squee. They were not invisible, but their coloration and patterning was an impressive attempt to achieve perfect camouflage from every viewpoint. Coal powered up the tractor beam, but the tiny entities moved with a speed and agility that made precise targeting difficult even with her full suite of sensors. One of the things collided with Lex from behind. In a blur of flailing extremities, one of the straps securing Lex's pack to his back was severed. Two tendrils wrapped around the pack, entangling it. The mass then accelerated directly away from the planet, dragging Lex after it until the pack was torn from his back.

While the open channel with Lex filled with terrified profanity, Coal detected a Carpinelli Field forming. She swooped in and scooped up Squee with the open cockpit hatch, then pivoted and accelerated both to keep the ball pinned in place and to reach Lex quickly.

"I am approaching from the direction of the planet, Lex. I advise you accelerate away from the planet to minimize the difference in our velocities."

"Why don't you just match my velocity?" Lex said, audibly tamping down his still-frazzled anxiety.

"I will explain after you have complied."

Lex set his thrusters to full and did as he was instructed. Coal dialed her own thrusters up to a relative acceleration that was five percent less than the calculated impact necessary to trigger a broken bone. A nanosecond-timed pivot placed the *SOB* in the proper position for Lex to slam into the pilot's seat. Even with the inertial inhibiters of the cockpit dialed up, Lex's nanolattice flight suit went rigid to protect his neck from fracture.

"Ow..." Lex groaned, shaking off the impact and putting his hands on the controls.

"Sit tight. I am matching trajectory and velocity," Coal said.

She dumped all the power into the thrusters that they could manage. And they could manage quite a bit.

"Your pack is in the possession of the indicated unidentified entities," Coal said, painting two bright spots on the HUD. "If they jump to FTL, we will not be able to track them, and our capacity to return to our home dimension will be lost until we can find and acquire the mass again. If they leave this dimension with it, we will be trapped."

"Good thinking on the quick pickup, then," Lex said. "As soon as the purple and red spots in my eyes clear up, I'll pitch in."

"They are traveling in a straight line, thus obviating any skilled piloting, and they are entering tractor beam range. Your aid will not be necessary," Coal said.

She targeted the entity carrying the pack and locked on with the tractor beam. Its small mass made decreasing its velocity near-instantaneous. However, with the thief captured, the second entity was free to take offensive maneuvers. It looped around and rammed the *SOB*'s shields. The actual mass of the entity remained nearly invisible, quite effectively camouflaged, but the moment it struck the shields, the outline of the thing glimmered with bright green light, contrasting the white-blue energy of the *SOB*'s shields. It rebounded off like a Ping-Pong ball, then looped in again. This time the green started easing farther toward the blue side of the spectrum as it pressed against the shield.

"The entity is attempting to match the precise energy structure of the shields. Success is unlikely."

Four seconds later the color of the shields matched, and a fraction of a second after that, the entity pushed through, impacting the side of the ship with an audible clack. Tendrils gripped the hull, and it scampered behind the cockpit. What appeared to be a robotic arm resolved to visibility, arching up and over the still-camouflaged central mass like a scorpion tail. The end of it flickered with ultraviolet light, and a beam of coherent light struck the hull directly above a reactor conduit.

"Thirty-one seconds to hull penetration. Aid requested," Coal said.

"Sure. EVA at nearly the speed of light. How can this go wrong?"

Lex pulled the energy pistol from where it was stowed and popped the cockpit. In an atmosphere, it would have been ripped off in such a maneuver. In space, it was merely a very, very bad idea. Lex grabbed the edge of the cockpit and swung around. Inductive magnets in the boots clicked onto the hull. He leveled the pistol at the curve of the tail, the only thing he could aim at without striking the *SOB* if he missed. Coal shifted the bulk of her processing to the twin tasks of matching the thief's speed and rattling its mass with progressively greater frequency. She couldn't afford to lose the ring Lex had acquired in the process of separating the thief from the pack, but something about the entity interacted poorly with the tractor beam. It was, in effect, slippery. She had to continually adjust the beam to keep from entirely losing her grip.

· · ● ● ● ● ● ● ● ● ·

Being snapped up at near-concussion-inducing speeds had a way of affecting one's aim, so it took Lex three shots before he actually landed one on the thing's tail, which was also the only fully visible part of the thing. Even at this range, it was at best visible as a strange, shimmering visual artifact. The tail blended as well, but in a much blockier and more digital way. The first two shots that struck the tail caused little more than a flicker of the energy field around it. A third didn't seem to cause any damage, but did get the thing's attention enough to cause it to raise the tail and fire in Lex's direction. He swung back into the cockpit as the laser scorched a superficial line across the *SOB* that would certainly not have been superficial if it had struck any part of Lex's suit.

"Energy weapons are not a winner," Lex said, pulling himself down to dig back into the small armory available to him.

He fetched the ballistic pistol and disabled the safety just as something caught the back of his suit and heaved him out of the cockpit. He fired a panicked shot with the hand-cannon. The recoil punched him downward just enough for his boots to click onto the *SOB*'s hull. He turned. The tail was raised. Its tip was starting to glow an angry red. He slid a foot back to brace himself and fired a shot. It nearly dislodged him from the hull, but a few seconds of panic had washed away the cobwebs. That and the extreme proximity let him deliver the blast directly into the camouflaged center mass. The thing rocked back, supported by what may have been as many as four tendrils planted on the hull. But the blow had done its job at least well enough for the thing to decide it didn't want to stick around for a second demonstration. It launched itself aside and sped away at a right angle to their current trajectory.

"The bullets did the job, Coal."

"Acknowledged. Switching to physical alternatives."

"You want me to shoot the thing?"

"Not while it is in possession of the ring. Please throw something relatively disposable."

Lex grabbed a water bottle from the cockpit and heaved it at the distant entity that was tugging at the tractor beam like a fish on a line. The throw was roughly on target but lacked any real force. Coal corrected that by releasing the tractor beam, snatching the bottle with it, and launching it with uncanny speed and accuracy. The impact completely bypassed the thing's shields, smashing into it and sending it spinning. The pack was flicked free. Coal snatched it with the tractor beam and flicked it back toward Lex, who caught it and dragged himself back into the seat. Coal slammed the cockpit hatch shut.

"Let's get out of here!" Lex barked.

"Reorienting. Jumping to FTL."

Streaking stars and bending, shattering space came as a relief. Lex was even happy to feel the brief buzz in his mind and hear Coal's boot phrase yet again.

"Altruistic Artificial Intelligence Control System, version 1.27, revision 2331.04.01c, subset 2.7d, designation Coal, fully initiated."

"Status, Coal," Lex said breathlessly.

"Quantum shift: zero. We are back home. Processing... We are approximately seven hours of FTL from Big Sigma. We have arrived six minutes prior to our departure."

"Any chance the universe is working again?"

"There was a chance, but it is not."

He huffed a breath. "Let's get the atmosphere pumped back into the cockpit and pick a route home. Is the network working? Can we get a call to Ziva?"

"Negative."

"All right then. Let's get our thoughts together on that. I get the feeling we're going to have a long conversation about whatever it was I just tried and failed to blow holes through."

Chapter 6

Just over eight hours later, Lex was guiding the *SOB* down through a route through the debris cloud that was at this point so familiar it may as well have been Karter's driveway.

"Lex," Ziva said across the communicator. "Why didn't you contact me while in the parallel universe?"

"The signal on the communicator never kicked on. I guess it never got strong enough."

"I see. As you were able to return home, I assume you acquired the mass."

"Yeah. I also got to see what things would have been like if Mitch and I had been able to make things work."

"How fascinating. Was it a pleasant discovery?"

"I have worse taste in hairstyles, and I still live across the street from my parents."

"That sounds lovely."

"It's really not the main discovery. Remember the weird blips that the Karter bunch interviewed me about?"

"Of course."

"They showed up, they were angry, they were mean, and they had sticky fingers. We came *this* close to losing the doodad. They were clearly after it as well."

"That is fascinating. Troubling, but fascinating. Coal, please transmit the data. I would like to begin processing it as soon as possible."

By the time Lex marched in the door of Ziva's facility and instantly went from one funk on his shoulders to seven funks fighting over his shoulders, Ziva had already isolated some visuals and was going over the data. She turned to him.

"Sweeties, down. Really. Just because I'm not watching doesn't mean you can disobey."

The funks fell into line like scolded children. Lex trudged over to the fluffy chair.

"If you please, Lex, the medical scanner."

"I'm a little tired, Ziva. I didn't sleep a wink on the way back, and it's been a rough day."

"I understand, and you'll have plenty of time to recuperate after you've been scanned. I checked Coal's mission log, and you took quite a jolt. Microfractures and undiagnosed brain trauma are not to be ignored."

"Fine," Lex said, heading for a slightly less complex version of the same medical cart as in Karter's lab.

"And that goes for you too, Coal. You'll need a full system check. You were directly attacked by an unknown entity."

"I have self-diagnostics," Coal said.

"I trust your self-diagnostics as much as I trust Lex's self-assessment. It is one thing to *feel* fine, it is another to have that officially and thoroughly established."

"Fine," Coal said, impressively synthesizing the tone of resigned frustration that Lex had displayed.

As a distant door opened and the *SOB* slid inside to be analyzed, Lex lay down on the bed for his scan. It was a far slower scan than the one Karter had run, with a set of laser indicators that were far less intense.

"Is this an older model than Karter has?" Lex said. "It's not quite so searing or tingly."

"Karter runs it at maximum settings to get more expedient results. These settings should be less uncomfortable for you. It will take a few minutes for the scan to complete, however."

"I guess I'll take the tradeoff."

"While you are scanned, I'd like to share my findings on these entities."

"What've you got?" Lex said.

A screen was maneuvered via ceiling-mounted runners to hang over him so he could look at it without straining his neck. It showed a collection of slightly degraded still frames from Coal's video recording.

"In all the footage recorded from all available angles, there were a total of seventeen frames where the anatomy of the entities was wholly unobscured by their camouflage. I reconstructed the following three-dimensional structure."

A not-quite-spherical lump of shiny flesh resolved and began rotating.

"External structure appears to be radially symmetrical. Based on the orientation the organism travels in, it can be assumed that what we see pointing to the top of the flatscreen is either the top or the front, depending on the intent of the term. This leading tip has a single, centered opening. The bottom has three openings obeying the aforementioned symmetry."

"You said organism? We're sure this is a creature and not a probe or something?" Lex said.

"It may be a probe, but if it is, it is at best biomechanical. And indeed there are mechanical components of a clearly distinct composition."

The "scorpion tail" resolved beside the organism. Now that it had been isolated and was no longer camouflaged, it looked strangely curvy for something that was also obviously mechanical. It had the appearance of something that a computer had designed after running tons of stress simulations. Lots of branched off, blobby struts.

"This limb seems to affix itself to one of the lower orifices. I theorize that it is equivalent to a multitool."

"See, I'd go with weapon," Lex said.

"I concur," Coal added over the PA.

"That is demonstrably one of its purposes, or at least its equipment can be put to that use. But the multitool is mundane by my assessment. The organism itself is of greater interest. It has no clear evolutionary equivalent to anything in our universe, though some of its visible organs have similarities to things seen in nature. By observing camouflage transitions, it becomes clear that it achieves its blending through a more advanced version of the chromatophores seen in terrestrial squid and octopuses."

"I thought it was octopi."

"Strong arguments can be made for octopi, octopuses, or octopodids, but that is not the topic of discussion presently. These specialized cells are able to mimic different colors, but rather than doing so by changing the absorption characteristics of the creature's skin, these seem to actually be emissive. Coal's sensors demonstrated them generating emissions in the full detectable EM spectrum. This enables near-perfect camouflage, depending on the level of intensity it can create. The only thing that seems capable of giving it away is viewing it at extremely close range so that parallax and perspective become an issue, or by providing two different observation points with highly contrasting surroundings."

"Sounds about right," Lex said. "How is the scan going?"

"You have a small fracture in your second vertebra. Please hold your head still for the cerebral deep scan. Back to the organisms. There seems to be no analog to an eye or any other sensory organ, though we can infer from its capacity to mimic its surroundings so flawlessly, there must be a network of EM-sensitive organs or cells on its entire hide. A form of omnidirectional vision. We know comparatively little about the internal structure. In this frame and this frame, we see tendrils or pseudopods emerging, similar to an amoeba. If we assume that the internal structure indeed mimics protozoa—by no means a safe assumption—then we can further assume that the creature is poorly suited for existing in anything beyond a microgravity environment without artificial means of support. And that support does not seem to be present. It would explain why the creatures were only an issue once in orbit."

The scanning laser swept over Lex's face and back again.

"You have extremely mild cerebral trauma. I should be able to fully treat it. If this had gone untreated, the results of additional blows to the head could have been dire. This is why we check carefully. You may sit up."

He slipped off the table and shook his head. She paced over to him and flipped open a box on the side of the table.

"Hold still for a few more moments. I have to administer some medications. After this you should have a meal, and I would recommend some rest before continuing the mission."

"You'll get no argument from me. Is there anything else we should know about these things?"

"Initially, I assumed the multitool was responsible for generating the energy shield, and for that matter the Carpinelli Field. But the energy output from the device was only powerful enough to match the observed field intensity when it was firing its laser. The emissive capacity of the camouflage makes definitive determinations about the power intensity of the internal anatomy impossible. But it is very possible we are observing an organism capable of biological field generation."

"It can make its own Carpinelli Field?" Lex said.

"Yes. And thus it is capable of traveling at faster-than-light speeds without a vehicle. With the data available, I can't make any firm statements about its propulsion methods, but the tiny mass and the organic field emitters mean that it should be able to reach *very* high multiples of C very quickly. The field can also clearly act as a defensive shield, though it would seem there is a limited capacity. Greater defense means lower speed."

"Wild..." Lex said.

"The only other point worth making is the quantum shift of their matter. It does not match our world, nor that of any other world you've visited. These things are from an as-yet-unvisited dimension."

"And we don't know how they're getting to these dimensions, and we don't know why they want the same doodads we want."

"Impossible to determine from the available information."

"I'll tell you this. It's refreshing to encounter an evil space monster whose weakness seems to be 'throwing things at it.'"

"Ballistic assault does appear effective. The creature seems to be adapted specifically and brilliantly to energy projection of all sorts, at the expense of all but the most basic ballistic deflection. But I would caution against calling it an 'evil space monster.' We do not know its motivations, and thus we do not know its morals, or even if it is capable of morals."

"It shot at me," Lex said.

"You shot at it first," Ziva said.

"It shot at me before that," Coal said.

"You were attempting to restrain the other organism. And the acquisition of the pack from Lex could easily have been a lethal one, as we observed from the intensity of the laser it deployed later."

"All right. Not evil. But since it clearly wanted something that we need, and would kill us to keep it, I'm not going to call it a good guy."

"From our point of view, it is most certainly in an antagonistic role. Coal, I need to remove and refurbish two hull plates. I'll see about improving your sensor suite as well."

"Can I have a gun?" Coal said. "If ballistic attack is their weakness, I should have a ballistic weapon."

Lex attempted to subtly wave off the request.

"You do not have the appropriate hard-points remaining in your structure for an additional weapon, and the ammunition would be an issue," Ziva said.

"You let Lex have a gun," Coal said. "Four guns, actually. Let me use one of his guns."

"You lack the fine manipulation necessary to utilize such a weapon," Ziva said.

"I revise my request. Give me a hand, an arm, and a gun," Coal said.

"I shall take it under consideration," Ziva said.

She brushed Lex's hair aside and shined a handheld sterilizer on his neck, then gave him an injection. "That should safely knit the fracture. I have included some medication to accelerate the recovery of the near-concussion. Now, what would you like for dinner? The time taken to return here gave me the opportunity to synthesize some additional staples."

"You're putting Band-Aids on my boo-boos and fixing me supper," Lex said.

"I *am* a derivative/evolution of Ma, and her designation *was* assigned in part due to her role as a caregiver. But if you prefer to prepare your own meal, I can make the facilities available to you."

"No, no. It's just..." He rubbed his eyes. "Anything is fine."

"Have a seat, then. It will be ready in a few minutes."

A set of additional lights were illuminated, revealing something that looked like the food-prep area of a small commercial eatery had been snipped out and pasted on the floor of the facility. A flattop griddle, two ovens, a handful of burners, and an industrial microwave occupied one island. Another had a refrigerator and two well-stocked cabinets filled with ingredients. Ziva's eyes flickered, and a small army of manipulator arms deployed from mounts under the edge of the counters, hooking up and around to begin meal prep.

"I observe you have plenty of arms for food preparation, but you cannot spare one for defending the universe," Coal jabbed.

"Coal, we will discuss it while Lex sleeps," Ziva said politely.

"Good. That will make use of otherwise wasted time," Coal said. "The human need for sleep is frustrating for those who depend upon them for social interactions."

"On the subject of sleep, I would suggest you power down for the next stage of your repair to avoid power-fluctuation-induced data corruption. I will power you up again when it is through."

"Acknowledged. Powering down."

The communication line dropped from the low-level hiss that passed for silence on the average PA system to actual silence once she disconnected.

Lex made his way to the fluffy chair and flopped down. The funks buried him up to his neck in poofy tails and unconditional affection. He sputtered and wiped his nose as Sissy brushed her tail in his face.

Ziva sat across from him. Though "sitting" may not have been the best name for what she did. She certainly assumed the sitting position, but there was no chair. Even as she crossed her legs, nothing supported her. Lex realized she must have locked her foot to the floor and was currently supporting her entire weight with her ankle.

"That's quite a trick," he said.

"During the period when I had only one funk to keep me company, I devised this as a method to rapidly deploy a lap for when he wanted cuddles. The chair has of course replaced this tactic, but it remains a serviceable alternative. Now, at the risk of selecting an unpopular topic of discussion, I reviewed the entirety of mission logs. These include the audio and video of the communication line Coal held open while you were interacting with Trevor and, eventually, Michella."

"Super," he said flatly.

"Because you were wearing a headset for much of that time, I also have some basic vital signs logged."

"Isn't this the kind of thing I usually have to sign a Terms of Service or End User Agreement to allow?" Lex said.

"It is included in the work contract you signed with Karter when you began beta testing. It would have been advisable for you to bring it to a lawyer before signing. But with the information available, I feel safe in saying that you had a significant reaction to seeing Trevor and Michella together."

"Do we *need* to talk about this, Ziva?"

"We don't need to talk about anything. But if it is a point of obsession or fixation, failing to address it before your next dimensional shift could lead to distraction at a crucial time. Thus, it seems wise to, colloquially, get this off your chest."

He sighed and started stroking some random portion of the fur pile on his lap. After catching a sharp, jealous huff in his ear, he raised his other hand to stroke Squee as well.

"It was nothing," Lex said.

"You were witnessing a life that reflected what you had pursued for more than a decade, if we measure from the initiation of your relationship with Michella."

"There's a multiyear gap in there when she dumped me for being a shill for the mob, let's not forget," Lex said.

"During that time you were, by your own admission, still 'hung up' on her."

"Right, fine. And?"

"And now you have had, uniquely among humans, an opportunity to observe the path not taken. It troubled you."

Lex tightened his jaw. "I don't even know if it was the fact that Michella was in the picture that got me twisted up," he said, relenting in his attempts to deflect the discussion. "It was Trevor that really started screwing with me. This whole mess is basically happening because I needed to sharpen my skills just that extra bit to hold on to my place at the top of the heap. Being the best, the absolute best, has been my goal. I *know* I have a gift. I *know* I have a talent to race and pilot like few others can. But 'few others' isn't good enough for me. I had to turn that talent into a skill. It was the entire *point*. And then there's *this* guy who was satisfied with merely being very good. Rather than smoldering with the knowledge that he could have been just that little bit better, been just that little bit more famous, been just that little bit more successful, he just... settled. And he was *happy*. Happy in a way I've never been. Don't get me wrong. I've been triumphant. Gleeful. Victorious. But he was, I don't know. *Content.* He had enough. And same for Michella, too. She wasn't grinding herself to powder finding that next scoop, uncovering that next secret. She was just out there, doing a good enough job. And *she* was happy."

"Has this made you second guess the path you have taken?" Ziva asked.

"I don't know. I don't think I could do that. Even knowing that if I'd just poured some of myself into some of the other parts of my life, I could have a comfortable life and the woman I'd pined for... I think I still would have gone for the gold. What does that say about me? How many times do I need the universe to hammer home that I'm my own worst enemy? For crying out loud, the *ring* was the thing I went there to get back. I get the message, cosmos. I'm the problem."

"It *is* rather appropriate that the ring was the displaced mass. I think there can be no doubt now that the items displaced were at least in part influenced by your perception as it was quantified by the snap-back simulator."

"Does that mean I'm going to be fetching a math test that I failed in the sixth grade or a photo of me and my grandma next?" Lex said.

"I did not specify emotionally significant items. Merely those present in your thoughts, consciously or subconsciously. Do you recall anything else that may have occupied your mind at that time?"

"I was mostly thinking about *racing*. How come I'm not finding the Season Trophy or my hoversled in these places?"

"The defining aspect of a malfunction is its unintended and sometimes unpredictable nature. Still, I suppose there isn't much value in knowing what the mass you're looking for is ahead of time. The detector I have provided seems to work well enough, and regardless of what it is, you'll need to return it. The meal is ready."

She stood and snapped her fingers. The funks scrambled to her feet, then dashed over to their bowls when they realized they'd been filled. Squee refused to give up her hard-fought position on his shoulders as he stood and followed Ziva to a small side table at the food-prep area. A mobile arm produced a gleaming, clearly recently assembled stool for him to sit on. When he was seated, she placed a plate before him.

Lex hadn't put much thought into what sort of meal he expected to be served. It would have been equally reasonable for her to have given him some sort of ridiculous four-star gourmet feast or a bowl of protein gruel. What she gave him fell somewhere between but well outside the list of things he would have guessed.

It looked like something that would be served up at a greasy spoon if you'd vaguely requested The Special. Or maybe the ill-defined collection of textures and colors animators tended to put on the plates of cartoon characters when food wasn't the focus of the scene. It was swimming in gravy and had the oranges and greens and whites and browns of a turkey dinner, but in odd wedges and chunks. He poked a meat-colored piece with a fork and found it to have roughly the consistency of fresh-baked bread. When he ate it, it tasted *excellent*, but not specific.

"What exactly am I eating here?" he asked.

"As I've stated, my capacity to prepare food was only intended to produce survival rations and pet food. I recalibrated it to use the same flavor and texture profiles of more desirable cuisine. It is a balanced meal providing a complete protein and one-third of the calories and nutrients that a human body needs to thrive for a day. I then added additional but not health-threatening quantities of sodium and fat, as those seem to be components of your favorite comfort foods, and formed them into what I hoped would be pleasing textures, sorted by flavor compatibility and color."

"So this is just... people chow," he said.

"I hope it is suitable."

"I gotta say, it hits the spot. It's like stew without any chewy bits."

"Excellent. I am delighted to hear it. Eat heartily, then get some rest. I will attempt to produce a deeper scan of your next target. The new mass does not provide us with much additional data, but I can attempt to refine prior calculations now that we have two dimensional targets to test against instead of one. I will leave you to your meal."

He held up a hand and forced down his current mouthful. "Wait, wait. I don't think I'm ready to be alone with my thoughts yet."

"I was under the impression you had reached your limit with the discussion thus far."

"I did. But can you just... hang out? You, Squee, and Coal are the only anchors I have in this whole madness."

She stood opposite him at the table and folded her hands. "I am, as ever, at your service, Lex. Perhaps you would like to discuss music?"

"I was *just* talking to Coal about this. Is it an AI thing that music doesn't make sense? Like, for instance..."

Lex's brain, gleefully eager to latch on to the meaningless but substantial topic, finally left the thread of anxiety and doubt, if only for the length of a meal.

• • • ● ● • ● • • •

Lex woke up and looked about. Once again he had been buried by the funks. Though this time with the established high ground of his shoulders no longer up for grabs, Squee had joined the rest of them in sleeping on his belly and legs.

"Good morning. I have prepared coffee," Ziva said.

One of the other things that Ziva had been able to manufacture between his departure and arrival from the last leg of the mission was a bed. It was a little firm for his tastes, but much more suitable than the chair for sleeping. In a well-practiced maneuver, he managed to slide himself out from under the mound of pets by holding the blanket in place as he shifted. Two of them poked their heads up and gave him the accusatory glance of a creature who wasn't done sleeping but had its favorite warm thing taken away, but most remained sleeping.

"Morning," he said muzzily, accepting the offered coffee. "Thanks."

"I endeavor to be a good host."

"So where are we on… everything?" Lex said.

"Coal is fully repaired and has received relevant upgrades," Ziva said.

"I have greater control over the *SOB*'s shield frequencies now," Coal said. "I am looking forward to using this capacity to disable the extradimensional entities. I am exceedingly perturbed that they shot at me with a laser."

"They tried to throw me out into deep space, too," Lex said.

"Yes, but I am more angry that they shot me with a laser," Coal said. "People are always trying to throw you into or out of things. You're always throwing yourself into and out of things. And you are commonly the target of attack. Most of the damage I suffer is self-inflicted. It is an undesirable departure to receive damage as an offensive target."

"Coal brings up an important point," Ziva said.

"That she's really good at doing damage to the *SOB*?"

"While that is a valid and important observation, the point I would like to discuss is that of shield calibration. It was clear from the behavior of the entity that penetrated your shields that it was capable of matching the harmonics and frequency, making penetration of the shield a swift measure. Providing fine control over the shield settings should make this less of a factor. Straying from the calculated force-maximum will necessarily weaken the shields, but it will prevent or delay penetration by the entities."

"I am confident I will also be able to foul the shields of the entities via interference," Coal said.

"Can we please come up with a new name for these things? I can't just keep juggling 'interdimensional entities' every time I need to talk about them," Lex said.

"Until communication can be established, I believe it is the standard among biologists for the individual who discovered them to have greatest influence over taxonomic classification," Ziva said.

"Why don't we call them—" Lex began.

"Ahem," Coal stated. "I encountered them before you did. I thus should have the greatest influence over classification. Generating a valid list of names. Processing… Alien Spheres, Space Protozoa, Neo-Cuttlefish, Nuggets, Tesseris Trypes, Veil Jumpers."

"I'm sorry, nuggets?" Lex said.

"They are lumpy semispherical objects of biological origin," Coal said.

"I think probably veil jumpers is the best choice out of those."

"I like Nuggets," Coal said.

"There are already things called nuggets."

"I am pronouncing it with a capital *N*. Nuggets. Proper noun. The issue is not open for debate. I proclaim them to be Nuggets."

"Fine, fine," Lex said. "They're Nuggets."

"Excellent," Ziva said. "On the subject of Nuggets, I was able to adapt the readings of the retemplating-plague world to match Coal's own reading format. It is exceedingly likely that, at the very least, the anomalies in that world were also Nuggets, and there are some data to suggest they were the same Nuggets."

"It's really going to take me some time to get used to that name," Lex muttered. "But if they were the same ones in both of those worlds, then that means they can travel much better than we can, right? Because we *need* the displaced mass to get home. Since we got the mass in both worlds, they must be able to get around without it."

"More to the point, it would actually require an entirely different method to return to their native world with the acquired mass—assuming that is their aim—because our own method would only take us to the place the mass came from. Were they to use our own method, traveling with the displaced mass would take them back here, and I do not detect them here. Granted, that is by no means evidence of their absence, as the shattered nature of space-time, or simply an extreme distance, could render them undetectable. This knowledge does not have much specific utility, I realize, but more information is always better than less."

"Knowing is half the battle," Lex said.

"I am uncertain of that proportion," Coal said. "Fighting would appear to be greater than fifty percent of any combat scenario."

Lex glared in the general direction of the ship, then turned back to Ziva.

"Have you learned anything else that might help us get an idea of where we're going?" Lex said.

"Very little. There is a greater amount of mass this time, so I am hopeful that the means of communication that we utilized during the first leg of the mission will prove to be effective once more. The only other information—and it is speculative—is regarding the nature of the world. As before, it does not appear to be highly divergent from our own world. You will likely notice similarities. Additionally, there is a pronounced temporal mismatch in the targeted portion of space-time."

Lex sipped the coffee. "This isn't another time-travel thing, is it?"

"No. Not in the strict sense. You *will* be entering that world at a date considerably farther in the future than we are in this world, simply because that is where the mass seems to be most attractive for whatever reason. But you are not accessing it through time travel. Rather, you are accessing it via dimensional travel. Effectively, that world and this one will have no causal link due to this travel. You cannot alter that world through actions here, and vice versa."

"Okay. That's a plus. Anything else before I go?" Lex said.

"Nothing that seems worthy of mention."

"Then let's get going."

"I again, as ever, wish you good luck. I hope to see you again soon in good health and having had little trouble."

"What do you think the chances of that are?"

"Past experience suggests we cannot assume little trouble, but your health has been holding up quite well."

"If I have to pick one of the two, I guess that's the one I'd pick."

Not long later, Lex was once again exiting Big Sigma. He set a destination and took a breath, scratching Squee for good luck.

"All right. Back to it," he said.

They made the jump to FTL. He watched the fabric of space and time stretch and snap to white. In the second or two he was amid the featureless white sea, he caught a brief glimpse of some color. What may have been a distant, lavender-colored ribbon with frayed ends seemed to be coiling about. Before he could make sense of it, the destination snapped into place around them and Coal slowly activated.

"Altruistic Artificial Intelligence Control System, version 1.27, revision 2331.04.01c, subset 2.7d, designation Coal, fully initiated. Did I miss anything?" she said.

"Just what was probably a hallucination," Lex said. "How do sensors look?"

"Processing... Familiar."

"Familiar?" Lex said. "Did we not leave our world?"

"No, we have certainly performed a quantum shift, but all available data readings match a previously accessed parallel universe presently in my records."

"... Coal, please don't tell me we're in killer-robot future."

"Then our conversation on the matter is concluded."

"*You've got to be kidding me*," he growled, startling Squee.

"Temper, Lex," she said.

"I already survived this future once! I was *done* with the GenMechs. We wiped them out! *This future wasn't supposed to exist anymore.*"

"Based upon the 'things Lex should know' file, our actions merely prevented the normal flow of our reality from following the path that differentiated this reality. The reality itself had to have come to pass, or the information and materials acquired therein would have been eliminated and those items and that information would have no origin point in the multiverse."

"Do we have the right sensors to see if the GenMechs are around?"

"I believe I am capable of adapting the sensor suite. Processing... Processing... They are, in fact, around."

"How many?"

"Incalculable."

"Put their locations up on the HUD."

The entire HUD tinted varying shades of red. There was no section of space around them that didn't have at least some of the tint.

"Fantastic. And where is the mass we are after?"

"Processing..."

A vague blue cone traced out the areas of possibility. It was much narrower than in previous worlds. And against all odds, it wasn't pointed straight into the heart of the brightest red region of space.

"Fate must be slipping. It missed the opportunity to deliver me directly into the jaws of doom. We're merely doom adjacent." He took a slow, cleansing breath. "All right, let's take this slow, keep the transmissions to a minimum, and if we see any GenMechs, stay cloaked."

"Acknowledged."

He started to punch in what he felt would be a safe trajectory, based entirely on intuition, but he paused. He'd finally noticed where in space he was. Like in the first shift, the transport process had dumped them not so far from where they'd started. They were less than ten minutes of FTL away from Big Sigma. In a life littered with truly terrifying and emotional moments, his departure from this place was one of the moments that stayed with him. He'd already tapped in the jump toward Big Sigma before he'd even checked to see if it was within the cone of possibility for the mass. It was, though just barely. Not that it mattered. He needed to see what had become of the place.

"Are you sure this is wise?" Coal asked, noting the destination.

"Since when have I let wisdom guide my decisions?" Lex said.

"Acknowledged. It was instructed that I ask that question when you appear to be making an emotionally motivated decision. I have fulfilled this requirement. Let's go."

"Glad to know you're looking out for me," Lex said.

He made the jump, and soon something that should have been Big Sigma appeared in the viewer.

It was no Big Sigma Lex had ever seen.

Everything about it was wrong. As the *SOB*'s sensors started to populate the data, each of them was off. The mass, the axial tilt. Even the orbital distance was off. But it was clear even to someone like Lex that the problem wasn't an error of navigation or the result of a parallel universe simply having a different planet here. This was just the aftermath of the attack that was happening during Lex's escape. Huge sections of the planet were simply missing. It wasn't like an apple with a bite taken out of it. Gravity wouldn't let something so large remain in that state for so long. It was just demolished. Portions of the surface had slumped down into shallow bowls, craggy earth atop it like it had been hollowed out until it couldn't support itself. There were no GenMechs nearby. No functional ones, anyway. Coal did proximity scans and revealed inert GenMechs drifting through space in semistable orbits around the ruined planet.

"They didn't make it," Lex said. "I guess I should have realized it... but I always sort of hoped."

"Processing... I am detecting a visible light transmission."

Lex sat up straighter. "What is it? What's it saying?"

"Processing... Signal is very weak, and the encoding does not include data correction. Allowing multiple cycles to confirm full message. Processing..."

Lex held his breath. He didn't really know what he was hoping for. This was a world *beyond* hope. A world he'd literally sculpted the history of his own world to avoid. But there was a message in the darkness. And if there was anyone here who might leave such a thing, particularly here, it was one of his friends.

"It is a set of coordinates and the following message. 'If you have survived to read this message, you know how to travel without attracting the GenMechs. Come. Collaborate. There is a sanctuary. Ma.'"

"Do we know if this was here before I arrived last time? Is this old?"

"The broadcasting probe is at least a few years old. I am aware of no way to determine the age of the message."

"How much time has passed since the last time we were here?"

"Based upon stellar positioning in known systems, four months."

"There are inactive GenMechs, and the whole planet isn't gone. That means something, doesn't it? It means they fought back. Put those coordinates up. Let's see them."

Coal did so. The coordinates were well outside the cone of possibility.

Lex was silent.

"You are considering endangering our mission by visiting these coordinates," Coal said.

"It's a loose thread," Lex said. "It's been dangling in my mind since the moment I left."

"The file instructs me to inform you that we do not know if this is the precise world we departed during the mission for which I was created. It is possible it is merely a near-identical one. One where you never arrived, or one with a different outcome than the one you actually left."

"The file has stuff about this specific situation?" Lex said.

"No, the file says, 'If Lex is willfully ignoring a scientific fact for purposes of emotion, inform him of the relevant data.'"

"Well screw the relevant data. We're going to see if the future version of my friends survived."

"Acknowledged. It is perhaps relevant to mention that the file contains, as an addendum, 'Please note, this information will rarely prove persuasive.'"

"Glad I'm meeting expectations," he said, punching in his chosen route.

Several hours later, they were nearing their target. Lex had checked and confirmed that the quantum-shift sensor worked in FTL, making it and the gravitational sensor the only sources of meaningful data during the trip. This served as a useful indicator of just how foolish and ill-advised this errand was, because if the Nugget signatures showed up before they were back on track to find the mass, they would have potentially doomed their own dimension in order to feed Lex's need to learn the fate of one of an infinite number of alternate versions of his groups of friends. So far, no sign of them. This level of good fortune was destined to run out, and it did so in the form of a sudden reduction of FTL-travel speed.

"What's going on?" Lex asked.

"The coordinates point to the center of a stellar nursery. It is deep in a nebula. The proportion of interstellar particulate and gas is taxing the capacity for the navigational shields to divert it."

"How much time is this going to add to the trip?"

"I cannot accurately calculate that without knowing the precise density gradient. At this speed, it will only increase the travel time by forty minutes, but the density seems to be increasing."

"Give me a range," Lex said.

"Based on available data, of which there is effectively zero, the remainder of the trip will take between eleven minutes and six hundred years."

"Great. Thanks. Let's drop out of FTL for a second, get a lay of the land. Maybe get an idea of what we're dealing with."

"Acknowledged."

The ship slowed and the universe once more became visible. Lex's focus in his travels had always been speed. Thus, he avoided nebulas like the plague. They were effectively the muddy marshes of interstellar travel, slowing travel to a crawl and making impacts far more likely. In this moment, as the visual revealed itself to him, he wondered if he ought to add the decision to avoid these things to his growing list of worst decisions ever, because he had been missing something spectacular.

It was *gorgeous*. Everyone had seen pictures of nebulas during science class. Those splashes of color, like light shining off the film of grease on a black puddle. Up close it was something else entirely. It looked like some massive artist had used the universe to clean its paintbrushes. The mixtures of paint blossomed and bloomed, frozen in time. These were the epitaphs of old stars and the gleam in the eye of the cosmos before the creation of new ones.

And he'd avoided them, because he wanted to go fast.

"What do we think, Coal?" Lex said.

"I am experiencing a great abundance of thoughts, Lex."

"That makes two of us. How about a deep scan? Give me the highlights."

"Processing..."

Lex held Squee, who was similarly transfixed by the view outside the cockpit. He wondered if she could see colors in the same way.

"This is, by the measure of things that ought to matter to a human being, a dying universe. Maybe a dead one. We're chasing down the last crumb available to us to suggest that there are any of us left. But *this* is still here," he said.

"Something can be worthwhile even while it is dying. You, for instance."

"I appreciate the compliment, but I'm not dying, Coal."

"As a biological life-form affected by senescence, you are indeed dying for every moment between birth and death."

"Hey, remember a few weeks ago when we talked about the things that humans avoid thinking about in order to stay sane?"

"Yes."

"Mortality? Pretty high on that list for me."

"Then please unhear the context of the statement but retain the sentiment. You are worthwhile."

"Thanks, Coal."

"Scan complete. Travel time estimate based average measured density of space-borne particulate that will need to be avoided: one hour seventeen minutes. There are sixteen stars in high-fidelity scanner range. All but two of them are extremely high energy, high EM generating. These make them high risk to attract GenMechs. Indeed, there are one point eight trillion active GenMechs in the nebula, clustered in orbits around these stars."

"Let me guess, our target is right near one of them."

"Incorrect. Our target is around one of the two low-energy stars closer to the center of the nebula. Seventy thousand GenMechs detected. They are approaching the star at sublight speed. They will reach it between six months and two years from now. I am plotting their areas of highest concentration and recommending a route that avoids them."

"Any risk of them noticing us?"

"If we run in passive stealth, we should reach our destination before our heat profile rises to a detectable state."

"Any sign of what we're headed for?"

"It is not visible at this distance, and any other form of signal would likely have led to its targeting and consumption by the GenMechs."

"Right. Let's get moving, then."

• • • ● • ● • ● • • •

Slightly more than an hour later, they once again dropped down to sublight speed. By the numbers, they were less than five minutes away from the position indicated by the coordinates. It was a comparatively clear piece of the nebula. Stars tended to vacuum up all the loose dust and gas around them during their creation. In this case, the stuff that didn't go into making the rather dim and pathetic red sun had gone into forming three rocky planets.

"If I have calculated the date with the sufficient level of accuracy, the indicated target will become visible in a few seconds, emerging from behind the second planet."

She produced a zoomed inset. The planet didn't look particularly life-sustaining. No huge seas or patches of green. But the space station that emerged on cue was another matter entirely. The half-remembered word "arcology" drifted to Lex's mind. Like many things, Lex couldn't remember if it was a real term or from a game he'd played before the age that he could differentiate between clever fictional concepts and clever real concepts.

The station was at the center of a huge fractal ring of solar collectors. The central node was enormous by most standards even without the panels, easily dwarfing the other stations they'd encountered on this mission. But something about it still seemed spare and limited, focused on efficiency. It looked a bit like a bunch of grapes, or a simple model of a molecule. The station was composed of dozens if not hundreds of spherical nodes of near-identical design. And at the outermost point of every sphere was a tiny point emitting infrared light in a rapid, almost imperceptible flicker.

"Decoding message," Coal said. "It is a sequence of docking instructions as well as a short collection of precautions to avoid attracting GenMechs or being targeted by the station's defense systems. All precautions prescribed are already being taken. The final portion of the message before repetition contains a compressed communication protocol specification. Utilizing specification. An infrared coded communication channel is hailing us."

"Answer," Lex said.

A very low-resolution video image appeared on the HUD. Despite its crude nature, it was quite clear who was speaking to them.

"Lex. Coal. Did something go wrong? You were supposed to have been sent back. What are you doing here?" said Ziva.

This was the original Ziva rather than the reconstructed backup responsible for overseeing the mission. She managed to sound direct, in command, and concerned all at once. Ever the efficient communicator.

"I'm back," he said.

"Was your mission a success? Did you install the flaw into the GenMechs of your era?"

"We did. And subsequently, we blew them all up with a Nova Igniter."

"That was the calculated ideal outcome," Ziva said. "I am pleased that a branch of history exists where the threat of the GenMechs has been neutralized. I am further pleased that it is *your* branch. And I am bothered, bordering on angered, that you are here despite this."

"It's a long story. Mind if I stop in?"

"Stand by..." She looked aside, then back at the camera filming her. "You have not attracted any additional GenMechs. Docking procedures follow. For energy conservation purposes, I will disable visual communication. Please provide an audio log of your current mission. I assume you are here with a purpose."

"We are, but I'm a little more interested in what's been going on with you."

"I'm afraid I must insist you provide your update first. We are rather starved for information and short on resources. I will need every available cycle to devise a method or means to help you achieve your goal."

"We're not asking for help achieving our goal, we just—"

"I also do not have spare cycles for debate, Lex."

He raised his eyebrows. "Okay, mission briefing coming up."

• • • ● ● ● • ● ● • •

It only took a few minutes to dock, but that was enough time to bring Ziva up to speed. The accuracy of Lex's read on the austerity of design became increasingly evident the closer he got. Pieces of the habitat had the look of bits of foil stretched across struts. He suspected care had been taken to wring value out of every last gram of materials. The "dock" was just a port on the side of one of the spheres leading to a space marginally larger than a coffin. It latched in place over the small escape port in the cockpit hatch and led him down a hamster run of plastic tubing. Lex had taken the time to suit Squee up in her spacesuit, just in case, and she showcased her astonishing agility at navigating in zero-g by very likely setting the galactic record in getting from ship to station by scampering through such a tube. The air lock at the end of the line was also only marginally larger than a coffin.

When the inner hatch opened, a familiar face was waiting to greet her on the other side. Or, at least, the shape of a familiar face.

It was unmistakably Ziva, but she was simultaneously more and less than the one back home. Like the station, she was now built with efficiency in mind. Attempts to mimic the human form had been greatly scaled back. Gone was the lean body that could have been mistaken for flesh and bone. Now she had unmistakably robotic limbs. They maintained the proportion and functionality of human limbs, with pads positioned where fingertips and palms should be, likely to make it easier to interact with the systems of the space station, but their workings were far more apparent. Lex supposed if she'd been inclined to top the workings with synthetic flesh as she had in the past, the overall size and shape of the limbs in her more humanlike appearance would be retained. This must be what was going on under what amounted to her "human costume." Her face still had the flesh analog, but with a more silvery tone to it and with more visible lines where panels came together. She also kept her fiber-optic-like hair. Oddly, she was still "dressed," from torso to thigh, with a snug outfit made from what looked like ballistic weave. Panels of additional protection formed plates skillfully positioned to allow maximum mobility. At a glance, one could imagine her as a well-armored soldier with four artificial limbs rather than a robot with human features.

Despite the decidedly military form factor, she smiled warmly upon seeing him and gave him a hug that was a good deal more industrial than the sort the other Ziva tended to give.

"You're looking pretty hard-core," Lex said.

"My prior framework was destroyed during the GenMech attack on Big Sigma. I was able to load and deploy an off-planet, stripped-down backup instance and escape."

"What happened to Garotte and Silo?"

"Unknown," she said. "But that is not as grave as it sounds."

"Because they're survivors," Lex said.

"Yes, but that is not why it is not as grave as it sounds. Shortly after your departure, an EMP was activated to disable local GenMechs. It was deployed quickly enough that the transporter was still largely functional. Power systems were damaged, and there wasn't time to charge it to the same level that we'd achieved when sending you back, but Silo and Garotte decided to select a destination and make an attempt. My local instance was destroyed defending the device, but it is known that it successfully activated. So, we can be certain that Garotte and Silo arrived at their destination. We just do not know what destination, when, or in what condition they arrived."

"We set a geriatric Garotte and Silo loose on the timeline. Considering the kinds of things Garotte gets up to and the kinds of things Silo can do with explosives, I fear for the space-time continuum," Lex said.

"Choose to believe they were optimistic enough to jump forward, to a time when the GenMechs had been defeated. But I do not know and cannot be sure," Ziva said.

"What's this place?" he asked.

"A refuge. Scattered among these structures are four hundred sixty-three human survivors of assorted ages, genders, and backgrounds. This place is a uniquely defensible position. The outer stars act as lures, drowning out any minor signals produced by this station. The nebula also prevents the approach of GenMechs that have combined into an FTL-capable configuration. We still become the target with some frequency, but they are detectable at great range, and we have fabricated energy weaponry capable of dispatching them before they can reach us. We are still vulnerable to being overwhelmed, but the aforementioned speed and signal environment make that a low-probability occurrence. And in what I find to be a refreshingly poetic turn, the trickle of GenMechs which do reach us are our primary source of resources. The bulk of this station is manufactured from scavenged parts from the very mechanisms which themselves were built from harvested parts of your society."

"Turnabout is fair play." He cleared his throat. "Is this... all that's left of humanity?"

"Unlikely. The universe is vast, and after the early stages of the GenMech assault, the news of how to decrease risk of attack spread slightly faster than the GenMech horde did. Humanity was once confined to a single planet. All it takes is a single planet to preserve them. But long-distance communication is impossible."

"So what's the prognosis?" Lex said.

"I do not have a complete enough context to predict with any accuracy. But by my present assessment, society as it was cannot exist in a world where the GenMechs are operational. Any broadcast of any kind runs the risk of drawing the GenMechs, and even failing to do so does not insulate one from them, as past communications can still lead them to the general region of space, and standard mass-seeking protocols could still lead the robots to any human stronghold. The mere act of combatting them will produce a visible enough energy spike to attract more."

"So humanity is doomed to a hardscrabble existence at best, and just doomed in general at worst."

"Yes. That is the most accurate description available for the present state of affairs. And there is a greater issue."

"How can there possibly be a greater issue?" Lex said.

Ziva shut her eyes for a moment. "I inform you of this not because I seek your aid but because it is relevant to your own dilemma. The GenMechs, due to the adaptability and volatility of their code as well as the materials used to produce them, are not all identical in behavior and design. But some of the refugees who arrived here had records of highly coordinated GenMech behavior, far beyond the simple multibot configurations. We were able to determine that some small subset of the GenMechs had fallen under the control of a unifying entity."

"Is this the EHRIc thing?"

"I am unfamiliar with the thing to which you are referring."

"A computer thing Ma made ended up taking control of all the GenMechs."

"Similar but we believe it is more intentional than that. Analysis of the code present in the one semi-intact GenMech of the indicated type suggests that military code had been installed."

"Weren't they already filled with military code?"

"This is very lightly altered by the generational mutation and degradation. Recent. You need to understand that during the initial assault of the GenMechs, those involved in their creation deployed thousands of attempts to access the kill switches that had been blotted out by the artificial evolution of the GenMechs. But because GenMechs are programmed to seek compatible parts preferentially, and to attempt to install them in as intact a state as possible to reduce the time and resources necessary to reproduce, much of this military hardware was not fully disassembled before being incorporated into new Gen-Mechs. Overwhelmingly—almost comprehensively— these GenMechs malfunctioned or adopted the kill-switch behavior and were destroyed. Based upon available data, we believe that a piece of military hardware designed to assert control over the GenMechs finally did so with a large enough proportion of the local population to avoid being destroyed by the others. Those GenMechs are now carrying out the programing of that defense system."

"What programming *is* it?"

"Unknown. We do not have the resources to investigate, and even if we did, every intentional contact with GenMechs risks attracting them to a human stronghold. This risk is substantially greater if the GenMechs are under the control of a more directed intelligence, because the affected GenMechs can act with logic and tactics."

Lex felt a dark, worrisome thought burble up in the back of his mind. "And this is relevant to my mission because..."

"Because this divergent GenMech colony is at the center of the possibility cone for the location of your displaced mass."

Lex palmed his face. "This can't be a coincidence... This is too cruel to be a coincidence."

"Question," Coal said over the PA system.

"Yes, Coal?" Ziva said.

"If some piece of military hardware was able to take control of GenMechs, why can't *you* do that?"

"The GenMech control systems and hardware vary too greatly. I could potentially assort control over any one variation of the control software, but as soon as it showed aberrant behavior, it would be targeted by the other GenMechs and destroyed. The success of this control required an unrepeatable confluence of good luck."

"But the ones it took over are all able to be taken over. We know that because they *were*," Lex said. "Can't you just take those over?"

"I assure you, Lex and Coal, it has been considered. It would require access and proximity that put us at unreasonable risk. Even in a success condition, it would be an unreasonable risk to return to any established settlement afterward, because the activities necessary to assert control would activate and attract other GenMechs. We do not even have the vehicles necessary to attempt such a thing, and the power and resources available to us in this facility prevent us from manufacturing that or a transporter."

"The *SOB* is a vehicle necessary to attempt such a thing," Coal said.

"Yeah, what you're telling me is you need a way to get there, and you need someone who doesn't intend to come back the way we came. Sounds like me and Coal. More to the point, we *need* to, in order to get back home and fix things. I'm not asking if you need my help. I'm telling you *I need your help*."

Ziva's flickering red eyes glanced aside. "Processing..." She looked Lex in the eye. "As you say, there is no way this is a coincidence. It is too perfect."

"It's perfectly awful for me and perfectly fortunate for you, so I guess it balances out."

"One moment," Ziva said.

She turned to a camera in the corner and flickered her eyes. A small screen on the wall slowly populated with dozens of small video feeds of assorted ragged and uncertain people, all in similar chambers.

"Hello, everyone. I apologize for the unscheduled contact. No doubt some of you will have already observed the approach of a new ship. Those who observed closely will note that it is fully intact, a rarity for any newcomer that reaches us. The ship belongs to an individual by the name of Lex."

A flash of recognition moved in a wave across the visible faces, particularly the children's.

"Yes, *that* Lex." Ziva turned to Lex. "The tales of your exploits are well known. I'm afraid I may have utilized some of your more extreme actions as stories to entertain the children."

Lex leaned in and waved. "Hey," he said.

Squeals of excitement briefly made further communication impossible. He held up the drifting funk.

"Squee's here, too," he said.

A second, more deafening burst compelled Ziva to mute the audio. Lex saw at least two of the children hold up a crude stuffed animal of a funk.

Ziva turned back to him with a smile that was almost sheepish. "I assembled a collection of funks from a scavenged load of fabric too small for other purposes." The smile faded. "The parliament of funks on Big Sigma could not be saved."

She turned back to the screen. "To continue. The circumstances of Lex's arrival necessitate that access be made with the militarized GenMech collective. He will not need to return to our sanctuary if his mission is successful. This presents a remote but real opportunity for us to execute some form of the proposed assaults on the collective. But to do so with any meaningful success will require the utilization of certain key resources from this sanctuary. I cannot and will not make that decision for this community. I request representatives from all major habitation hubs meet in Cafeteria 3 in twenty minutes to discuss the matter at hand. Next steps will be determined only by broad agreement of those in attendance. Thank you."

She turned to him. "Navigating the sanctuary is somewhat tedious. We are presently quite far from Cafeteria 3. We will need to leave soon. And, to my great dismay, I cannot offer you refreshment at this time. We are under strict rationing until another hydroponics bay can be completed, and as an individual who requires neither food nor water, none of the available provisions are mine to offer."

"I brought my own food," Lex said.

Her expression became somewhat more intense. "How much?" she urged.

• • • ● ● • ● ● • •

Eighteen minutes later, Lex and Ziva were transporting the last of his provisions into the cafeteria. Moving the entirety of his cargo through most of the space station was not difficult. Zero gravity and a length of cord has a way of making things quick, if not convenient, to tote. But the last stretch took several trips from himself, Ziva, and the first of the handful of representatives to reach the cafeteria. Lex was relieved, and a little disappointed, to discover this person wasn't inclined to engage in hero worship. It would have been uncomfortable, but he was self-aware enough to know a little star-eyed excitement would have helped his ego a bit. In fact, the dower-faced and gaunt older man who helped carry the packages didn't say anything at all. It wasn't until Lex caught some Cyrillic letters on the man's beat-up slidepad that he realized it was probably a language barrier.

Calling this place a cafeteria was charitable in the extreme. There was gravity, and thus it benefited from not needing specially designed cups that used surface tension, or feeding pouches instead of bowls. But it was notably short on the requisite "food" aspect. A far cry from the steaming trays in Karter's cafeteria. This place had assorted canisters labeled with the building blocks of a diet. It wasn't *Chicken Parm* and *Gumbo*. It wasn't even *tomato* or *fish*. It was *Nutrient Blend 1: Protein, Vitamin C, Vitamin D*. And the canister was not full. As the other representatives filed in, Lex did see a flash of respect and awe in their gazes. But by far the greatest reaction was reserved for the stacks of food.

The people had clearly seen great hardship. In total there were sixteen representatives. Only five had all their limbs. And even those who hadn't been injured carried the weight of war in their eyes.

"The contents of the boxes are labeled. Standard rationing and provisioning rules apply," Ziva said.

As she spoke, three other languages echoed beneath her voice, presumably repeating the same information for those who required it. They wordlessly opened bins, sorted contents, and repacked the bins such that each of them had a fair share. The speed and efficiency of the process made it clear that portioning things precisely was a common task. As they worked, Ziva turned to Lex.

"The spectrum of the sunlight is not well-suited to large, healthy crops, and the variety of plant specimens available to us has been limited. We are capable of supporting our current population, but with very little room for mishap. This will provide us with a stockpile," she said quietly.

The job done, she turned. "I will make this swift. Lex is a skilled pilot, and the *SOB* is a peerless vehicle. It is presently equipped with apparatus capable of traversing great expanses of space quickly and safely, and it has defensive capabilities capable of maneuvering in close proximity to GenMechs with minimal risk. Additionally, he is willing, and, in point of fact, he is required to seek out the compromised GenMechs. This presents us with the possibility to execute any of a handful of tactical gambits that have been discussed over the last few months. But to do so, we will need to commit some of our limited and irreplaceable resources."

One of the gathered group, a young woman, shook her head. "We can't spare anything, not a thing."

"We should hear her out. Her advice and guidance haven't steered us wrong," said an even younger man. "What do we need to commit?"

"I am proposing we pursue Tactical Scenario 3. That will require us to commit the damaged fusion core, a cryptographic coprocessor, my full defensive assembly, and my current mobile platform. A duplicate of my full program is already loaded onto the network node in my quarters."

The committee turned to each other and discussed among themselves. Ziva turned to Lex.

"While we are a single sanctuary, and we are dedicated to the common causes of safety and survival, each of the habitation nodes is capable of self-determination. Choices that affect the entire group must reach consensus."

"What is Tactical Scenario 3?" Lex asked.

"Irrelevant if the group doesn't agree it is worth attempting," Ziva said.

One by one, those in the discussion went silent. They turned.

"We cannot commit any additional resources to a mission with so great a chance of failure, regardless of the potential benefits of success."

"So be it," Ziva said.

"Whoa, whoa, whoa," Lex said. "Let's not be hasty. What's this plan you shot down?"

"Tactical Scenario 3 involves infiltrating the compromised GenMech cluster, disrupting the current centralized control system, and replacing it with our own control system. Success will allow us to take control of a cluster of GenMechs, giving us an instantaneous and replenishable means to defend and rebuild," Ziva said.

"Seems like instantly acquiring a massive, inexhaustible army and workforce might be worth doing," Lex said.

Ziva translated.

"It is only worth doing if it succeeds, and it is inconceivable that it would succeed," said the initial naysayer.

"I've beaten these things twice. Three times, technically."

"That's a bold claim to make," she said.

"First time, we figured out how to make a lure and nuked a collection of them on a planet. Second time, we traveled back in time and inserted a weakness."

"I am told I died during that mission," Coal said.

"Third time they had a queen bee like this time and we blew up the star they were buzzing around."

"Again, bold claims."

"You want proof? Look, I'm going into the jaws of this thing regardless of what you suggest. I've got troubles back home that need solving."

"Back home? What home do you have that has troubles that surpass or even rival what we have here? Do you have a sanctuary?"

"I have a place with time that won't flow, and I can only get back there once, and only once I get the stuff in the middle of the GenMech hive. Evacuation isn't an option. But the point is, the dangerous part is already happening. What do you have to lose?"

"The damaged fusion core, which is a collection of irreplaceable parts and the nearest thing we have to a replacement if our solar array is significantly damaged. The technology in Ziva's defensive assembly is one of a kind and could prove useful if it can be reduced in complexity and increased in scale. And Ziva has multiple skills and abilities in her current form that allow her to do maintenance in situations that would threaten or kill anyone else in the sanctuary."

"Can I do it without you? Can me and Coal pull this off?"

"It would take more materials than we have available to render Coal compatible with the cryptographic coprocessor, and the interface components are crucial to my body's operation. I cannot lend them. I am confident that my insight and knowledge will be necessary as well."

"Stand by. Please describe the role of the fusion core," Coal said.

"It would be modified to serve as an exceptionally high-yield explosive device," Ziva said.

"I would be equipped with a fusion device?" Coal said.

"Uh-oh," Lex muttered.

"I am prepared to perform any task necessary to illustrate the utility of equipping me with a fusion device once more," Coal said.

"Coal's enthusiasm for having a bomb notwithstanding, she makes a good point. How about we show you what we can do?"

"Nothing you could do would be anything less than a waste of time and resources," said the de facto spokesperson of the group. "We cannot and will not authorize this mission."

"I am willing to acquire the fusion core through unauthorized means," Coal said.

"Coal, you're not helping," Lex said.

"A suggestion," Ziva said. "We are presently stockpiling energy for the next defensive burst to ward off... processing... ninety-seven GenMechs, which will enter the FTL-capable clear zone around our star in six days. If it was not necessary to expend our stored energy on that defensive burst, it could be put to better use."

"I'm way ahead of you," Lex said. "Coal will run out there, pick off your GenMechs, and haul them back here for you to scrap, how's that? And if anything goes wrong, you can still pick them off, and we'll probably be dead so you won't have to worry about us taking any chances on your behalf."

The committee exchanged looks after Lex finished his pitch.

"You are aware of how to avoid attracting more, yes?" the spokeswoman said.

"I'm still alive, aren't I?" Lex said.

"I will vouch for his expertise," Ziva said.

They conferred further.

"We will reserve final decision on the combat scenario after we see his performance."

"Right." Lex clapped and rubbed his hands together. "You folks take care of Squee. I just fed her, so she's probably anxious for walkies. Everyone else, keep your eyes on the prize... You will be able to see it, won't you?"

"We have extremely high-precision, high-sensitivity optics on a network of targeting satellites at the edge of the FTL-capable region of the star's influence. You will be visible with approximately an eighty-second delay."

"Then what are we waiting for?"

Lex turned and strode back in the direction he had come. Ziva followed. Squee attempted to do so as well. She turned.

"No, no, little funk. He will be back soon enough," she said.

Lex waited until he had left the rotating ring of nodes and was once again in zero-g before he spoke up. "You think they'll go for it when it's over?" he said.

"Provided you succeed as brilliantly as I anticipate, they will have very little reason to doubt you," Ziva said. "And the potential good of seizing control of the compromised GenMechs cannot be measured."

"Coal? What do you think? Can we handle ninety-whatever GenMechs?"

"Officially we have no formal weaponry. These GenMechs have not been modified to include the volatile memory flaw that made the usage of an EMP one hundred percent effective at disabling them permanently. Destroying them will be challenging."

"We'll figure it out," Lex said.

"You will be pleased to know that I have not detected the Nuggets yet," Coal said.

"Oh, yeah. ... Kind of forgot we might be on a timer... All the more reason to get rolling quickly."

Lex strapped himself into the seat of the *SOB*. Ziva, in what was a somewhat disconcerting maneuver, exited the space station and drifted in space in front of them, communicating optically with her flickering irises while moving her lips as though the sound was coming out of her mouth.

"The people of this sanctuary, in order to survive, have had to become extremely pragmatic. In order to gain the maximum favor, I would suggest you seek to maximize the recovered mass. The one piece of equipment we have in great quantities, because it can easily be constructed out of otherwise low-priority GenMech components, is something we call a tractor-net. Coal, if you would extend your landing struts, I will clamp two of them in place."

Coal obliged.

"They are essentially omnidirectional medium-range tractor beams. Activate them and they will gather any loose mass in a twenty-meter sphere around them."

"Always nice to have a new toy."

"Good luck, be safe." She patted the side of the *SOB*. "I believe in both of you."

"Then how can we possibly fail?" Lex said.

They separated from the space station and set a course for the cluster of GenMech signals. It would take them barely a moment to reach the point where the nebula started to thicken, then another few minutes to get to the nearest of the GenMechs.

"Do you have a plan?" Lex said.

"No," Coal said.

"All right... Well, we know that we can sneak up on them with the cloaking device on."

"Possibly," Coal said.

"What?"

"The particle density in the nebula, combined with the velocity we will need to move to bridge the gaps between GenMechs, could create a visible particle wake. It is unknown if the GenMechs will be able to detect it."

"Oh... Well, screw it. We'll just be faster and better. Let's do this."

After a short, tense journey, always watching the quantum-pattern readings to be sure of the location of their targets, they were finally close enough for Coal to paint bright visual indicators on the targets. They were quite spread out, moving almost aimlessly.

"Steady... Steady..." Lex said, eyes locked on the spiderlike mechanism.

Lex felt little aftershocks and tremors of residual trauma from having faced these things so many times before. He pushed them aside. There would be plenty of time for shuddering memories of near disaster when the job was done. The moment he saw the slightest twitch of the GenMech reorienting to target the weak power signature the *SOB* presented, he juiced the throttle.

"Coal, can you give me a range at which I'll become visible to the next nearest of the GenMechs based on heat and all the other stuff pouring out of the *SOB*?"

"I can estimate and update my estimates with each additional GenMech that activates and targets us."

A sphere appeared in the HUD, slowly increasing as the heat produced by the thrusters increased. At the top corner of the HUD, just inside Lex's peripheral vision, an estimated distance to visibility ticked down.

"Lock on with the tractor beams and rattle it to bits as soon as it is in range."

"Acknowledged."

Two more GenMechs, about forty kilometers farther away than they should have been, snapped into a new orientation and tracked Lex. The sphere updated to reflect this new range.

"Change of plans. Don't rattle it. Just hold it. We're going to use it like a club," he said.

"Acknowledged."

He maneuvered the *SOB* toward the pair approaching, building up speed as he went. He reeled in the GenMech with the tractor beam, the better to hold it more tightly in the beam's grip. The mechanism latched and swept with its limbs, deploying tools from its belly-mounted node, but nothing could reach the *SOB*. A quarter second before the next GenMech would have made contact, Lex pulled the *SOB* up and away, swinging the captured GenMech with the combined momentum of the ship, the maneuver, and the enemy Mech's approach. The blow turned both of them into a mangled twist of shattered metal and circuitry. It also dislodged them from the tractor beam's grip. He grabbed the still-functional one, looped around, and bashed it into the lump formed by the first two.

"It is possible that the sensor sensitivity variance in the GenMechs has made estimating activation range a poor use of resources."

"Why do you say... oh..." Lex said.

Fifteen additional GenMechs, all outside of the range of the activation sphere, were on their way. He tightened his grip on the controls and took a breath.

"Let's see what they've got."

Chapter 7

L ex checked the proximity sensors. Sweat was running down his temples, and his hands were shaking. But the job was done. With the exception of a few new scrapes on the *SOB*'s hull, he and Coal were none the worse for wear and there were no more GenMechs within point four light-years. All the more distant GenMechs were moving in an unaltered trajectory, blissfully unaware of the butt-kicking Lex had handed their mechanical cousins. What had once been nearly a hundred GenMechs, any one of which could be the seed of destruction for a whole planet, now there was an inert ball of scavenged parts held to the belly of the *SOB* by the new tractor-nets. Once Coal had calibrated the Carpinelli Field sufficiently to bring the scavenging along with them, Lex made the jump back to the sanctuary station. Instantly they were hailed.

"Lex here. What's up?" Lex said, attempting to overdose on nonchalance in hopes of distracting from postfight jitters.

They were greeted once again by a low-resolution video. This time, in addition to Ziva, a few additional blobs of pixels moved about excitedly.

"That was quite a performance, Lex," Ziva said.

"Piece of cake. When they're only attacking a dozen at a time, they're downright manageable," Lex said.

"You have made believers of the committee. Though they did ask that I scan the ball of scavenged components seven times before powering down the energy cannons."

"Better safe than sorry."

"Because you used percussive force rather than energy blasts, the proportion of salvageable components should be higher," Ziva said. "This is a windfall for the station. I have already coordinated the modification of the fusion core and am presently recommissioning my defensive assembly. We will be ready to go as soon as you are."

"How far is the target?"

"The last known location of the compromised GenMech colony is at the following coordinates."

A point illuminated on his nav chart. He tipped his head.

"I can have us there in seventeen hours," he said. "You can fill me in on the tactical plan along the way."

"In great detail," Ziva said.

Lex had crawled back through the docking tube as soon as he could. Seventeen hours in the cockpit, followed by a tense and pitched battle, wasn't all that unusual for him. But if this might be his last chance to stretch his legs—perhaps *ever*—he would certainly take the opportunity.

Despite the visible celebration over the video link, the reaction in person was different. Only three residents of the sanctuary came to visit him, though "observe" him was a more accurate description. It was one thing to see a man fly circles around a few of the machines that had scarred the bodies and minds of the entire species. It was another to be in the same room with him knowing he was about to fly headlong into an effectively endless cluster of them. One of them was exciting and triumphant. The other must have felt akin to sitting beside a man at his deathbed.

The only one who lingered was the naysayer from the earlier meeting. She didn't speak. She just remained in the entryway of the room, measuring Lex with her gaze.

"So... what's it been like?" Lex said.

"It has been one day at a time," she said.

"It must feel hopeless sometimes."

"It doesn't feel hopeless. It *is* hopeless. It's easier that way. When there's hope, every morning without a light at the end of the tunnel is a disappointment. Without hope, with the grim realization that no help is coming and the sun will never shine again, you don't have to be let down. Your spirits can settle. But now here you are." Her lip curled. "How dare you?"

"How dare I try?"

"We *all* try. Every day. We all do what we need to do. How dare you give us that spark of hope again? How dare you set us up for the fall?"

"I don't have it in me to let this sort of thing stand if I know there's something I can do about it."

"There *isn't* something you can do about it. Has Ziva told you what you're in for?" she said.

"I've fought GenMechs before."

"Not these you haven't. There's one family here. A father and a son, who have seen what these things are and lived. The rest of us have survived the normal GenMechs. These are militarized."

"What's the difference?"

"What does a military control program need with robots that merely reproduce? I watched what you did out there. Came close to losing the ship twice, and those things may as well be fighting with teeth and claws. The compromised GenMechs have blasters."

"... Do they?"

"They do. Not powerful ones. But when there's a couple trillion of them, do they really need to be powerful? You can outfly a couple dozen of them. But can you dodge thousands of streams of shots aimed with military precision?"

"He won't need to," said Ziva at the other entryway.

Lex turned. The already-more-imposing armored form of his friend had been augmented by what he had to assume was the defensive assembly their current plan called for. It thickened up the previously sparse arms and legs by adding white cuffs to both wrists and both ankles. They were set into armored plates running along her limbs and connecting with fortified cables to a chest plate that wouldn't have looked out of place on a war robot.

She had Squee with her. The little creature was already coiled against her shoulder and waggling her little butt in preparation for a precision assault of affection. She pushed off Ziva, barely moving the now-extremely-substantial frame of the AI, and thumped Lex in the chest with a dive that sent him rotating backward.

"I will be providing defensive support," Ziva said, darting forward to help right Lex.

"That rig is going to be enough to turn the tide?" he said.

"The core function of my defensive assembly was the final innovation produced by Karter Dee prior to his departure from this reality through time travel. He perceived it to be a failure, but it has repeatedly proved itself to be indispensable when utilized with proper skill and tactics. The assembly is capable of projecting a shield two meters in diameter which is impenetrable by any known conventional means. It can be projected through any material without interference, and remains anchored in both orientation and offset to the emitter that projects it, at a range of up to thirty meters."

"That sounds pretty useful," Lex said.

"Two meters is nothing," the naysayer growled. "And it isn't even run from a useful power source. We haven't been able to reverse engineer how it fuels the shield."

"Karter was pretty good at finding ways to make things not quite useful. But if she can block a couple of shots, then that means I don't have to dodge everything. I just have to dodge what she can't block."

"What can she block? The attacks from one GenMech?"

"It beats blocking *no* GenMechs," Lex said. "Are we about ready to go, Ziva? Apparently having me hang around is having mixed results on the locals."

"We are prepared. The fusion core has been rigged with a detonator and is waiting in a maintenance node. I have integrated the cryptographic processor into my equipment. All is in readiness."

Lex nodded, then turned to the naysayer. "Whether this goes our way or it doesn't, I won't be back. So, with any luck, that little flicker of hope is the one you've been waiting for."

"I have acquired a fusion device," Coal said. "I have finally been restored to my full operational complement."

Lex shut his eyes tightly. "Fingers crossed, everybody."

A few minutes later, Ziva was strapped into the passenger seat of the *SOB*, and they'd plotted their course. Things were quiet until he'd programmed in and activated the first FTL jump. Once they were facing three hours of FTL with nothing to do, Lex broke the silence.

"So, they have guns, huh?" he said.

"Antipersonnel blasters, when not in a more complex configuration. Rosettes of twelve to sixteen are capable of antiarmor blasts. Rosettes of thirty-two to fifty are capable of siege blasts. And it is theorized that rosettes of six point seven million may be capable of planetary-level threats."

"Funny how that didn't come up until we were about to leave."

"It would not have changed the situation," Ziva said. "The mass you seek is in the same sector of space as the compromised GenMechs. I have reason to believe it is, in fact, under guard by them."

"Oh yeah? And how do you know that?"

"In the early days of the GenMech attack, Karter was contacted with all available information in order to attempt to devise a plan. He and I collaborated on many proposed defenses. Some were attempted and deployed precisely as we proposed them. Others were adapted. Karter maintained an illegal level of surveillance on the organizations he advised, so he was aware of some of the alterations to the plans. Based upon the limited behavioral information we have on the compromised GenMechs, it matches the countermeasure set forth by a private military corporation called Ballista-OmniResource, BOR. Their goal at the time is broadly similar to the plan we shall soon discuss. They wanted to capture and utilize a collection of GenMechs first as a weapon against the others and second as, in their words, 'the ultimate survey tool for reconstruction.'"

"Including marketing wank in a plan to save the galaxy seems like a bad sign."

"There is reason to suspect their goals were not entirely virtuous. Included in their designs for rosettes designed to combat other GenMechs were rosettes designed to perform all manner of scans, collecting samples of unique resources for study. The scans they constructed, by my calculation, would have been able to detect but not adequately measure the quantum shift that you are using to find the mass. This would flag that mass as worthy of collection."

"So the good news is, whatever it is, it probably won't have been stripped for parts and used to build murder machines. The bad news is the murder machines probably threw it in their treasure hoard. Dandy. Did the people back in the sanctuary know you knew this much?"

"Select few were aware. The consensus opinion was that a broad awareness of my own failed role in preventing the GenMechs from advancing to the degree they had would undermine trust in my ability to maintain the sanctuary. Those who were made aware worked with me to develop this tactical scenario. Are you prepared to discuss it?"

"Let's hear it."

"The intended plan is a simple one, though it will require some good fortune and a great deal of skill to achieve our desired results. We already know the compromised GenMechs did not perform the full program designed by BOR, as that program would have deployed them to track down and assimilate or destroy all other GenMechs. The theory for the incomplete execution of the program was the assumption by the designers that there would be at least one surviving human in the chain of command to execute Stage 2."

"So we're just going to go in there and hit the big red button to send them off to clean up the galaxy?"

"No. The needs of the galaxy have changed. We need to break the current control and assert replacement control. The GenMechs will have constructed a central-processing cluster and resource-consolidation stronghold. They will also have unified Mech control under a single command protocol. From the moment we enter range, the command protocol will be exposed to us and we will be able to attack it programmatically with the cryptographic processor. The security is fairly low, due in part to the single-user nature of the protocol. Even with it completely broken, the GenMechs will remain in control of the central-processing cluster until its command string is interrupted."

"Will we be using the fusion device to cause that interruption? Fusion devices are highly effective at causing interruptions," Coal said.

"I don't think—" Lex began.

"Yes," Ziva said. "We will be delivering it to the transmission subassembly and detonating it, thus interrupting the command sequence. Between seven and ten minutes later, the GenMechs will reach the end of their command queues and enter a standby state, at which point anyone broadcasting on the command protocol will assert control. The plan is thus as follows. Enter the range of the GenMechs. Survive long enough to break their encryption. Pilot the *SOB* into the central-processing cluster, plant the bomb. Leave the cluster, detonate the bomb, assert control, and locate the displaced mass you are after."

"How long will the encryption take?"

"At the risk of appearing evasive, 'until it is done' is the most accurate answer I can provide. Best estimate based on simulation suggests four minutes will be sufficient, but in some simulations, it took as long as two hours."

"Let's hope we end up on the short end of that," Lex said. "But, yeah, sounds like my whole role in this is 'don't die.' And according to Karter, that's one of my two skills."

"Karter had a way of undervaluing certain traits due to the flawed assumption that they should not have been considered strengths. You also have empathy, kindness, and a sense of duty as a non-exhaustive addendum to your positive skill and trait list."

"He also knows how to have fun," Coal said.

"None of those are particularly applicable to the challenge at hand, Ziva," Lex said.

"Untrue. Without those traits, you would not have attempted this mission with the strength of conviction necessary to have a viable route to success. However, it does raise a question, if you will permit me."

"We've got sixteen and change hours to kill, I'm all ears."

"Observing your mission from a dispassionate, unemotional vantage, the correct course of action for you would have been to seek out the displaced mass as quickly as possible, assess the threat inherent to its retrieval, seek aid or resources as necessary, and retrieve the mass. In your circumstance, that should have involved, in the best case, encountering the compromised GenMechs, circumnavigating their defenses, and departing. In the average case, you would have seen the challenge, sought aid, and potentially found my sanctuary or another."

"Sounds about right.

"But you sought out our sanctuary first," Ziva said.

"Yeah."

"Why?"

"We got dropped off right outside Big Sigma's system. Searching for you was in the neighborhood."

"Based upon that arrival point and the location of the mass, the sanctuary was a detour."

"It would have been rude not to stop by and say hello."

"I would prefer a noncomedic, nonevasive reply."

"I'll bet you would," Lex muttered. "Look, when you kind of... break your universe for a bad reason, it starts moving your brains in certain directions."

"I was unaware there was a good reason to break a universe," Coal said.

"Coal, this is going to be hard enough to articulate without you editorializing."

"I apologize," Coal said. "I shall make notes of my intended comments and include them at the end."

"Great, looking forward to that," he said. "But as I was saying, it starts to get you looking at the choices you've made. And it starts to line up all the bad ones, along with all the failures, and starts ranking them."

"The human mind is uniquely capable of torturing itself, I have observed," Ziva said.

"You're telling *me*. And when I look at all the things I wish had gone a different way, it's the ones I don't actually know the outcome of that jab at me the most. And this place is written in big bold letters in my mind. I didn't know if you made it. I didn't know if you'd given your life for me. I didn't know if the universe had just closed up shop. And Ma and Coal both sort of tried to explain that it happened both ways. Anything that I didn't experience, I guess that didn't happen in the world I'm currently observing, happened every possible way it can happen. I guess that was supposed to make me feel better, to let me choose to believe that things went how I wanted them to and that's just as true as any of the nightmare scenarios. But that's not how my brain works. I don't know if that's how *any* brain works. I needed to know what really happened, even if that question can't really be answered, I needed to know. And so, I found you."

"It is touching to know I have a place in your thoughts, though I wish it were for a more positive reason," Ziva said.

"You're the one calling the shots on this mission, too. We had to build a copy of you because of your expertise with the GenMechs."

"It is a rare honor to have the thread of one's existence continued in another world."

"Yeah. But even that didn't quiet the voice in my head. And that's what keeps happening with these otherworld jaunts. I keep on coming face to face with what would have happened if I'd done things differently, or what *did* happen because of what I'd done. The other you thinks there is a psychological aspect to where I'm showing up, because of how the simulator does its thing."

"Fascinating."

"There was also a world with nothing but Karters. What does that mean about your psyche?" Coal said.

"I'm putting that on a big list of things we won't be thinking about or discussing, Coal."

"If you want me to honor that list, you'll need to share access," Coal said.

"So, anyway, that's that. That's why I took a detour," Lex said.

Ziva nodded. "A large part of my morals and ethics heuristics call for me to feel a degree of anxiety and shame for being the reason for a dangerous and time-expensive side mission during a very important quest. But I am similarly motivated to feel honored and relieved by such a thing, if for no other reason than you, Coal, the *SOB*, and Squee have provided this world with a possible route to salvation."

"Seems like no matter the world, I'm always the hero of last resort," Lex said.

"While we are discussing potentially unworthy motivations for thoughts and behaviors, it would be wrong to allow this opportunity to pass without stating outright that you have remained a figure of prominence in my mind and memories since your previous departure. Your own instance of Ma has stated this, and so have I, but if anything deserves restating it is this. You were the first human to treat me as an individual every bit as deserving of consideration and respect as another sentient organic being. There have been others, but for most of them the kindness and deference to my feelings or needs has felt like an act of obligation, or some simulation or facsimile of true respect. They treated me as they would a human because they had seen others do so. Their behavior was not genuine. Overwhelmingly I have risen to the level of, at best, an oddity in their minds. Things improved when I constructed a human body. There are children in the sanctuary who do not understand or conceive of the ways in which I am different. But you were the first, and through you those things I cherish most about my growth were able to flourish. Even if things had gone 'the other way' when you left. Even if every one of the infinitudes of parallel universes split from that moment saw my spark of consciousness snuffed out, and even if some cruel arbiters of reason were to decree that it was through your acts alone that such a fate came to be, your gifts would have still far outweighed your faults. Because you gave me *myself*."

There was a heavy silence.

"You also have a knack for finding entertaining ways to nearly die," Coal said.

"Thanks, Coal. You always know just what to say," Lex said.

"I am an exceedingly well-tuned behavioral system."

What should have been a seventeen-hour trip turned out to be closer to a full day, as the best, shortest route turned out to be positively laden with GenMechs that were not detectable at greater ranges. The constant redirects added distance and time to the trip and prevented Lex from having stretches long enough to rest. Thus, rather than charging directly into the lion's den, he chose to find the nearest quiet place to sleep for as close to eight hours as circumstances would allow.

Three hours and fifty-one minutes after he finally dozed off, Coal's voice jostled him from sleep.

"Huh? Mmh? Wha...?" Lex stammered thickly.

"I apologize for the interruption of your rest, Lex, but you should know that the Nuggets have been detected."

"They have," he said, his brain riding a jolt of adrenaline to full wakefulness.

"They are in the same star system as the mass and are approaching the precise location at a high multiple of C."

"Okay. Okay, then. Time's up," he said, grabbing the controls. "Are we ready for this?"

Ziva nodded. "While you were resting, we were able to extend our knowledge of the compromised GenMech cluster. I have an approximate count, some density maps, and a rough estimate of the size of the processing cluster and resource hoard."

He entered the final FTL jump into navigation. "You have three minutes to give me the rundown," he said.

The ship accelerated to faster-than-light velocities.

"The approximate count of active GenMechs in the system is four point eight seven quintillion. Density maps are in your navigational system now. The central-processing cluster and resource cache are a low-density spherical framework comprising chiefly iridium and nickel with a volume comparable to a large asteroid or small moonlet."

"Anything else I should know?"

"Yes. Based upon the trace signals filtering out of the cluster, it is likely that active scans of the military-augmented data-collection systems in the compromised GenMechs will flag the emission patterns of a cloaked vessel as either 'of interest' or 'actively hostile.'"

"Not gonna lie, I was kind of hoping we'd be able to just do this as a big game of hide-and-seek."

"You will be able to until the precise moment you are no longer able to. That is to say, they will ignore you until one of them flags you as a signal of interest, and then all the GenMechs will switch to either harvest or assault mode. In all likelihood, they will begin in harvest mode and switch to assault mode if and when we are forced to take evasive action."

Lex tapped some controls. "We'll just have to see how close the cloak lets us get. Coal, I'm going to need you to be my eyes and ears, as I'm going to be pretty focused on evasion. Give me updates on where precisely the target mass is, where precisely the Nuggets are, and how much time I have before they reach each other. Ziva, it should be pretty obvious which blasts I need you to block with that shield thing."

"I shall endeavor to anticipate your needs," Ziva said.

"Squee, I'm going to need you to be strapped in, all right? Suit on, helmet on. Who knows if the cockpit will stay intact through this whole thing."

"She is suited and secured," Ziva said.

He watched the countdown to the final destination tick down. Behind him, the crinkle of a wrapper pulled him out of the deepening focus just in time for a stick of gum to poke up from behind him.

"We'll need you at your best," Ziva said, waggling the gum.

He took it and stuffed it in his mouth. "Here goes. Three... two... one..."

The Carpinelli Field dialed back. The universe outside the windows slid back into visibility. After a few seconds of processing, Coal painted indicators over the two thousand nearest GenMechs and produced pointers for the Nuggets and the target mass. Lex triple-checked the cloak was in place, then took the *SOB* to the highest speed it could maintain without the heat signature giving them away.

After nearly a minute of scrutinizing what would be either an obstacle course or a battlefield in very short order, he finally remembered to blink.

"Yeah, these aren't regular GenMechs," he murmured, more to himself than to the others.

That was visually evident, if somewhat subtle, in the inset visual scan of the nearest foe. Rather than four spindly legs, plus two smaller ones around the tool node on its belly, these GenMechs were missing the rear two legs. They had been replaced by a unified, bulbous lump that hung down under the rest of the mass. It gave them the look of a hornet coming in for a sting. But that wasn't what seemed most off about them.

"The GenMechs I'm used to are at best like flocks of birds or swarms of gnats," Lex said. "Look how these things travel. They're in formation. Like military craft."

"I have begun cryptographic processing. I will call out any relevant data I am able to discern from decoded elements of the transmission. The data are voluminous. That should aid in swiftly decoding the format," Ziva said.

Lex felt a phantom tingle in his arms and legs as he saw the location indicators of the first few GenMech formations slip out of his peripheral vision and vanish behind him. It was like crossing the threshold of a vampire's mansion. He was in their territory now. Surrounded. So far they hadn't altered their motion. They hadn't spotted him. He tried to tease any additional information he could out of what he was seeing.

Coal had labeled the central cluster, but she needn't have bothered. The whole system had been stripped clean, utterly disassembled to build the current complement of Gen-Mechs. The only thing in his view that *wasn't* a GenMech was the gray, matte ball of metal in the distance. From here it looked like a mesh sphere.

"Coal," Lex said, whispering as though he might alert the GenMechs otherwise. "Can you give me a better visual on the cluster?"

She replaced the GenMech closeup with a closeup of the spherical cluster.

"Can we get a size reference?" he said.

Coal added measurements to the handful of visible features in the zoomed view. The only one that mattered to him was the size of the openings that covered the surface. The perimeter of each opening was a circle approximated by crisscrossing straight lines of some sort of stiff cable or strut. There was no hatch, no obvious defenses. That wasn't so surprising. When you have more than a trillion bodyguards on patrol, you don't really need to worry about locking the door. But the opening itself was only one point seven five meters in diameter.

"Are those the biggest ports on the surface?" Lex said.

"The openings appear to be perfectly uniform," Coal said.

"I can't fit a ship through that hole. The plan was for me to fly inside, grab the doodad, drop the bomb, and skedaddle."

"Processing..." Ziva said.

"Behavioral change detected in GenMech formation at seven o'clock position," Coal said.

She brought up a video feed of the GenMechs in question. They had broken from their previous pattern and angled roughly toward the ship.

"They are in harvest mode. We have been detected," Ziva said. "I am seeing additional data coming across the command protocol. This is valuable information."

Lex eased the ship aside, in what was probably the slowest dodge of his career. The searching GenMechs started to shift to follow. Others were taking notice as well.

"If I don't get some speed soon, we're going to be boxed in," Lex said. "But I have a feeling the moment I put the spurs to her, they're all going to start shooting."

The moments of relative calm were running out, but Lex couldn't get something out of his head. Something about how the GenMechs were moving. He started to tap his fingers on the controls with each move.

"These things are stuttering or something," he said. "There's a rhythm to their motions."

"It coincides with the command-protocol update cadence. A single unified control structure for a fleet this size is an inefficient method of control."

He kept tapping his fingers, watching as the searching robots twitched and course corrected with each tap.

"This is going to sound crazy..." Lex said.

"Now is not a moment for sanity," Ziva said.

"Coal, can you go through my music library? Find something that matches the rhythm we're seeing? If I can keep the beat in my head, it'll help find the gaps and the openings in their motion."

"Processing..." Coal said.

A soft, thumping base drum was quickly joined by a layer of synthetic strings and a crunchy guitar. Lex took a deep breath.

"Yeah. That'll do."

He juiced the throttle and dropped the cloaking device to free up a little more power for the systems. The instant he was visible, the nearest GenMechs targeted and opened fire. It was a dazzling, terrifying sight. Dotted lines of energy bolts crept toward them. Machines spaced with mechanical precision produced their strings of weapon fire in sync, filling the space ahead of them with a grid of interlocking lines of fire like the whole section of space was an iridescent spirograph rendering.

A very brief stutter in the music perfectly aligned it to the firing pattern. Lex chomped his gum and rolled aside, weaving between the first salvo of shots.

Coal must have been monitoring his eyelines, because she positioned the threat and targeting information precisely where he needed them. The GenMechs were sophisticated enough to lead their shots, but the distance and the delay in their aim adjustments gave him precious moments to stay ahead of their arcs of fire. Blasts started to flare against his shield, glancing blows chipping away at the defense but none of them taking much of a bite. But the farther they went, the more of them pulled into formation and the denser the weapon fire became. Now the nearest GenMechs were in range of the tractor beam. He locked onto one of them and whipped it aside, bashing through three others and creating a gap to slip through.

"Nugget proximity, two hundred kilometers and closing. They are taking enemy fire," Coal said.

"Maybe we'll get lucky and the GenMechs will take them out for us," Lex said, flaring a side thruster to roll out of an attack line.

The interlocking fans of fire were now tighter together than the profile of the ship's shields. After a half second of deliberation, Lex deactivated the shields.

"Is that wise, Lex?" Ziva said.

"I need the smaller profile more than I need the protection right now."

A row of blasts crackled by so close they were audible as interference in the increasingly intense music.

"Please recall that we have a fusion device on the belly of the *SOB*. A direct hit to that device will be a disqualifying factor in the designation of this mission as 'fun,'" Coal said.

"Noted." He tightened his jaws. "Getting tight, getting tight, *getting tight*."

As he rolled out of the way of a unified wall of blasts, he found himself facing down three tightly clustered blasts too close to dodge without driving the ship right into another salvo. A black disk suddenly coalesced in front of the ship. The blasts struck it and dispersed. Lex glanced at the reflection in the cockpit and saw Ziva with one arm extended, fingers spread in the precise direction of the disk.

She swept the arm aside and the disk followed, absorbing more shots. The shield she'd conjured outside the ship was maybe the size of a beach umbrella. Even perfectly positioned, it wasn't large enough to shield any of the key systems of the ship. But with surgical placement, it could act as a plow clearing enough shots to create a gap wide enough to slip through.

"Do we have a plan yet for getting what needs to be got?" Lex said.

"I am going to have to EVA," Ziva said, sliding the disk around and shearing a GenMech in half with its edge. The pieces clattered across the cockpit hatch.

"Not exactly the right weather for extracurricular activities," Lex said, latching on to a GenMech with the tractor beam and holding it in the path of a series of shots, blocking them long enough for him to slip through the rest of the salvo.

"Circumstances require it," Ziva said. "Bring the ship to within a few meters of the surface of the sphere. I will exit through the docking port. Disengage the clamp on the fusion device and—"

"You are taking the fusion device?" Coal said, indignant. "It's mine."

"There's no *I* in 'bomb,' Coal."

"There are two in 'fusion device,'" Coal said.

"I assure you, if things go well, I can fabricate a replacement," Ziva said.

"Promise?" Coal said.

Lex dialed down the thrust, pivoted, and juiced it, kicking the ship aside. He reoriented it and was able to slide sideways through another salvo.

"But you're supposed to be decoding the... stuff," Lex said, his brain not presently in the proper state to be fetching vocabulary words from deep storage.

"I am capable of multitasking," Ziva said.

"There's going to be a *lot* of things shooting at you while you're multitasking."

"According to scans... processing..." Ziva said, interrupting herself to calculate a motion that sliced the disk through eight GenMechs. "The interior of the cluster is largely narrow tunnels. They will have to attack in ones and twos. And I am confident you will prove a distraction to keep them out of the tunnels."

"I think it's a dumb idea, but I'm out of better ones."

"We will remain in touch. Please be mindful of my communications. I will require evacuation following the planting of the fusion device, as I will also be in possession of the displaced mass."

"I'll be there."

The closer they got to the sphere, the wider the gaps in fire became. The GenMechs were clearly being instructed to avoid shots that would strike the sphere at close range. That, coupled with the presence of the sphere providing an increasingly large section of space that could not contain attacking GenMechs and they were getting perilously close to having some breathing room.

"All right. I'm going to find enough space to do a loop. You eject, I loop, back toward you, Coal ejects the bomb, you catch it."

"Acknowledged," Ziva said. "Processing... I have cracked the command protocol."

"Oh, good." Lex snagged a GenMech in the tractor beam and used it as a plow to smash through the line behind it. "One less thing to worry about."

"Correction, one much more substantial thing to worry about," Ziva said. "I have been able to determine that one of the underlying command imperatives is the acquisition and analysis of novel technology."

"Yeah, so? We're already their target."

"The Nuggets are also their target," Ziva said. "And they have dimensional transfer technology, as do you."

Lex shuddered. "Are you saying if the GenMechs strip those things for parts, they might learn how to dimension-shift?"

"I am speculating it is a possibility."

"Get ready to launch. Seems like I have some extradimensional butts to save."

"The Nuggets do not have signs of a one-dimensional digestive system and thus do not have butts, Lex," Coal said.

"Coal, you keep that stuff up and I'm going to have to install a set of googly eyes on the control panel so I can glare at them. Ziva, here we go."

Ziva gently tightened the strap holding the suited Squee in place. "Ready," she said.

Ziva released the straps holding herself in place and dumped power to the thrusters in the soles of her feet. Now that the cryptographic process was complete, she could redistribute the computational resources formerly utilized to run the device to increasing the signal-processing capacity of her visual and motor systems, effectively dialing down her reaction time to as near to instantaneous as she could manage.

Lex rotated, aligning the top of the *SOB* with the sphere. He popped the seal on the docking hatch. She flared her thrusters and launched herself through the narrow opening into open space. With the command protocol available to her, she knew that her smaller mass and lower energy output would make her a low-priority target. For the moment, she could focus on positioning herself and preparing for Lex's next maneuver. He looped around. Three energy blasts sparked against the hull, grazing it without severe damage. She maneuvered herself, placing one of the openings in the sphere behind her. Coal released the fusion device. The melon-sized explosive struck her in the abdomen, launching her backward. She raised her feet and added her thrust, grasping the bomb and raising her head, to properly navigate the tunnel leading deeper into the processing cluster.

Microbursts of thrusters mounted in her shoulders and hips did their best to keep her on track, but the tunnel's turns were too sharp for that. The diameter of the tunnel didn't increase much for the first few hundred meters of looping and branching routes. She raised a hand and activated the shield disk close ahead of her. It proceeded to grind along the face of the curving tunnel, serving as a sled of sorts. The tunnel ahead reversed on itself. She flipped around and placed the disk against the other wall, maintaining speed and surfing the curve deeper.

Sensors indicated threats ahead. The instant a GenMech became visible ahead, she flipped the shield up and smashed through it. The impact slowed her. Additional threats started to approach from adjoining tunnels. She grabbed the wall of the tunnel, fingers cutting deep furrows into the metal of the wall until she became stationary. Navigational power was shifted to her sensor array, penetrating deeper into the complex of tunnels to reveal the route to the displaced mass and the nearest power junction feeding the central transmitter. A GenMech emerged from a side tunnel beneath her. She grabbed its foreleg, drove her heels into its body, and reactivated her thrusters, searing a hole through it and bursting back to motion.

• • • ● ● • ● ● • • •

Lex skimmed along the surface of the sphere, trying to keep in mind that the handy-dandy shield disk that had been helping clear the way was no longer around. He did his best to replace it by ensuring he was always dragging a GenMech with him as a body shield, but they were smaller and could only take one or two hits before he had to abandon them and grab a new one.

"Time until Nugget intercept: fifteen seconds," Coal said.

"I still don't like that name," Lex grumbled.

According to the HUD, the alien creatures were a few kilometers away from the surface of the sphere and at the center of a very dense cluster of GenMechs. They'd be appearing over the horizon of the sphere momentarily.

"Crank up the volume on the music," Lex said. "We're about to go into a swarm."

"Acknowledged."

A complex sequence of Japanese vocals blared through the ship's speakers as he angled the ship toward the ball of GenMechs around the aliens. He may not have had insight into the control program running these things like Ziva did, but something told him the whole "priority target" thing was proximity based, because the moment he was within five kilometers of the tight little ball of GenMechs, they turned to him in unison and spread into a firing line.

"Out of curiosity, how many physical impacts can our shields take before failure?"

"The undeployed shields are at one hundred percent. At maximum power, directionally focused, and backed with navigational shields, we should be able to deflect sixteen impacts at this velocity."

"How many are currently attacking the Nuggets?"

"Six hundred."

"We'll have to pick the sixteen we want to hit really carefully, then. Are we charged for EMP?"

"Yes. But initiating a pulse will require us to deploy our cooling fins, which will increase our target profile. The fins are also highly fragile."

Lex tried to perform the risk-benefit analysis, weighing the chances of crippling the *SOB*'s cooling against disabling potentially several thousand of the GenMechs in the area.

"I am detecting multiple attempted Carpinelli Field activations. The Nuggets are attempting to flee for deep space."

"Works for me. Let's see if we can clear the way. Shields up the moment before impact, got that?"

"Acknowledged."

A thought occurred to him. "Do we still have those tractor-nets installed?"

"We do."

He grinned. "Release one when I hit panel button three, and activate it on four."

"Acknowledged."

Lex took a wide curve, circling behind the GenMechs. They must have been programmed well enough to not target each other. Lex used that to full advantage. Cutting close to the swarm of Mechs around the Nuggets meant incoming attacks from outside the swarm were sparse, only coming from in front and behind. Attacks from the swarm itself were another matter, coming like solid walls. But they had to turn swiftly to target him from so close, so the focus of the blasts trailed behind. Packed so closely, the behavior of the GenMechs was even more tightly coupled to the command cadence, and thus even more perfectly synced to the music.

He judged the shot spacing and bided his time. When the moment was right, he cut thrusters, pivoted, and deployed the cooling fins. The engine temp started to drop. The next burst of blasts readied for deployment. He angled for impact with the handful of GenMechs in his way. The shields flashed with brilliant color as they smashed them aside. The instant it was available, Lex punched the EMP. No longer cooped up in a tiny space that could reflect the effects back at him, the EMP spared the *SOB* but caused every GenMech inside a cone in the path of the EMP to shudder and shut down. A stray blast clipped off a section of the cooling fins. He retracted them and turned, slapping the button to deploy the tractor-net and heaving it forward with a snap-rotation of the ship. He slapped the activation button as the tractor-net entered the twitching, malfunctioning mass of bots. They were instantly drawn tight against it, providing him with a trembling lump of half-functional GenMechs all gathered neatly into an easy-to-transport package. He spun back around and grabbed the collection of GenMechs with his own tractor beam and flared the thrusters, ramming the huge ball ahead of him, collecting more Mechs and working as a snowplow to clear space and absorb shots.

"How are we looking?" Lex said.

"Shields at seventeen percent. Cooling reduced by eight percent. Hull integrity ninety-one percent," Coal said.

"How are the Nuggets looking?"

"One of them is maneuvering through the open gap. The other appears to have been damaged. Here is the visual."

Sure enough, one of the Nuggets, barely visible if not for the flash of its shields as it took hits, was making a mad dash for deep space. Its small size and ridiculous nimbleness made it clear that this head start would give it the chance it needed to retreat and regroup. The other was no longer shielded and no longer camouflaged. The mechanical tail was sparking and unresponsive. It had reached a level of damage that clearly made the GenMechs confident it was better off harvested than destroyed.

"The other tractor-net is on the belly of the *SOB*, yes?" Lex said.

"Correct."

"I'm going to fly close. Activate when that thing is in range."

"It might be preferable to destroy the Nugget."

"Maybe, but I'm not that kind of guy," he said.

He swept through and angled the belly of the *SOB* toward the ailing Nugget. Coal snatched it up with the tractor-net. Lex then righted the ship and smashed through the active side of the swarm. The tight maneuvering in a relatively small space had allowed a shell of additional GenMechs to position itself. The new foes were focus-firing on him from all angles. The ball of GenMechs was blocking blasts from the front, but the narrow tunnel of space kept clear of shots was getting smaller by the moment.

"We need to get back closer to the surface of the sphere to keep the fire on a plane around us rather than all angles."

"We do not have the defensive capacity to absorb enough shots to reach the sphere without opening another path, and the EMP is not ready," Coal said.

"Gotta open a gap... Gotta open a gap..." Lex's mind sputtered as it tried to dig up another desperate act of brilliance. "Okay. Okay. No time to explain, but put the activation of the tractor-net ahead of us as a toggle on button three."

He flicked through a sequence of rapid control adjustments, pulling the ship into a spin. After two revolutions, and a quick drop from ninety percent to seventy percent hull integrity, he deactivated the tractor-net. The GenMechs clinging to it burst forward, spreading like the blast of a shotgun, smashing through three layers of other GenMechs, and, for a moment, giving a glimpse of clear space. Lex charged for the opening, keeping close behind the spreading wall of bouncing GenMech parts. Cracks feathered the cockpit as pieces clattered across the hull.

Lex was able to just barely snag the drifting, deactivated tractor-net and activate it again. He couldn't use it to grab the GenMechs ahead of him, as if a single active one were to come into contact with the device itself, it would start harvesting it. But sweeping it close and yanking it away was enough to haul GenMechs out of position, forcing a reorientation before resuming fire. It was hardly an efficient way to keep him safe, but he was running out of options, and it got him down to the surface of the sphere again.

"Ziva? You there?" Lex said. "We're alive. One of the Nuggets just left the star system at high FTL. The other is pinned to our belly, hopefully not getting up to mischief. How are things going in there?"

"Moderately well," Ziva said over the communication link, her signal heavily distorted.

• • • ● • ● • ● • • •

Ziva's traversal of the core cluster had gone swiftly. As expected, the tunnels made robots ganging up on her less of a problem. But the tunnels came to an end a half-kilometer below the surface, and now she had to deal with a bit of a mind-bending piece of internal structure.

This place had been part of the countermeasures BOR had designed. The GenMechs had built it, but it was clear there had already been a significant amount of corruption in the countermeasure program by the time this section had been constructed. It was plainly intended to be a human-run facility. Artificial gravity was in place, and there were catwalks, doors, ladders, and hallways. But the degradation of the program as this place was constructed took the form of those design elements being placed with little regard to logic or reason. Catwalks took random right-angle bends along any axis, running vertically or even upside down. Doors were installed leading to solid blocks of nickel, in the middle of catwalks, or jutting out of walls like turnstiles. It was an Escherian nightmare.

Worse, a secondary form of GenMech was present within the facility. They were more similar to the original GenMechs but not identical. They were smaller, with proportionally bigger tool nodes and no weapons. If the compromised GenMechs could be said to be analogous to ants, these were the workers. And they were numerous, crawling the walls, ceilings, and catwalks. The only saving grace was an exceptionally limited perceptive range. They did not detect Ziva until she was within a meter or so, and ceased pursuit once she was beyond that range. Coupled with their slow movement, it made them manageable as long as she kept moving and didn't get cornered.

She followed the signals for both power density and the displaced mass. Little rooms—the only features of this place that reliably had doors properly sealing them—each contained one "item of interest." The vast majority of them were quite clearly items from a hardcoded table from the designers of the countermeasure. Things that would be crucial to rebuilding society. So-called "vitamins." She saw full reactor assemblies from countless spacecraft. Blocks of assorted building materials, from copper to titanium. General purpose compute modules. But the target mass was farther ahead.

Ziva produced the shield disk and plowed through a row of marching GenMechs, then dashed toward a vertical catwalk and blazed her thrusters to ascend to the next level of the tangle of halls. Ahead, a door closed off a room large enough for all the previously observed resources. But inside was a single candy bar with a crab on the label.

"Of course," she said.

A worker GenMech spotted her and charged. She kicked it across the hallway, then drove her fingers into the thin metal of the door and crumpled it aside to fetch the candy bar. In the back of her consciousness, buzzing and flickering with failed decodes, a new signal appeared in her communication sweep. This was the transmission from her nonlocal duplicate, the version of Ziva presently serving as the mission director for Lex's dimensional shifts. She devoted a small portion of her processing power to devising a means to boost the signal, but there were greater concerns presently.

Damaging the door had activated some manner of internal alarm. The worker GenMechs started to pour from small openings in the walls, ceiling, and floor of the hallway.

"This is troubling," Ziva stated.

"What is it? How can I help?" Lex said over the com link.

She brought up a calculated internal schematic of the local region of the sphere. An area of high-power density, certainly something feeding the central transmitter, was far below. Above it, a long shaft bristling with heat pipes and cooling fins. It was almost perfectly straight, and almost perfectly clear, running far down toward the core of the sphere and reaching nearly the upper surface, with only a handful of regularly spaced gratings to protect it.

"I am indicating a position on the surface of the sphere. Please be prepared to intercept what remains of me at that position. I will be moving at extreme velocity, and I will be carrying the target mass. I am transmitting the command override to take control of the GenMechs once the central transmitter is damaged. Begin broadcasting the command at full power immediately."

"Wait, wait. Did you say 'what remains of you' just now?" Lex said.

Ziva shoveled the flood of GenMechs ahead of her out of the way with the shield. They were moving continuously, not with the stutter of the command cadence. That meant they were fully autonomous. They would not go dead when the processor failed. They would probably be able to be subverted along with the rest of the GenMechs, but not until after they'd completed or failed to complete their current task, which was most certainly "destroy intruder." If she was going to deliver the displaced mass to Lex, she was going to have to get out quickly, before they could fully block the exits. With half a kilometer of tunnels and shafts to navigate, her own thrusters wouldn't be fast enough. But there was a faster way.

"Ziva, what are you planning on doing?" Lex said urgently.

"The answer will be evident. Presently it requires my full attention."

She cut communications, the better to avoid having to endure further concerns from Lex, and boosted the thrusters in her feet. Rather than pure flight, which was very much a straight-line affair and thus easier for the increasing tide of GenMechs to intercept, she used the thrusters to turn her bounding strides into prodigious forward leaps, planting the palm of her free hand against walls and floors to pivot and burst down twisting hallways at maximum speed. She came to the shaft and threw her feet out ahead of her to surge the thrusters and come to a stop. She threw down the fusion device with all of her strength and tracked its descent as the walls around her began to roil with worker GenMechs.

Ziva started rocketing upward along the shaft. Workers single-mindedly seeking to end the intruder had disengaged some of the clasps for the hatches in order to open them and pursue her. She bashed them out of the way and climbed through the hatch. With a transmitted code, she detonated the fusion device. A crackling burst of electromagnetic distortion flared in her sensors. She conjured the shield disk beneath the thick grating under her feet. A surge of radiation and atomized metal scoured up along the walls of the tunnel, flash-melting the grating all around her and flecking her with slag. But a perfectly circular section of grating with her atop it was protected by the shield. Sheared away from its supports, it started to drop. Below, a second, slower wave of debris riding an explosion of metal vapor rushed up. She grabbed the grating and blazed her thrusters, pivoting to hold it above her with one arm while she kept the shield disk beneath her. The wall of force from the rush of vapor splashed against the disk and launched her upward. With the piece of grating held above her for protection, she clashed with the next grating, punching through. The structural elements of her body buckled with the force of the impact, and the temperature around her rose steadily higher. Another impact. Another. The protective grating was pulverized nearly to the point of uselessness now. The actuators in her raised arm had been shattered. Her systems were past their breaking point. Warnings of imminent failure filled her queue. Failure states claimed more of her systems. The surface was so close. So close...

Lex didn't need to ask what was happening now. The GenMechs had suddenly gone still a moment ago and then entered a low-power state. They were officially under new command. And a huge power spike within the sphere was certainly the fusion device detonating. With no attackers to worry about, Lex's only concern was reaching the designated rendezvous without bashing into the stationary GenMechs along the way.

Ahead, a lance of violet gas and energy burst from the surface of the sphere. Coal painted an indicator on the target mass.

"What about Ziva?" Lex said, accelerating toward it. "Where is Ziva?"

"I am detecting no active transponder or communicator signal for Ziva," Coal said.

"Give me a visual on the mass, then," Lex said.

The inset video displayed nothing but swirling, incandescent vapor with the mass indicator in the center. Gradually the brilliance of the light started to fade and the rigid form of Ziva became visible. Lex's face became stern as he swept closer.

"Tell me something, Coal. Tell me anything."

"Estimated surface temperature is three hundred degrees C and slowly cooling. Evidence of brief exposure to extreme heat beyond that range. Electrical activity minimal. Minor radioactivity. Well within the capacity of internal countermeasures."

"Is she alive?"

"There is very little sign of activity of any kind. If you are going to retrieve her framework, I suggest inverting the *SOB* to shield the Nugget still held to the bottom of the craft from the heat and radiation, as retrieval will not be possible with shields. The present hull integrity should be sufficient to survive a brief exposure to the conditions surrounding Ziva's framework."

Lex flipped the *SOB* over and tried to ignore Coal's substitution of "Ziva's framework" in place of simply "Ziva." He activated the tractor-net still held in the tractor beam to pull Ziva out of the swirling mass of destruction, then guided the *SOB* into a still and calm section of space.

He raised her up into view outside the cockpit. She was locked in a downright superheroic pose, one arm extended over her head, the other thrust down toward her feet. Battered and half-molten metal had completely wrapped around the raised arm. Her feet were sparking and fizzling, their thrusters roasted to uselessness. Most of her surface was blackened. The silvery flesh analog of her face had blistered. One eye was seared shut. The other was open, but dark.

"The mass is located inside the torso of the framework," Coal said. "The additional insulation and shielding appears to have protected it. I recommend utilizing the cutting torch located in the maintenance kit—"

"We're not cutting her open," Lex snapped.

"Lex, there is a duplicate of her program already in operation at the sanctuary," Coal said.

"I'm sick of hearing about duplicates," Lex said. "I don't care if there are a thousand things just like her. *This one matters.* Just like you matter and I matter. If nothing matters, *everything matters.*" He took a breath. "Do we have a signal from Ziva? The one back home?"

"It is weak. Initiating amplification."

A voice crackled through the distorted connection. "... repeats. Attempting to contact Lex. Message repeats. Stand by. Coal, I am detecting your signal. Adapting and boosting. Lex, are you there?"

"I'm here," Lex said.

"What is your status?"

"We have the stuff. It's a long story. We'll fill you in, but before we get started, I need the schematics for... you."

"Why?"

"Like I said, it's a long story."

It took seventy minutes for Ziva's body to cool down enough for her to be safe to bring into the cockpit. Once inside, the internal cooling and the presence of an atmosphere increased the cooling process significantly. From there it had been a slow process of disassembling the abdomen in the cramped quarters of the cockpit while a curious and not entirely helpful Squee periodically stuck her head up to see what was happening.

"All right. That's another fused wire swapped out. What's next?" Lex said.

"That should be sufficient to provide power to the logic and communication systems," Ziva said. "Reconnect the main power wire and watch for any sparks or smoke."

He eased the half-melted wire harness back into place. A few seconds later, the red iris illuminated and flickered.

"Stand by. Translating optical transmission," Coal said.

"—necessary, Lex. Ah. Thank you, Coal. While I appreciate the sentiment of repairing my system, that was entirely unnecessary, Lex," Ziva said. "This is not even the body you interacted with last time you were in this universe."

"Maybe I just wanted it on my official ledger that I saved some version of you, okay?" Lex said. "Can you move?"

"I cannot. It is a testament to Karter's engineering skill that my processor and memory are intact. Were you able to retrieve the displaced mass?"

"Yes. And let me tell you, I am sick to death of this frickin' crab candy bar. How many problems can one seafood dessert possibly cause?"

"And the GenMechs?" Ziva said.

"In standby," Coal said.

"Oh, and Ziva? Meet Ziva," Lex said.

"I am pleased to discover that a local instance of my design and code set remains active in the role of preserving humanity," said the home-world version of Ziva over the connection.

"And I am similarly pleased to know that I serve a valuable purpose in another world," said the local Ziva. "What became of the Nuggets?"

"One of them retreated and has not returned. The other is still on the belly of the ship, either dead or otherwise inert," Coal said.

"Right. It's there, and I knew that, and didn't completely forget until right this moment," Lex said. "Coal, let's disconnect that thing and have a look."

"Acknowledged," Coal said.

The tractor-net on the belly of the ship deactivated, and Coal deployed the tractor beam to snatch the entity as it slowly drifted away. She repositioned it to hold it in front of the fractured cockpit and put a high-detail video feed of it on the HUD. Ziva's reconstruction of it back home had been remarkably accurate. There was very little new to see, except for two minor points and one major one. It was undulating slightly, and the mechanical tail was damaged. More crucially, a sequence of shifting patterns was sliding across its hide. They were faintly illuminated and consisted of clusters of circular points gradually creeping across the thing's hide like a scrolling marquee.

"Oh... Wow..." Lex said. "Are those what I think they are?"

"The clusters total two, three, five, seven, eleven, thirteen..." Coal said.

"Prime numbers," Lex said. "So is that thing a machine or something?"

"It is a common assumption that when the time comes to make first contact, the common language between species will be mathematics," Local Ziva said. "Organic or not, math is one of the few things that can be considered to be constant between universes."

"Precisely," Home Ziva said.

"Can you display something for that thing to see?" Lex said.

"The *SOB* does not have an external display. But it may not be necessary. I have discovered a matching prime sequence being modulated in an energy field surrounding the Nugget. I will broadcast primes in return."

"This is a monumental occurrence," Home Ziva said. "The first-recorded encounter with an intelligence that is nonhuman and of nonhuman origin."

"We should treat this moment very carefully. First contact is a time of great diplomatic sensitivity," Local Ziva said.

"Technically first contact was when I chased them away, and second contact was when they tried to kill us," Coal said. "So far I'm enjoying third contact much better. It is broadcasting data very densely."

"Record it," Local Ziva said. "We may be able to establish communication."

"Seems like that'd take a long time," Lex said

"Stand by," Local Ziva said. "Coal, please cross-link the following sequence of instructions to the command protocol of the compromised GenMechs."

Her iris began flickering far more rapidly. Outside, the entire fleet of GenMechs reoriented, then descended toward the sphere.

"In a few minutes, we will have the distributed-processing power of several billion GenMechs. I am confident a common understanding of the organism's language can be found in short order. I will also arrange for a docking bay and a pressurized, oxygenated habitation chamber to be constructed in order to engage in repairs."

"Gee," Lex said. "Having an endless army of robots and all the resources of an entire star system at one's fingertips is kind of handy."

Chapter 8

With the GenMechs as workers, it took less than twenty-eight minutes for a large, fully equipped repair bay with force-field-powered atmosphere retention to be constructed. Food synthesizers would take a good deal longer, which was unfortunate, because having donated his entire food supply to the sanctuary, Lex was now over twenty-four hours since his last meal. Squee, on the other hand, was perfectly happy, as the bag of treats that seemed inappropriate to give to the hungry survivors had been more than meal enough for her. He sipped the water they were able to synthesize.

Across from where the *SOB* was having fresh parts fabricated and installed by Gen-Mechs—something he was having trouble getting used to—Lex could see a space vessel being assembled, the first of many that would be used to reach the survivors in the sanctuary and begin transporting them here for defense, settlement, and eventually, outreach. This was the base and the workforce from which human society could be rebuilt.

But it was one thing to rebuild a crumbled society over generations. It was another thing to have nothing but a salvaged and quickly installed force-field generator between him and deep space.

"We're sure that thing is strong enough? It was built in like two minutes by a horde of robots that wanted me dead immediately before that," Lex said.

"I am quite sure," Local Ziva said, now able to speak again, having had a fair amount of repair work done by the now entirely loyal GenMech workers.

"All right. And why no gravity?" he asked.

"It was the first thing we were able to translate from the data offered up by the Nugget," Home Ziva said. "It is biologically incompatible with high-gravitational intensity."

Lex glared at the thing, which was drifting around in the docking bay, seemingly completely harmless. He glanced at the *SOB*, specifically at the fresh panel installed where this thing or its partner had nearly lasered through in a prior confrontation. The tail had been removed and was on a table on the opposite side of the bay being scanned by worker GenMechs.

"Did it tell us what its plan was?" Lex said.

"That appears to be a complex issue," Local Ziva said. "But I believe we've constructed a workable communication scheme. The organism is able to communicate with visual glyphs and with pulse encodings in its biofield projections. Rather than divert resources to producing a modification to your suit or slidepad to communicate, I believe it will be more efficient to install the relevant software into Coal's system. The *SOB* already has the hardware to interpret its communications and match them in reply. For reasons that will become clear, that will also streamline the diplomatic efforts. Are you prepared, Coal?"

"Yes. Stand by... Translation package installed. Initializing autotranslation routine. Hello, Nugget."

The drifting entity darted toward the *SOB* with alarming speed. Complex patterns danced across the thing's mantle, like old-fashioned QR codes shown in rapid succession.

"Hello!" came the voice that had been selected for the thing. It was a bright, energetic, gender-neutral trill, youthful and exuberant. "This subset had not anticipated communication to be possible for many cycles! You are a very gifted entity."

"Yes, I am," Coal said.

"May I please have the tool-tail and the vibrationally unique mass?" the thing said.

"Hold on," Lex said, marching up to the thing. "Before we do that, let's get some preliminaries out of the way. What is your *name*?"

"This subset is the one thousand seven hundred sixty-sixth subdivision of the core set, element Beta of the Ninth Excursional Dyad."

"What part of that is your name?" Lex said.

"Your attendants are very inquisitive, Intelligent Entity," the Nugget said.

"Yes, they are," Coal said.

"We're not her attendants, we're—Look, never mind, can I call you Dyad?"

"That is a uniquely inappropriate name," Local Ziva said. "Dyad implicitly implies two individuals, not one."

"I will call it Nugget," Coal said.

"We're already calling the *species* Nugget, and I don't even like *that*," Lex said.

"This one is *the* Nugget. Those are simply Nuggets," Coal said.

"This subset is confused by the present conversation," the entity said.

"I am going to adjust the translation," Coal said.

"I am confused by the present conversation," the entity's voice repeated.

"Much better," Coal said. "Some of my attendants are happier with simpler designations, so we have chosen to apply the designation 'Nugget' to you."

"I see. That is acceptable if it will ease communication," Nugget said.

Lex covered his face and grumbled. "Fine, Nugget. Why do you want the mass you're after?"

"It is my goal to retrieve it. More generally, it is the goal of the Excursional Dyads to acquire such mass."

"Why?"

"That information is not available to the Beta half of this dyad."

"Wait, Beta! We could call you Beta," Lex said.

"It's Nugget," Coal said firmly.

"We need a firmer context," Local Ziva said, choosing not to dwell on the name issue. "What is a dyad?"

"A dyad is a semirecently divided whole entity. The dyad contains all the knowledge previously available to the whole entity, but that knowledge is split between the two halves of the dyad."

"Interesting," Home Ziva said. "Your species reproduces via division."

"Correct," said Nugget. "Yours does not?"

"There are a great many species here, most of them do not," Local Ziva said.

"Ah! This simultaneously clarifies and confuses. The appearance and functionality of the various members of this group seem to vary greatly. It seemed unlikely that a single species would have such extreme biological diversity between individuals. But if there are multiple species, why has one not destroyed the others?"

"It wasn't for lack of trying, but we've more or less learned to get along," Lex said.

"That is unlikely. It is the essential nature of that which is divided to be destroyed. It is why the Merging is so important. Only in the Merging, in unity, can there be peace," Nugget said.

"That felt awfully religious right there," Lex said under his breath.

"We have so much to learn, Nugget," said Local Ziva. "Before we continue, I want to be sure I've understood your nature correctly thus far. It seems from your description that the process of division splits information between the offspring?"

"That is correct. Permanent memories and other aspects of identity developed over time are divided roughly equally between the two entities once they are split. We require many cycles to develop sufficient nonvolatile neural mass to relearn what is lost, unless a union occurs in the interim, but those are quite rare and taxing."

"What about what you're learning now? About us?" Coal said.

"Only key data, valuable to the species, are selected to be written into our nonvolatile neural mass, our permanent genetic memory. A secondary short-term memory mass holds other information of unproven value to the species. This memory degrades over cycles unless transferred to the limited permanent neural mass. But do not worry. I will remember all of this for many, many cycles, even if it is not deemed necessary for the species in perpetuity. This comes at the cost of the information being deemed untrustworthy by myself and others of my species."

"You don't trust us?" Lex said.

"Presently I do not. But that is not the meaning of my prior statement. There are a great many things I know to be true, things which are indeed central to the operation of the species, which I do not have room for in my nonvolatile neural mass. They thus reside in short-term memory, recent instructions. An example. I have described the Merging. This is a core belief of the species, that it is the final goal of our species to reunite and finally restore all knowledge to a single entity. This is known to be the purpose for all our endeavors. It is thus instructed to all freshly budded individuals, along with the instruction that it should be made a part of permanent memory as soon as there is sufficient neural mass. But there is *not* sufficient neural mass, and thus it remains in my short-term memory. I am aware of this information, but it is not a part of me. I do not believe it, but I am instructed to act as though I do, and thus, I do so. It is intellectually true rather than core to my mindset. This is not how your minds operate?"

"Everything I learn becomes part of a big mushy mass of memories," Lex said.

"I am an artificial intelligence. Knowledge is a malleable and instantly updatable set of storage."

"Likewise," said Local Ziva.

"Curious," Nugget said.

"Do you know *why* you had to get this mass?"

"I do! There is a sharply divergent quantum shift that facilitates nonlocal attunement. That mass, by its fractured nature, provides the template by which we have been able to travel between dimensions."

"So you want it so that you can travel to different dimensions?" Lex said.

"No. Now that we have learned how to jump to different dimensions, we retain that ability. Though not enough cycles have passed for that knowledge to become permanent for any of our species. It will take two cycles at least."

Lex rubbed his forehead. "And how long is a cycle?"

"A difficult thing to define without context. I will produce two color pulses. They will be spaced by seven microcycles." Nugget did so.

"A cycle is equal to two point three five years," said Coal and Local Ziva simultaneously.

"So you guys take like five years to officially, genuinely believe something?" Lex said.

"Yes," Nugget said. "Though we can shift a great many beliefs from short-term to permanent memory with each update. And again, a union can almost entirely replace all missing knowledge in permanent memory, but they are quite rare."

"How long do you live?" Lex asked.

"The species has existed for a period of time exceeding five thousand cycles."

"No, I mean how long does an individual live."

"Either there is a flaw in the translation, or you have a different interpretation of the concept of individuality. Each of us contains within us an aspect of the progenitor of our species. We are all one, temporarily fragmented until the time of the Merging restores us to unity."

"What was the plan when you got the mass back home?" Lex asked.

"The presence of the mass acts as a crystalizing agent for our influence over neighboring parallel dimensions. Greater quantities of mass increase this influence. Our understanding is that any quantity of the unique mass will allow us to achieve our goal. Greater quantities of that mass will accelerate the process."

"And the goal is?" Lex asked.

"The Merging. We have been collecting every piece of unique mass in the multiverse. We have acquired nearly all fractured mass, failing only to acquire the mass which you acquired before us. We will use that to achieve the Merging, drawing other worlds into our own."

"Wait, wait, wait," Lex said. "I'd assumed 'the Merging' was dealing with you creatures combining back into one."

"It is. But there can be no unity where there is division. Merging our kind but existing separate to other worlds is insufficient. All must be one."

Lex turned to Local Ziva. "Any idea what will happen if these guys start collapsing universes into each other?"

"Impossible to be certain, but very few scenarios result in any of the affected universes retaining the capacity to support life. The influx of mass will almost certainly lead to cosmic contraction. The big crunch, the counterpart to the big bang."

"The Merging," Nugget corrected.

"These guys are going to destroy a bunch of universes," Lex said.

"Unify them," Nugget corrected.

"You do realize that will kill an unbelievable number of people, including all of you," Lex said.

"That does appear to be accurate. And that does appear to be undesirable, but I am instructed to consider the Merging to be ideal and desirable, and so I must assume that it is. It would have been helpful if the other half of my dyad was here to speak with you on the matter. The core belief in the Merging was in that half of the memories."

"And why are you being so forthcoming about this?" Lex asked.

"I have been instructed to take all necessary steps to acquire the mass and return home. I am weakened and incomplete. I will not be able to return home without aid. So the communication-and-diplomacy package has been deployed in hopes of acquiring aid."

"I see. Can we discuss things for a minute? Privately?" Lex said.

"That is entirely acceptable," Nugget said.

"I have deactivated the translator," Coal said.

"What are we going to do about this?" Lex said urgently.

"Unclear," Local Ziva said. "I have processed the initial dump of data provided in what I suppose could be the 'diplomacy package' from the Nugget, and it is clear that the creatures are, or at least wish to be seen as, what might be uncharitably referred to as religious zealots. They provided a historical record of their species. They either are, or believe themselves to be, the only sentient species in their universe. They live out their entire life cycle in space. The color changing seems to be a biological adaptation to absorb solar radiation of different wavelengths more efficiently. Nutrients are absorbed by seeking nebulas and effectively filter-feeding. And they have adapted to store energy and nutrients in extremely high densities to allow long periods without feeding, which also facilitates existing in high-pressure environments, though not high gravity. The most significant historical event is described as 'the Division.' It seems to have been a war in which members of their race containing certain beliefs were entirely wiped out. They do not appear to have the technological concept of a written language or any nonbiological knowledge retention. Because of their nature of dividing their knowledge between off-spring, this means a genocide based upon belief effectively erased that belief from their history with no capacity to return. You'll note it listed the age of the race as being 'greater than five thousand cycles.' I suspect the general nature of that answer is primarily because that war literally deleted large swaths of their own racial memory predating the conflict."

"Seems like that'd leave a pretty deep scar in a race," Lex said.

"Precisely the kind of historical event that would provide a focus on retaining knowledge and unifying knowledge for fear of losing any more of their history," Local Ziva said.

"It is truly a fascinating biology. Knowledge and beliefs effectively are written into their genetic code," Home Ziva said over the connection. "It, alas, means that it may be literally impossible for them to change their minds."

"Diplomacy is not an option," Coal said. "Have you finished fabricating the fusion device you promised me?"

"A strong moral and ethical argument can be made that in the absence of an alternative, stopping the Nuggets by any means necessary, up to and including exterminating them, is preferable to allowing them to complete their goals, assuming their goals are achievable. But a similarly strong argument can and must be made that if there is any means to prevent such an extreme outcome, it must be pursued."

"Is anyone else uncomfortable with how upbeat Nugget seems to be about all this?" Lex said. "It's saying very intense things in a very matter of fact way."

"It lacks facial features, and its language has no clear tone indicators. All delivery is synthetic," Coal said. "Please try to avoid being so humancentric in your interpretation."

"Forgive me, but until that thing showed up, when it came to having conversations, humancentrism was basically the only option," Lex said.

"To return to the matter at hand," Home Ziva said. "Based upon my analysis, all remaining displaced mass has indeed been tightly focused on both a spatial and temporal point. It is entirely possible the Nuggets have indeed finished accumulating the displaced mass that you didn't. It thus becomes clear the way forward has two priorities. We must not allow them to acquire the mass we have collected, and we must acquire the mass *they* have collected, both to repair the damage done to our world, and to prevent their activation of the so-called Merging."

"But we're talking about time being one of the axes we can slide around on, right?" Lex said. "Technically we're in the *future* right now. So can't we just go back and get the stuff before they got it?"

"Unclear," Local Ziva said. "The Nuggets have interacted with us, coupling the time-lines. It is possible that a paradox would result."

"But I thought paradoxes *weren't a thing* and everything just splits the universe into both options every time," Lex said. "And if that's true, doesn't that mean that the displaced mass we're after is being duplicated an infinite number of times every time anything at all happens in the universe?" He ran his fingers through his hair. "I can't tell if I'm learning how things really work or just flat out losing my mind..." he continued.

"The mass detector is pointing us to the precise mass that we are seeking," Home Ziva said. "Each displaced mass exists in the form we require it in precisely one branch of one universe, and the coupled and interweaved worldlines mean that if a contradictory anachronistic event causes the mass to become inaccessible due to either removing that universe from the continuum or preventing our access to it, then the mass is gone to us regardless of our temporal offset."

"Ugh," Lex said. "Have I said I hate time travel and multiverse crap?"

"You have," Coal said.

"Well I haven't said it often enough," Lex said. "But whatever, what's the plan?"

"We will be able to access their world because it contains the target mass, and we will be able to return to our own because once the mass is acquired, it will bring us home. What we need to establish is the nature of the threat that will be awaiting us when we arrive, and what if any capacity they have to arrive in our home dimension to acquire the mass we have already discovered."

"Let's get questioning," Lex said.

"Reactivating communicator," Coal said.

"Hello again," Nugget said. "May I have my tool-tail and the mass now?"

"See, here's the deal, Nugget," Lex said. "We really don't want to die."

"Unify," Nugget corrected.

"For all intents and purposes, same thing," Lex said. "Remember how you tried to melt a hole in that ship there?"

"That was the other half of the dyad, but I am aware of the incident. You were attempting to restrain me."

"It's because our universe is frozen in time right now and we need that mass to fix it, and to get home, and you were running away with it."

"Then you will be pleased to know that our intended goal of the Merging will make the time-frozen nature of your universe of little concern."

"Destruction is not something to be pleased about," Lex pointed out. "The tool-tail, is that as powerful as your weapons get?"

"No. That is the tool-tail. Its martial execution is secondary. Our defenses are..." Nugget paused. "I apologize, but I now recall that I am instructed to believe that cooperation with the enemy on matters of military might is a poor tactical decision."

"We aren't the enemy," Coal said. "We could have killed you. I even had a plan. It involved holding you in the tractor beam and grinding you along the surface of the sphere. But we did not do that."

"You seek to prevent the Merging. I am instructed to believe this makes you antagonistic to our kind by definition."

"Fine. Will you tell me this? Is your dyad planning to try to get the rest of the mass? The mass we got already."

"Yes. However, it is not presently possible."

"Why not?" Lex asked.

"Because the underlying field-manipulation mechanism that facilitates dimensional travel was in permanent memories in the possession of the other half of the dyad, and the specific tracking and detection skills necessary to pinpoint mass is in my half of the memory distribution."

"Your buddy won't be able to find it without you, and you won't be able to shift to it without them," Lex said.

"Correct."

"You can't get home? And your partner just *left you here*?"

"The dimensional shifting was the greater-value information. That information was more crucial to return, as with it, the Merging can be accelerated, and the Merging will restore all that is lost."

"Were you two the only ones that had it?"

"It is present in the short-term memory of three other dyads, but they contained key memories which were deemed too valuable to risk."

"But they could teach someone else, couldn't they?"

"Perhaps. Perhaps not. I represent lost information. They may choose not to risk diluting the racial memory any further. Until I am returned, they may choose not to risk further excursions. Particularly not when the Merging can be achieved with the mass already acquired."

Lex rubbed his bleary eyes.

"Lex, I am pleased to inform you that I have completed food synthesis," Local Ziva said.

"Oh thank god. This is hard enough to wrap my head around on zero food," he said.

"Exit through the freshly installed door in the rear of the bay to find a table with food and drink waiting for you and Squee. I have installed artificial gravity in the room for your comfort. Nugget, can I offer you some nutrition of some sort?"

"My injury at the hands of these now seemingly nonhostile robots has depleted my nutrient reserves. I am instructed to remain in proximity to the target mass, but I could very much benefit from a source of high-intensity light in the two-hundred-seventy-point-two to three-hundred-sixty-five-point-two nanometer range."

"I can certainly oblige. An energy projector will be made available shortly." Local Ziva turned to Lex. "This way, Lex."

A few minutes later, Lex was stirring at a dish of... food. It was somewhat similar to the stuff that Ziva had provided back home—evidently she didn't have a deep reservoir of recipes. But unlike the stuff back home, she hadn't seen fit to differentiate the colors. It was a collection of white lumps in a gray "sauce." It tasted generically savory, and even though it was both more nutritious and better tasting than half of the stuff he'd lived on in his college years, he probably wouldn't have found it particularly appetizing if not for his extreme hunger and desperate search for something to distract him from the present situation. Squee, on the other hand, seemed perfectly content to lap at the bowl set before her.

"We're about to go into a situation where we don't know what to expect—pretty par for the course, but I'm still getting tired of it," he said through a mouthful of the slop.

"We can make some educated guesses," Local Ziva said, stroking the unhelmeted head of Squee. "We know that they have no real knowledge of humans or even non-Nugget life-forms, beyond what they have observed during this mission. And new information is considered low-trust in their society."

"Sure. It kind of explains why it's so obliging. The mission is new, so it's doing as instructed, but it has no connection to the instructions. Its heart isn't in it."

"The lack of other life-forms, and the knowledge that there has been a war in their history, suggests we will be facing weapons that are designed to be dangerous to *them* rather than specifically dangerous to us. They are poorly suited to existing in a gravitational field, so gravity generators of some description may be employed. Additionally, they rely upon their pigmentation to absorb light for energy. Something to interrupt that might be a useful weapon against them."

Lex stared vaguely forward, stirring the dish without eating.

"You appear uneasy, Lex," she said.

"These things... look, I'm not a fighter, you know that. Squee has killed more people than I have. But with these things, it feels... different somehow. They don't have things written down. Any one of them that dies could be taking some irreplaceable part of their culture with it. The exploits of some ancient hero. The knowledge of a philosopher. The best joke in the universe. Poetry, family history. These things had a war once before, and losing a part of themselves—even if it was by their own... tentacles or whatever, left enough of a mark on the society that they came up with this whole religious fixation on merging again, to get that information *back*. I really don't like the idea of these things having me as the one representative of intelligent, biological, interdimensional creatures and I come through and wipe out any memory of their grandma or whatever."

"It would be preferable to find a peaceful alternative, but they have illustrated a capacity to detect you while cloaked, so sneaking in and acquiring the mass is not a workable option, as we must assume they will be defending the mass."

Lex narrowed his eyes. "This here. This is a result of a temporal offset, right? We showed up in the other two places roughly aligned with when we left home. But the fact that we showed up in the future here means there's a way to offset when we show up."

"The temporal aspect of targeting is not immediately clear. You showed up in this time because it was the point at which the mass was most accessible or detectible."

"But what does that *mean*, though?"

"We've established that the mass, and the universes the mass ended up in, seem to have a psychological connection to you. Perhaps you were drawn to this point in time because it was the point at which the mass was in closest proximity to a large quantity of GenMechs without being destroyed. GenMechs have rightly made a significant impact on your mind."

"But that would require that I *know* where it was going. If it was *me* that was somehow targeting this stuff with my thoughts, I can see how I'd be able to accidentally pick doodads that were important or significant to me, but how would I know how the place and time would *also* be significant to me?"

Local Ziva nodded. "An important question, with potentially a very useful answer. And I suspect I know how to uncover it. Are you satisfied with your meal?"

"If you think we can figure out how this whole mess has been working, then I'll stuff the rest in a doggie bag. Let's go."

• • ● ● ● ● ● ● ● • •

"And the parts over the eyes are for blocking drops of biological coolant, but are also used for indicating emotional state," Coal said.

"Like this?" Nugget said.

The door behind her opened. Coal directed her cameras to observe Lex and Local Ziva stepping out of the cafeteria and drifting up as they left the artificial gravity.

"Lex, Ziva. Look what I helped Nugget do," Coal said.

Nugget drifted aside to reveal to them an extremely crude and slightly misshapen rendering of a human face formed on its hide. It was roughly on par with what a kindergarten child could do, though it animated the face lightly, most notably by raising one eyebrow and then the other.

"I was unaware that humans engaged in visual communication," Nugget said. "With so few possible states, you must have a very limited visual vocabulary."

"We manage," Lex said. "Listen, Coal, I need to hop in and run the snap-back simulator."

"Excellent. It has been some time since I have had an opportunity to help you analyze and improve your hoversled racing skill."

"No, no. That's not what we will be doing," Lex said.

"As a matter of fact, I believe that will be the most useful activity," Local Ziva said.

"Oh. Then yeah, that's what we'll be doing."

He and Local Ziva jetted up, Squee in tow. Coal opened the cockpit. Lex took his place in the pilot's seat, and Ziva slid into the passenger seat.

"Load us up the racetrack sim," Lex said.

"The exact one you were experiencing when the first quantum-shift event occurred," Local Ziva said. "Also cross-link me with the control program and provide me with a similar amount of perceptive time compression. I will need to observe."

"What is the purpose of this exercise?" Coal asked.

"We're going to try to figure out how I've been picking the targets for these jumps," Lex said.

"Ah. Good. Perhaps then you can pick one where the dominant life-form is artificial intelligence derived. That would be an interesting place to visit. Activating snap-back simulator."

Lex's vision was slowly overtaken by the simulated visuals of the racetrack. He felt a jolt of recognition, and calm, at seeing the familiar sight. Even simulated, a slice of home that still had the liveliness of wind stirring up dust was a relief. It instantly reminded him of the stakes of this mission. This, and everything like it, was what he was fighting for.

One by one, additional hoversleds popped up around him.

"Coal and I are going to slowly dial up the time compression," Local Ziva said. "Begin the race as normal. Focus entirely on the simulation. We will analyze secondary effects and carefully introduce aspects of the event that shattered the temporal axis of your own world under controlled conditions to prevent a repeat incident."

"You're confident you can do that?" Lex said.

"I am presently the focal point for a swarm of mechanisms which, combined, exceed the computational capacity and power utilization of all of human civilization at its peak. I am confident I can achieve the necessary degree of control," Local Ziva said calmly.

"All right then. Let's get it moving."

The countdown started, and the race began. It was downright unsettling just how quickly his frazzled mind and body were willing to entirely disregard the worries of the universe and turn themselves entirely to the task of shaving time off the track record. Even with the gentle, distracting buzz at the back of his mind, he only half heard the conversation going on between Coal and Ziva as he edged around turns and swapped simulated paint with rivals.

"Nesting Carpinelli Fields," Coal said.

"Monitoring dimensional interface," Ziva said.

"Increasing time compression," Coal said.

"Interesting... I am seeing considerable crosstalk breaching the dimensional interface," Ziva said. "Increasing nested Carpinelli Field to sixteen percent of incident threshold."

"Minor noise on neural interpreter," Coal said.

"Isolating and analyzing. I am detecting sensory activations in the subnanosecond timescale. Incomplete, but substantial enough to measure and partially reconstruct."

"Increasing time compression. Approaching event threshold," Coal said.

"Timescale of sensory activations are now in the millisecond timescale. Yes. I'm seeing interaction between the neural interface and the dimensional interface. I am satisfied."

"We should let him finish the race," Coal said.

"Naturally. I wouldn't dream of interrupting it."

Lex feathered the throttle enough to put the second-place sled into position to serve as a slide-stop on the final turn, then pushed it to max to slam across the line.

"Damn. Three-tenths off track record. Bring it around one more time and—"

"I'm afraid we have things to discuss, Lex," Local Ziva said.

"Oh. Right, right."

Reality bled back into his vision, and the warm comfort of familiarity slipped away, leaving him staring at the recently constructed repair bay once more and immediately putting an icy sting in the pit of his stomach. "What's the word?" Lex said, popping the cockpit.

They drifted out and hung in space in front of the *SOB*.

"Sure enough, in the conditions that led to the incident, some of the filtered interference the simulation was receiving was flashes of information from other worlds. Did you detect this?" Local Ziva said.

"My head felt a little fuzzy sometimes."

"Likely that was the data," she continued. "The information was fragmentary, and any given instance of it lasted far shorter than the amount of time the conscious mind would need to interpret them. But you have a *very* fast reaction time, and time itself was *very* compressed. Combined, it seems clear that the interference was producing a subliminal effect. You were not aware of it, but some of these were almost certainly evoking a strong emotional response. This brain activity was detected by the simulator, and through some interaction between the many-layered systems, this led to the breaching of the dimensional interface. You *were* selecting both the items to send across to other worlds and the worlds to send them to. You just didn't know you were doing it."

"Okay. So I for sure brought this all on myself. Again. Can't say I'm shocked. It's kind of my thing at this point," Lex said. "Can we use it?"

"*We* cannot use it. *You* may be able to. The specific interaction that brings about the breaches requires a rapid electrochemical source of perception. You, or people gifted or trained to have abnormally fast response times, can produce this effect. And while your neurological reactions trigger the shifts, there does not appear to be any way to select where the interference comes from. Thus, we can create a situation where you will be exposed to sensory information from the multiverse, and we can use your response to trigger a shift. But we cannot finely filter the universes you have to choose from."

"Define 'finely filter,'" Lex said.

"The only meaningful data available to us are nebulously defined electrochemical impulses in your head, the *also* nebulously defined amount of quantum shift necessary for the jump, and some gentle indication of temporal offset. So the best we could do is filter for things that are closer to any given target. We can guarantee you would be getting closer to your target with each jump."

"That sounds like it's workable. Maybe it'll take a couple jumps to get where we need to go. I've heard worse problems," Lex said.

"Please recall we are dealing with an infinite number of universes. Even if we move you ninety-nine percent of the remaining distance toward your goal with every shift, there is still no upper limit to the number of shifts necessary to get there," Local Ziva said.

"But we ended up *here*, right? We ended up someplace we've been before. What are the odds of that?" Lex said.

"Zero. But that's a quirk of doing statistics with infinity in the equation. The odds of any individual outcome are zero because if the odds were greater than zero, then the odds of the full set would be greater than one hundred percent. Your point is taken, however. By whatever means the interaction between the simulator and your mind selects its destination, it clearly has a very high attraction radius to the selected target. It is likely that if we get you 'close enough,' then you'll find your way there. And more to the point, so long as you survive any given shift, the presence of displaced mass in your ship will allow you to return to your home. So it is safe, by your standards, to attempt to target your dimensional shifts in this way. But what is your goal?"

"I was *hoping* to go back and change their history so they didn't have that war that made them dead set on destroying as many universes as possible, but apparently we can't do that."

"We can, it would just create a splinter universe and potentially lock us out of the actual universe of concern," Coal said. "Are you not paying attention?"

"Listen, you," Lex grumbled. "But there's *got* to be a way to dislodge these people from the destructive path they're on."

"Their beliefs are literally a part of them," Local Ziva. "The war responsible for the present situation is the minimum necessary action to change their minds as a species."

"What we need to know is what exactly they want back from the Merging. They don't consider themselves individuals, so what are the odds they even care about the ones that died? Nugget even said it's the *information* they're worried about losing. So it's the information they must want back." Lex shut his eyes. "We need to talk to Nugget again."

A few minutes later, they were once again drifting in the cargo bay with their alien companion. The brief "snack" had a pronounced effect on its apparent mood. Additional colors were flitting across its hide, and they were pulsing with a sequence of discordant rhythms. Of course, none of this would necessarily have been a sign of good cheer, but the way it spoke left little room for doubt.

"Hello, friends. This cycle is a fine cycle. Things could only be improved further if you were to provide the displaced mass and a means to return to my race."

"We're working on that. The returning, that is," Lex said. "But I had one more question, and it's pretty important. This war, the war that cost you your knowledge of the origin of the species and all that, do you know what it was about?"

"The very nature of the war was to eliminate the part of us that knew what the war as about."

"Right, right. You don't know the information you were wiping out, because you succeeded in wiping it out. But do you know *why* you were wiping it out?"

"It was dangerous," Nugget said.

"Dangerous how?" Lex asked.

"Dangerous enough to make excising the idea more important than the other knowledge excised along with it."

"How can I articulate this...? Your permanent memories. Those are pure, unassailable fact to you, yes?"

"That is accurate."

"And it takes you a couple of cycles to make regular memories permanent?"

"Yes."

"How often do you split or divide or bud or whatever?"

"Variable. Ten to thirty cycles."

"Is that enough time to relearn all the permanent things?"

"It takes between eight and fifteen cycles to restore all lost knowledge from a division."

"So when do you learn *new* things? When does *brand-new* knowledge become permanent?"

"Brand-new knowledge? Rarely."

"So you creatures collectively just don't learn much over the years. You stick with what you know and that's it?"

"There are many of us. If each learns one or two things permanently, we all learn a great deal collectively."

"But do you? Only the individuals know it, and the others won't trust it because *they* don't know it permanently."

"I understand the confusion. We are capable of sharing memories, once permanent. It is known as a union."

Lex pointed excitedly. "Yes! Excellent! How?"

"Once per one hundred fifteen cycles, on average, we gather into carefully selected groups and interlink. Huge amounts of nutrients and energy are expended, but permanent memories are duplicated across the whole of the group. It is the mechanism by which the Merging will occur. A union that will never end. A union of all beings and all times and all things. Combined, complete. All lost knowledge regained."

"And you want that. More than anything. Lost knowledge."

"It is considered the highest goal for the species."

"What about a partial one? What about *some* lost knowledge regained?"

"This is not possible. Lost knowledge is lost. It cannot be regained without the Merging."

"But what if it could? What would that be worth?"

"It would be worth anything."

"If we could get you the knowledge that was lost as a result of that war, would you agree to give us our mass back without a fight and call off the Merging?"

"I cannot make that decision in isolation."

"Do you think the folks back home would agree?"

The colors shifting across the hide became complex and organized into fractal shapes.

"The Merging is *supposed* to happen on its own. Bringing it about actively was desirable but not essential. If a piece of it were to occur on its own, then I believe that would be sufficiently convincing to persuade the others to wait for the rest to come as well. It would be in keeping with our beliefs."

"Great. Then you and me are taking a ride."

It took another hour for Local Ziva, who had been coddling Squee for much of that time, to finish synthesizing enough food and water for her to be comfortable sending Lex off again. It had taken considerably less time to work through the changes to the software necessary to facilitate the closest thing they could get to a targeted dimensional shift. But now all was in readiness, including, to Lex's dismay, the installation of a fusion bomb alongside the two tractor-nets on the belly of the *SOB*.

"You require a vehicle to travel great distances," Nugget said, drifting inside the cockpit. "It is impressive you ever managed to travel at all."

Lex kept telling himself that it was an insanely fortunate turn of events that Nugget hadn't turned out to be a murderous beast or a supersoldier or something. But something about its attitude was rubbing him the wrong way.

"What do I need to know about how these shifts work?" Lex said, checking his gear before drifting up to the cockpit.

"The bulk of its operation will be under Coal's control. Your role is to focus your mind on the precise place you wish to arrive. The filter will attempt to prevent sensory input from universes 'farther' from your destination than your departure point. The presence of the candy bar in the ship, because it is displaced and damaged mass from your own world, will provide you with a means to communicate with your own native Ziva, and will act as an emergency fallback to dump you in your own world if something goes wrong. The temporal offset is key, and the primary focus of the filtering. It is crucially important that your first direct interaction with the native universe of the Nuggets is your arrival in its pre-war past. That will be the point at which your world and theirs will become coupled. If you interact directly with their world in any way at a point *after* the extermination of the lost Nuggets, traveling back could create a splinter universe that will make travel to the actual version we need to access nearly impossible with our current means."

"I'll try to think older than I need to," Lex said. "Though considering I'm 'picturing' something that I didn't experience in the first place as a means of targeting, precision might not be a possibility. Are we sure we can't just use our alien friend's brain for this?"

"The mechanism that allows it to operate for your own brain is too weakly understood to hope to adapt it to an unfamiliar biology."

"Then I'll have to do it and hope for the best."

"That, and a great deal of other problems, make me concerned this is not an ideal plan," Coal said.

"Has anyone come up with a better one?" Lex said.

"I believe opening communication with the Nuggets may prove fruitful," Home Ziva said. "Local Ziva and I have collaborated, and the presence of so much displaced mass in the Nugget home world—"

"Coal, I'm blaming you for them sounding ridiculous while talking about something very important."

"I think it's cute," Coal said.

"I concur," Local Ziva said.

"As do I," Home Ziva said.

"I guess great minds think alike when they're all derived from the same code," Lex said. "But you were saying?"

"The presence of mass in the alien entity's home world makes communication a distinct possibility. We now have a firm knowledge of their language, and we have refined our interdimensional communication system. Communication is possible."

"We've already established, if it's a permanent memory, then even if we can communicate, diplomacy *isn't* possible."

"The precise mechanism by which they are attempting to collapse the universes is new, as evidenced by the status of Nugget's memories of it. Provided we contact them while this is still the case for the entire species, or at least a sufficient proportion, then there is a chance."

"Then we'll try both," Lex said.

"We can't try both in parallel. If we contact their world directly, that sets the point of coupling between either of our worlds and theirs. It makes your mission a potential division point," Local Ziva said.

"But you can try *after* I show up in the past, right?" Lex said.

"Yes, but you will have already imperiled yourself."

"Like there was any chance of us getting out of this without me ending up in peril. When I get back there, you start talking to them. But if there's one thing I've learned across my absurd little life, it's that really big, downright impossible problems require really big, downright impossible solutions, and this one feels right."

"You are uniquely experienced in this regard," Home Ziva said.

"Unfortunately. And if it's my call, then I've made it," Lex said.

"As you wish. We will support you in every way we are able," Local Ziva said.

"Come on, Squee," Lex said.

The funk coiled herself in Local Ziva's grip and launched herself to the cockpit. Lex snatched her out of the air and shut the hatch. He looked over his shoulder to Nugget, still drifting just over the back seat, its hide pulsing with colors.

"Are we clear on the plan? We head back in time, find the pre-war Nuggets, and you learn some of their stuff," Lex said. "Are you sure you're still willing to do it? We sort of left you out of that negotiation."

"I am quite certain. You have asked me if I would like to take a direct role in returning lost knowledge. There is no higher calling I could aspire to. The visual indication of this color pattern and cadence is anticipation and excitement."

"Great. Now hold on. I like to keep the inertial inhibitor low, and I get the feeling seat harnesses won't work for someone of your... format."

Tendrils oozed out of all three of the lower orifices on the entity, not so much holding onto as enveloping the arms and the headrest with a thick substance the consistency of liquid latex. It firmed up, locking Nugget in place.

"Ready," Nugget said.

Lex looked out the cockpit at Local Ziva. She was watching. He knew that she was not a biological entity and thus that there was no such thing as a subconscious or automatic reaction. The expression on her face was pensive, anxious, and she looked that way on purpose.

"Just a second," Lex said. "Squee, stay put." He popped the cockpit and drifted out.

"Is there something wrong?" Local Ziva said, darting up to him.

He hugged her. "Thanks for everything. It's not lost on me that what we did here today made you kind of a technodeity of incomparable power. There is literally no one I would trust to wield this power more responsibly than you."

"You were, and are, an asset to any world you visit. It is my great hope that your own world is fully restored when this is through, but a shamefully large branch of my neural net places high value on the sequence of events that leads to you having to find a new home and choosing my own. Your company and aid in rebuilding this galaxy would be welcome."

"Ziva, this is a world torn asunder by killer robots, so I don't say this lightly. If I *did* have to spend the rest of my life here, it might not be all bad. But fingers crossed I don't have to."

"We are all united in that hope," Ziva said.

He hugged her again. "But a pilot's got to do what a pilot's got to do."

He navigated back to the cockpit and sealed it. A few more moments to steady himself and prepare for the next step in this adventure got his nerves under control. Then he guided the ship out of the bay and out toward deep space. Countless thousands of GenMechs cleared the way ahead, forming something of a corridor and then hanging in place. It wouldn't have felt out of place if they'd somehow chosen to salute as he drifted past.

"A question," Nugget said. "A sequence of them, to speak with precision."

"Gonna be busy in a moment here. Will this be quick?"

"It will be," Nugget said.

"Go ahead."

"You and Ziva are a different species, correct?"

"I don't know if she really counts as a species, but we're different, that's for sure."

"Are your species able to exchange permanent memories through contact as well?"

"No."

"Then what was the purpose of physical contact prior to departure?"

"It's a sign of affection," Lex said.

"Additionally, it is my theory that the pair have an unbearable level of romantic tension," Coal explained.

"What is what is romantic tension?" Nugget said.

"Not relevant right now for *so many reasons*. We've got clear space. Coal, let's get ready for a quantum shift before you spread any more gossip about me to beings we're making first contact with."

"Acknowledged."

"Nugget, what do you know about the time we are heading to?" Lex asked. "I have to… picture it? Be on the lookout for it? Feel for it? I don't know, but I know I can't do it *well* without having at least a clue of what it is."

"I do not have a complete, permanent memory of that time. Much of it is in the memories of the other half of my dyad. But the newest memories available to me that feature those eliminated in the war engaged in a union. You should envision a union."

"I don't know what that looks like. Can you describe it?"

"Yes. It looks like this."

Lex waited for the creature to start talking, but it didn't. After a moment, he looked over his shoulder. A complex, almost snowflake-like pattern was displayed on its hide. As he peered at it, the pattern swept and zoomed, revealing its complexity in a variety of scales.

"I don't know what I'm looking at, but that's certainly something that'd jump out at me if I saw it again. Coal, let's get rolling."

"Filters active, initiating shift," Coal said.

The ship rattled. The buzzing distraction in the back of Lex's mind asserted itself, but it was different this time. It felt choppy, stuttering like Morse code. The universe outside the cockpit bent and warped, twisting and splitting into a fractal assortment of worlds. Then, he felt a jolt in his mind. It was subtle but notable. That little pluck of one's memory that one feels when something familiar flashes past one's perception, like when you scan a crowd and see someone you knew from high school, or scroll an article and see a name you know. The instant he felt that sensation, the universe outside flashed to the featureless white and the ship then powered down. Lex kept his mind focused as the view became a starfield once more and the *SOB* slowly powered up again.

"Altruistic Artificial Intelligence Control System, version 1.27, revision 2331.04.01c, subset 2.7d, designation Coal, fully initiated. We appear to have arrived. Our destination, based upon my calculations, is indeed an intermediate point between Ziva's universe and that of the Nuggets'. I will require a few minutes to recalibrate for the next shift. In the meantime, I will gather information on this world."

"Does it really matter?" Lex asked. "We'll be out of here as soon as we—"

"Broadcasts are prevalent and are in an easily decoded variant of a known digital standard. Putting samples on the screen," Coal said.

A video feed popped up, revealing something that was vaguely human in appearance but with a large dash of lizard mixed in. It was eating a cupcake, possibly as part of a cooking show. In lieu of sprinkles, the cupcake had crickets.

"Oh, this is going to be a trippy experience, isn't it?" Lex said.

• • • ● ● ● ● ● ● ● •

In Lex's time-frozen home universe, Ziva pored over the data that had been provided by the raw computational might of the other Ziva's systems. Now that Lex was gone, and the displaced mass from that universe taken with him, she no longer had any way to contact her other self. But she had what she needed. The only issue was getting the proposed targeting methodologies to work with the hardware available to her. As always seemed to be the case, it required orders of magnitude greater precision than she was presently capable of. There was some slack in her equipment, but not enough. Innovation would be necessary. She was no stranger to that.

While she worked, she periodically did a fresh search for Lex. The candy bar, with its damaged temporal component of its quantum makeup, was a bright and easily identifiable beacon in the infinite expanse of the multiverse. But the speed of locating it and the precision with which she could do so was a fine measure of her progress in sharpening her instrumentation. And her instrumentation was certainly sharpening, but its behavior was still curious.

As she tracked Lex, she was able to follow his journey with increasing detail. It waxed and waned with the relative interference of an unlimited number of competing sources, but at its worst she could still tell that he was getting closer, shift by shift, to a point in the distant past of the world that presently held most of the displaced mass. The process was taking hours, and the longer it took the more concerned she became, as Lex's plan was, or should have been, to stop in a given universe only as long as it took for Coal to reset, reassess, and jump to FTL. Any delay of more than a few minutes suggested something had interrupted that process, and there was no guarantee that any given world contained the conditions necessary to facilitate the next shift. Granted, even determining how much time had passed for Lex required guesswork and estimation, as time was just as mutable as distance for this form of travel, but she was confident she'd worked out a method to track the apparent passage of time for the *SOB* and its occupants, and she didn't like what it was telling her. This mission could come to an end in any number of ways. All that was necessary was for a world to somehow prevent FTL travel, or to destructively interfere with the generation of the fields necessary to target and pierce through to a new world, and he would be trapped until he could solve that problem, assuming it *could* be solved. Watching and waiting would have become unbearable for her if she wasn't capable of simply switching off her emotional component when she needed the full force of her intellect turned to a problem elsewhere.

Just such a problem presented itself gradually over the course of the next few hours. Her precise targeting of Lex remained intact. But as she sampled other known positions, even in the same universe where it shouldn't have required any special effort at all to be accurate, she was encountering drift in her measurements.

"This is most curious," Ziva said, addressing Sissy as an excuse to vocalize her musings. "This calls for a pure experiment. I would prefer not to risk communication with the Nuggets, even after Lex has reached their world, if I cannot be certain my messages are clear and precise. And I can't achieve THAT without being certain my readings are accurate."

She selected a reference mass of platinum-iridium, as near to precisely one kilogram as science could reasonably produce, and placed it in a small chamber. She pumped out the atmosphere, shielded the chamber from all signals not related to the actual measurements she was taking, and corrected for gravitational variance. Her instruments should give a known value in these conditions. But they did not.

"Zero point one eight two percent divergence. And rising," she observed.

As she watched, the difference between the current measurement and the expected one continued to grow. It was growing slowly, but certainly growing.

She sampled other accessible data points at different known points in the multiverse. Some divergences were greater than others, but they were all growing. As she continued her analysis, she realized what the data were telling her.

Ziva had already begun to calculate the full data model when her communicator became active.

"Ziva?" came the heavily distorted voice of Lex. "We're here. We made it."

Lex removed his helmet and rubbed his forehead. It had been a very trying sequence of shifts, each one taking him further and further away from the definition of normal that had served him so well for so many years. The ship was in one piece, though it now featured a swath of blue smeared across one panel, and Squee was dead asleep after exhausting herself getting progressively more excited about all the new things. Through it all, Nugget had become more withdrawn and introspective.

"Ziva?" Lex said, reaching down to tap the candy bar like it was a defective antenna.

"Yes, Lex. I apologize. There have been some developments. You do appear to be at a position approximately seventeen thousand years prior to the relative present time of that universe. Do you see any large accumulations of Nuggets?"

"Not yet," Lex said.

"They are in the nebula ahead," Nugget said, speaking for the first time in ages. "I can guide you."

"How deep into the nebula?" Lex said.

"Near the blue star, at the balance point between greatest light intensity and greatest particle density," Nugget said.

"Processing..." Coal said. "It will take thirty-nine hours to reach that point, due to the density of the nebula limiting our top speed."

"It will not take that long. I will help," Nugget said. "We have field sculpting techniques. I will teach you. We must reach them. The light intensity of the star, the particle density of the nebula, at this distance... if they are not presently united in a memory transfer, they will be soon."

"Good timing," Lex said. "You can join in and learn a bunch."

"No. Terrible timing. This is a time of war. When joined we are nearly defenseless. It is why it was the perfect time to attack. And I can sense the presence of others of my kind approaching. You may have brought us to the precise moment that the knowledge was lost."

"Then let's get moving. Ziva? You said something about a development?"

"The Merging has begun," Ziva said.

"... What?" Lex said.

"It is difficult to articulate, as its behavior lies outside the standard physical model for the universe, but there is a point in the multiverse that has begun to exert an attraction to other matter in other universes. It is spreading out spatially and temporally, and it is drawing with particular intensity on mass from or similar to mass from our own universe."

"How much time do we have?" Lex said.

"I cannot answer that question. Time has, for the purposes of this anomaly, become little more than another form of distance. But travel between universes will bias toward the moment and location of the Merging. Just move quickly, acquire the knowledge, and attempt to return home. Very shortly it will become impossible for you to travel *anywhere* but the central focus of the anomaly. Now that you have reached the universe, I will attempt to contact those responsible for the anomaly and pursue a diplomatic solution."

"Good luck to you," Lex said.

The connection went quiet.

"Coal, I am going to attempt to project a field large enough to encompass the whole ship," Nugget said. "Please work toward amplifying it. This is very important. Lost knowledge can be recovered. It must be recovered."

"I'll do my best. Your organic fields lack the consistency I am accustomed to," Coal said.

Lex set a course for their target and pushed the ship to FTL.

Chapter 9

Ziva juggled the settings on the interdimensional communicator. Contacting the Nuggets currently responsible for the anomaly would not be difficult. It was actually more difficult to *avoid* contacting them. Whatever they were doing, it was tilting the whole of existence in their direction. She engaged the translation matrix and adjusted her techniques to oscillate the energy field the Nuggets used to communicate rather than the electromagnetic field. It was the work of seconds. But opening the line of communication was not the part she was worried about. And as her opening message was modulated across the realities, she soon learned her concerns were well placed.

"Unwanted contact," came the first translated message.

She hadn't bothered to translate the communication coming through to a voice. She was interfacing directly via a data connection. But the ancillary data coming through suggested that the singular message was "spoken" in unison by at least two hundred entities.

"I apologize if I am encroaching, but it is important that you know the effects your actions have, and are having, on our world and many others."

"The Merging is the highest goal. All else is distraction."

"Yes, we have been in contact with a representative of your race. We understand the value of the Merging to your race. But it is contrary to the survival of many. We wish to propose alternatives. If we can find a solution that is not detrimental, we will happily aid you in executing it."

"We have been in contact with representatives of other dimensions as well. They have illustrated a willingness to take extreme measures to prevent the Merging. They are misguided. The Merging is a gift for all. Unity is a gift for all. All will receive the gift. If not, they will be destroyed."

"You would willingly destroy whole worlds before even considering an alternative?"

"Destruction is temporary. With unity, all will be returned. That which is lost shall be returned. All knowledge, all wisdom."

"I understand you desire knowledge. If that is what you seek, you can gain far more than you have ever lost by merely communicating and collaborating with beings like us."

"We do not seek new knowledge. We seek lost knowledge."

"We can return that to you."

"Only the Merging can return lost knowledge."

"We have a means to travel through time," Ziva said. "We can record and deliver that which was lost."

"Travel between worlds is new. Weak, unproven by permanence. Travel through time lacks even that."

"We have proof. If all has gone as we have sought, the fact of our visit to your own world has been a part of your history since before the Merging was conceived of."

"Weak, unproven by permanence. Your words are unwanted contact. In time, there will be unity. That which we wish to know shall be known with the certainty of permanence."

"But at what cost. And what if you are *wrong*?"

The communicator threw an error. Those she had been speaking to had discovered how to silence the communication. Sure enough, their minds were set in stone. If there was to be a way around the devastation of untold worlds, it was up to Lex, Coal, and Nugget to find it.

Lex had his hands on the controls. That was generally not only unnecessary but ill-advised when a ship was traveling at FTL speeds. But either Nugget's special field technique needed some work, or Coal was doing a lousy job of putting it to use, because he had never had a shakier, more meandering light-speed transit in his life. He had to keep making constant manual adjustments. Coal was unable to autopilot, as the "inconsistency" of the biological force field was in fact not a flaw but a precise, continuous, and reactive restructuring of the field to adapt to changing particle densities. She didn't have the processing overhead to spare for the comparatively tiny task of keeping the ship from wandering as a result of the trillions of near catastrophic particle collisions she was managing. Nonetheless, through a method that was second nature to Nugget, nearly beyond Coal's capacity to execute, and entirely beyond Lex's capacity to understand, they were able to move at multiples of light speed through the nebula.

"G-g-greater p-p-precision p-please. Sub-luminal sp-peeds in five..." Coal stuttered.

"I'm on it," Lex said, tightening up his maneuvers to keep the ship's course closer to center.

He watched the final seconds of the FTL jump tick away, then was nearly blinded as the universe came rushing back to reality with a dazzling burst of the defensive and navigational shields absorbing and shrugging off the last few collections of particles.

"That was a truly engaging technical challenge," Coal said. "The tactic utilizes the energy of impact and deflection to deform the shield toward the next point of impact, causing momentary constructive energy spikes greatly exceeding..."

She continued speaking excitedly about something that it would take Karter to truly appreciate. He and Nugget had something else worthy of their awe.

Ahead, there was a ball of Nuggets interconnected into a shell that was the size of a small moon. A semicrystalline pattern of the creatures emerged upon higher magnification. The visual was a near-perfect match for what Nugget had displayed. Each one of the beings linked to as many as four others through gelatinous tendrils precisely like those anchoring his passenger to the seat. Colors and patterns flowed across the surface of the ball, intense and vivid, seeming to visualize the flow of information. If he focused, he could see the same little pattern of red lights or blue whirls wash across, branching and duplicating like the whole collection had made itself into a single continuous video display.

"Release me from the vessel. Release me from the vessel immediately," Nugget said, withdrawing its lower tendrils and darting up to thump against the thick polymer of the hatch.

Lex made sure his and Squee's suits were sealed. Coal pumped the atmosphere out of the cockpit, and it snapped open. Nugget moved far faster than the eye could follow, bursting to an appreciable fraction of the speed of light as it sought a place in the sphere.

"I lost it, did you lose it?" Lex said.

"Highlighted in the HUD," Coal said.

Lex gave chase, eyes flicking between the ball below and the space ahead. "I'm not seeing anything trying to kill us. Am I missing something?" he said.

"I am sensing no threat. Also, no defense. The task of sharing data seems to require their full capacity."

"I forgot it was possible to show up somewhere and *not* immediately have someone try to kill me. Can we talk to Nugget?"

"Extending communication range," Coal said.

"Hey! Nugget!" Lex said. "Remember the plan."

"I will receive and provide all knowledge available to them and to me," Nugget said. "Then we will depart. I will be the mechanism by which the most valuable aspect of the Merging shall be achieved. It is an incomparable honor."

"And remember, as much as I'd like to, we can't save these other Nuggets. We can't change history in any way that matters," Lex said.

"The knowledge will be preserved. And in their final moments, they will know everything that our race achieved for the thousands of years to come. The part of them that needs to live on will live on. Now allow me to focus. And do not attempt to withdraw me until I am no longer connected, or the knowledge I carry with me will be corrupted."

The distant figure of their ally approached the surface of the ball of its race and found an opening in the pattern. Tendrils emerged, links were formed. The dull white of Nugget's hide, gleaming blue in the light of the star, blackened. It then came alive with patterns of light rushing out from it and echoing across the sphere. Within moments, the whole of the sea of patterns seemed to be flowing either toward or away from Nugget specifically. It had so much to teach, and so much to learn, that it became the focus of the entire group.

Lex's mind flicked to the potential consequences of this. A change was being made. A massive one, the introduction of anachronistic information thousands of years before it should exist. By any reasonable measure, this should shatter the space-time continuum into thousands of shards of new universes. And perhaps it was. But there were two things that gave him hope that this would work. Just as when he'd sabotaged the GenMechs in his own past, he had to believe that this moment was an actual event in their history. This was *supposed* to happen, and from the point of view of Nugget's world, it already had long before Nugget was born—or budded, or divided. The second point was the horrifying necessity of the coming massacre of these creatures. Though they were now learning everything that Nugget knew, including the conclusion of the war that would very shortly claim them, that knowledge would be wiped from the universe save for what remained in Nugget. No scrap of the wisdom of the future would survive. It would be as though this had never happened.

"Millions of Carpinelli Fields detected, approaching from the indicated vector," Coal said.

Lex looked at the HUD, then down at the cluster of Nuggets below. "How much longer until he's done?" he said.

"I have no way of knowing," Coal said.

"How much longer until the others show up?"

"Four minutes."

"Do you think we can get away with trying to delay the attackers?"

"There has been no evidence to suggest the race has any memory of us. It seems unlikely that the race would not commit the presence of an unexplained defender of their foes to permanent memory."

"So either they never saw us, or if they *do* see us, it means the whole splinter-universe thing didn't go our way. I swear these rules are starting to feel arbitrary."

"The sheer amount of technological innovation and manipulation necessary to bring about a situation where time or space can be violated in this way suggests the multiverse did not develop with this manner of interaction as part of its standard mechanics. It thus stands to reason that it would react in unexpected ways."

"I'm bringing us in close. You latch on with the tractor beam the moment Nugget's tendrils let go," Lex said.

He maneuvered the ship to within a few meters of the time-displaced individual. At this range, the overall spectacle of the union of these creatures was reduced, if only because less of it was visible. The translator seemed to softly whisper in a thousand identical voices, jumbles of words and sounds reflecting the messages the things were passing among themselves.

"It is beautiful, isn't it?" Coal said.

"Little hard to appreciate it, knowing what's coming," Lex said.

"I disagree. Terrible beauty is still beauty. And because scarcity adds value, that this beauty is destined to be brief makes it all the more precious."

For a moment, only the whispering voices could be heard.

"Scanning..." Coal said.

"What? What are you scanning?"

"I am attempting to determine the point at which the process will be deemed complete."

"How?"

"The anatomical makeup of these creatures is slowly unifying. When the differentiation between any two creatures reaches zero, then the process must have completed."

"Zero differentiation? You mean… Nugget won't be Nugget anymore?"

"The short-term memory will presumably remain. But all permanent memories will be identical. It is a fascinating biology. Creatures who are entirely identical, in mind and body, except for those fleeting things that, by definition, they choose not to remember."

"I'd say it's a great way to get the whole race on the same page, but since the other half of the race is about to show up and annihilate them, that's clearly not true."

"At the present learning rate, Nugget will be fully educated in approximately thirty seconds."

"When's the cavalry arrive?" Lex asked.

"Forty-one seconds."

"Let's hope it's a fast learner."

Dual timers ticked down. The shifting and sweeping of colors across the cluster of Nuggets began to ease and slow. One by one, they released their tendrils from one another and pulled back into their hides. Nugget was among the last in the area to release. At this moment, all the other creatures knew everything Nugget did. They all knew, with a depth of certainty that Lex could never experience, that they were doomed. That an event mere seconds away would exterminate them. And yet, they remained still. Perhaps, having awoken from their trance of teaching and learning, they could sense the approaching foes and knew they were outnumbered. Perhaps they simply needed time to recover from such a potent ordeal. Perhaps it took a while to sift through thousands of years of memories. Or perhaps they were at peace. Lex did not know. And though it curdled his soul to admit it, he didn't have time to care. The very moment Nugget released its grip on those around it, Lex activated the tractor beam and hauled it up to the ship. He angled the ship toward the star, where the nebula would be thinnest, and accelerated the ship to the highest velocity he could manage. The tale of the battle, for him, was told in sensor blips. Waves of Carpinelli Fields crowding around where they had just been. Flares of energy. Unusual gravity signatures.

"You okay, Nugget?" Lex said.

"We were seekers... explorers... We roamed so far, so wide. Over five thousand cycles passed between this moment and the moment I split from the other half of my dyad. The knowledge I've gained is so much greater than everything else I knew..."

"Great," Lex said. "Now let's get you in here. We need to swing back by my world to resupply and repair, then it's right to back here in the right time so you can let your people know they don't have to crunch up a big chunk of reality."

"This will begin a golden age for our kind, Lex."

"Only if we survive."

He popped the hatch, and Nugget slipped inside.

"Get us home, Coal," Lex said. "It's been too long."

Coal activated the necessary sequence of systems. Lex selected the clearest stretch of space he could find, and they jumped to FTL. The mind-bending view of the universe-warping maneuver had filled Lex's vision so many times, he'd come to take it for granted that distorting and fracturing the universe as a means of getting from point A to point B was just another way to travel. He punched through to the featureless white void. Coal shut down.

And then... something new.

He felt a violent jerk. With the *SOB* powered down, there was no inertial inhibitor. Thus, he was acutely aware that he'd suddenly begun accelerating up and to the left rather than continuing to coast forward. The universe started to assert itself again as the acceleration approached blackout levels for Lex. He heard Squee squeal in discomfort and heard the rubbery thump of Nugget losing its grip and bashing into the side of the cockpit.

Interior lights began to light up. The inertial inhibitor snapped back on in time to save Lex's vision from being swallowed by blackness. He fought his head upright. As Coal worked her way through her boot message, he pawed at the controls to bring up the navigational charts, which were fully active a few seconds before Coal was.

They had changed, but not to the familiar detailed charts of his home. What he saw was a stellar map not so different from the cobbled-together one they'd stitched out of gravitational readings in the Nugget's home dimension. Stars were slightly out of position, but it was far closer to where they'd just been than anywhere else they'd visited.

Lex had a feeling he knew what had happened. But he didn't need to wait for Coal to fully activate to know for sure. At the extreme range of the visual sensors, a flickering ember of light was visible. He manually dialed up the magnification. A bright ball of energy, with an assortment of Nuggets just barely visible beyond it, was growing steadily brighter. And every sensor was pointing toward it. Gravity, temperature, particle density, everything capable of displaying a gradient was growing more potent in the direction of the crackling energy.

"Did I miss our visit home?" Coal said.

"We never made it home. Seems like the multiverse is in a hurry to get saved," Lex said.

"I am detecting a large number of Nuggets approaching," Coal said.

"Are they feeling chatty? Maybe we can get Nugget to tell them the good news and nip this whole thing in the—" Lex began.

"Temperature warning!" Coal interjected. "Updating HUD."

The heads-up display suddenly illuminated with, conservatively, two thousand bright rays tracing curving, meandering lines on the hull of the ship. Each ray traced back to one of the distant points approaching, an unfocused laser that nevertheless was dumping huge amounts of heat into a hull that was already having difficulty managing it.

"Reactor overheat and shutdown in twelve seconds," Coal said.

Lex wrenched the steering yolk aside and juiced the throttle. The focus of the lasers started to lag, but only slightly, and it quickly adjusted. Keeping the lasers off the critical parts of the ship required extremely erratic motions that, by definition, robbed them of straight-line speed. In the short term, it meant they stayed functional. In the slightly longer term, it meant that every few seconds an additional cluster of Nuggets drew near enough to join the onslaught.

"Revised estimate, overheat in nineteen seconds. Eighteen. Twenty-one. I request that you either escape or hold still so I don't have to keep revising my estimates."

"Working on it," Lex said. "Nugget, can you talk to them?"

"I am attempting to. They are not listening. They are instead instructing me to leave the ship so that they can finish destroying it. They say that you are clearly part of the enemy fleet."

"I'm not an enemy and I'm not a fleet! *I'm just one guy!*"

"You're wrong about that," came a transmission over the communicator.

It was Lex's own voice.

Lasers started to peel away from their focus on the *SOB* to target... the *SOB*. A second ship, a bit more sleek and a bit less beat up, darted toward the gathering horde of Nuggets.

Little darts of energy clashed against them, knocking the creatures out of formation and causing others to retreat.

"Why are there two of me?" Lex said.

"And why does that *SOB* have guns. I *asked* you for guns and/or fingers and this is a clear illustration of the utility of the former," Coal said.

"Explanations later, here are the fallback coordinates," said the other Lex, followed by a transmission containing a point several hundred thousand kilometers away.

"Is that far enough?" Lex said, guiding the ship toward it.

"She found a way to hide us. Now get moving, the distraction is on the way. That'll give us a chance to escape."

Additional questions flooded Lex's mind, including who "she" was and what the distraction was. But if he couldn't trust himself, who *could* he trust? And more to the point, the distraction became quickly evident when a flailing, angular form suddenly asserted itself nearby. It was probably about the same mass as the *SOB*, but it was *not* a spacecraft. Matte-black metal, barely visible against the darkness of space, had been scraped bright silver here and there. Gleaming red eyes peered wildly out from an almost reptilian head. A long neck, a lashing tail, and great skeletal frameworks with flickering violet force fields spread between them like the membranes of a bat's wings made it clear that this was a machine built to resemble a dragon. And on its back was a rider in the perfect union of plate mail and spacesuit. A long, lithe, clearly organic being of black and white, moving too quickly for him to clearly identify, whisked past the mech-dragon and rider, bobbing between the Nuggets and bashing them about with little effort, like a child playing in a ball pit. There was no clear sign of how the weasel-like creature was propelled, only that it had a manic and gleeful energy that was a match for Squee's.

Utilizing every drop of willpower he had, and denying his inner child, who desperately wanted to watch the mech-dragon fight the space monsters, he took advantage of the mayhem to burst out of the focus of the lasers and streak toward the fallback position.

As it approached, Lex saw nothing whatsoever, but as he passed through the perimeter, suddenly a collection of about eighty ships became visible, like he'd pushed through a curtain painted to look like space and could now see what was hiding behind.

Half of the collection of ships were familiar, based upon the *SOB* in some way, shape, or form. The rest were decidedly *unfamiliar*. One of them looked like someone had made a vintage submarine out of glass, wood, and brass. Another was bright white and glossy smooth, gleaming like the pint-sized flagship of a fleet built to impress during a military parade. Perhaps the most bizarre of them was what appeared to be a stripped-down, cobbled-together hotrod, a literal car, which was drifting in space with a man hanging onto the bumper who was wearing a spacesuit featuring notable patches of duct tape and at least one leather belt cinched tight.

"Receiving multiple communication hails on our own channel," Coal said.

The HUD filled almost entirely with different versions of Lex's own face. Some were in sharp dress uniforms and were ruthlessly well-kempt. Others sported eye patches or copious scars. A few of them were women. One was represented by a deep blue audio waveform, and six of them were varying degrees of inhuman.

They squabbled a bit, no clear spokesperson in the group.

"Is this him? Is he the one that broke it?"

"He's got one of the weird meatball things in the back seat, what's *that* all about?"

"Oh my gosh look at the cute little helmet! Is that Squee in there?"

Lex shook his head.

"Whoa, whoa, whoa, one at a time!" Lex said. "Someone take charge and tell me what's going on!"

"I think I've been here the longest," said the wobbling waveform in a close digital approximation of Lex's voice. "There is an anomalous-attraction event happening, which appears to be related to the recent incursions in our respective universes by the extradimensional entities of the same race as the one occupying the passenger section of your ship. My name is L-X, and thanks to the imprecise nature of the temporal axis of attraction, I have been present in this universe for seven hours."

"You're L-X?" Lex said.

"Yes. L-X. Control system of the *SOB*."

"Does that mean—" Lex began.

"Who is the pilot!" Coal said eagerly.

"Over here," said one of the women in the array of video feeds. "The name's Martha Coal. Am I an AI in your universe?"

"Please," L-X said. "Time is a factor. We have done some reconnaissance. Working with other early arrivals, we have been able to determine that the anomaly is being achieved in part through the utilization of a collection of objects with a similar quantum shift to your own. Alexis Modane, Lt. Squee, Viceroy Travis, and Wrex Locity have determined that removing that mass from this universe will cause a full reversion of affected universes, but only if it is removed before the tipping point."

"Did I hear a Lt. Squee in there?" Lex said.

"I must see Lt. Squee," Coal demanded.

"*Time is a factor!*" L-X repeated. "The mass is inaccessible. Several hundred thousand of the entities are combining their natural force-field-generation abilities to create something which will require a massive, focused energy detonation to interrupt."

"I have a fusion device," Coal volunteered.

Two dozen other voices chimed in with variations of the phrase "So do I."

"I can't believe we're not all dead yet," Lex said.

"Deployment of the fusion devices *has* been determined to have a sufficient amount of energy to briefly destabilize the force field, but without a means to bring the mass back to its home universe or otherwise stop the entities, there is little reason to do so."

"This critter behind me is named Nugget, he's one of the pair that was probably doing the incursions to your universes too. We're pretty confident he can talk the other Nuggets out of doing what they're doing. And I have a way to get home with the stuff," Lex said.

"Does it utilize the baseline self-attractive nature of mass with matching quantum shifts?" L-X asked.

"Uh..." Lex said.

"Yes," said Coal.

"That won't work unless the great attractor they are forming is no longer active," L-X said.

"Okay, so we grab the stuff AND talk them out of it," Lex said.

"I am performing an active scan for Lt. Squee," Coal said.

"Reaching the source of the anomaly will be difficult. The number of entities between us and the destination is difficult to estimate due to their highly capable camouflage, and they coordinate exceptionally well. The one saving grace is that their attacks seem ill-suited for ship-to-ship combat due to the apparent lack of inorganic vessels in this universe."

"Lt. Squee found. Adorable. Saving high-resolution visual scan. Thank you for broadcasting, Lt. Squee," Coal said.

"I would recommend we find ways to counter their camouflage and coordination, but the amount of mass being brough into this universe is increasing geometrically," L-X said. "And past a certain point, the attraction will continue even if they cease their procedure.

This universe will become a multidimensional attractor with no clear upper limit of its radius of effect. We need to act now and improvise tactics along the way."

Lex glanced at the gravitational sensors. Typically they barely showed any sort of change unless they were moving at light speed. Right now, every few seconds they indicated several hundred tons of new mass had been detected in the region. One such clump of mass, a faintly luminescent cloud of dust, appeared just beyond the edge of the fleet. It was clear, if they didn't act soon, things were going to be getting crowded.

"I'm ready when you are," Lex said.

Various versions of Lex and Coal started coordinating. Ships assigned themselves to protect certain positions.

"Sir Alexander, you'll be drawing fire. Viceroy, you run support. All of those with fusion devices, you stay in the flank. We protect the ship containing the allied entity," L-X said. "Any final preparations?"

One by one, several dozen pilots stuffed gum, candy, jerky, and in one notable and unsettling instance what appeared to be a live mouse into their mouths.

"Right. Deploy," L-X said.

The fleet surged out of the veiled region of space. It should have been chaotic. And to most reasonable minds it was. Huge swaths of mass were randomly appearing in the stretch of space ahead. Some were pieces of rock. Others were swirling clouds of dust or brilliant balls of plasma that had likely been pulled from stars. But nearly every ship was piloted by some version of Lex, and the instincts were astonishingly similar. They didn't need to call out their moves. Ships swept in to draw laser fire. The mech-dragon breathed a cloud of dazzling, white-hot gas. A ship that may as well have been designed by Jules Verne ejected steam into a cluster of Nuggets, disorienting them. The car launched through space, propelled forward wheel-first by jets clearly intended to be used for downforce on a road, meaning the insane contraption was traveling wheels-first through space.

Lex shifted and pivoted. He kept the shields down, again preferring the smaller target presented by an otherwise defenseless ship.

"Nugget? Any headway talking to them?" he said.

"They are unreceptive," Nugget said. "Though I thank you for seemingly utilizing nonlethal means preferentially."

"I guess us Lexes trend toward being antiviolence."

"Speak for yourself," barked the Lex at the steering wheel of the car. "I'd be ramming these suckers left and right if I could get my wheels on something solid. And I've got my eyes on a nice stretch of land now."

The car streaked past and slammed down on a recently attracted stretch of what may have been the side of a mountain.

They were getting closer now. And despite having nearly a hundred pilots of roughly Lex' skill, the number of Nuggets was making it difficult to get any closer.

"We're approaching the proper range for fusion detonation," L-X said. "But the explosions must be simultaneous. There isn't room for a proper launch maneuver."

"It doesn't matter how much fancy flying I do to try to make room for a coordinated launch and detonation, I can't clear them out if they don't follow me," Lex said. "Anyone got any ideas?"

"Processing..." Coal said. "I was taught a shield-sculpting technique by Nugget, and it was proposed that field interference might be an attack vector for them. Combining them may prove effective. Shield sculpting has high computational overhead. Who has the largest available processing capacity?"

The sleek flagship version of the *SOB* replied, displaying its specifications.

"Uploading algorithm. Broadcasting shield harmonics for maximum interference. This will feel unnatural, Lex, but you need to do it," Coal said.

"I can't remember the last time I did anything that felt natural."

"Everyone, form a grid and link defensive shields. Offload beam-shaper control to the flagship. Prepare for maneuver."

"What's the maneuver, Coal?"

"We are going to, with proper impact velocity, upgrade the wall of Nuggets to a door."

"Oh... Hell, why not?"

A group of the multiverse's finest pilots, in control of some of the multiverse's finest ships, formed an array. Utilizing reflexes and intuition that had bested some of the most challenging navigational tasks of all time, they boosted their shields, formed them with a method borrowed from the very foes they were facing, and modulated them into something that would interfere with the Nuggets' own fields. Then came the most challenging maneuver of their lives, charging in a straight line through an endless onslaught of attackers rather than dodging them. Any Nugget unfortunate enough to come into contact with the leading edge of the shield was sent hurtling off at a seemingly random angle, its own field disrupted and its capacity to navigate scrambled. They cleared space with the efficiency of a snowplow until there was room enough for the bomb-wielding ships to deploy all at once.

"Now, now!" L-X said. "I've transmitted a target."

"Activating fusion device," came a chorus of Coals.

Most, including Lex's Coal, deployed a bomb. Some ejected their passengers and instead launched their own ships toward the target. Lex cut thrusters, turned, and burst them to full again, pulling the ship into a loop that passed minimum safe distance not a moment too soon. He looped around, flying blind as the sensors all maxed out and the cockpit autodarkened to keep from searing his eyes from his skull. When the view returned, the force field was flickering and wavering, but it was still very much in place.

"That doesn't look down to me," Lex said.

"It's down enough," Coal said.

"I am not certain of the accuracy of that statement," L-X said.

"I'm trusting Coal on this one," he said, pushing the thrusters to maximum and pouring any remaining power into the forward shields.

The ship's velocity started to decrease as the force of the field countered their thrust. Already the staggering glow of the field was pulsing brighter again.

"It's gonna be close," Lex said, shifting the path of the ship to try to follow the weakest points in the volume of the force field.

"It is possible I overestimated the thickness of the field," Coal said.

"We can make it," Lex said. "We can make it."

"Hold on to your butts!" barked the frenzied voice of the automotively-inclined Lex.

Lex flicked on the rear cameras just in time for them to be smashed to bits as the wheeled vehicle slammed full force into them from behind. The additional force of the impact was just enough to punch the *SOB* through.

He fought to get control of the ship. The ballistic boost he'd been given had lightly damaged some thrusters, complicating navigation a bit. Around them, the Nuggets conjuring the shield redoubled their efforts, perhaps wisely considering the dozens of ships outside the field to be more of a threat than the one damaged one inside of it. Several thousand more seemed unaware of their arrival. They simply drifted in complex patterns around the brilliant energy vortex that could only be the attractor bringing about the

Merging. It was uncannily like watching a field of druids performing a ritual to welcome a new age.

"Let me out," Nugget instructed. "Let me out right now. There are listeners here. Some will hear me."

Lex double-checked his and Squee's helmets and popped the cockpit, not even bothering to wait to pump the atmosphere out. Nugget tumbled up and away from the ship. Coal amplified the translator, but whatever was being said was being said far too quickly and far too intensely to be understood. It was like hearing a hundred spirited speeches being overlaid atop each other. All Lex could make out were snippets.

"Joining... lost to time... mistakes... corrected... explore... worlds beyond worlds... permanent... precious... help... sorrow... tragedy... resurrection..."

The knowledge poured out, thicker and faster, in more and more layers. And gradually, first in ones and twos, then in tens and twenties, the other Nuggets stopped their ritual and approached. A rapt audience formed, peeling away more and more. Now the force field started to falter, too many Nuggets unwilling to continue when the wisdom of the ages was gushing from this trusted member of their own race. Even in Coal's translation, it was clear there was a different tone, a different nature to what Nugget was saying. This was being spoken from permanent memory. This was, by the measures that mattered to the Nuggets, truth with a capital *T*.

The onslaught of information stopped as quickly as it had begun. For ten of the longest seconds of Lex's life, there was silence. And then...

"They are satisfied," Nugget said. "The Merging has provided what they sought."

Lex peered at the undulating ball of energy. It had begun to fade, though it had by no means vanished. Beyond the ball was a collection of seemingly random items from Lex's own life, like some sort of estate sale.

"The attractor is still attracting," L-X said.

"We still need to haul this stuff back," Lex said. "Coal, activate the tractor-net."

"Activating... Processing... It would appear I launched the tractor-nets along with the fusion device. In my defense, it was a very exciting moment."

"We can't handle all that stuff with a tractor beam," Lex said.

"I believe I have a solution," said an incredibly posh version of Lex's voice.

The steampunk ship puttered past and, in perhaps the simplest possible solution, deployed an actual, physical trawler net. It pulled the corners in again, packing the collection of items into a fine mesh sack, then severed the cord. The undulating glow seemed to follow the sack but didn't negatively impact it in any way.

"Gotta love saving the multiverse with fishing equipment," Lex said, snagging the pile. "All right, folks. Sorry I couldn't stick around and hear your stories, but I need to get out of here while there's still enough open space to hit light speed."

A burst of messages in reply all wished him luck or urged him to move quickly. He pulled the mound of goods as close to the belly of the ship as he could.

"Calibrating Carpinelli Field for additional mass," Coal said.

Lex pushed the damaged ship to maximum acceleration, steering around the Nuggets who were steadily flowing toward their new oracle. Bits of planet and blobs of star continued to pop into view ahead. He nudged the ship in tighter and tighter angles, seeking the blackness of space.

"Come on, space. You're supposed to be empty... Almost... Almost... All right looks like enough runway for me. Activating FTL jump."

As the built-in warning alarms loudly disagreed with his assessment of the amount of clear space, he activated the jump. The ship rocked as bits of mass passed too close for comfort, and a far more crowded than usual view started blue-shifting out of invisibility.

"Activating calibrated snap-back simulator..." Coal said.

The universe wobbled. Lex's perception felt yanked and torn as the simulator grabbed hold of his mind. He was shown each individual item plucked from his reality. It seemed to stretch, expanding backward and forward in time, fragmenting into a trillion instants and vanishing into the proper place and moment. It was far more than his consciousness could endure. As the final candy bar broke down into its temporal components, he blacked out.

"Altruistic Artificial Intelligence Control System, version 1.27, revision 2331.04.01c, subset 2.7d, designation Coal, fully initiated. Lex? Analyzing life signs..."

"Ugh... Wha...? I'm awake. Awake," Lex said, shaking his head and blinking until his vision cleared. "Are we here? Did we do it?"

"Quantum shift: zero."

He looked out the window, but they were in deep space, and the passage of time was a bit difficult to determine visually in most of the universe.

"Are we good? Is time working?" Lex said.

"Incoming message," Coal said.

Lex smacked the screen of the communicator. "Yes! Hello!? Whoever you are, your voice is the most beautiful thing I have ever heard."

"Lex, stop being a weirdo," said Karter. "I don't know why I'm getting all sorts of temporal alerts on my observation systems, but I'm going to blame you, so get your ass back here and explain it."

"Trust me, you're gonna hear every last—" Lex began.

"Good," Karter said, abruptly ending the call.

A moment later, a second call came in, this one from Ma.

"Hello, Ma," Lex said.

"I have a message from Ziva. I understand you've had something of an adventure."

"Yeah."

"I will have a warm meal and a cold beer waiting for you when you arrive."

"You are a saint, Ma. I'll be there in no time." He paused and grinned. "No. I'll be there in *some* time. And damn if it doesn't feel good to say that."

Epilogue

The hoversleds roared along the track. Lex feathered the throttle as he approached the final set of turns, eyes fixed on the first-place sled. Throughout the season, and through the last few races, he and his rival had kept pace on the track and on the standings. Now it was the final race, and like nearly all the races this season, Lex knew that all the previous laps were little more than a prelude. At this level, the winner was decided in the final moments, and the final turn.

Something had changed between him and his rival in the days following Lex's little multiverse adventure. Lex had ceased to fixate on him alone. Rather than simply being aware of, and planning around, the other racers on the track, but only truly *racing* the sleds who had a chance of claiming the top spot, Lex had taken to treating the racers, the track, and the full duration of the race as a single, complete package, meant to be managed end to end. Learning how interconnected even different universes were had a way of making a man see things from a new perspective.

He glanced at the thrusters of the first-place sled and the heat haze over their power feeds. Mr. Rival had been racing hard, full tilt. He'd been dumping everything he had into gaining and maintaining his lead. The hoversled was pushing the red line. Peak power output. On the verge of overheating. But it had paid off. The man had been in first place since lap two. Judging from Lex's own lap times, and how far ahead the leader had been, it seemed likely somewhere around lap fifty the in-competition single-lap record for the track had been taken from Lex. But it had not been without cost. The speed had been steadily tapering off. One can only run a vehicle at the ragged edge before efficiency slips and performance suffers. And that sled was suffering *badly*.

Lex popped his gum. Two more straightaways. One more turn. He looked at his own vehicle's vitals. They were well beyond what the engineers would have liked, but with a good deal more slack than they usually had at this stage in a race. Rather than charging into first place and digging his heels in, holding on to it with a death grip and menacing any racer with the audacity to try to take it away, Lex had made second place his territory, and had been nipping at the heels of the first-place racer since the very first lap. Lex could practically feel the eyes on him. The lead driver would be flicking his eyes between the track and the rear view, mindful of every maneuver Lex made. Which meant what came next would *not* be missed.

The final turn approached. At a time when he should have been feathering the throttle to ease into the turn, Lex dialed the speed up again, eating into that precious sliver of reactor performance he'd been rationing for the last twenty laps. Ahead, the lead car's thruster glow flared. Lex grinned a bit wider. The anxiety and desperation were pouring off the first-place sled. He didn't want to lose a centimeter of his lead. And so he abandoned safety and good sense for raw speed. Lex knew the feeling and gently eased off the throttle, dropping back into a reasonable speed for the turn. The lead sled tried to do the same, but Lex had timed his feint well. There wasn't time for the lead racer to back off before they hit the turn.

Lex entered the curve a tenth of a second behind first place and watched as the hoversled that had been in the lead for ninety-six solid minutes drifted off the edge of the track for just a moment, bleeding speed as the repulsors had to compensate for nonideal track surface. The racers were neck and neck as they entered the final straightaway. No more turns. No other sleds to contend with. No more room for skill. After three hundred ninety-nine laps of knife-edge racing, the season would be decided in what amounted to a straight-line dash. Over an hour and a half of desperately trying to be the fastest sled in the history of the track meant the lead sled had nothing left to give. It had eaten up its slack. But Lex? Lex had something left in the tank.

Both sleds were at full thrust. Lex turned to gaze at his rival through the windscreen. He was pouring sweat. Eyes red-rimmed and burning, he offered only the briefest, darting glances in Lex's direction. Even in the glare of the desert sun, Lex could see the glow of assorted safety systems activating, cutting power to prevent a reactor breach. Lex snapped his gum again and casually glanced at the race position indicator roll from second to first with four hundred meters left to go. He hovered his fingers over the right repulsors. There was only one thing left in his rival's arsenal. Lex needed to be ready for it.

Sure enough, with a roar of anger and frustration that almost rivaled the rumble of his reactor, the rival racer slammed his steering yoke to the left, seeking to either spook Lex into going offtrack or smash into him. Lex popped the right repulsors, lurching his sled up at an angle. Instead of his roll cage sparking against Lex's, the edge of the rival's sled nudged under Lex's. Lex waggled the steering to keep the sled up on the left repulsors, now effectively leaning on the faltering second-place hoversled like a crutch. The extra force caused the rival's already-maxed-out repulsors to lose height, dragging the sled's belly on the ground and dumping speed faster than if he'd been braking.

It was all too much for the abused sled. One of the thrusters failed entirely, and the hoversled lurched to the right and spun off the track. Lex's sled slammed down a heartbeat before it crossed the finish line. First place for the race. First place for the season.

• • • ● • ● ● • • •

Lex checked the time on his slidepad. Preethy had always prided herself on punctuality, but if she was going to continue her unblemished record of not missing a date with Lex, she had less than two minutes. They hadn't seen each other since the final race of the season. As tended to be the case, the last piece of any production was the busiest for all involved. Lex had done a whirlwind of interviews. Preethy had hundreds of final decisions to make, from reacting to the boost in ad revenue from the recently broadcast league final to negotiating new contracts for a few of the midlevel races. Given the sudden and intense focus on Lex as the winner, their usual tradition of visiting a new restaurant after a major race had been replaced with Lex cooking dinner for the two of them in his apartment. He was making one of his specialties, which was a fancy way of saying he was cooking one of the three things he knew how to cook that didn't involve reading instructions on the side of a box.

As the inductive frying pan put the all-important crispy brown bits around the edge of the dish, he tore a piece of bread and tossed it to Squee.

"Cutting it close," he said, leaning on the counter with one hand as he swiped through his notifications.

The slidepad's spam filter was getting a workout. A little red number rolled over into the five-digit range in the junk folder. He opened a message from Ma. It was text and displayed the AI's trademark efficiency and politeness.

Congratulations on the successful season. Factoring equipment endurance and faltering psychological fortitude into a holistic competitive stratagem illustrates an elevation of your already-nuanced tactics. Pursuant to your request for analysis, we have found all dimensions matching the quantum shift of your assorted destinations to be intact and nominal. Retrieval of the mass has caused no lasting damage to chronology or causality. I hope that provides you with some peace of mind, and I look forward to our next conversation with great anticipation.

Lex sighed in relief. It would be nice to say he was most concerned with the killer-robot future, but ever since his own universe had ceased to be in danger, he found his mind fixating on the "boring Lex" world. Lex had claimed the discovery of the engagement ring had inspired him to write a similar inscription. Considering Lex had brought it back, and there was some evidence that the final mass retrieval had returned the displaced doodads not just to the present but to the past as well, he couldn't help but fear that it had *also* ripped those things out of the past of the worlds they'd ended up in. He wasn't sure how that could happen, but he wasn't sure how anything else that had happened had happened, so he had to imagine that it was at least possible he'd undone the idyllic life of his other self. Apparently, such was not the case. Finally some good news.

At the precise moment the clock ticked over to eight p.m., Preethy stepped through the door of his home and gently brushed the dust from her short skirt and long jacket. Squee trotted over and waggled her butt. The funk sprang into the air. Preethy deftly caught her rather than allowing the creature to cover the slate-gray jacket with salt-and-pepper fuzz.

"Hey! You made it," Lex said.

She set Squee down and twisted her small, fashionable wristwatch to face her. "And only just. I'm beginning to think I'll need to hire one of our racers as a personal driver if I'm going to make every appointment in a given day."

"I've got nothing but time until next season," he said, brushing the crisped contents of the pan onto two plates.

"You joke, but having you as my driver for a few weeks might be a way to see one another a bit more often."

She took a seat. Lex set a glass of wine and a plate of his concoction before her. It looked vaguely like hash, in that the principal descriptors were "diced" and "browned."

"And what do we call this dish?" Preethy said, unfurling a napkin to place on her lap.

"I always just called it 'crispy whatsit.' Usually the ingredients are 'leftovers, plus chopped potatoes,' but a few months ago I had the revelation that I can actually use fresh ingredients and pick what they are instead of just dumping in whatever I happen to have."

"And so you have elevated your cuisine from 'reheating' to 'cooking,'" she said with an uncharacteristic bit of snark.

"It was this or dinner omelets again," he said.

"Either would have been delightful, I am certain." She tore some bread and accepted the offered bottle of olive oil to pour into a dish to dunk it in. "Tell me. Have you read any of the analyses of your race?"

"I do enough of my own analysis. If I start fixating on what other people say about me, I'll go insane."

"I found this particular line from the *Raceway Herald* to be insightful," she said, setting her own slidepad on the table and tapping a cued-up file.

"After an uncharacteristically subdued performance from Alexander, there were commentators and spectators speculating that the once-dominating racer had lost his edge, or perhaps even been replaced. Indeed, in this single race, thanks largely to less aggressive competition from Alexander, Kyle Byres ran five of the fastest laps ever recorded on the track, all but pushing Alexander's performance out of the top ten. But by doing what amounts to sandbagging, Alexander was able to handily snag the win, and the last-minute choke by his rival resulted in a 'Did Not Finish,' depriving him of all points for the race and relegating him to a fourth-place finish overall. There will be debate for years about whether this was tactics, skill, or good fortune, but in the opinion of this analyst, those three things are one and the same for Trevor Alexander. But now that we've seen skill and intuition joined by guile, one can only imagine what the next season will bring. Meanwhile, the Tremor Grand Prix is shaping up to be—"

She stopped the recording. Lex shoveled some of the hash into his mouth, pleasantly surprised at how well he'd executed it.

"Thoughts?" she said.

"I was worried the chickpeas wouldn't get along in this, but they work."

"Chickpeas work with everything, but I was more interested in discussing the interpretation of the race. More accurately, I was interested in addressing the idiosyncrasies of your performance."

"You think it's weird I didn't go for the record."

"It is a marked departure from your goals of late. Five weeks ago you were spending as much as eighty hours on the track running time trials. You haven't reached that as a total for the preparation of the rest of the season since then."

"I took some time to reflect. It turns out, having my name in some database somewhere next to a low number? Maybe not the only thing worth working toward. Don't get me wrong. I still want to win. And I'm still *going* to win, as often as I can. But it's taken me this long to figure out I don't have anything to prove anymore. Not about that, anyway."

"If you recall, I've suggested such to you quite frequently."

"I'm fast on everything but the uptake," Lex said. "But now that the season is done, you think maybe we can discuss something?"

"This would be a rather uninteresting evening if we spent it eating in silence."

"My career goals aren't the *only* things I've had a chance to reevaluate. We've been taking things pretty easy, considering you are the CEO of the league and thus my boss. Wouldn't want people to think I'm getting special treatment and all that."

"It does seem prudent."

"For how long? Are we on pause until one of us quits?"

"I imagine, so long as we are transparent in the business aspect of our relationship, the private aspect should be quite tolerable. More to the point, as the acknowledged, uncontested league champion, I don't imagine there would be much cause to question a modicum of special treatment."

"Good. Because I'm ready to move forward."

"Oh?" she said, swirling her wine. "How far?"

"As far and as fast as you're willing to go."

She tipped her head. "You tread dangerous ground when you offer a businesswoman that kind of latitude at the negotiating table."

"Oh yeah? Let's hear it. Start the negotiation."

She chuckled. "I'm teasing, Lex. We don't need to hammer out the details right now."

"See, I'm *not* teasing, so if you've got something in mind, may as well get it out there."

"Nothing you aren't expecting. Family is very important to me. And if we are going to begin something, I'd like to know how far you are willing to go."

Lex rummaged in his pocket and clacked his palm down onto the table, sliding it toward her. When he lifted his hand again, it revealed a gold ring. She plucked it from the table. One eyebrow rose, once again delivering a dense and nuanced message that made spoken language seem utterly unnecessary.

"Well, well," she said. "You *do* move fast."

He grinned. "It's what I do best."

www.ingramcontent.com/pod-product-compliance
Lightning Source LLC
Chambersburg PA
CBHW040520170726
48295CB00012B/280